John Wilson Croker

The Croker papers

The correspondence and diaries of the late Right Honourable John Wilson Croker

John Wilson Croker

The Croker papers
The correspondence and diaries of the late Right Honourable John Wilson Croker

ISBN/EAN: 9783337196615

Printed in Europe, USA, Canada, Australia, Japan

Cover: Foto ©Andreas Hilbeck / pixelio.de

More available books at **www.hansebooks.com**

THE

CORRESPONDENCE AND DIARIES

OF THE LATE

RIGHT HONOURABLE

JOHN WILSON CROKER, LL.D., F.R.S.,

SECRETARY TO THE ADMIRALTY

FROM 1809 TO 1830.

EDITED BY

LOUIS J. JENNINGS,

AUTHOR OF 'REPUBLICAN GOVERNMENT IN THE UNITED STATES.'

IN THREE VOLUMES.—Vol. I.

WITH PORTRAIT.

LONDON:

JOHN MURRAY, ALBEMARLE STREET.

1884.

LONDON:
PRINTED BY WILLIAM CLOWES AND SONS, LIMITED,
STAMFORD STREET AND CHARING CROSS.

PREFACE.

———◆———

A few words of explanation may be necessary concerning the papers which are submitted to the public in these volumes.

The letters of Mr. Croker from 1811 to about 1833 were chiefly to be found in twenty-eight large volumes; from 1833 to 1857, they were scattered in great disorder through scores of bundles of miscellaneous documents, most of which yielded nothing likely to prove attractive to the general reader. But, mingled with tax receipts, appeals for alms and loans, friendly invitations, applications for office, and formal notes on business affairs, were many letters of the highest political importance, and others of almost equal value relating to the social and literary life of the first half of the present century.

The preliminary work of reading, sorting, and making selections from this immense collection consumed the greater part of a year. In the end, I found that although there were serious gaps in the correspondence, for which Mr. Croker's Trustees are unable to account, yet that a great mass remained which could not fail to be of unusual interest to the public, and of great value to the future historian. Mr. Croker's correspondence was chiefly carried on with men of distinction in various walks of life, and it ranged over every topic which engaged popular attention. Mr. Croker's own letters were written in a singularly light and sparkling vein;

and his friendships included most of the eminent statesmen of his day, and all who had made public life illustrious—except, of course, on the side of the Whigs. He gave his friends, when he wrote to them, the best he had to give, and they dealt in the same spirit with him. The result, after all deductions, was a correspondence which presents a contribution to the history of our times not surpassed in general interest, or in historical importance, by any similar records which have been brought to light during the present century. The curious series of incidents which preceded and attended the Ministries of Mr. Canning and Lord Goderich ; the letters of Sir Robert Peel, which throw so powerful, and from some points of view, so new a light, on his entire character and career; the full details concerning the negociations which went on within the Tory party in the critical month of May, 1832 ; the narrative of the circumstances attending Peel's second great conversion in 1846; the remarkable conversations with the Duke of Wellington ; the statement made to Mr. Croker by George the Fourth, clearly with a view to its publication ; the secret history of many political events which hitherto have been only darkly visible to the public—these are among the features of the Croker Papers which will command universal attention. And it will be found that the literary and social interest of the collection is scarcely less original and attractive.

The systematic arrangement of these papers, the process of condensation, the frequent necessity of choosing from several documents bearing upon the same subject that which seemed the most worthy of publication—all this was a most difficult and heavy task, requiring upwards of another year for its completion. My first and greatest desire from the outset was to let the correspondence speak for itself, a long and patient study of it having convinced me that it afforded a complete vindication of Mr. Croker from the injustice with which one writer after another, each imitating the other, had treated him. It is too often the first word that decides the estimation in which a man is to be held. It happened that Mr. Disraeli, inflamed by personal dislike and pique, spoke that word about Mr. Croker, and others echoed it, some of them from Mr. Disraeli's motive, and others without well knowing what they were doing.

But although it seemed clear that the correspondence should be allowed to tell its own tale, a connecting narrative was indispensable. In endeavouring to supply this, I have presented the main facts connected with Mr. Croker's life, together with such explanatory comments as appeared to be essential in reference to the public events which are directly mentioned in the correspondence. To have gone beyond these limits would have led to the attempt to construct a long and formal biography of Mr. Croker, for which there is not adequate material; or to write the political history of this country from 1809 to 1857—an undertaking which would have been still more remote from the scope of the editor's duties.

The narrative portions of these volumes are therefore brief, as brief as they could properly be made; for it seemed to be a most important part of the business of an editor to interpose as little as possible between the reader and Mr. Croker or his correspondents. The editor is aware that his own work may, in consequence, have a slight and fragmentary appearance, but this was inevitable, since it was designed to form a mere link of connection—unobtrusive, but not, it is to be hoped, superfluous.

It would be too much to hope that no error whatever will be found in a compilation which deals with so many hundreds of names and dates and personal allusions; but if any mistakes have thus far escaped detection, it may honestly be pleaded that it is not because the most anxious care and attention have not been bestowed upon the work throughout every stage of its preparation. Finally, the editor is desirous of acknowledging with gratitude the great assistance he has received from Mr. Murray and from Mr. John Murray, jun., in the laborious task of reading the proofs, and in suggesting appropriate and necessary notes. These notes are placed within brackets when they refer to the diaries or letters, but the brackets are omitted when the editor has appended them to his own remarks. The very few notes furnished by Mr. Croker himself have his initials attached to them.

October 1884.

CONTENTS OF VOL. I.

—————

CHAPTER III.

1814–1816.

CHAPTER IV.

1817–1818.

CHAPTER V.

1819.

CHAPTER VI.

1820.

CHAPTER VII.

1821.

CHAPTER VIII.

1822.

CHAPTER IX.

1823–1824.

CHAPTER XIII.

1828.

LETTERS, DIARIES, AND MEMOIRS

OF THE

RT. HON. JOHN W. CROKER.

CHAPTER I.

1780–1809.

Misrepresentations of Mr. Croker's Character—Birth and Parentage—The
Croker Family—Early Recollections—School Life—The Father of
Sheridan Knowles—Trinity College—Mr. Croker's Removal to London
—The French Revolution — Letters to the *Times* — First Literary
Productions—His Practice at the Bar—Marriage to Miss Pennell—
Elected to Parliament in 1807—Friendship with Canning—Catholic
Disabilities—Mr. Perceval and the New Member—First Acquaintance
with Sir Arthur Wellesley—Colonel Wardle's Charge against the
Duke of York—Canning and the Premiership—Letter from Charles
Arbuthnot—Mr. Croker appointed Secretary of the Admiralty—Letter
to Lord Palmerston—Croker's Performance of his Duties—Memo-
randum on his own and Mr. Perceval's Position—A Scandal in the
Admiralty — Firmness of the New Secretary — Foundation of the
Quarterly Review — Mr. Croker as a Political Writer — His great
attention to Facts and Details—Characteristics of his Style and
Workmanship.

FEW men whose names are known to the public have
received harder usage than John Wilson Croker. All whom
he offended by his articles, or by articles which they thought
proper to attribute to him, took care, sooner or later, to
exact vengeance. In his lifetime he never replied to any of
these attacks, although he could not have been insensible to

their injustice. After his death their bitterness was redoubled. He was exhibited to the view of the world as "the
wickedest of reviewers," with a "malignant ulcer" in his
mind; a man who employed his faculties "for the gratification of his own morbid inclination to give pain." These
were the softest words which Miss Martineau could find to
say of him while the grave was still open to receive his
remains. She thought that Mr. Croker had done her a
wrong. In 1839 a severe article upon her ' Illustrations of
Political Economy' appeared in the *Quarterly Review,* and in
1852 there was a notice in the same pages—not altogether
complimentary, although not severe—of her 'History of
England.' Smarting under these criticisms, Miss Martineau
struck back at Mr. Croker, and yet he was not the offender.
He had nothing whatever to do with either article. In like
manner Lord Macaulay, who almost avowedly wrote from
motives of revenge, placed it upon record, though the record
was not published till after his death, that he was a "bad, a
very bad man: a scandal to politics and to letters." These
are examples of the portraits which have been drawn by his
political and personal adversaries.

On the other hand, when we get fairly behind the scenes
of his life, we find that Mr. Croker was the close and
intimate friend of many of the most eminent men of his day,
and not only their friend, but their adviser in every great
emergency which befell them. They attached an extraordinary value to his opinions, and trusted in him to a degree
which is rare either in public or in private life. Never was
he known to betray this confidence. His discretion and his
sturdy common sense could be depended on to the last
extremity. Political differences sometimes cost him the loss
of a friend; no man can take an active part in public affairs
without being required, sooner or later, to pay that penalty.

But his sincerity was never called in question by those who were compelled to part company with him. He was severed from most of his acquaintances only by the hand of death. " Our friendship," wrote one of them—the Earl of Lonsdale —" has lasted fifty years without a cloud." He had the cordial respect of Mr. Canning, of the Duke of Wellington, of Sir Robert Peel, and of every Conservative leader, from Mr. Perceval down to the late Lord Derby ; and he enjoyed the confidence and esteem of many who were habitually opposed to him in politics,—as Sir Robert Peel himself became in the latter part of his career. In private life we find him free from blame or reproach, devoted to his home, overshadowed as it was by the loss of his only son ; deeply attached to his kinsfolk, and never turning a deaf ear either to friends or strangers who came to him for help, and who could prove that they deserved it.

Such is the man who is presented to us when we see him as he really was. The immense correspondence of all kinds which he left strips away disguises. If he had been the unjust, selfish, and bad man described by his foes, this correspondence would have told the tale. That his character was not without defects, assuredly he would have been the last to pretend. He sometimes held extreme opinions, and was extreme in his way of advocating them. He was of a combative disposition, ever ready for a fray, and seldom happier than when the cry of battle rung in his ears. He was a redoubtable opponent, as his enemies found out to their cost ; and a man who struck so hard, and so often, was sure to make many enemies. But any fair-minded reader who dispassionately considers his life and work, with the aid of the materials which are now produced for the formation of a right conclusion, will speedily be convinced that, so far from being wholly " bad," the vehement controversialist had, after all, a kindly heart and a generous nature; and that in everything he undertook he was animated by a lofty sense of duty, which alone would entitle him to respectful recollection.

John Wilson Croker was born in Galway, on the 20th of December, 1780. His father, John Croker, was for many years Surveyor-General of Customs and Excise in Ireland, and it is recorded, on the sufficient authority of Edmund Burke, that he was "a man of great abilities and most amiable manners, an able and upright public steward, and universally respected and beloved in private life." His mother was the daughter of the Rev. R. Rathbone, of Galway. On his father's side, he came of an old Devonshire stock, the name of Croker being commemorated in a well-known distich of the county :—

> "Croker, Crwys, and Copleston
> When the conqueror came were at home."

When Mr. Croker had made himself a power in public life, his assailants derived some kind of consolation from referring to him as a man of "low birth and no principles—the son of a county gauger;" a description which, though purely imaginary, was not more inaccurate than the account which was given of him at a later period by writers or politicians who had winced under the sharp strokes of his pen.

Not very long before Mr. Croker's death, he happened one day to be in the library of the British Museum, when he recognised a face which he had not seen for many years. It was that of an old schoolfellow, Mr. Justice Jackson, of the Irish Common Pleas, and the meeting occasioned to both a feeling of surprise, for on his way to the Museum that very morning the Judge was assured that Mr. Croker had died several years previously. The two friends fell into conversa-

tion, and shortly afterwards they exchanged a few reminis-
cences of their early lives. These letters afford us a glimpse
or two of Croker's school days. "Your father and mine,"
wrote Jackson, "were friends and brother officers in the
Revenue. I was sent to Portarlington School very young,
and I was placed under your protection. You were then at
the head of the school, and *facile princeps* in every branch of
our course. You were also a great favourite with our master
Mr. Willis, and with Monsieur Doineau, the French teacher,
the principal assistant. They were proud of your talents
and acquirements, as being likely to redound to the character
and credit of the school. I perfectly well recollect that you
had at your then early age translated almost the whole of
Virgil into English verse."

To this Mr. Croker replied (December 4th, 1856) :—

Your memory, I think, exaggerates my poetical diligence.
I am pretty sure that the first eclogue and the first book of
the Æneid were all of Virgil that I translated. Pope's
Homer I had by heart. The old Lord Shannon had given
me one when my father once took me (*æt.* 10) to Castle
Martyr. I dare say I knew of no translation of Virgil, and,
stimulated by the example of Mr. Pope, was resolved to fill
up that chasm in English literature. I don't think that this
noble ambition had recurred to my memory from my leaving
Portarlington up to the receipt of your refresher of yesterday ; but that hint has recalled it, and I now could repeat
a line or two. But I still believe that I got no further than
the first eclogue and Æneid. But I was an early dabbler in
political squibbing. There happened to be an election for
the county of Cork severely contested, and prolific of a
deluge of lampoons. I forget the date : I suppose about
1789. There were three candidates. A Mr. Morris was one.
He was my father's and, I suppose, Lord Shannon's friend,
and I wrote at least one *prose* piece on his side which was
printed ; it was a dialogue. I wish I could recover it. As
I was born in the last days (20th) of Dec., 1780, I could have
been not yet *nine.* It is probable that this election had
something to do with my father's visit to Castle Martyr, and

Lord Shannon's notice of me. I wonder whether I also *lisped* in numbers : I should rather say *stuttered ;* for you will perhaps recollect that I had a most distressing impediment in my speech, for the cure of which I was sent to an academy kept in Cork by one Knowles, who had married one of the Sheridans, and professed to remedy cacology and teach elocution, after the manner of old Sheridan. Thence, about 1792, I was transferred to Portarlington. From Willis's I was sent for a year or two to a more classical school, where there were but half-a-dozen boys, kept by the Rev. R. Hood, also at Portarlington, whence, in November, 1796, a month before I was sixteen, I was entered at Trinity College, Dublin, where I found Tom Moore a year or two above me, and met of my own class Strangford, Leslie Foster, Gervais, Bushe, Fitz-Gibbon, Coote, &c.

It was not until the time when this memorandum was written—the last year of his life—that Mr. Croker took any interest in verifying his early recollections. He had never felt sure, for instance, that Sheridan Knowles was the son of "one Knowles" who kept the school in Cork, and in November, 1856, he wrote to the author of the 'Hunchback' to make an inquiry on that point. The reply began with the words, "My dear old schoolfellow," and continued thus :—

I remember you well, for you were, of all my father's pupils, my dear lamented mother's favourite. She loved you for your constant good spirits, and a cordial frankness that drew you to her—for she was frankness and generosity itself. Of all my schoolfellows, you are the only one, except one of the Atkinses, whose face and figure I have before me now. It is a fact—but where is the wonder, when you were pointed out to me by my dear mother's love ?

A note in Mr. Croker's handwriting, appended to a brief sketch of his career which was published many years ago, states that the efforts of Mr. Knowles to cure the impediment in his speech were never entirely successful, and that after leaving this first school, he was sent to another which was originally founded by French refugees. Here, no other language but French was ever spoken, and he attained, he tells us, a "perfect facility in reading, writing, and speaking that language. I was then removed to the classical school of the revered Richmond Hood, who, a few years later, became the classical tutor of Sir Robert Peel. From Mr. Hood's school I was sent, when a little under sixteen, to College, and, oddly enough, my tutor was a Dr. Lloyd, as Peel's was another Dr. Lloyd."

It was in 1796 that Mr. Croker was entered at Trinity College, Dublin, and although he had not then completed his sixteenth year, his remarkable abilities appeared from the first to have attracted the attention of his associates. The "Historical Society," which had then a high reputation, admitted him as a member, and he not only distinguished himself greatly in its debates, but upon several occasions received medals for essays, which were characterised by an unusual degree of literary power. His first acquaintance with Thomas Moore began at this period, and the correspondence which ensued between them was rarely interrupted until the death of the poet, although political ties and other circumstances often threw them widely apart. It was not until Lord John Russell published Moore's Journals that Croker, the most staunch and faithful of friends, had any reason to suspect the faithlessness of Moore.

In the first year of the present century, Croker went to London, and entered himself a student of Lincoln's Inn, having made up his mind to follow the profession of the law. He arrived in the capital armed with good letters of introduction, and soon found many friends; but it does not appear that law exercised so great a fascination over his mind as literature. The French Revolution had produced a powerful impression upon him, as it could not fail to do on any observant and thoughtful man, and his first contributions to the press were on a subject which he continued to make a profound study for many a year afterwards. They were in the form of letters to Tallien, and were published in the *Times*—probably the first introduction which Mr. Croker obtained to that journal. He subsequently held relations of a most friendly and confidential kind with the chief proprietor.

I was lodging and boarding, wrote the late Mr. Jesse, the naturalist, with a Miss Robinson in Middle Scotland Yard, about fifty-seven years ago, when Mr. Croker became an inmate. The society in the house consisted of four or five very pleasant men, and Mr. Croker soon became the life of the party by his wit and talents, and his constant readiness to provoke an argument, which he never failed to have the best of. In these lodgings he employed himself in writing political letters on the French Revolution, addressed to Tallien, which appeared in the *Times* newspaper. I frequently took them for him to Printing House Square. He probably knew more of the history of the Revolution in France, and had written more on that subject, than any man living.

A year or two later he assisted Horace and James Smith Mr. Herries, and Colonel Greville, in starting two publications, neither of which was destined to attain a long life—the *Cabinet* and the *Picnic*. The fire has died out of most of the epigrams contained in these forgotten pages, and it would not be a profitable task to seek to rekindle it. A little more interest belongs to some fragments of table-talk which Mr. Croker amused himself by collecting at that time:—

Old Doctor Stopford (Bishop of Cloyne) stopped once at Mr. Phillips', a clergyman of his diocese, who entertained him very hospitably and, *inter alia*, with some fine fish. When the Bishop was stepping into his carriage to go away— "My dear Phillips," said he, " you have been extremely kind to me and there is but one thing more which can add to my obligation, that is to drown yourself in the river which produces your excellent fish, that I may give your living to my son Joe." "I thank your lordship," replied Phillips, " but I would not even hurt the last joint of my most useless finger to save your lordship, your lordship's son Joe, and all your lordship's family from the gallows."

This Doctor Stopford was an intimate friend of Swift's, and I daresay this strange speech to Phillips was but an imitation of the Dean's *brusquerie*.

When Archbishop Wake waited on King George II. to complain of the famous blackguard song written by the Duke of Wharton on the Archbishop, and the latter, to convince the King of the justice of his complaint, gravely began to read the verses, the old monarch, in an ecstasy, at one stanza cried out, " Bon! Bon!" "How, sir," said Wake, "do you call such execrable ribaldry good?" "Oh, que non," replied George correcting himself, " c'est mal, très mal, c'est exécrable ; mais il faut avouer que le drôle a de l'esprit."

Several other literary ventures occupied Mr. Croker's attention in 1804 and the succeeding year. One was a satire on the Irish stage, entitled 'Familiar Epistles,' which hit the fancy of the public so thoroughly that five editions were disposed of in less than a twelvemonth. 'An Intercepted Letter,' in which the society of Dublin was caricatured, had even a greater success, for it received the hearty praise of Miss Edgeworth, and speedily ran through seven editions. At this time Croker had attached himself to the Munster Circuit, to which Daniel O'Connell also belonged. His practice was good, and the Revenue cases which came to him by his father's influence formed not the least lucrative part of his business. Few men at his age find lying before them so fair and promising a field for their exertions.

Two events were now approaching which were destined to exercise no small influence in shaping his future career. One was his marriage, in 1806, and the other was his election to Parliament, in 1807. In his choice of a wife

Mr. Croker always accounted himself, and with reason, one of the most fortunate of men. He found a partner who was absolutely devoted to him, and whose first and last thought was to promote his happiness or advance his interests. She was the daughter of Mr. William Pennell, who subsequently became British Consul-General in South America, and was a lady of great firmness of character, yet of a most kind and gentle disposition. "Do not," he wrote to his friend Mr. E. H. Locker,* "indulge yourself in fancying my dear wife to be one of those fine and feathered ladies who have a little learning, a little language, a little talent, and a great deal of self opinion. She is nothing like this—she has none of what Sir Hugh Evans calls affectations, fribbles, and frabbles. She is a kind, even-tempered, well-judging girl, who can admire beauty and value talents without pretending to either, and whose object is rather to make home happy than splendid, and her husband contented than vain—in truth she is all goodness, but for literary talents, she has, as yet, none, and her indifference on this point becomes her so well that I can hardly wish for a change." Mrs. Croker, however, took more interest in literary studies and pursuits than her husband at that time imagined, and her judgment, as he afterwards gratefully acknowledged, was always sound and good.

They lived to celebrate their golden wedding in 1856, surrounded by many devoted friends; but, unhappily, the son, upon whom was set all the affection which was not given to each other, died in the full promise of his childhood—a blow from which Mr. Croker never fully recovered. Whenever he spoke or thought of his son, even in the midst of the greatest successes of after years, it seemed

* The son of Commodore Locker, and father of Mr. Frederick Locker. Mr. Croker and Mr. E. H. Locker continued on terms of intimacy for many years, but the correspondence which took place between them was not of great public interest.

as if his bereavement had happened only the day before.   In course of time, his adopted daughter—his wife's sister, afterwards Lady Barrow—succeeded in partially removing the heavy sense of bereavement from his heart, and the affection and true womanly helpfulness of his wife were a constant source of consolation to him.   His chief pleasures in life were always found in his own home, and the friends in whose society he most delighted were his own kindred.

It was in the year of his marriage that Mr. Croker made his first attempt to enter Parliament, for the borough of Downpatrick, but, although the influence of the chief local family was on his side, he was defeated.   In the following year there came the collapse of the Grenville Ministry, "All the Talents," and again Mr. Croker resolved to storm Downpatrick, and this time he succeeded.   He took his seat in May, 1807, and lost no time in accustoming himself to the new arena in which he was to strive with fortune :—

"I spoke very early," he wrote, on the margin of an inaccurate biographical sketch, "indeed, on the very night I took my seat.   Some observations of Mr. Grattan on the state of Ireland, which I thought injurious and unfounded, called me up,—nothing loath, I dare say, but quite unexpectedly even to myself; and though so obviously unpremeditated and, as it were, occasional, I, in after years, was not altogether flattered at hearing that my first speech was the best.   I suspect it was so.   Canning, whom I had never seen before, asked Mr. Foster to introduce me to him after the division, was very kind, and walked home with me to my lodgings."

Croker was in favour of some measure of Catholic Emancipation ; so was Canning.   Starting from the point of view common to them both, they soon became friends.   It was evident, however, that the time was not ripe for the removal of Catholic disabilities.   Mr. Perceval, the leader of the House of Commons, and the Duke of Portland, the Prime Minister, were opposed to any change in the law. Mr. Perceval's opinions were well known. " I could not conceive," he said on one occasion, " a time or any change of circumstances which could render further concession to the Catholics consistent with the safety of the State." Mr. Croker endeavoured to convince the public that there was danger in any further delay. In a pamphlet entitled ' A Sketch of Ireland, Past and Present,' published anonymously, but which reached a twentieth edition, he contended that " the Catholic lawyer, soldier, sailor, gentry, priesthood, and nobility should be admitted to all the honours of their professions and ranks. The priesthood, however, should be independent of foreign control, and paid by the State." The ability with which these views were advocated attracted Mr. Perceval's notice, and in the course of the next few months the young Member had shown so many signs of aptitude for Parliamentary life that Sir Arthur Wellesley, then Chief Secretary for Ireland, requested him to take charge of the Parliamentary business of his office during his absence in Portugal.* This was the beginning of a confidential relationship between the two men which continued without a moment's interruption down to the death of the Duke of Wellington in 1852.

There is, it has been explained, no regular diary of Mr. Croker's in existence, but frequently he made a memorandum upon public events as they took place, and the following relates to this period :—

June 14*th*, 1808.—Dined early with Sir Arthur and Lady Wellesley in Harley St., in order to talk over some of the Irish business which he had requested me to do for him in the House of Commons, as he was to set out for Ireland next morning on his way to Portugal. After dinner we were alone and talked over our business. There was one point of

* Sir A. Wellesley left England in July 1808, and returned in the ensuing autumn.

the Dublin Pipe Water Bill on which I differed a little from him, but could not convince him.   At last I said, perhaps he would reconsider the subject and write to me from Dublin about it.   He said, in his quick way, " No, no, I shall be no wiser to-morrow than I am to-day.   I have given you my reasons : you must decide for yourself."   When this was over, and while I was making some memoranda on the papers, he seemed to lapse into a kind of reverie, and remained silent so long that I asked him what he was thinking of.   He replied, "Why, to say the truth, I am thinking of the French that I am going to fight.   I have not seen them since the campaign in Flanders, when they were capital soldiers, and a dozen years of victory under Buona-parte must have made them better still.   They have besides, it seems, a new system of strategy, which has out-manœuvred and overwhelmed all the armies of Europe.   'Tis enough to make one thoughtful ; but no matter : my die is cast, they may overwhelm me, but I don't think they will out-manœuvre me.   First, because I am not afraid of them, as everybody else seems to be ; and secondly, because if what I hear of their system of manœuvres be true, I think it a false one as against steady troops.   I suspect all the continental armies were more than half beaten before the battle was begun.   I, at least, will not be frightened before-hand."

No favourable occasion for the display of Mr. Croker's debating powers arose till the following year, 1809, when Colonel Wardle brought forward his charges against the Duke of York, Commander-in-Chief, of corruptly sharing with his mistress, Mary Anne Clarke, the profits arising from the sale of commissions in the army.   There could be no doubt of the sway which this woman—who was the daughter of a French polisher and the wife of a builder—had gained over the Duke, although she was by no means in her first youth when he became acquainted with her, and had never been over-burdened with moral scruples.   She was a mercenary and designing creature who had led a wild and worthless life ; and she was doubtless quite capable of spreading abroad the impression that the surest road to advancement in the service was to gain her favour, and that her favour was only to be secured by money. In 1807 the Duke's acquaintance with her ceased.   She then formed an intimacy of the same kind with Colonel Wardle, her pension was withdrawn, and in revenge— as no one can now doubt—she accused the Duke of participating with her in the proceeds of the scandalous sale of military appointments.*   The House inquired into the charge, and after a searching investigation, in which the King's favourite son was certainly not spared, the Duke was exonerated from the main accusation, although it was justly held that in many respects his conduct had been most rash and reprehensible. The minority, in fact, was large enough to render the Duke's resignation necessary.   Mr. Croker took an active part in these proceedings, on the side of the Duke, and it was admitted that the art with which he sifted the evidence of the witnesses, and the great address and skill shown in his speech in reply to Sir Francis Burdett, tended very greatly towards bringing about the Duke's formal acquittal.

His pamphlet on Ireland, the abilities he had shown, the strongly favourable impression he made on those who conversed with him on public business, all served to mark him out thus early for public employment, and Mr. Perceval appears to have approached him on the subject more than once.

Memorandum by Mr. Croker.

April 18th, 1809.

Having occasion to mention to Mr. Perceval, whom I met in the House of Commons, some circumstances relative to giving up the Dublin Paving Bill, after we had settled that topic, he said, "But, Croker, you are all this while taking a great deal of trouble for us, and no care of yourself. Can

---

* It is said that Mrs. Clarke died so recently as the year 1880, aged 95.

you not think of anything we can do for you? Be assured
we have every disposition to serve you." I replied that I
was much obliged by his voluntary introduction of this subject, but that I had not turned my thoughts to anything for
myself, except that I should have liked, for the sake of
learning business, to have been private secretary to the Chief
Secretary for Ireland. The conversation ended by his repeating that I should look about for something suitable, and that
the Government would be happy to serve me."

Upon the resignation of the Duke of Portland, Canning
had hoped to be made Prime Minister, but he had not yet
discovered the secret of securing the good will of the King.
The following letter, from the Secretary of the Treasury,
enters somewhat fully into the position of affairs in 1809 :—

Mr. Charles Arbuthnot* to Mr. Croker.

Treasury Chambers, September 23rd.

MY DEAR CROKER,

I am sure you will not expect me to say a word upon the
painful subject of the duel.† On the other more general subject of the resignations I will write you a few hasty lines.
The Duke of Portland's state of health made his resignation
necessary. The question then was who should be his successor? Canning thought that the Minister ought to be
in the House of Commons, and he was aware that the choice
must be between him and Perceval. He felt that Perceval,
having led the House, was the obvious person to become
Minister; but he stated distinctly that in the event of such
an arrangement he himself should retire. In short, he would
not consent to remain in office unless he were Prime
Minister.

Perceval, on the other hand, though of the same opinion as
to the expediency of having the Minister in the Lower House,
would have consented, and entreated Canning to consent,
that the Duke's successor should be some third person in the

---

* [The lifelong friend of the Duke of Wellington. He lived with the
Duke, and many interesting facts connected with their intimacy will be
found in the course of this work.]

† [Between Lord Castlereagh and Canning.]

House of Lords; and I really believe that he would not have objected to any person for that situation whom Canning might have chosen to select. I know even that there was a doubt in Perceval's mind (who has the best regulated ambition I ever witnessed) whether for the general good he should yield to Canning's pretensions; but his friends and relations would never have consented to such a lowering of himself. And so, alas, our two former champions in the House of Commons have for the time separated; but their separation has been painful to both, and there has been nothing between them but the extreme of cordiality. When it became certain that the loss of Canning was not to be avoided, the King directed his remaining servants to submit to him what they considered to be the best new arrangement.

Their opinion has been (and it is now given to the King) that under the present circumstances their endeavour ought to be to form an Administration upon an extended basis; that the admission of Lord Sidmouth and his party might by counteraction produce a diminution instead of an addition of strength, and that a junction, upon equal terms, with the Grey and Grenville party would be that which would be most advisable. To this the King has consented, and should the offer be accepted with the cordiality with which it is made, I shall flatter myself that, notwithstanding the unfortunate loss of such talents as Canning has, we may still have such a strong Administration as the exigencies of the country require.

You must be aware that as yet no arrangement can be made; I can therefore tell you no more than that the disposition of Perceval towards you is as kind as you can desire. I will write to you again in a day or two.

Ever yours,

C. A.

The hopes raised by the concluding paragraph of this letter were not destined to remain long unfulfilled. In October Mr. Croker was offered the appointment of Secretary of the Admiralty, under the circumstances which are sufficiently explained in the following letters, written forty-one years afterwards:—

Mr. Croker to his wife. Extract.

July 28th, 1850.

After dinner I read some of the letters written by Charles Long and Lord Mulgrave to the late Lord Lonsdale about the time that I came into political life, which of course amused me. Lord Mulgrave writes to Lord Lonsdale, in October, 1809, to say that he had written to offer the Secretary of the Admiralty "to Mr. Croker, who was active, quick, and intelligent, and who might go off to Canning if he were not attended to." In this last point, at least, Lord Mulgrave was mistaken, for before the offer was made me, I had already answered Mr. Canning that I could not take his view of the differences in the Cabinet.

Mr. Croker to Lord Palmerston.

West Molesey, Surrey, 14th June, 1850.

MY DEAR PALMERSTON,

Will you forgive me for troubling you *inter tot et tanta negotia*, with two questions, which I know not any one else who can answer?

The first is purely literary:—Is there any ground for a doubt lately raised that your father was the author of the pretty lines beginning,—

> " Whoe'er like me with trembling anguish brings
> His heart's whole treasure to fair Bristol's springs? "

I suspect the doubt to have arisen from a different inscription, I believe to your mother, in Romsey Church, but of course not his.

The other is rather personal and historical. Ward, in his Memoirs, just published,* states in terms of compliment (which I am far from deserving) that you and I owe our appointments in the Admiralty to the discernment of Lord Mulgrave. Now Lord Mulgrave wrote me the official proposition, and was very cordial and kind to me, but I owed the appointment to the Government, and especially to Mr. Perceval, by whose

* ['Memoirs of the Political and Literary Life of Robert Plumer Ward.' 1850.]

desire Lord Mulgrave made the official proposition. If you have no objection to tell me, I should be glad to know how it was with you. If you have the slightest, pray have no scruple in leaving my curiosity ungratified. My own impression was, that your station and University character suggested you at once to the framers of the new Government, and that if anybody in particular rang the bell it was old Lord Malmesbury.

Ever, my dear Palmerston,

Faithfully yours,

J. W. CROKER.

Lord Palmerston to Mr. Croker.

Carlton Gardens, June 17th, 1852.

MY DEAR CROKER,

There is, I believe, no statute of limitation as to epistolary debts, and you know by your own experience, no doubt, that letters have often remained unanswered by men overwhelmed with business from pressure of occupations, and not from any want of good will towards the writer, and therefore in clearing off "the gathered chaos of five office years" (if I may take a liberty with our great poet) I cannot refrain from assuring you that nothing but an endless repetition of "too much" every day prevented me from replying to two letters of yours which I received long ago, and which you may by this time have forgotten. The replies, however, which I should have given if I had answered your letters at the time, would have been that the verses were my father's, and that my appointment to the Admiralty was given me by the Duke of Portland at the request of Lord Malmesbury the diplomatist.

Well, here we are now, two "statesmen out of place," and I should be very glad to renew our companionship; and if I should chance at any time to find myself in your neighbourhood, I will not fail to do so.

Yours very sincerely,

PALMERSTON.

Mr. James Smith to Mr. Croker.

Basinghall Street, December 28th, 1809.

MY DEAR CROKER,

My brother and myself are much mortified at our inability to accept your kind invitation.

You certainly have a lien upon Horace in respect of ship's licences, and so had some Secretary in the days of Augustus, if we may judge from the following ode :—

> " O navis, referent in mare te novi
> Fluctus. O quid agis? fortiter occupa
> Portum."

If I am late in the offer of congratulations upon your appointment, you will not on that account doubt the sincerity.

I should long since have paid them personally but was prevented by considering that you must be too much occupied at the office to receive any visits other than those of business.

There is a book published * (which I will send for your perusal to-morrow) containing a history of the late memorable row at Covent Garden Theatre, with the fugitive rhymes that have been written on that event. Of the latter, the pieces signed " H " are my brother's, and those signed " I," with the addition of " Heigho, says Kemble," proceed from the pen of

Dear Croker,

Yours most sincerely,

JAMES SMITH.

Mr. Croker retained this post until 1830, and it has always been admitted that the Board of Admiralty never had a more efficient, zealous, and industrious Secretary. He once wrote to Thomas Moore (October 26th, 1811), inviting him to call at his office, saying, "I should be glad to see you whenever you happen to pass my way. I am almost always to be found at my desk." This was literally true. He was very seldom absent from his duties, except during the time of his annual holiday. "For two and twenty years," he wrote to Mr. Murray, in 1838, "I never quitted that office-room without a kind of uneasiness, like a truant boy; and this feeling still clings to me." A recent First Lord of the Admiralty has said that all which is best and most business

* ['Rejected Addresses.']

like in the department was the legacy of Mr. Croker. He
quickly made himself master of the details of work connected with the office. This thorough competency for his
duties rendered him indispensable to the successive First
Lords under whom he served, and it partly helped to
explain the great influence which he exerted on all who
came into contact with him in his official capacity. He once
referred to himself in the House of Commons as a "servant
of the Board," but Sir Joseph Yorke, a former Lord of the
Admiralty, promptly remarked that when he was at the
Board "it was precisely the other way." The spirit in which
he began his duties is indicated in a letter to his wife :—

October 12th, 1809.

I am now thoroughly and completely in office, and up to
my eyes in business, the extent of which is quite terrific;
but with good assistance (which every one seems ready to
give me) I hope to be able to get on. I must attend regularly from nine in the morning till four or five in the evening.
I therefore shall rise early, and walk or ride for half-an-hour
before I come to office. Direct to me now to the Admiralty,
but you need not write "private," as I open *all* letters myself :
tell this to Mrs. Casey, and desire her also to direct to me at
the Admiralty.

From Mr. Croker's Journal.

In the summer and autumn of 1809 some differences grew
up in the Cabinet, which broke out into general notice by
the strange event of a duel between Mr. Canning, Secretary
of State for Foreign Affairs, and Lord Castlereagh, Secretary
of State for the War Department. This duel took place on
the 21st September (Thursday), on Putney Heath. Lord
Yarmouth, Castlereagh's first cousin and second, told me
afterwards that Charles Ellis, who was Canning's second,
was so nervous for his friend's safety that he could not load
his pistols, and that Lord Yarmouth either loaded Mr.
Canning's pistols for Mr. Ellis, or lent him one of his own,
I forget which, but I think the latter. Nothing could exceed

the coolness and propriety of conduct of the principals, and Ellis's incapacity does him honour. Yarmouth drove Castlereagh to the ground (which was on Putney Heath, just beyond a cottage on the left of the road to Roehampton), in his curricle, and the conversation was chiefly relative to Catalani, who was then in high fashion, and Castlereagh hummed some of her songs as they went along.

The differences in his Cabinet and his own bad state of health induced the Duke of Portland to resign ; and Mr. Perceval, who had been his Chancellor of the Exchequer and manager of the House of Commons (after a fruitless attempt to obtain the accession of Lords Grenville and Grey), proceeded to form an Administration, in which he was the First Lord of the Treasury.

Nobody had resigned Cabinet office but Lord Castlereagh and Mr. Canning. Lord Castlereagh's place was filled by Lord Liverpool, and his at the Home Department by Mr. Ryder, but this was after some delay. Lord Bathurst, who had held the Board of Control, took the Foreign Seals *ad interim*, till it should be known whether Lord Wellesley, then in Spain, would accept them. Mr. Pole,* who was Secretary of the Admiralty, succeeded Mr. Dundas in Ireland, and Lord Mulgrave, at Mr. Perceval's request, offered that place to me.

I was in Ireland at the time I received these letters, and thought it right to lose no time in coming to London, there to give my answer, because, though the office was a very high one, and much better and greater than my age, connexions, or expectations led me to look to, yet the precarious tenure which I should have of it, and the difficulty of the situation itself (at that period particularly, the Walcheren expedition having just failed), induced me to pause before I took so decided a step as throwing up my profession, which was almost my only means of livelihood. I was not, to be sure, very high in my profession ; but by the assistance of the revenue business, which my father's interest and great knowledge of revenue affairs secured me, I had made in the years previous to this time from 400*l.* to 600*l.* a year. I was, besides, fond of the profession itself.

When I arrived in London, on the morning of the 10th of October, I first saw Arbuthnot, Secretary of the Treasury, who told me all the news of the day ; but, as to myself, he said, I *must* accept, though I should be sure of being turned

* [Rt. Hon. Wm. Wellesley Pole.]

out in a week, for that I was bound in honour to obey Mr. Perceval's wishes, who had thought so kindly of me; that when he wrote to desire the accession of Lords Grenville and Grey, he had determined, if they came in, to accept the Seals of the Home Department, and had declared that he stipulated but for one appointment, which was that I should be his Under-Secretary. I could, after this, have no doubt what to do, so I waited on Mr. Perceval, and accepted the office with many thanks. Next day I was appointed in form, and took my seat at the Board.

The selection of a young and comparatively unknown man for such a post naturally gave rise to considerable outcry, but to this Mr. Croker paid little heed. A more serious difficulty presented itself in less than a month after his appointment, and at first it seemed probable that it would render his resignation inevitable. The circumstances are related in the following memorandum, which bears no date, but was evidently written towards the close of Mr. Croker's life :—

I believe the fury of political parties never ran higher— they certainly in my threescore years of experience never ran so high—as on Mr. Perceval's accession to office; and amidst a storm of accusation and reproach, of course a very prominent topic would be the appointment at such a crisis (it was the depth of the Walcheren disaster and the height of Buonaparte's triumph on the Continent) to such an office as Secretary of the Admiralty of a " young " and " briefless " Irish barrister, though the epithets were rather overstrained— for I was eight-and-twenty, and I had made professionally in the year before I came into Parliament 600*l.* But it certainly was *un peu fort*, and only to be accounted for by the straits to which the extraordinary circumstances in which Mr. Perceval was placed [had reduced him] and [by] his personal partiality for me. The outcry was very violent, and some accidents, with which, in fact, I had nothing to do, came in to increase the clamour. But luckily I was able to assert and keep my position, and I never heard, and do not believe, there was any complaint of my official conduct. I was at least not wanting in diligence and activity.

Within a month, however, of this unexpected and enviable

appointment, you will be surprised to hear that I resigned it.
It happened that, paying a more minute attention to details
than my two predecessors had happened to do, I saw reason
to suspect a serious defalcation in a public accountant of high
rank and respectability, and refused my signature to an
additional issue of money till the last issues were accounted
for. The person implicated was a *protégé* and personal
friend of the King, George III., to whom he represented that
this young Irishman, who knew nothing of his business,
refused his signature, which was a mere routine form, and
thus impeded the ordinary current of the public service. The
King sent for Mr. Perceval and desired him to have an
explanation with me. I could not then have known or
imagined the extent of the defalcation, still less could either
the King or Mr. Perceval; but the officer himself did, and
pressed his royal patron to stifle my *capricious* opposition,
which could be the more easily and properly done because
nothing had transpired, and all that was to be done to set all
right was that I should sign the same routine order that my
predecessors had always signed. This was pressed upon me
with an earnestness proportioned to the interest which the
King's prompter had in the affair, but in the meanwhile
I was silently examining the former practice, and I soon
satisfied myself that it was a case of disgrace and ruin to the
individual, and a loss of at least 200,000*l.* to the public.
This grieved me to the heart; I was grieved to be the
involuntary cause of so great an affliction to individuals—
grieved to oppose the wishes of the King, who at first took
a very anxious interest in the affair—grieved to embarrass
Mr. Perceval—grieved to lose my high and lucrative office,
but, seeing no alternative between the results and an
abandonment of my own duty, I adopted them, and placed
my resignation in Mr. Perceval's hands, who, sorry as he
was, could not but admit that I was right, and I really
believe would have himself resigned rather than have compromised an affair of which by this time he saw the whole
importance. Upon his explanation, the just and upright old
King came round much more readily than Mr. Perceval had
anticipated, and not merely approved of my proceeding, but
sent me through Mr. Perceval a most gracious assurance of
his satisfaction at my zeal in doing my duty, and, he added,
my firmness in resisting his own first suggestions under
a misunderstanding of the case.

Mr. Croker's firmness and integrity throughout this affair increased the high opinion of him which Mr. Perceval had already formed, and the vigour and tact which he displayed in the debates on the unlucky Walcheren expedition confirmed the reputation he had previously gained. But although he was assiduous in the discharge of his parliamentary and official duties, he found time to pay some attention to those literary pursuits which had been the first to win his affection. All the routine duty which fell upon him—and he had to write or sign hundreds of letters every day, answer innumerable questions, and waste much of his time in personal interviews—did not prevent him getting through an astonishing amount of literary work. Perhaps this was the part of his day's task to which he turned with the greatest zest. He was at all times the master of a clear and manly style, and in none of his compositions does it show forth to greater advantage than in his letters. Political writing was somewhat artificial and ponderous, as a rule, when Mr. Croker entered the field; but his lighter hand and more dexterous touch were at once recognised as indicating the arrival of a new-comer who would be formidable, and whose support it was therefore desirable to secure. Imitations of the letters of "Junius" had been only too plentiful, but originality of style and thought were not common, and it was easily to be seen from the first that Mr. Croker was master of these advantages. Some of his early efforts had been in verse—epigrams on the names of London streets; a few pasquinades; and a spirited poem entitled "the Battles of Talavera," which was highly successful, and which Lord Wellington appears to have read with "satisfaction."

Badajoz, Nov. 15th, 1809.

My DEAR SIR,

I am much obliged to you for your letter of the 20th October, and your poem, which I have read with great satisfaction. I did not think a battle could be turned into anything so entertaining. I heard with great pleasure that you were to be appointed Secretary of the Admiralty, in which situation, I have no doubt, you will do yourself credit, and more than justify me in any little exertion I may have made for you while I was in office.

Ever, my dear Sir,
Yours most sincerely,
WELLINGTON.

But although Mr. Croker wrote verses, he never pretended to be a poet. The weapon which he handled best was prose. In this year of his appointment to the Admiralty, a publication made its appearance which was afterwards to afford him great scope for the display of his highest literary powers, and to which he became devotedly attached—the *Quarterly Review.* It was the chief pride of his life to be associated with this famous periodical, and his best original work was done for its pages. He delighted to be included in the list of its founders, but he was not at first a contributor; ten numbers had been published, and among them all there was but one article by him—in number three. But from 1811 down to 1854, with the exception of an interval between 1826 and 1831, he seldom failed to supply an article for every number of the *Review,* and sometimes he wrote three or four articles, every one of which was tolerably sure to attract immediate notice. Although his strength lay greatly in political discussion, he was one of the most entertaining of writers in the general field of literature, and few men equalled him as a critic. It has pleased many persons to speak of Mr. Croker as if in his day he wrote all the political

articles in the *Quarterly*, whereas he was the author of comparatively few. As he said in a letter to Mr. Lockhart, in
1834, " for twenty years that I wrote in it, from 1809 to
1829, I never gave, I believe, one purely political article—
not one, certainly, in which party politics predominated."
Mr. Croker's range was, indeed, a wide one; from the
slightest of society novels, or the latest book of travels,
to the gravest treatise on affairs of State, nothing came
amiss to him. He took immense pains with his articles;
he would ransack all England to verify an important statement, or clear up a doubt about a fact. If the disputed
point related to family history, he would go to the fountain
head for information, and never failed to get it and to make
good use of it. In those days, it must be remembered,
the newspapers did but a small part of the work which
they undertake now, and the great movements which were
impending in political parties were known to the public only
by vague rumour, or were kept confined to the knowledge of
a few well-informed men. It frequently happened that news
of the gravest importance was first made known to the
country through the medium of the political article in the
Edinburgh or *Quarterly Reviews.* Almost always that article
was founded upon intelligence which had been communicated
by the heads of the Ministry, or by the originators of some
measure which was soon to become the universal theme of
discussion. It is evident from Mr. Croker's correspondence
that he went for the foundation of many of his essays to the
men who alone could rightly know all the facts with which
he had to deal, and thus in many cases an almost complete
draft of the political article was supplied by the Duke of
Wellington, by Sir Robert Peel, by Lord Stanley (Derby),
or by some authority of equal weight on the question of the
day. The case which Mr. Croker had thus prepared was

always stated with great force and pungency, although to the reader of the present day the style may sometimes appear a little too elaborate and strained, while the mannerisms which characterize so many of Mr. Croker's printed compositions—entirely absent from his letters—especially his excessive use of italics and capitals, give them an archaic appearance which does not always correspond with the matter itself. The raw material for much of the political history of the present century, from 1809 onwards, will be found scattered in profusion, though mingled no doubt with strong partisan opinions, in the pages of the *Quarterly Review.*

In all his articles, and in everything that he did, accuracy and truthfulness were most diligently sought for by Mr. Croker. His opinions, it must be confessed, were sometimes prejudiced and one-sided; for he was an avowed party man of the old type, although his party zeal certainly did not exceed that which we find in his opponents of the *Edinburgh.* But he always sought to ground himself thoroughly in the *facts* with which he had to deal. He was often taunted with the great importance which he attached to dates, but dates are very important things in history, and it is a pity that some of his critics did not borrow his respect for them. He invariably wished to test every statement before committing it to paper. If that was a fault, it is to be regretted that historians and critics of more or less eminence have not always shared it with him. On the margin of a printed sketch of his life, in which the writer had dwelt upon the "exaggerated" value which he attached to "trifles," Mr. Croker wrote:—"I dare say that this may be true, for I feel that I am disposed to think nothing a trifle—not merely because *nugœ in seria ducunt,* but because I think and find that the smallest and apparently most indifferent trifles are always indicative of *something*—often something of importance. In many not unimportant instances, both in private and public life, I found the benefit of a minute attention to *trifles ;* and so I believe every man would say who narrowly consulted his own experience." It was this regard for accuracy which made him so indefatigable in the preparation of the celebrated edition of Boswell's 'Life of Johnson'; the facts which he brought to light were of the greatest interest at the time, and they will be prized more and more as the persons to whom they relate are removed to a greater distance from successive generations of Boswell's readers. In the same way, his essays in the *Quarterly Review* on the various collections of family papers which were published during his day—the "Malmesbury Papers," the "Buckingham Memoirs," and similar collections—brought a world of new information to the subject, and in some cases they possessed a higher value by far than the book on which they were founded. The method in which he set about preparing for any labour on which he was engaged will come out very clearly in the course of these pages, and it will be admitted that if Mr. Croker's strong feelings on certain political questions some- times interfered with the coolness of his judgment, he never failed to approach his work in a thoroughly honest and con- scientious spirit, and seldom lost sight of the first and most imperative obligation which every writer owes to the public.

CHAPTER II.

1810–1813.

THE complete series of Mr. Croker's own letters, carefully copied into well-bound volumes, begins in 1811, and extends to 1834. Within this period, and especially between the years 1814 and 1830, scarcely anything of importance appears to be missing; before the first date, and after the last, the correspondence must have been somewhat irregularly kept, although a large proportion of the letters received by Mr. Croker was preserved. His replies to these letters are, in many cases, not to be found. It is probable that during the first year or two of Mr. Croker's official life, he gave little attention to his private correspondence; his time was almost wholly taken up with the routine duties which daily pressed upon him, and with his parliamentary work. He had been a little more than a year in his new position before there seemed to be a probability of his losing it. In 1810, politics were in a highly unsettled state, and the general expectation was that a change of Ministry could not be long deferred. The derangement of the King (George III.) recurred in so decided a form that little hope was entertained of his recovery by the most sanguine of his friends, and it was well known that the doctors looked upon his case as hopeless. The friends and advisers of the Prince of Wales were openly opposed to Mr. Perceval's Ministry, the Prince himself hated the Prime Minister, and lists of the new Administration were circulated in every club in London. It was supposed that Lord Grenville and Lord Grey would be at the head of the coming Government, and that Henry Brougham would take Mr. Croker's place at the Admiralty. It could not be doubted that Mr. Perceval's position was as weak as it well could be; he was not popular in the country, and before his accession to power, as well as afterwards, events ran steadily against him. The Walcheren disaster, the Peninsula expedition, the appointment of Sir Arthur Wellesley as commander — everything was regarded by the people with more or less disfavour and suspicion. Mr. Croker was, to all appearance, fully justified in the conviction that his tenure of office was very precarious.

During the debates on the Regency Bill, Mr. Croker delivered a powerful speech in the House of Commons in favour of the Ministerial proposition, and it soon appeared that the Prince of Wales had no intention of doing anything to bring about the removal of Mr. Perceval in favour of his Whig friends. It afterwards turned out that he was not very anxious to assist them even when the death of Mr. Perceval gave him a fair opportunity of doing so. So far from being willing to see Lord Grey in office, for instance, he declared that he would have abdicated if Lord Grey had been forced upon him ;* and thus it befell that a Tory Minister, Lord Liverpool—who has been much ridiculed by a Tory Minister of our own day as the " Arch Mediocrity "—was put in the place of the assassinated Premier, and remained in power from 1812 to 1827.

There are no letters from Mr. Croker of any consequence in relation to the Regency debates, but in June, 1811, he briefly touched upon public affairs in a communication to a friend :—

I hear from a good hand that the King is doing much better than the public reports would give us ground for believing— this is the only circumstance of any interest which I have to communicate. The few. people I see all come to me with hopes. One hopes for a Russian war, another for a Spanish victory, a third for an American peace, and a fourth for an American war. As for the two latter, I have not even the means of forming a hope or a fear. About Spain I am at this moment very anxious, and about Russia I sincerely hope she may not break with France too soon. A feverish and jealous peace I think more useful than unconnected and uncombined war. Such a peace might end in a general war ; such a war could but end in a general subjection.

But the greater part of Mr. Croker's correspondence at this period is of literary or social interest. In the two following letters, Walter Scott requests Mr. Croker's acceptance of the ' Lady of the Lake ' (published in 1810), and expresses his thanks for ' Talavera ' :—

* "Three times that day, before dinner and after dinner, he declared that if Lord Grey had been forced upon him, he should have abdicated." Lord Russell's ' Memoirs of Moore,' i. 360 ; Buckingham's ' Memoirs of the Regency,' &c.

Walter Scott to Mr. Croker.

Edinburgh, May 3rd, 1810.

My dear Sir,

This comes to entreat your obliging acceptance of a certain square volume called ‘The Lady of the Lake.’ I am now enabled to send her to my friends as the Romans of yore used to lend their wives, and greatly it is to my own relief; for never was man more bored of his wife (and that’s a bold word) than I am of the said Lady. I hope, however, you will find her agreeable company for an evening or two—and I don’t think you will be disposed greatly to abuse me for using your cover for another copy to be left at Hatchard’s for Canning, who did me the honour to wish to see it as soon as possible. I would you were all together again, and am apt to hope it may yet come round.

Believe me, dear sir,

Ever your truly obliged,

Walter Scott.

Oct 10th, [1810].

My dear Sir,

I drop you these few lines, not to engage you in correspondence, for which I am aware you have so little time, but merely to thank you very sincerely for the eighth edition of your beautiful and spirited poem and the kind letter which accompanied it. Whatever the practised and hackneyed critic may say of that sort of poetry, which is rather moulded in an appeal to the general feelings of mankind than the technical rules of art, the warm and universal interest taken by those who are alive to fancy and feeling, will always compensate for his approbation, whether entirely withheld or given with tardy and ungracious reluctance. Many a heart has kindled at your ‘Tala᾽era’ which may be the more patriotic for the impulse as long as it shall last. I trust we shall soon hear from the conqueror of that glorious day such news as may procure us “another of the same.” His excellent conduct, joined to his high and undaunted courage, make him our Nelson on land, and though I devoutly wish that his force could be doubled, I shall feel little anxiety for the event of a day in which he is only outnumbered by one-third. Your acceptable bulletin looks well and auspiciously. The matter of Lucien Bonaparte is one of the most surprising which has occurred in our day—a Frenchman refusing at once a crown, and declining to part with his wife, is indeed one of the most uncommon exhibitions of an age fertile in novelties as wonderful as portentous. •

> Believe me, my dear sir,
> > Ever your truly grateful,
> > > WALTER SCOTT.

Concerning 'Talavera,' Mr. Murray sent him a note in April of this year to inform him that he had printed another edition, and adding, " it has been more successful than any short poem that I know, exceeding in circulation Mr. Heber's ' Palestine ' or ' Europe,' and even Mr. Canning's ' Ulm ' and ' Trafalgar.' "

In the following letters, some incidents of the French war, of a kind which at that time were by no means uncommon on our coasts, were brought to Mr. Croker's notice :—

> *Mr. (afterwards Sir John) Barrow to Mr. Croker.*

> > Ramsgate, July 18th, 1810.

We had the mortification of seeing *two* colliers captured the other evening close under the North Foreland, when not a single cruiser was in sight, except *one in Margate Roads.* See if there is not a Lieutenant Leach commanding the " Cracker " gun-brig, and if that gun-brig is not on the Foreland station. This gentleman, I understand, has a house at Birchington, where he usually *sleeps,* and for this purpose Margate Roads is a very convenient place for his vessel to lie in. The Admiral must be remarkably good-natured to grant him this indulgence, so advantageous to the enemy's privateers.

> > Ramsgate, July 27th, 1810.

Last night, about eight o'clock, I had the mortification of seeing from my window two French lugger privateers very quickly take possession of an Ordnance Hoy close astern to the Galloper Light, and in the face of our whole squadron in the Downs, not one of which attempted to move a peg. Without pretending to much knowledge of naval tactics, I cannot help feeling, as everybody here feels, that there is some mismanagement of our naval force in the Channel, or the enemy would not dare, in the height of summer and during fine weather and broad daylight, come over and beard us close to our own coast; it is mortifying enough to hear people publicly crying out, "Aye, this is what we get for paying taxes to keep up the navy; a French privateer is not worth capturing, she will not pay the charges of condemnation." If there be truth in this, Mr. Yorke * will have the merit of curing the evil by the promotion of Brown and Maxwell.

I am, dear Croker,

Yours faithfully,

J. BARROW.

Mr. Perceval to Mr. Croker.

Sunday, Nov. 11th, 1810.

DEAR CROKER,

I thank you for the sight of H.'s pamphlet.† I have run through it, I cannot say *read* it, for it requires much more *reading* than I have had time yet to give it. It is in many parts very able—in all very specious; in many, however, I presume to think, very fallacious, and particularly unfair in keeping out of sight so much as it does the circumstance of interrupted commercial intercourse with the Continent which in my opinion is sufficient, together with the causes which he mentions, to account for almost all these symptoms and phenomena which he ascribes solely to the supposed excess in our paper circulation. The truth probably lies between the two extremes of opinion upon this point; but the practical danger and difficulty of this experiment, so immensely in my mind at least, weighs down the mischief,

---

* [Mr. Charles Yorke, The First Lord of the Admiralty.]

† [The pamphlet referred to was published in 1810 by Mr. Huskisson, and was entitled 'The Question Concerning the Depreciation of our Currency Stated and Examined.']

which he supposes to exist from the over-issue of paper, that I should consider the measure he proposes as tantamount to a Parliamentary declaration that we must submit to any terms of peace rather than continue the war, which, I apprehend under his project, would be found utterly impossible.

Yours very truly,

Sp. P.

Memorandum by Mr. Perceval inclosed in the above.

I do not know that what is written on the accompanying pages is worth your perusal, but it explains a little more what I allude to above respecting the interrupted intercourse in commerce with the Continent, which I conceive to be so very material a part of that question.

" It is absurd to suppose that any other process can be necessary than that of restoring things to their natural course " (the last member of the last sentence of Huskisson's pamphlet, *see* page 149).   I would ask any man who has read nothing upon this subject but Huskisson's pamphlet, whether he can believe that it is in the power—*the physical power*—of Parliament to restore to their natural course *all those* things which most materially bear upon the present question?—and if it is not possible, how idle is it to say that nothing else is necessary than to restore things to their natural course.

His mode of doing it is for the Bank to buy up gold, and to resume their payments in specie.

But supposing his view to be correct respecting the depreciation of our circulating medium (which, to say the least of it, I conceive to be a most exaggerated view of it), can any man say that our *want* being (as Huskisson supposes it to be) to get more gold into this country from foreign countries (which cannot be brought here either by the Bank or any one else but by purchasing it with some equivalent), will any man say that these orders of the enemy, which impede in so great a degree, if they do not absolutely prevent, the introduction of our manufacture and merchandise into the Continent (by which alone we can purchase the gold from the Continent), are not some of the circumstances, and some too of the most operative, which make gold an article so

D 2

difficult to get and to keep here?—or that there are not circumstances which must be removed before "things can be restored to their natural course"? Yet over these circumstances Parliament has no control.

We want gold, and Huskisson supposes it to exist in sufficient quantity on the Continent. Our warehouses are clogged with merchandise which the Continent would be most glad to purchase, but their tyrant will not let them; if he would, we should get their gold in exchange. Till, then, such an alteration takes place in the world as will admit of the freer intercourse in trade, no measure can be effectual as to the object of acquiring that gold but one which may at once prevent our buying those articles from the Continent which they wish to sell, and which we indispensably *want*—I say *indispensably*, if we are to carry on the war; and that shall put a stop to that immense foreign expenditure which, as long as the war continues on, would drain out of this country every new importation of gold and silver which any purchasers, however extravagant of the Bank, could possibly procure.

The difficulty of getting trustworthy news from the Continent at this period was great, and it is well known that no one displayed greater enterprise and spirit in the endeavour to overcome the difficulty, and to satisfy the very reasonable demands of the public for prompt information, than Mr. John Walter, of the *Times*—the son of the original proprietor. The *Times* had its special packet-boats running, but they were frequently interfered with under one pretext or another, and the Government officials did not scruple to try by every means in their power to enable their own organs to leave the independent journal far behind in the race. Mr. Walter was not to be beaten. His organisation and plans were so perfect that in 1809 he was able to announce the capitulation of Flushing two days before the news was otherwise known, even to the Ministry. Early in Mr. Croker's official career Mr. Walter addressed several letters to him on the subject.

Mr. John Walter to Mr. Croker.

Printing House Square, May 9th, 1811.

SIR,

I take the liberty of addressing you upon a subject which has been suggested to me in relation to the procurement of French papers. The difficulty of obtaining these has increased lately to an extraordinary degree, to overcome which a plan has been proposed to the following effect.

It is pretty certain that no French journals whatsoever can be procured but by the means of smugglers. A person of this description, who is in collusion with a French officer near a certain port, is willing to exchange this contraband traffic in which he has been hitherto engaged for one which is perfectly innocent with respect to its operation upon the public revenue, namely, the conveyance of French papers only to England. He feels disposed to engage in this traffic, if he could be well assured of certain facilities which seem to be necessary to the execution of the scheme. Government, I apprehend, will be no less desirous than myself of obtaining the information contained in these papers. I do not mean to ask the permission in this instance directly, but only to know, in the way of information (if you would have the goodness to satisfy me), whether there would be any impropriety in requesting the Admiralty to grant this man's vessel a protection for the purpose above specified, upon the sole condition that no smuggled goods whatsoever should be transported by him. With this understanding, I should, of course, transmit you the papers received with all possible dispatch.

As I before specified, I only wish now to inquire whether there is any impropriety in making the application, engaging, so far as I can possibly be answerable for the conduct of the person employed, that the object of his voyages shall be totally remote from anything connected with contraband trade.

I have the honour to remain, Sir,

Your most obedient servant,

JOHN WALTER, Jun.

Neither the assistance given to him by Mr. Croker, nor any other consideration, could lead Mr. Walter to sacrifice any portion of that spirit of independence which always characterised him. When, on the assassination of Mr. Perceval, it was perceived that the old Administration was substantially to remain in power, the proprietor of the *Times* took the first opportunity—only nine days after Bellingham's fatal act—of expressing his opinions to Mr. Croker, in his usual manly and straightforward way :—

Mr. John Walter to Mr. Croker.

Wednesday night, May 20th, [1812].

MY DEAR SIR,

I learn from the evening papers that no important changes will take place in the Administration. This, I confess, appears to me to be a circumstance of that nature which must oblige me to consider attentively the part I ought to take in so perplexing situation of things. I have much to thank you for on the score of friendly communications, and many motives for personal esteem and respect ; but I cannot, I fear, extend these sentiments much beyond yourself, or at least not to the general body of the Administration, as it is at present likely to be composed. I hope, therefore, you will not think me taking too great a liberty if I frankly inform you that I must hesitate at engaging by implication to support a body of men so critically situated, and so doubtful of national support, as those to whom public affairs are now likely to be entrusted. This political separation, however—if such it be—will produce no breach on my part of personal esteem ; but it might seem unfair in me to receive farther assistance, when I cannot make the return, which I have hitherto done with so much pleasure.

I remain, with great respect, my dear Sir,
Your faithful and obliged servant,
JOHN WALTER, Jun.

Mr. Croker to Sir Richard Keats.

March 31st, 1812.

Mr. Yorke and Sir Richard Bickerton left us [the Admiralty] on the 25th instant, Sir Richard to hoist his flag at

Portsmouth, and Mr. Yorke to rear turnips at his saline farm at Bonington. The latter is really a loss to the public service; he was indefatigable in his attention to his duty, and I believe acted in the most conscientious manner in the discharge of it; but we had been very unlucky in his time, and so many untoward circumstances, together with a disposition naturally anxious and nervous, rendered him at last heartily tired of the Admiralty; and he insisted on retiring, very much to the regret of the Government, and I even believe of the Regent.

Lord Melville * is a most amiable and worthy man, and very good at business, and I am mistaken if he be not popular with the service and the country. I am sure he will desire to be so with both. The French have a little squadron at sea, which we miss, as Skirmish in the play misses the bottle; I hope, like Skirmish, we shall catch it at last.

J. W. C.

Mr. Croker retained his office under the new Prime Minister, although he differed from Lord Liverpool on more than one issue of the day, including the question of Catholic Emancipation. He supported the Catholic claims, as Mr. Perceval had justly said, on "true no-Popery principles." His views may be gathered from a reply to an address from the Roman Catholic electors of Down, thanking him for his votes in Parliament:—

I beg you will state to them that I am happy to have deserved their approbation; I felt it was my duty to be in my place in Parliament on every part of that important question, and to give my decided vote for what appeared to me to be a measure of just and liberal policy and of national conciliation.

The failure of that measure and the consequences which must follow from the temper with which the measure itself was received in Ireland have given me sincere pain; but it is a consolation to me to think that for that failure I am as little responsible as for those consequences; and that in one

* [The new First Lord.]

of the closest divisions that ever took place in the House of
Commons on a great national question where the parties
were, if I may use the expression, *neck* and *neck*, and where
a single vote was of the utmost importance—I am, I say,
well pleased to think that I was not absent from my duty.

While he retained his office, however, he was unsuccessful
in retaining his seat for Down, and his opponent, who
represented the anti-Catholic interest, was elected.   For
Mr. Croker himself a seat was secured for the borough of
Athlone.

It is well known that Lord Wellington was much annoyed
and harassed by the hostile criticisms which pursued him
throughout his campaign in the Peninsula.   His feelings on
the subject are forcibly described in the following letter :—

Lord Wellington to Mr. Croker.

Cartaxo, December 20th, 1810.

My dear Sir,

I am very much obliged to you for your notes to the
4th inst., and I am happy to learn that the King is doing
so well.

In regard to affairs here I must continue to do what I think
will be good for the people of England under all the circumstances of the case, and not what I learn from this or from
that print will please them.

The licentiousness of the press, and the presumption of the
editors of the newspapers, which is one of the consequences of
their licentiousness, have gone near to stultify the people of
England ; and it makes one sick to hear the statements
of supposed facts, and the comments upon supposed transactions here, which have the effect only of keeping the minds of
the people of England in a state of constant alarm and
anxiety, and of expectation which must be disappointed.

In the early part of the campaign all was alarm and
gloomy anxiety ; the British army was doomed to destruction,
and I was to be well thought of if I could bring any part of
it off the Peninsula without disgrace.   Then came the battle
of Burgos, and nothing would then suit the editors of the

newspapers but that Massena's army should be destroyed, although it was 20,000 men stronger than mine in that action; and, making a very large allowance for reinforcements to mine in the retreat, and for losses to the enemy in their advance, the numbers must have been nearly equal in the first days in October. Those who have seen or know anything of armies are aware that a combined army made up as mine is, and always has been, partly of recruits and in a great measure of soldiers in a state of convalescence, and composed of officers unaccustomed to the great operations of war, is not equal to a French army; and those who have been engaged with a French army know that it is not so very easily destroyed, even by one equal to contend with it. But nothing will suit editors (friends and foes are alike) but that the enemy should be swept from the face of the earth; and for a month they kept the people of England in trembling expectation of receiving the accounts of an action which was to relieve Europe from the yoke of the tyrant.

Then every word in a despatch is not only scrupulously weighed and canvassed, but synonymous terms are found out for, and false arguments are founded upon, expressions to which meanings are assigned which never entered into the contemplation of the writer. All this, I conclude, for the instruction of the people of England!

I really believe that, owing to the ignorance and presumption and licentiousness of the press, the most ignorant people in the world of military and political affairs (excepting the domestic politics of their own country) are the people of England; and I cannot but think that I act wisely and honestly towards them to do what I think is good for them, rather than what will please them. At the same time it is shameful to see the negligence of these same editors (who are so acute in respect to expressions and dates and reasonings in the despatches of a British officer) in respect to the lies of the 'Moniteur.' In the last paper which I have received I see a letter of Massena's, published in the 'Moniteur' of the 23rd November, supposed to have been written on the 3rd of November, and to have been carried by General Foy. A little reflection would show the editors that General Foy could not have gone the distance in the time. In fact he left Massena on the 7th of October. But the letter which is published states that the paragraphs in the English newspapers about his distresses are falsehoods. It might have been

expected that this attack upon their veracity might have
attracted their attention! But what are the paragraphs
alluded to, and when were they published?

They were the paragraphs published in consequence of
the letters sent from here on the 13th and 19th October.
Now I expect that Massena has never seen either English or
any other newspaper or letter (excepting those which I have
sent him) since he entered Portugal in September; but unless
he received these paragraphs by flying pigeons, and if he had
had the best post in Europe, he could not have known on the
3rd of November at Alenquer of the paragraphs written in
London in consequence of letters from Portugal of the 13th
and 14th October. This despatch, therefore, of the 3rd of
November is manifestly forged. But nobody in England
could find it out!!

Then the supposed statement of General Foy is as false
evidently as the letter from Massena is spurious. I don't
appeal to my despatches for the truth of the fact, but to
Massena's intercepted despatches, the originals of which were
sent home to Government and were published, and which
contradict every word of it. But how interesting it is to the
people of England and to the world to show them that the
whole system in France is falsehood and fraud, and that not
a word of truth is ever published in France, particularly
respecting the affairs of the Peninsula; and whatever proofs
of these facts may have been drawn from these papers and
from the circumstances known to the whole world, not an
editor has taken the smallest notice of them. On the contrary, I understand that, when these publications reached
England, notes were changed, and it was again supposed
we were in a bad way. Even now it is represented, and with
success, that England must pay the expense of feeding the
people of Lisbon!!!

However grievous it is, and however injurious to the
country, I cannot avoid laughing when I reflect upon all this
folly; and I don't know why I have taken the trouble of
writing you so much upon it. I shall either fight a battle or
not as I shall find it advantageous. The enemy have suffered
enormously, and at this moment, including Spaniards, I have
the inferior army by *ten thousand* men. But there is a great
deal of difference (particularly in the blood to be spilt)
between fighting in a position which I choose or in one in
which the enemy choose to fight! And the difference makes

the question which the London editors and their readers
cannot comprehend. There are, besides, some other considerations to be weighed upon which I will not trouble after
having written you so long a letter about nothing, but to
which it is obvious that these same wise gentlemen have
never adverted.

Ever, my dear Sir,

Yours most faithfully,

WELLINGTON.

During the year 1812 there occurred the serious differences
with the United States which led to war between the two
countries. English seamen who deserted the Royal service
were glad to enter that of the American Government, where
they deemed themselves secure. The captains under whom
they served refused to allow their vessels to be searched by
British ships, and in this course they were sustained by the
authorities at Washington. The dispute had been going on
ever since the outbreak of the war with France, and France
herself had injured the commerce of the United States more
than England, by the restrictions she had placed upon
American trade. This was felt and acknowledged at the
time in the United States, and there was a great opposition
to the war, the Federalists maintaining that it was unjust,
while the Democrats supported it because it tended to assist
France in her struggle with England. The Federalists even
held a Convention in Connecticut to oppose the continuance
of the war ; but the struggle lingered on for nearly three years,
and was ultimately brought to an end by the Treaty of Ghent
(Dec. 24th, 1814), in which the right of search was not even
mentioned, so that, so far as regards official cognizance, the
question was left precisely where it was at first.

In the course of the controversy in 1812, Mr. Croker
published a pamphlet explanatory of the position taken by
the British Government. It was entitled 'A Key to the

Orders in Council,' and was confined to a recapitulation of the decrees and orders issued by Great Britain, France, and the United States, since 1806. But the naval glory of England was tarnished by the successes of the American naval force,—especially by the surrender of an entire British squadron of six vessels to an American squadron of nine, on Lake Erie. The English vessels were, as a rule, unequally matched, as was shown clearly enough in the first action which was fought—that between the *Guerrière* and the *Constitution.* At first sight, it appeared to the English people that their frigates had been defeated by ships of equal size, but it was soon ascertained that the American ships were one-third larger than the English in size, complement, and weight of metal, and that they were in fact line-of-battle ships in disguise. They were fully able to cope with the smaller description of British vessels, which at that time were classed in the line-of-battle. Opposition newspapers were loud in their outcries against the Naval Administration, and charges of neglect and incompetency were plentifully showered on the Admiralty. Mr. Croker met these attacks in a series of clever letters published in the *Courier* newspaper, under the signature of "Nereus," and at the same time he rendered a much greater service to the British seamen and the nation by persuading the Cabinet and the Admiralty to allow him to issue a confidential circular, which he believed would produce important results. The following is the circular :—

My Lords Commissioners of the Admiralty having received intelligence that several of the American ships of war are now at sea, I have their Lordships' commands to acquaint you therewith, and that they do not conceive that any of his Majesty's frigates should attempt to engage, single handed, the larger class of American ships, which, though they may be called frigates, are of a size, complement, and weight of metal much beyond that class, and more resembling line-of-battle ships.

In the event of one of his Majesty's frigates under your orders falling in with one of these ships, his captain should endeavour in the first instance to secure the retreat of his Majesty's ship, but if he finds that he has an advantage in sailing he should endeavour to manœuvre, and keep company with her, without coming to action, in the hope of falling in with some other of his Majesty's ships, with whose assistance the enemy might be attacked with a reasonable hope of success.

It is their Lordships' further directions that you make this known as soon as possible to the several captains commanding his Majesty's ships.

Mr. Croker always maintained that there was nothing in these instructions to prevent an officer from fighting if he thought he could do so with success; the Admiralty merely assumed the responsibility of restraining high-spirited men from unnecessarily seeking a contest with ships of nominally the same class but which, in reality, were far superior in strength. This fighting spirit led to the celebrated duel between the *Shannon* and the *Chesapeake*, in which the British commander won. It was, however, a somewhat barren victory. The circular issued by Mr. Croker was successful in its object. No more unequal fights took place. In illustration of the difficulty the Admiralty had in obtaining correct information, Mr. Croker used to say that when one of the American large frigates was at Spithead shortly before the war broke out, some officers were ordered to visit her and report the result of their inspection. They expressed the opinion that she differed but little from our first-class frigates, though, as it eventually turned out, she was in every way superior.

It is in this year also that the first letter of Robert Peel to Mr. Croker is to be found among the correspondence.

They had already been friends for a long period, and doubt-less had corresponded, but a diligent search has failed to bring to light any letter of Peel's earlier than that which follows. Peel was at that time, it will be remembered, Secretary for Ireland. The letter relates to the refusal of Canning and Lord Wellesley to join the new Adminis-tration on Perceval's death, and their failure to make any coalition which would have sufficed to form the basis of another Government :—

Mr. Peel to Mr. Croker.

Dublin, Oct. 30th, 1812.

My dear Croker,

Lord Melville wrote a letter to you which he allowed me to read, and the subject of which you are, of course, now fully apprized of, and which I destroyed, as it could not have reached you before your arrival at the Admiralty.

I am sorry that the parliamentary aspect is not so good in England as I trust that it is with us, and I am much surprised at the accession of strength which from your letter Canning and Lord Wellesley appear to have acquired.

I am not, however, much alarmed by it, as I trust and believe that the House of Commons, after what has passed will support Lord Liverpool against either or both of them combined. As for Lord Wellesley, I consider him a sort of appendage to Mr. Canning—incumbrance, perhaps the latter would say. I should think his Lordship could not be very well satisfied when he found that the change of a moment in Mr. Canning's determination to accept office saved him the trouble of de-liberating whether he would succeed the Duke of Richmond or not.

I hope we may fight out this battle as we have fought out many others ; there was a time when I should have had less fears, and when perhaps, from every private and public feel-ing, I should have seen our little champion go forth with his sling and with his sword, and bring down the mightiest of his enemies, and felt prouder in his triumph ; but there never was a time when I felt more determined to do all I could to

support the Government on its present footing and on the
principles on which it will meet Parliament.

If I understood, as I believe I did, the offers made to
Canning, I think they were fair ones, as he himself must
have thought when he accepted them; and as to keeping him
down, the Government know his power too well not to wish
to have it exerted in their favour.

I think in the worst event we shall gain one here, in the
best we shall have six friends in the place of six enemies,
but that is supposing three of the old members who remain
in to be equally friendly, and three of the new ones to have
the disposition which is now attached to them.

I am, dear Croker,

Yours affectionately,

ROBERT PEEL.

In another letter Peel gives some account of his mode of
life in Ireland :—

I have survived the hospitality of Ireland hitherto, contrary to my expectation. I have scarcely dined once at
home since my arrival. I see no great prospect of it for
some time to come, excepting with about twenty-five guests.
I am just opening upon the campaign, and have visions of
future feasts studded with Lord Mayors and Sheriffs Elect.
I fancy I see some who think that the Government of
England have a strange notion of Ireland when they put a
man here who drinks port, and as little of that as he can.
The Governor of the Bank remarked with horror that I was
not fully impressed with the necessity of toasting the glorious
memory.

One of the great troubles of Mr. Croker's life at the
Admiralty arose from the avalanche of applications for office
which fell upon his desk day after day and year after year.
At that period, when official favour was all that was required
to get a man into the service of his country, everybody occupying an official position was beset with applicants for place,
and Mr. Croker appears to have been besieged from morning

till night. His friends were importunate, and yet he had no places to give away. He was very chary indeed about using his influence over the Board of Admiralty, for he considered that it was no part of his duty to recommend any person for employment, and he was strongly opposed to anything which savoured of jobbery in public offices. Some of the applications which were sprung upon him by intimate personal friends were so far beyond the bounds of decorum or reason, that they provoked retorts which could not have been very pleasant to the unfortunate office-seekers. The following may be taken as examples:—

Mr. Croker to ———.

June 8th, 1812.

A young man came to me yesterday with a letter from Mrs. ———* to request of me to "make him a mid-shipman." I cannot conceal from you my surprise and concern that Mrs. ——— should write to me on matters of business, about which ladies can know nothing. If she had asked you to do this, you would probably have been able to tell her that I have no more to say to the *making* of mid-shipmen, as she calls it, than to the making of archbishops, and that if even I had the power, it might be prudent, before the poor young man was sent over here,† to ask me whether I was inclined to exert it. You could also have told her that ——— was not a person concerning whom I was likely to be interested, as I know as little of the uncle as of the nephew. You might also perhaps have told her that no captain will take a young man as midshipman whose friends cannot allow him thirty or forty pounds per annum. You finally would have informed her that a man turned of nineteen years of age is more than six years too old to begin a sea life, and that he would be entering on the profession with the most deplorable prospects. And having told her all this, you would have saved the poor young man the expense and

* [The wife of the gentleman to whom Mr. Croker's letter was addressed.]
† [From Ireland.]

mortification of a journey to London, where he does not know a soul, and where he cannot meet anything but disappointment, and perhaps ruin.

To another Friend.

If Mrs. F—— is the daughter or the sister of my father's late friend, Major F—— (whom I never saw in my life), she might have known that my name was not *Croaker;* and when she next laments that the Board of Admiralty does not answer Mr. L——'s letters, though its Secretary does, pray hint to her that Mr. L—— knows little of his profession if he does not know that the Board of Admiralty never does write a letter (and indeed I hardly see how it could), and that it is for this reason that it has a Secretary.

It is quite evident, however, that Mr. Croker's kindness of heart induced him to exert his influence in various ways for the benefit of such of his friends as seemed to have a fair claim upon his consideration. Thus he obtained an appointment for Mr. Thomas Scott, who was described by his brother, the great novelist, as " a very honest and pleasant fellow." At a later period, he endeavoured to get a son of Robert Burns a clerkship in the Mint, but failed. In 1813, he had some share in placing Robert Southey in the post of Poet Laureate, which had been offered to Scott and declined. Southey accepted it under an implied condition which is now taken for granted on all sides.

Robert Southey to Mr. Croker.

Streatham, Saturday Afternoon.
[Probably in September, 1813.]

Twenty years ago, when I had a reputation to win, it would have been easy for me to furnish odes upon demand on any subject. This is no longer the case. I should go to the task like a schoolboy, with reluctance and a sense of incapacity for executing it well ; but unless I could so perform

VOL. I.   E it as to give credit to the office, certain it is that the office could give none to me.

But if these periodical exhibitions were dispensed with, and I were left to write upon great events, or to be silent, according as the spirit moved, I should then thankfully accept the office as a mark of honourable distinction, which it would then become.

I write thus to you, not as proposing terms to the Prince, an impropriety of which I should be fully aware, but as to a friend who has more than once shown me acts of kindness which I had no reason to expect and by whose advice I would be guided.

In the previous month of May, Southey had published his 'Life of Nelson,' a work which he had expanded from an article in the *Quarterly Review*, at Mr. Murray's suggestion. Mr. Croker at once formed the opinion of this performance which has ever since been entertained by the public; and he wrote to Southey an encouraging letter, prophesying that the book would always be 'The *Popular* Life of Nelson,' and entering into some interesting particulars concerning the battle of Copenhagen, and Nelson's famous refusal to obey the signal to discontinue the action.

Mr. Croker to Robert Southey.   Extract.

May 7th, 1813.

On the subject of the Copenhagen fight, I have an observation or two to make to you, which I have from the best authority, namely, my friend Admiral Domett, now a Lord of the Admiralty; at the period of the battle, Captain of the Fleet to Sir Hyde Parker.   Domett, as you will easily believe, exceedingly regretted the signal of recall made by Sir Hyde, but he gives a reason for it highly honourable to that officer.   "I will make the signal of recall," said Sir Hyde, "for Nelson's sake; if he is in a condition to continue the action successfully, he will disregard it; if he is not, it will be an excuse for his retreat, and no blame will be imputed to him."   And though Domett, not at all agreeing in this fine-

spun distinction, urged him, by every possible reason, not to
make the signal, at least not until a personal communication
could be opened, he persisted in doing so, because he thought
he was thereby removing the responsibility, in case
of failure, from Lord Nelson.   However, therefore, this
famous signal may derogate from Sir Hyde's character as a
seaman, or as a man of foresight and boldness, it at least
does credit to his disinterestedness and generosity of mind;
and Domett assures me that he was well aware at the
moment of the consequence to his professional reputation of
the step he was then taking, but he thought the fire was too
hot for Nelson to oppose, that a retreat was probably to be
made, and that it would be cowardly to leave Nelson to bear
the whole shame, if shame there should be, of the failure.

It was about this time also that Mr. Croker's acquaintance
was renewed with Thomas Moore, who had taken offence at
some allusion to him in print which he imagined had proceeded
from Croker.   Moore's vanity was easily wounded at any
time.   On this particular occasion, Moore wrote to Mr. Croker
expressing his regret for the coldness with which he had
treated him. " I have long thought," he said, " that I was a fool
to quarrel with you, and by no means required your present
conduct to convince me how much you are, in every way,
superior to me."   Moore had been assisted by Mr. Croker out
of a serious difficulty in connection with his Bermuda appointment (Registrar to the Admiralty Court), the duties of which
the poet found it convenient to discharge by deputy.   This
probably accounts for the fervour of his protestations of friendship. " In warmth of feeling," he declared, " I will not be outdone, and I assure you it is with all my heart and soul that I
enter into the renewal of our friendship."   With his gratitude
for the past was mingled a " lively sense of favours to come,"
for he attempted soon after this to induce Mr. Croker to help
him in a project, which he had much at heart, for clandestinely
selling his appointment to his deputy—a proposal, as

Moore coolly admitted in his letter (December 22nd, 1809), which "sounds very like one of those transactions which *we patriots* cry out against as unworthy of the great Russell and Algernon Sydney." Mr. Croker declined to undertake this commission, but he gave him some counsel which, had it been followed, would have saved Moore from the embarrassments brought upon him by his deputy a few years later.

Mr. Croker to Thomas Moore.

Nov. 13th, 1813.

I wish I could give you any more agreeable advice on the subject of your office than that which I before have given, namely, that you should yourself go out and look after your profits. I have no doubt that they are well worth your doing so, and in your (since acquired) character of father of a family, I really think it is your bounden duty to look after your family interests. It is very unpoetical, and very un-Irish, and very unromantic to attend to worldly cares, but if not attended to they at last become too strong for the most poetical head and the most ardent heart.

The following letter is of an earlier date, but it may fitly be placed here, in further illustration of the respect which Moore at this period felt for Mr. Croker.

Thomas Moore to Mr. Croker.

Keyworth, Lancashire, May 22nd, 1812.

MY DEAR CROKER,

I dare say you have heard of my having appeared suddenly to my friends in the new characters of a husband and a father. If I were quite sure that you feel interested enough about an old friend to wish to know the particulars of my marriage, you should know them. At all events, I hope it will give you pleasure to learn that, though I thought it necessary to conceal the business so long (from every one but my friends Rogers and the Dowager Lady Donegal), yet the moment the revelation took place, all my friends took the excellent creature I have married most cordially by the hand, and Lady Loudoun and Lady Charlotte Rawdon were among the first to visit her. They knew the story, and could not but respect her. I should have been most happy to have made her known to you, but I found it impossible to stand the expenses of town, and therefore made a hasty retreat into Lord Moira's neighbourhood, where, with his fair library and a happy home, I hope to live a life of peace and goodness, and to become at last, perhaps, respectable.

I am glad to take the opportunity of troubling you with the inclosed letter to show you that I am not unmindful of your good opinion nor indifferent to your remembrance of me.

Ever yours,

THOMAS MOORE.

It need only be added that Mr. Croker never gave Moore any cause of offence, unless it was in declining to become a party to the trafficking in public offices which the poet was so eager to undertake, but which he candidly acknowledged was unworthy of a true patriot.

Mr. Croker to his Wife.

August 15th, 1813.

The Plymouth telegraph* announces another complete victory of Lord W. over Soult on the 30th. When I went to the Prince with the news this morning he embraced me with both arms. You never saw a man so rejoiced. I have seen him again to-day, and you cannot conceive how gracious he is to me.

We were very pleasant yesterday, and H.R. Highness has asked me to go to the Pavilion Wednesday and Thursday, or as long as I can stay.

---

* [The news was sent by the old system of telegraphing—that is, by the semaphores on the tops of the hills,—to the Admiralty. This naval telegraph had its terminus on the roof of the Admiralty, and thus it happened that Mr. Croker received the news first, and was able to communicate it to the Prince Regent.]

The victory referred to was that gained by Wellington over Soult, in the battle of the Pyrenees. The intimacy with the Prince Regent, begun a few months before this letter was written, was continued after the Prince succeeded to the throne; and it led to the king imparting to Mr. Croker his own story—which was not always the same story—of his relations with Mrs. Fitzherbert. Mr. Croker, however, was much too sincere and plain-spoken to be a model courtier, as the Duke of Clarence discovered when he had official dealings with him at the Admiralty.

CHAPTER III.

1814-1816.

ONE of the advantages incidental to the office of Secretary of the Admiralty in Mr. Croker's day was the opportunity which it occasionally conferred of obtaining a passage in a King's ship to some foreign port—a privilege which was highly valued, not only because it was much pleasanter to make a voyage in a vessel of the Royal Navy than in an ordinary merchantman, but also because in that disturbed period, when hostile ships were encountered on almost every sea, a comparative degree of safety could be enjoyed in a Royal frigate. Many were the applications which Mr. Croker received for these favours, which, after all, he could only secure by using his influence with the commanders of the vessels, for he had no power or authority of his own to grant them. As a matter of course, however, the influence of the Secretary was great, and it seldom failed to accomplish the desired purpose. But there were seasons when nothing whatever could be done, and this happened to be the case in July, 1813, with reference to Lord Byron, who was anxious to make his way to Greece, and who applied to Mr. Croker to help him. He was obliged to return an answer to the effect that he knew no captain who was going out. A few weeks later, Mr. Croker took the trouble to seek out the captain of the *Boyne,* and to get the desired permission. Either Lord Byron changed his mind, or he could not get ready in time, for he did not sail by this vessel. A little later, in reply to a similar request from Mr. Canning, Mr. Croker was obliged to make the following explanation, which serves incidentally to show how reluctant he was all through his life to ask for anything for himself: " A young lady, a cousin of my own, who had been residing with Mrs. Croker these last five years, and who was ordered to Lisbon for the same cause as the young lady you mention, sailed in a merchant vessel this day week, in a convoy protected by three King's ships, in none of which I could take the liberty of asking a passage for her."

Another application of Canning's is worthy, perhaps, of passing notice from the fact that it solicited Mr. Croker's good offices in favour of Mr. Gladstone " of Liverpool," whose son, the future Prime Minister, was then not five years old :—

Mr. Canning to Mr. Croker.

Liverpool Office, May 16th, 1814.

My dear Sir,

Now that the general question of convoy is disposed of, I am earnestly entreated earnestly to entreat your re-consideration of the particular case of a ship for which, if a licence is not obtained to sail without convoy, her voyage will have to be undertaken at a heavy loss.   It is the ship *Kingsmill* of Liverpool, belonging to Mr. Gladstone, destined for the East Indies—a ship of between 5 and 600 tons, armed— "a small frigate in appearance"—and capable of beating off any ordinary privateer that might attack her.   She is quite ready to put to sea this week.   She is a venture of 40,000*l.*, and the delay of waiting for a convoy would be highly detrimental to the owner.   That she was not ready for the last convoy which sailed is to be attributed to the novelty of the undertaking.   The singularity of the case seems to preclude any danger of its being considered as a precedent for licences for merchant ships of smaller force.

I am ever, my dear Sir,

Very sincerely yours,

GEORGE CANNING.

There was a transient gleam of peace in 1814—the calm which preceded the last great storm which Buonaparte was destined to create in Europe.   Mr. Croker profited by this lull to go to Paris in the autumn, and he immediately occupied himself with the work of tracing out every spot which had been made memorable by the great revolution—the event which he was never weary of studying.   He had collected a large library of French journals, tracts, broadsides, and other contemporary documents relating to it; and he once had some plan in his mind of writing a 'History of the Revolution.'   At this time, however, Mr. Croker was bent not so much upon literary achievements as upon the task of endeavouring to get a suitable memorial erected to the hero of the Peninsula in the Irish capital, Irishmen of every class having made known their desire to do honour in some way to the name of Wellington.   Mr. Croker was strongly in favour of a column, but his advice was not taken, and the miserable design to be seen to-day in the Phœnix Park was substituted for it.

Mr. Croker to the Secretary of the Wellington Fund.   Extract.

October 7th, 1814.

I quite agree with the Committee in its predilection for a pillar.   I was one of the pillarists in the Nelson case, and only wish our column had been one of more magnificent dimensions.   Great height is the cheapest way and one of the most certain of obtaining sublimity.   Ten thousand pounds will build you the highest column in the world, and will produce an astonishing effect; fifty thousand pounds would not serve to erect an arch, and when it was erected you would have it doubted which, it or the Royal Exchange, was the more magnificent object; therefore I exhort you to keep to the columnar form.   Whatever you do, be at least sure to make it *stupendously* high; let it be of all columns in the world the most lofty.   Nelson's is, I suppose, about 150 feet, the London monument is 202, Trajan's about 150, Antoninus' 122, or, as some have it, 180.   Buonaparte's in the Place Vendôme is, I think, near 200.   I wish therefore that you should not fall short of 250 feet, and I should prefer to have it exactly from the first layer of the base to the crown of the statue 300 feet.

Not only had Mr. Croker become by this time a regular contributor to the *Quarterly Review*, but he was associated with Mr. Peel and Lord Palmerston in supplying political squibs and lyrics to the *Courier* newspaper, resembling in general features the 'Anti-Jacobin' and the 'Rolliad.'   The verses are chiefly parodies of Moore's 'Irish Melodies,' or of Byron's songs, and are far above the ordinary level of such compositions, although there is nothing so remarkably brilliant in them as to call for their republication.   Most of the allusions to persons or events would now be pointless; the spirit of the verse has long since evaporated.   The various pieces were collected and published in 1815, under the title of *The New Whig Guide*, and for many years afterwards quotations from them were common in periodical literature.   A work of a different kind was undertaken by Mr. Croker in the autumn of 1815—a retrospect of the chief incidents in Bonaparte's career, prepared for the *Quarterly*. The escape from Elba, the Emperor's defeat by the Prussians at Ligny, and his overthrow at Waterloo, were events which caused everything else then going on in the world to be put out of sight and forgotten. In March, Mr. Croker sent the following account of the state of affairs to his friend Canning, who was then Ambassador Extraordinary at Lisbon :

Mr. Croker to Mr. Canning.

March 13th, 1815.

You will already have heard by your post from Madrid that Buonaparte has landed in France ; and the English papers will tell you all the details as far as they have been published. I can only add that my private letters from Paris are very satisfactory. Great *inquiétude*, but it is that of loyalty, and my friends describe the crowds that throng the Tuileries as evincing the best spirit possible. But I have also seen letters that state that there is a good deal of indifference with regard to both parties. The fact I take to be this, that the nation is fully content with the Bourbons, that the higher officers who have something to lose are likely to adhere to the king ; that the great class of *réformés*, who are as ill off as they can be, must be inclined to take tickets in Napoleon's lottery, and that the common soldiers to a man are Bonapartists ; but the whole people is so volatile, that their conduct will be determined by the first accidental successes of either party, and with this opinion you may easily believe that I am not quite so much at my ease as most other people are.

Our riots, which are a good deal exaggerated in the public papers, are subsiding, and never were, I think, at all serious ;. but you know how timid all constituted authority is on such occasions.

The messenger who was employed to convey to the Rothschilds in London the news of the Victory of Waterloo, was ordered to call upon the King of France (Louis XVIII.), at

Brussels, on the way. He did so, and then proceeded to the Rothschilds. After they had extracted from him all the information that he possessed, they sent him on to Lord Liverpool, the Prime Minister, in order that the Government might receive tidings of this great event.

Lord Liverpool could make nothing out of the man, and after examining and cross-examining him for some time, he felt increasingly sceptical as to the authenticity of the news which he brought. He then sent for Mr. Croker and told him that the messenger had come from Waterloo with the tidings of victory, but that his story was confused, and it was therefore difficult to accept it as genuine. Thereupon, Mr. Croker began to question the man, with all his legal acumen, but he succeeded no better than Lord Liverpool in making the narrative intelligible. When about to give it up in despair, as a last resource, and by a sudden impulse, Mr. Croker questioned the messenger as to his interview with the French King, and he asked him how the King was dressed. The messenger replied, " In his dressing-gown." Mr. Croker then asked him what the King did and said to him, to which the messenger replied : " His Majesty embraced me, and kissed me !" Mr. Croker asked, "How did the King kiss you ?" "On both cheeks," replied the messenger; upon which Mr. Croker emphatically exclaimed : " My Lord, it is true ; his news is genuine," and so, in truth, it proved.

In July, 1815, Mr. Croker took advantage of his annual holiday to pay another visit to Paris, then in the midst of the excitement produced by the victory of the Allies. His notes and sketches made at that time, and forwarded regularly to his wife, present a curious picture of the French capital during the English occupation. Mr. Peel and Mr. Vesey (afterwards Lord) Fitzgerald accompanied him on this journey.

Mr. Croker to his Wife. Extracts.

Paris, July 12th, 1815.

The town is full of troops, particularly Prussians; but there are a good many English; it was amusing to us to see the old Life Guards patrolling the Boulevard last night, as they used to do Charing Cross during the Corn riots.

I got up this morning three hours at least before my companions, walked through the Palais Royal, where I found a strong English guard. I spoke to the soldiers, and they were rather surprised to see me. They looked very strange amongst this blue-coated nation. I then went to the Carrousel, where about 2000 Prussians are bivouacked: they are very picturesque and savage.

The King appeared last night at the windows of the Tuileries when we were at dinner, and I really never heard such shouts and cries and other demonstrations of joy as he was received with; and as we came along through the whole country, all the villagers cried "Vive le Roi!" with great enthusiasm. As we drove into Abbeville, where the garrison were savage Buonapartists, the townspeople huzzaed and cried "Vive le Roi!" as we came in, to the great vexation of the military who attended us through the town.

When I went to Castlereagh's, he said he had sent for me to meet the Duke of Otranto (Fouché) and the Count de Jaucourt, the Minister of Marine, to concoct measures for the capture of Buonaparte. Jaucourt came with Fouché's apology, and an appointment that we should all meet at a conference at Talleyrand's that evening.

I was so detained by writing the draft of the paper that was to be submitted to the Conference that I came late for dinner. We were all English except Marshal Prince Wrede, the Bavarian, a good-looking, agreeable, gentlemanly man. After dinner we went and walked in the Tuileries, to see the people dancing and singing and shouting under the King's window. I never saw so gay, and hardly a more touching, scene. After idling there for a couple of hours, we went to Talleyrand's to do our business, and there we found a little kind of *male* assembly. There were Talleyrand, Fouché, and Jaucourt, Marshal Gouvion St. Cyr, Pozzo di Borgo, Prince John of Zuhlenstein, the Duke of Wellington, &c., &c. You may be sure I was rather glad to see all those heroes and rogues " de si près." I did not get home till one o'clock. My comrades were both in bed; they, I hear, went from the gardens to the Palais Royal, where they indulged themselves with a peep at some of the gaming houses; Fitzgerald lost 10 louis, and Peel, more lucky, won 5.

Thursday, July 13th.—I lost a good deal of this morning in doing business with Castlereagh and going to the bankers. We found our poor bankers in trouble; Blucher had demanded a contribution of 100 millions from Paris, and, as it was not paid, he shut up the 'Change and arrested all the bankers, M. Perigeux among the rest. The Emperor of Russia, however, whose bankers they are, has saved these persons out of the clutches of the *Vieux Diable;* but he swears that he will make them pay the money. The Prussians are very insolent, and hardly less offensive to the English than to the French. The Duke says that they actually forget that there is a British army in Paris. They had mined the two piers of the Pont de Jena, next the Champ de Mars, and had endeavoured, as I saw by the marks of explosion, to blow it up! but they have been stopped, and no mischief is done.

Friday, July 14th.—I went to see Denon; he is very low-spirited for the loss of his friend Buonaparte, and because Blucher has quartered a guard of Prussians on him who are very unpleasant guests. He thinks the Gallery is likely to be *plundered* of *its plunder.* He, however, was exceedingly civil to me, and if *I* had been *agreeable,* as the girls say in England, he would have kissed me on both cheeks. He was the last person that Buonaparte saw before he went away. Buonaparte spoke very little, but he desired him to tell him all he thought, which Denon says he did, and that B. heard all with great composure and *sang froid.* When they were about to part, Denon was much agitated and affected; Buonaparte put his two hands on his shoulders, and said, " Mon cher, ne nous attendrissons pas; il faut dans des crises comme celle-ci se conduire avec sang froid." Denon almost cried when he told the story. He says he told Buonaparte that he had committed two great faults, one in leaving the army, the other in getting into discussions with a deputation of the Chambers, which grew too strong and factious for him to manage, and which began to discuss the rights of citizens when they should have provided against the common enemy. In speaking of the battle of Waterloo, Denon said to Buona-

parte, "You have been beaten *moitié malheur, moitié trahison.*"
This we observed escaped him by accident; he complained
greatly of the Prussians, expressed great anxiety for the monuments, and said that he was "*malheureux* to have to do with
a *bête féroce, un animal indécrottable, le Prince Blucher.*"

Saturday, July 15*th.*—We went to the Gallery of the
Louvre at 11 o'clock, and stayed there a couple of hours.
We met Apsley, and all four went off to see the English
army encamped in the Bois de Boulogne. An army encamped
does not answer the expectations one entertains of it. It
looks more like a fair than anything martial, for you see
very few red coats worn. The soldiers had made themselves
nice little huts with the boughs and branches of trees, and
I think that the mischief they are doing to the wood will in
the end improve its beauty, as they break the long formal
lines of the rows of trees, and cutting down half-a-dozen
leave one or two standing here and there. On our return
Fitzgerald went to the Palais Royal, and Peel and I went
wandering through the town. We afterwards dined at
Roberts's, a gaming tavern, where we had an excellent dinner,
but it cost us 24 francs each. After dinner we went to the
Variétés. My gentlemen, not understanding a syllable, got
tired, and would not sit it out. I did, and saw, besides the
'Singe Voleur,' which I had seen before, 'Sage et Coquette'
and 'Les Pensionnaires'; the last was agreeable enough, but
none of them were very *risible*. I have not yet see Potier.

July 16*th.*—The Père Elysée sent us an order for the King's
Mass, where we went at half-past 12. There was a greater
crowd than when you were there, and as there was not
a court mourning, everything was much gayer. After the
mass, we followed the King on his return. He showed
himself with Monsieur and the Duc de Berri at the balcony
that looks towards the garden to a very loyal multitude that
were assembled below. We afterwards went through the Salles
des Maréchaux, de la Paix, and du Throne, into the gallery.
We were the only people not in uniform, but the Père passed
us on quite well. We here saw Marshals Marmont, Augereau,
Massena, Kellerman, Moncey, Macdonald; the latter was not
dressed as a marshal, but as a peer of France. He went the
other day to the King dressed as a National Guard. Has he
the good taste to be ashamed of belonging to such a corps as
the Marshal's, or is he forming some design to distinguish
himself from them? One thing surprised me exceedingly;

the army and the great majority of the officers belonging to it went off south of the Loire, yet there were yesterday at the Tuileries at least three times as many general officers as we could have under the most favourable circumstances collected at a *levée* in England, and those there wore orders, stars, and ribbands "par boisseaux." Peel said that, on *an average,* every man in Paris would have *two* crosses. I saw one man yesterday with 6, twenty with 4 or 5, and hundreds with 3 different orders at their button hole. Prince Wrede the other day at dinner wore 6 stars, and I believe he has one or two that he did not wear; in fact, the greatest distinction our people have here is that they are without them.

The Emperor of Russia and the Emperor of Austria rode twice yesterday past our balcony with an immense staff. The Emperor of all the Russias is a greater dandy than ever; he had a *levée* of the English generals to-day, at which he was very civil; he made them a little speech, in which he said he was proud to make acquaintance with the officers of so gallant an army. The King of France, at his *levée* of English officers, "congratulated them on their glory, and thanked them for their generosity towards his poor subjects." At present the English are in high favour with the Parisians, less, I fear, from their own merits, than from a contrast with our worthy allies the Prussians. The latter are, however, decamping out of the city; their bivouac in the Carrousel has already disappeared. . . . We came round the Boulevards home; all along the Boulevards there were puppets and punches and merry-go-rounds and the like; but not much music and not much *gaiety* to my notion. In general we observe that all the women are loyal; the men seem a good deal divided, but the majority, the decided majority, of all who are at all "comme il faut" are for the King. What good boys we are! we are all in bed by 12. Fitzgerald does nothing but sleep; he goes to bed at 11, and makes his appearance in 12 hours after. Peel also is tolerably lazy. I rise at half-past six, and read and write, and dress myself till nine or half-past, and then I have still an hour to wait for my breakfast.

July 17*th.*—We dined yesterday at Castlereagh's with, besides the Embassy, Talleyrand, Fouché, Marshal Gouvion St. Cyr, and the Baron de Vitrolles, Lords Cathcart, Clancarty, Stewart, and Clive, and two ladies, the Princesse de Vaudemont, a fat, ugly old woman, and a Mademoiselle Chasse, her friend, a pretty young one. At so quiet a dinner you may judge there was not much interesting conversation, and accordingly I have not often been at a dinner of which I had less to tell. The wonder was to find ourselves at table with Fouché, who, to be sure, looks very like what one would naturally suppose him to be—a sly old rogue; but I think he seems to feel a passion of which I did not expect to find him capable; I mean *shame*, for he looks conscious and embarrassed. He is a man about 5 ft. 7 in. high, very thin, with a grey head, cropped and powdered, and a very acute expression of countenance. Talleyrand, on the other hand, is fattish for a Frenchman; his ankles are weak and his feet deformed, and he totters about in a strange way. His face is not at all expressive, except it be of a kind of drunken stupor; in fact, he looks altogether like an old fuddled, lame, village schoolmaster, and his voice is deep and hoarse. I should suspect that at the Congress his most natural employment would be keeping the unruly boys in order. We dined very late—that is, for Paris, for we were not at table till half-past six. We afterwards went to the Théâtre Feydau, where we had 'Richard Cœur de Lion' and 'Les Héritiers Michau.' The latter is a pretty little piece made last year on the King's return. I shall tell you the story when we meet.

Think of the Buonapartists having the audacity to wear little marks of distinction, signals to know one another. These last few days the sign (no longer the violet) was a *red* pink, in opposition to the white pinks; and on Sunday night a serious riot took place on the Boulevard St. Martin between two of the King's bodyguard and some *red pink men*, who insulted and pursued them till they took refuge in one of the theatres, which the mob were going to storm, but that the guard was called out, which put an end to the tumult; but, notwithstanding this disaffection of the blackguards and soldiery, I really never saw more general or unequivocal testimonies of loyalty than one sees in the generality of the people. I am sure last night at Feydau the bursts of joy and triumph at every allusion flattering to the King exceeded what could under any circumstances like the present have been expected.

Late last night Castlereagh sent me a copy of a note from Fouché, announcing that Buonaparte had gone on board the Bellerophon, Capt. Maitland. He, it seems, wanted to stipulate for *conditions*, but that, being refused, he said he would throw himself on the Prince Regent's hospitality.

I went this morning to Castlereagh's, to hear something more on the subject, but he had no further particulars. The fact was published in the *Moniteur*, and the account concluded with a statement that thus ended an enterprise conceived by Buonaparte and executed by him with the assistance of MM. Labédoyère, Ney, Soult, La Valette, Bassano, and others. The list of names is generally said to be a designation of the individuals whom it is intended to punish, and folks are so charitable as to suppose that their old friend Fouché gives them this notice that they may make haste to escape. Castlereagh tells me that what the old rogue says of this last revolution is this, that he confesses that there was a conspiracy (he calls it a union) of some Jacobins (he calls them patriots) at Paris for the purpose of operating a political change, but that Buonaparte was no party to it, and that they did not think of him; in other words, they wished for neither the King nor the Emperor, but what they intended he did not say, and, with all his cunning, perhaps he did not know. While this was going on, Buonaparte heard of it, and resolved, with the assistance of his military friends, to take advantage of the mines against the King that the conspirators had laid. He landed, the King was betrayed on all sides and was driven out. Of all this fine story I believe little more than the last part. Castlereagh says what interest has Fouché now to tell a lie? I reply, "first, the natural inclination to lying which the Devil and all his disciples are admitted to possess." Secondly, he wishes to clear himself from the disgrace of serving two masters within ten days, God and Mammon, and would have us believe that he did not plot with Buonaparte to turn out the King, and a little after concert with the King the means of keeping out Buonaparte; and thirdly, he wishes to enhance his own importance and that of his party, by insinuating that it was powerful enough to think of overturning the King's government without any assistance from Buonaparte. I therefore, begging the Duke of Otranto's good pardon, am satisfied either that there was no regular conspiracy at all, and that Buonaparte came with his usual and characteristic audacity to try his luck previous to the final close of the Congress, or else that to the list of traitors published by his Excellency the Duke of Otranto, we should add the name of the notorious M. Fouché.

At a quarter-past one we went in full dress to the Tuileries to be presented to the King; there were about thirty persons,

Russians and English, to be presented. Among the latter, Lords Stewart, Clancarty, Alvanley, Clive, Sir W. Colthurst, Sir John Shelley, the gentlemen of the Embassy, and ourselves. The King told me he was happy to *revoir* me, hobbled round us all, and said in English, "Gentlemen, I am very glad to see you all here." We then went to pay our respects to Monsieur. He recollected me perfectly, and the first word he said was, "Well, you have got Buonaparte aboard your squadron." He then reminded us that it was to-day just a month from the battle of Waterloo, "Quelle superbe bataille." He spoke to everybody, and did his part of the farce well enough. We then went in a body to the Duke de Berri's; but here we only wrote down our names.

July 19*th.*—After looking at about 5000 men of the Austrian army, who were drawn up along the Boulevards (for the purpose of being reviewed by the two Emperors and the King of Prussia), we set off for Neuilly, where we breakfasted with Sir Lowry Cole, in a very nice villa on the banks of the Seine, which was assigned to him as his quarters. After breakfast we set out, Apsley, Peel, and Cole on horseback, Fitzgerald and I in the barouche; we first went along the river-side to St. Cloud, which we found in possession of old Blucher and his staff; the great hall was a common guard-house, in which the Prussians were drinking, spitting, smoking, and sleeping in all directions. No mischief, however, had been done, except to one old china jar, which had been broken by accident in the billiard-room. The gallery was perfectly *intact.* Blucher occupied Buonaparte's own apartment, and we did not see it, as we had no mind to disturb the old man; but I hear that a good many, even English officers and others, have helped themselves to books out of the library as marks of triumph.

Peel and Fitzgerald are gone to visit the Catacombs. I went to pay a visit to my new friend, the Minister of Marine, who has asked me to take a family dinner with him, and Madame de Jaucourt, to meet General Becker—the officer who was charged with the surveillance of Buonaparte, that I may hear some details from him on the subject of his late transactions.* M. de Jaucourt told me a few particulars which

* [General Becker received his commission to keep Napoleon under surveillance in June, 1815. *Vide* Las Casas, 'Mémorial de Sainte-Hélène,' I. pp. 28–32.]

he had had from General Becker. Buonaparte he described as much depressed—as sunk into a kind of *mollesse*, and very careful about his personal ease and comfort. Now and then he had fits of talent and activity like those of his better days, and seemed inclined to throw himself into the interior of France and continue the war; at other times he proposed to set out in the night in a small schooner, to endeavour to pass the English squadron, and so get to America, or "se livrer au hasard." In this latter proposal he meant to include only Bertrand and Savary; but Madame Bertrand, who accompanied them, wept, and "se désolait," and protested and entreated against both those plans; she said it was cruel to separate her from her husband and more cruel still (as she would not leave him) to expose her to the chances of war or of the waves. General Becker represents Buonaparte as glad to seize even this excuse for abandoning plans neither of which suited his personal disposition, and to have affected to yield to Madame's entreaties in giving himself up to the English. He took on board with him only three boxes of gold; each not heavier than a man could carry, which, therefore, might be of perhaps 50 lbs. weight, which at 5*l.* the ounce would make each box of about 4000*l.* value. He also had some diamonds, particularly a very fine necklace, which he took the night before he went from his sister Hortense.

July 20th.—General Becker did not add much to his former information about Buonaparte, but what he did say gave occasion to La Place to say that Buonaparte, great as he was in prosperity, was never able to bear up against a reverse, under which his talents, resolution, courage, all vanished when he had most need of them.

Becker showed us a copy of Buonaparte's letter to the Prince Regent, in which he says that driven out of home by internal factions and foreign enemies, he came, like Themistocles, to sit on the British hearth, and to claim the protection of our laws from the "plus puissant, plus constant, et plus généreux de ses ennemis." In reading this, when I came to " *Thémis-tocle,*" who certainly was the last person I expected to meet there, I could not help bursting out into a loud laugh, which astonished the French, who thought all beautiful, but " *Thémis-tocle* " sublime and pathetic. I called the whole letter a base flattery, and said Buonaparte should have died rather than have written such a one; the only proper answer to it would have been to have enclosed him a copy of one of his *Moniteurs,*

in which he accused England of assassination and every other
horror. La Place said that Buonaparte ought to have died, if
not by his own hand (which, however, he seemed to think
would be better than not dying at all), at least in battle. I
said, he preferred living like a *Grecian,* to dying like a *Roman.*
They all seemed to agree that he had no *heart,* either in the
sense of magnanimity or feeling; and M. de Jaucourt told us
a saying, *un mot,* of his mother : " et pour le cœur, Napoléon,
il en *voulut."* She meant to say that he had a *disposition* to
feel ; just enough to make him wish that he had had a heart.
Madame La Princesse said she had heard him say that he had
le cœur à la tête, on some particular occasion, and that one who
was by said afterwards, that he was glad he had it anywhere.
I told them that an Englishman (I meant Douglas) who had
seen him in Elba, had found him very amiable ; upon which
they all cried out in chorus, " *du tout, du tout :*" no, he was
great and splendid and what you will, *mais pour aimable non,
du tout ;* and men and women vied with one another in
asserting the brusquerie of his manners. Becker said that in
his way of conferring a favour he always diminished its value,
and instead of *giving* one anything he *threw it at his head.*
They seemed to think that he was fond of Marie Louise and
had treated her with great attention—but he never opened
his lips about her in this latter period ; when General Becker
said something to him, as they were walking in the garden
of Malmaison the day before they set off, about the Austrian
court and its policy, Buonaparte gave him a little slap on the
lips with the back of his hand, and said laughingly, " tais toi,
tais toi, mon ami, tu ne connais rien à ces gens là." And of
course the subject was never renewed, though Becker had a
great wish to have heard him speak of the Empress.

   Whenever he talked of the battle of Waterloo, he accused
Ney of losing it by making an attack without orders, which
he said divided his forces and his *attention.* It was good to
hear Becker talk of the battle having been gained, and merely
lost afterwards by an *accident.* I asked him if he had ever
known a battle lost, but by an accident of the same sort ; and
the Princess said that if the General had any way of
reducing war to a certainty and abolishing accidents and
chances, she would go to battle herself. I think all the
French laughed very good-humouredly at the General, who,
however, did not seem inclined to admit that the French were
beaten, and was quite sure that they *ought* not to have been.

Becker, however, was not personally an admirer of Buonaparte, for he accused him of great military ignorance in all his wars, not knowing the true principles of manœuvring, and carrying everything by the mere waste of human life. "Diable," said he, " when I joined his army and saw his mode of operating, I no longer wondered that all the other armies were made weak to strengthen his."

Yesterday we dined with the Duke of Wellington, and found him in exceeding good spirits; he was ready enough to give details of his battle, but as Peel sat between me and him, he had almost all the benefit of his Grace's communicativeness. He is to have his review on Monday; we wait for it, and afterwards shall set out. The Duke expects to surprise the Sovereigns by showing them 65,000 men, as no one here thinks he has above 20,000.

This morning the three sovereigns, the Dukes of Berri and Wellington, with Blucher, Schwartzenburg, &c., passed part of the Prussian army in review. Lord and Lady Castlereagh, Mr. Planta, and I went in our barouche, but we found they would not let the carriage go along the Boulevard, and as the troops were to pass the Sovereigns in the Place Louis XV., I took them to the Bureau de la Marine, which is at the corner of that place and the Rue Royale, which leads to the Boulevard ; so that we had, through the politeness of M. de Jaucourt, an excellent view of what passed. I certainly never saw so fine a military sight; there were in the whole about 12,000 men. I counted them exactly and found there were eleven regiments of infantry of the line and two of chasseurs, each of 8 companies of 80 men; that made 8320 rank and file. The cavalry were one regiment of superb cuirassiers— the finest thing I ever saw—a regiment of light dragoons, one of hussars, and one of lancers, all very fine in their kinds, each regiment was composed of 6 troops at 68 rank and file a troop, in all 1632 men ; the artillery consisted of 24 6-pounder brass guns, many of them marked N, which had been taken from the French, and 8 12-pounder guns and howitzers; the artillerymen and their escort were 629 ; in the whole 10,581, rank and file—to which, if the officers, sergeants, and drivers are added, there must have been above 12,000 men. It was, altogether, much the finest sight of the kind I ever saw, particularly when one considered the distinction of the personages present, and the place in which they were assembled. But whether it be (as I fancy it is) that the people of Paris are not so prone to gather into crowds as we are, or that they are sulky and would not come out, I cannot tell, but there really was no concourse of spectators ; even where the sovereigns stood, I believe I exceed when I say there were 200 persons assembled to look on ; though the place would have easily contained 20,000.

July 22nd.—Went to Lady Castlereagh's, who had a supper; Peel and Fitz. were lazy, and would not dress themselves to come. I had rather not have gone, but as I had promised her verbally, I thought it would be rude not to go. The greatest folks there were the Duke, who wore seven stars on his coat, the Prince Royal of Bavaria, and the Prince of Saxe Coburg. I thought it stupid enough, and came away in about an hour. The only pleasant thing I saw or heard was the Prince of Bavaria endeavouring to speak English ; he is, it seems, a great John Bull, and is highly flattered at being told that he speaks *English* like an *Englishman,* and of course his Royal Highness finds people enough to tell him this ; but I doubt whether he finds one creature who understands a syllable he says. I stood by him last night for ten minutes, and I had not the least suspicion whatsoever that he was not speaking German. Sir Watkyn Wynn is here, and the joke is that Sir Watkyn has taught the Prince English ; the fact is that poor Sir Watkyn is almost as unintelligible as his Royal Highness, and, when they are conversing together, one is inclined to admit that the flattery of the courtiers is not *altogether* ground-less, and *that the Prince talks English like a Welshman.*

[Written at sea on the voyage home.]

Wednesday, July 26th.—The weather was now [at Brussels] exceedingly bad—cold, and more continued rain than I ever saw, except at Cork when I used to go the *summer circuit ;* so that we saw little of Brussels or its environs. We went in the first instance to call on the Duke and Duchess of Rich-mond, who had heard of our coming and wrote to press Peel to stay with them for some days ; but the necessity in which I was of being in London on Sunday prevented the possibility of this, as Peel would not leave me, though I pressed him to do so ; but in fact it would have been inconvenient and un-pleasant both to him and me to have separated. We sat the whole morning at the Duke's till about 4 o'clock.

We dined of course at the Duke's, when, besides ourselves,

the only strangers were a Colonel Stewart, who was come to see a wounded brother, and Colonel D'Oyly, of the Guards, himself wounded at Waterloo. Yet our party was not a small one, for we had the Duke and Duchess and Ladies Mary, Sarah, Georgiana and Jane, and after dinner three young lords and three young ladies more were admitted to the dessert. We did not get home till one in the morning.

Thursday, July 27th.—We breakfasted at home. Though the weather was still very bad, we were obliged by our want of time to go to Waterloo; so the Duke, the Duchess, and Lady Mary called on us in their landau at 11 o'clock, and we set out. The road goes straight from the town for 10 or 12 miles through the forest, which, in spite of the horrid weather, we thought very fine. It is a *pavé* the whole way, and well for us it was, for with the rain which had been falling the last ten days and quantity of waggons and cannon which had passed it, the *terres* on each side were now quite impassable; indeed, they were black and muddy and deep, like an Irish bog, and the whole way along was strewed with soldiers' hats and caps, broken arms, bones of horses, and other reliques of an army. Waterloo is a little town about half a mile long, prettily situated on the other side of the forest, but distant from the scene of the action about a mile and a half, and separated from it by a couple of pretty woods. Beyond these woods is the little village of Mont St. Jean. Here the Duke had sent his horses for us, and we mounted to ride over the field while the ladies returned to Waterloo. As the Duke had seen the whole action up to 3 o'clock on the 18th,* and had been since twice over the ground and knew all the particulars, we could not have had a better guide, and he conducted us over the whole of the ground. Without such a guide we should have seen but little; for one might have passed along the two roads that lead through the ground, nay, might have ridden over it without finding out that anything very extraordinary had passed there. When clear of the woods I have mentioned, you see a great undulating plain, without a hedge or tree, and nothing but two or three farm-houses visible for miles. This plain or succession of little hills is all under tillage, and was covered at the day of the battle with high corn and clover; in many places the oats and clover had

* [It is scarcely necessary to remind the reader that it is the Duke of Richmond who is here referred to.]

grown up again; in some places the farmers had already
ploughed up the ground, but in others, where the action had
been hottest, the marks of trampling, &c., were still visible.
The whole of the extent when you came to ride over it was
strewed with the cartridges and waddings of the cannon;.
letters which had been thrown out of the pockets of the
killed and wounded, and the torn remains of hats, caps, and
helmets.   You also could see the graves into which the dead
had been thrown, sometimes singly, sometimes two or more·
at a time, and in many places by fifties and hundreds.   The
farm of Hougoumont, which was the right of the action, was·
totally destroyed, the house and offices burnt and battered
with shot, the trees around it (for it had an orchard and a
little wood) cut to pieces; its courts and ditches strewed with
caps and cartridges, and the fields around it broken up with
graves.

On several parts of the field we saw people searching for·
some remains of plunder, but they had not got much, as·
the whole had been already carefully gleaned over by the
peasants; two boys had two English Lifeguardsmen's swords.-
All the peasants of Mt. St. Jean and Waterloo have collected
great quantities of spoil—clothes, swords, helmets, cuirasses,·
crosses of the Legion of Honour, &c., which they offer to you for·
sale.   At first these things were bought by the curious cheap
enough; now the purchasers are more numerous and the
commodity rarer, and therefore their prices are much
enhanced.   The Duke has bought a dozen of cuirasses taken
from the bodies of the French, and Peel bought a very hand--
some one for two napoleons.   I bought *for you* a little cross
of the Legion of Honour, which had been taken from a dead
French officer; this cost me one napoleon.   I also gave one·
franc a-piece for half-a-dozen of the broken eagles which the·
French soldiers wore on the fronts of their caps.   The Duchess·
made me a present of the orderly book of one of the French
regiments, which she had bought, and these, with the things·
I picked up myself on the field, are all my spoils.

The very morning after the battle the peasants were ordered
to bury the dead, and when the Duke of Richmond rode over·
the field on Wednesday morning all the bodies had been
already stripped and plundered.   This part of the ceremony·
was performed by the fair sex.   The most valuable part of·
the soldier's dress to the plunderers were the shoes and
stockings, which of course they made great haste to lay hold.

of, except only the stockings of the Highlanders, which could be of no use to them, and therefore one saw their bodies, in other respects naked, lying with their plaid stockings on; but this is enough on this subject. We rode back as fast as we could to Waterloo, having got wet to the skin; in the meanwhile, when the Duchess and Lady Mary had laid out a lunch of sandwiches and wine, which they had brought with them, to which the woman of the inn added an omelette and some of the Flemish pancakes called *gaufres*, while Peel and the ladies were cheapening spoils from the villagers, I went to the stove and dried myself. It was in this little inn that the Duke of Wellington had his quarters. On the morning of the battle the poor landlady was weeping and bewailing her danger, but the Duke, she said, encouraged her, and said, slapping her on the shoulders, "*C'est moi qui répond de tout*, personne ne souffrira aujourd'hui des Français excepté les soldats." In this house the Prince of Orange had his wound dressed.

Opposite to the inn door is a curious little chapel, in which one monument is already erected to an officer who fell in the action, a Capt. Fitzgerald, of the Lifeguards, I am told; his poor wife brought out a leaden coffin to remove the body, but it would not go into it, and she was obliged to bury him at Waterloo. Some bodies which had been buried have been taken up and sent to England. One officer, the Duchess told me, of the name of Lindsay, was so disinterred, and, though he had been a fortnight in the earth, when they took him up to remove him he was not in the slightest degree changed; he had been buried in his clothes, and was immediately recognised by his friends. This seems to me very surprising. Some very extraordinary cases of wounds occurred in the action, which I heard of at Brussels. One officer received a severe wound in the shoulder as, it was thought, from a ragged ball, but when the substance came to be extracted it turned out to be a tooth; some poor devil's head had been, it is supposed, knocked to pieces by a cannon ball, and his tooth had been driven into this officer's arm. Another officer had his thigh dreadfully lacerated, and the substance was lodged so deep that the extraction was exceedingly difficult; when it was taken out it was found to be a piece of five francs, and two pieces of one franc each; these two must have been shot out of some other person's pocket, as he declared he had not had them in his own. A soldier, Somerville's surgeon told him, had a ball through the forehead which came out behind, yet is alive and doing well. I have heard twenty other such stories, but these are quite enough to exercise your faith.

We dined again with the Duke of Richmond, and as we could not get away before, and were to be off at dawn of day, I endeavoured to persuade Peel not to go to bed for two or three hours, but to hasten on to Ostend as the wind was fair, and to get there in time to have our carriage embarked; but he would not, which, as afterwards turned out, was very unlucky. He was very stout about travelling all night and every night when we left Paris, and seemed only to fear my laziness or reluctance, and made several speeches in its praise; but the second night, I fancy, did not please him as well as the first, for he said no more on this subject, and seemed a good deal annoyed; and this night, though we were to be in bed but three hours, he was decidedly unwilling to come on.

We are now lying at sea with our sails flapping, and shall think ourselves well off to be at Ramsgate or Deal with the next afternoon's tide.

On Peel's return to Ireland after this trip, he was two nights and a day crossing from Holyhead to Dublin—a journey which now occupies on the average about four hours.

Mr. Peel to Mr. Croker.

Dublin Castle, August 8th, 1815.

MY DEAR CROKER,

Let me know what you paid the man at Dover for me, for I forget the amount of the charge. Pray have the goodness to send me, if you can, a copy of your Waterloo plan, for I have lost mine. I find here plans of the battle from officers who were in the engagement, who have no more notion of it than they have of craniology.

I had a passage of thirty-three hours from Holyhead—two nights and a day. Wretched beyond description—a strong N.W. by W., if such a wind blows. I mean westerly, with just enough inclination to the north to make it a completely foul wind. The packet was full of passengers. The men were all sick, and the women and children thought they were going to the bottom, and filled up the intervals of sickness with a chorus of lamentation, and cries of "Steward, are we sinking?" which would have been ludicrous enough for half an hour, but, like other good things, wearied by constant repetition.

I always thought Bonaparte must have mistaken La Haye Sainte for Haute St. Jean; but after all, I think Lord Wellington's is the best account of the battle.

Yours most affectionately,

R. Peel.

The general political events of 1815 are not touched upon in any of the journals or papers which Mr. Croker left behind him. The agitation which sprung up respecting the supply of corn, the adoption by the House of Commons of a Bill prohibiting the importation of wheat when the average price was under eighty shillings a quarter, the riots which took place in London, the discussions on the Bank Restriction Act—on none of these subjects is there a single letter or memorandum. It must be assumed that Mr. Croker had not yet begun to write with such fulness on political affairs to his friends as he did in later years. The only documents of any interest, apart from the diaries which were sent to Mrs. Croker from Paris, relate to the quarrel which took place between Peel and O'Connell. In this curious affair, Mr. Croker was consulted by Peel, although he seems to have had no part in making the arrangements for the hostile meeting. It was something which was said by Mr. Peel in Parliament that produced the misunderstanding; and according to a memorandum drawn up by Mr. Justice Keogh, Peel, after uttering the objectionable words, sent Sir Charles Saxton to O'Connell, not exactly to deliver a message, but practically to express his readiness to receive one. A correspondence ensued, and the result of it was, as described by Mr. Justice Keogh, that "Mr. Peel sent a message to O'Connell through his friend Colonel Browne," while another duel was arranged between the intermediaries who had at first been employed, on account of a misunderstanding which had arisen between them. It was finally arranged that all the parties should meet at Ostend, and Mr. Peel and Sir Charles Saxton proceeded there, having taken every precaution to avoid the vigilance of the police, who had got scent of the intended affray.

Mr. Croker to Mr. W. Gregory.

September 12th, 1815.

As Peel slept at Maidstone last night, I took the opportunity of running down with Browne to see him. Indeed, I had intended to go on with him; but we gave up that plan, for reasons that appear good even to me, anxious as I was to accompany him. He was in the finest spirits, and as unaffectedly gay and at his ease as he was when we were going to Dover two months ago on our tour to Paris. We parted this morning at Maidstone. He will embark probably this evening's tide, and will sleep at Calais to-night, and to-morrow night at Ostend.

Mr. Peel and Sir Charles Saxton reached Ostend without interference, but O'Connell and his second, Mr. Lidwill, were arrested in London, and bound over by Lord Ellenborough to keep the peace, and not to leave the country before the first day of the ensuing term. The belligerents returned to Ireland pretty much as they went, and Mr. O'Connell seems to have proceeded no farther in the affair; but in November Mr. Lidwill was still not satisfied, and he insisted on having a meeting with Sir Charles Saxton. This meeting took place, and Lidwill, after receiving his adversary's fire, discharged his own pistol in the air, declaring that he felt bound thus to act in consequence of the stringency of the undertaking entered into by him before Lord Ellenborough. Meanwhile, Peel had followed Sir Charles Saxton to the Continent, with the intention of challenging Lidwill for certain words which he (Peel) construed as insulting; but when he heard that Lidwill would only fire in the air, he resolved not to offer the challenge. O'Connell, who had already "killed his man," as the saying ran, declared that he would never again fight a duel, and here the whole affair—which caused a considerable stir at the time—came to an end. Peel's own comments on the incident in November may perhaps be worth preserving :—

Mr. Peel to Mr. Croker.

Dublin Castle, Nov. 20th, 1815.

MY DEAR CROKER,

I know *I can trust you,* and therefore I have no hesitation in writing to you. A person calling himself Major Lidwill sent in his name the day before yesterday to Saxton, and told him *Lidwill was then at Calais.* Saxton said, "I shall be there too very soon." The Major replied, "If you are there before *us,* leave a note at the Post-office." This was all that passed, and he did not explain the contradiction. Saxton sails to-night. I have sent by him a *special retainer* to Lidwill, desiring him to remain on the Continent. I shall soon follow Saxton—probably before you can answer this—however, try. Let me know *by special express* whether you have heard anything about Lidwill—whether he has appeared in the Court of King's Bench, &c., &c. I presume he has not, and that he means to go at all risks; but he is such a fellow that I should wish to be quite certain that he is gone before I start to follow him. There would be something absurd in again finding him a *détenu.* I place implicit confidence in you. No one here but Browne, Saxton, and myself know of Lidwill's communication.

Yours affectionately,

R. P.

MY DEAR CROKER,

Here I am, notwithstanding your advice, which I received between Cerneoge and Corwen. I am just going to embark, and to escape all apprehensions of arrest, which (as this will be the fifth night which I have passed without changing my clothes) I think I deserve. We had a passage of forty hours from Holyhead, but, notwithstanding, I only left Dublin last Friday night. I think I could prove to you I have acted for the best.

Yours most affectionately,

My dear Croker,

ROBERT PEEL.

Do not let the *Courier* insert my name for the next fortnight. My father takes it in. Every letter from Dublin to him will be stopped. I hope he will learn nothing of my departure from Dublin.

R. P.

The year 1816 opened with a general anxiety to reduce the burdens which had so long pressed heavily upon the people. At one period (in 1806) the income-tax had been raised to two shillings in the pound, and the people had borne it without complaining; but when the war was over, they naturally considered that they had a just claim to be relieved. Mr. Vansittart proposed to reduce the tax by one-half, but the House was in no mood to submit to a compromise, and it rejected the proposition by 238 to 201 votes. The Opposition, however, determined to beat the Government in a still more effectual manner, and it was thought that the best opportunity would be afforded by throwing out the Navy Estimates. When the attempt was made, Mr. Tierney led the attack, and Mr. Croker repulsed it in a manner so brilliant that he added greatly to his reputation as a debater, and was offered a Privy Councillor's office, "which I declined," he wrote afterwards, "as I did similar propositions, for I had early made up my mind to remain Secretary of the Admiralty." In 1857, Lord Hatherton (formerly Mr. Littleton, Secretary for Ireland under Lord Grey's Government), happened to meet Mr. Croker, and recalled to his mind the old encounter with Tierney. This led to a

correspondence which throws sufficient light on the somewhat remarkable circumstances connected with the mis-
directed onslaught of the leader of the Opposition.

Lord Hatherton to Mr. Croker.

Hastings, July 26th, 1857.

MY DEAR CROKER,

I regret that my detention at this place still prevents my
sending you a copy of the memorandum you asked for. It
shall not be delayed a day after my return home.

There is no reason, however, why I should longer delay
to give you my recollection of the very brilliant scene
between you and Tierney, to which I adverted when I had
last the pleasure of seeing you.

It must have occurred in the year 1816; as the occasion
of it was the presentation by the Government of larger Navy
Estimates in that year, the first year of the peace, than had
been voted in the preceding year, the last year of the war.

Tierney, on the motion for the Speaker leaving the Chair
to go into the Committee of Supply, made a very formidable
attack on the Government for this demand.

Warrender followed in reply; but you rose immediately
afterwards, and made in effect the defence of the Government. But the affair I spoke of must, I think, have occurred
subsequently in the Committee of the whole House. For I
well remember that you and Tierney spoke frequently in
rapid succession to each other; he enforcing and varying his
attacks, and you instantly and successfully repelling them.
The battle was between yourselves only, and continued for a
considerable time; parties in the House cheering their com-
batants in a state of great excitement. The passage of arms
was so rapid, that I can only describe it in general terms;
and can give no account of it beyond this, that you
proved that in every instance the first year of peace had
been more expensive in the Naval Department than the last
year of war. But I retain at the distance of more than
forty years the most vivid recollection of the scene, the most
brilliant of its kind I remember in the House of Commons
during the twenty-three years I was a member of it.

I heartily concurred in the policy of the Government with
respect to its proposed plan of armaments at that time; and

felt much interest in its success. I can recall to mind no instance of a similar attack on a department so triumphantly repelled.

On the restoration of peace, after the war with Russia last year, I thought it might be useful to call the attention of Sir Charles Wood to those discussions. But to my surprise I could find no record of them. The debate on Tierney's motion is given. But no notice is taken of those discussions in Committee. Although it was not customary in those days to give debates in Committee at any length, I expected to have found some notice of so exciting a scene.

I remain, my dear Croker,

Yours very sincerely,

HATHERTON.

Mr. Croker to Lord Hatherton.   Extracts.

February 1st, 1857.*

In the beginning of 1816 the ministerial defeat on the Property Tax and the public impatience for the reduction of the war establishments, together with some accidental defeats on minor points connected with the army, and especially the Admiralty, contributed to suggest to the Opposition a short cut to office by a *coup de main* against the navy estimates. The moving these estimates was generally considered in the first instance as a matter of form, and their reference to the Committee of supply a matter of course. All the struggle was to be in the Committee.

It was the official etiquette that the senior lay Lord should make the motion, and not the Secretary, who might have been naturally expected to be better acquainted with the details. This practice arose from two causes—first, the official rank of the Lord over the Secretary; the Lord speaking in his own name and that of his colleagues, while the Secretary was only an individual member of the House; and secondly, because (till our own day) the Secretary was not looked upon as a political officer, did not change with ministries, and took no part in political debate. This etiquette fell in with the Opposition scheme.

---

* [This letter was written six months before Mr. Croker's death.]

The senior lay Lord happened to be Warrender, a much cleverer fellow than he was generally thought, but who knew nothing at all of the Navy Estimates; the object was, therefore, to demolish Warrender at once, to negative going into Committee where the sea Lords and I would have been able to explain or justify details, and thus by so flagrant an affront overthrow the ministry at a blow. For this purpose Tierney, then the real leader of the Opposition, with the additional authority which his being an ex-Treasurer of the Navy gave him, was himself to lead the onset. The Government were wholly unapprized of the scheme, and it happened (from a curious circumstance, but too complicated to repeat) that I did not expect the debate that night, and had not even brought down the office red box containing my detailed notes on the estimates which I hardly expected to want that night, or at least not so early in the evening! The box was left on my desk at the Admiralty, whence if necessary, it might be had.

We knew nothing of the intentions of the Opposition, but I remember we were somewhat surprised at the numbers and the eagerness they exhibited, and the tone in which Tierney in some preliminary conversation about the loan had menaced us with an utter defeat "in half an hour;" and certainly, if he had not based his hopes on a most extraordinary blunder, he would have succeeded. In a most able and forcible speech he examined and contrasted the late war and present peace estimates, and showed by the indisputable figures that the estimates, so far from being prepared with any pretence to economy, were, every where and in all branches, enormously increased. "What could be done with such derisive, such insulting documents, than throw them back in the face of the Government?" You may recollect the enthusiasm of the Opposition as this speech proceeded, and the uneasiness at our side. But it was no surprise to me. *I* was prepared for it, and was waiting quietly on a back bench for Warrender's reply, which I knew might be complete. In the meanwhile Castlereagh grew alarmed, and beckoned me down to sit by him, and he asked me "what answer could be made to all that." "Oh," said I, "Warrender has a full answer that will blow it all away in five minutes." "I," exclaimed Warrender, "I know nothing about it." "What," said I, "have you not the memorandum I gave Lord Melville and you yesterday, or at least notes of it?"

"No," said Warrender, "Lord Melville said they were old stories, and had nothing to do with these times." "Good Lord!" I said, "and where is the memorandum?" "I put it back," said he, "in the bundle you gave us."

"But you can state the facts," said Castlereagh. "It will be of no effect," I replied. The facts are only a series of *figures*, which nothing but the identical figures can substantiate. "But where," said C., "is the paper?" "At the Admiralty in a red box."

Billy Holmes,* very much alarmed at the aspect of the House, volunteered to dash away for the recovery of the red box, and brought it me in a wonderfully short space of time, and there I found my memorandum, which was an abstract of the *last war* and *first peace* estimates ever since the treaty of Ryswick, in all of which the peace estimate for establishments exceeded the war estimate, and proved that *naturâ rerum* it must of necessity do so. The estimates are of two classes; first, for *active* service; second, for the establishments; the active service called the *"vote of seamen"* was for ship's victuals, ammunition, wear and tear, and wages, &c., of 145,000 men: say 100 sail of the line. When peace came, 80 of the 100 sail were paid off, and reduced the expense of *that* estimate which fell to nothing, while they and their various expenses were transferred over to the *establishment* estimate, commonly called " the Navy Estimate;" which, of course, was proportionally increased in all its branches. The simple reading of this memorandum, and the evidence of the figures *in every ease* from the treaty of Ryswick, changed the face of the House in a moment. Our opponents were ashamed of Tierney, and Tierney was ashamed of himself to be taken in such a mare's nest; and the mortification was the greater, for he had been a party to the same process as Treasurer of the Navy in 1803. The thing was so obvious that, though I had taken pains (for I never spared pains) to work it out, and had given it to Melville and Warrender as general information, I really did not expect that any one, least of all an old fox like Tierney, would have ever given me an opportunity of using it, but my diligence was rewarded by good luck; and I certainly never saw in Parliament so sudden and so complete a turning of the tide of victory.

* [Mr. W. Holmes, commonly known as "Black Billy," was then acting as the Treasury Whip.]

It was celebrated at the time in verse and prose. This is the history, and a curious secret history it is, of the *first* of the two occasions mentioned in your letter, and which fortunately the little circumstances of the *red box and despised memorandum* fixed more strongly in my mind than the subsequent affair.

This, the first really important debate on which the fate of parties was staked, took place on the 25th of March, 1816; but it had ended so disgracefully for the Opposition, that, though there was no longer a hope of turning us out on the Navy Estimates, their *amour propre* induced them to try to make a rally for their own characters, and Tierney, Brougham, and Baring, all of them in after life personal friends of mine, and the two latter intimate and affectionate ones, got up that second scene which as relates to Tierney and me you have so graphically described. But on this occasion, though I was assailed on all sides and by such formidable antagonists, I was not under the difficulty in which I was the first night of coming in as a subordinate and auxiliary. I had not now to send Billy Holmes for my "red box." I had all my papers in my hands and in my head, and I do believe that single-handed (as Castlereagh good naturedly said) I completed that night the success which I had begun on the 25th.

It was in consequence of these debates that Castlereagh soon after sent for me and offered me from Lord Liverpool, a Privy Councillor's office, which, as I have told you, I then, and twice afterwards, declined. If I had accepted, where should I have ultimately been? Should I have been submerged in the Lethe of time even more completely than I am—like Calcraft, Courtenay, and many others; or should I have been tottering down the day after to-morrow to the House of Lords, with Glenelg, and Goodrich, and Monteagle, and Brougham and yourself, and twenty others? It is not worth a conjecture; I am sure I should never have been happier, nor I hope more respectable. I filled an important office in glorious times, and with illustrious colleagues and friends, of whom I am more proud than I ever could be of any successes of my own.

Ever, my dear Hatherton,

Yours sincerely,

J. W. CROKER.

P.S.—I have been very ill while writing this letter, which must account for blots, and perhaps blunders, but with reference to the allusion to contemporaries, friends and foes, made peers, let me add a curious circumstance. I have been once to see the new House of Lords, and while I was there, Brougham, I think, first, and then Monteagle spied me out, and came down to the Bar to shake hands with me (it was since the beginning of my illness), and indeed I think half the House, or more, did me the same civility, and this called my attention to a fact that I think not unimportant to constitutional history. There were, I think, about thirty peers present; and we observed that there was not one, not a single one, with whom I had not sat in the House of Commons, including the Duke of Wellington and the Chancellor. It shows how completely the House of Commons has been the nursery to the House of Lords.

Mr. Croker gained another success in Parliament during this year by inducing the Legislature to purchase the Elgin marbles, now in the British Museum. His exertions called forth a warm acknowledgment from Lord Elgin. " I perceive," wrote Lord Elgin, " in this hasty sketch [referring to a newspaper report of Mr. Croker's speech] not only the well-informed and triumphant supporter of my cause, but the animated and, I may say, friendly vindication of my conduct. It has ever been a source of great astonishment with me, that without its having earlier been at all an object of attention with you, you should, with such perfect ease, have made yourself master of the whole question, as much, I may venture to say, as it can be understood; and that you should at once have seized, with precision, details which one should imagine nothing short of personal inspection or professional study could have brought to particular notice." Everybody now acknowledges the almost priceless value of these relics of the Acropolis, but in 1816 it was very difficult to induce the House or the public to regard them as worth the relatively small sum which was paid for them, and which, it was acknowledged, did not suffice to cover the outlay actually incurred by Lord Elgin. Lord Byron and others attacked Lord Elgin bitterly for despoiling the Acropolis, but since then it has been almost universally admitted that the marbles of Phidias were only saved from destruction by a safe home having been provided for them in England.

Mr. Canning to Mr. Croker.

Lisbon, January 24th, 1816.

My dear Sir,

If Blackford communicated to you, as I desired, the contents of a letter which I wrote to him, in October I think, (but which by the way he has never acknowledged), you will have been prepared for my application for a ship of war, and for my request (I hope not an unreasonable one) that it might be allowed to touch with me at Bordeaux.

I have had the satisfaction to hear from Lord Liverpool that I may expect a frigate here in March, and that Lord Melville has been so good as to promise that the instruction which I requested shall be given to the captain.

I trust to your kindness that you will have had in view for me as good a captain as Briggs (better there cannot be); and if a *cleaner* ship than the Leviathan, I know no other improvement that I could wish.

Is it necessary that the Admiralty should have a direction from the Secretary of State for this employment of a frigate? In the uncertainty, I have thought it safest to write an official letter (or despatch *rasée*) to Lord Castlereagh, which I take the liberty of inclosing to you, to be forwarded if you think it necessary; if not, to be put into the fire.

Is it necessary that I should trouble you with a list of myself and my establishment? or will it be sufficient generally to state that *to* Bordeaux the cargo will consist of ourselves, four children, a governess, three females, and five or six male servants; and *from* Bordeaux, of myself, and three or four servants? Add to this two or three horses and two carriages, if there be room for them; and baggage somewhat out of proportion to our reduced numbers; which, however, neither eats nor drinks.

So much for business.   Now will you allow me to ask you whether it would be possible to get something of pleasure out of this frigate consistently with the public service? Have you any instructions to send to Gibraltar?   I have a great desire to see that place; and indeed it is a shame to leave this part of the world without having made an attempt to do so.   Ten days, or at most a fortnight, would be sufficient to carry me there from the Tagus and bring me back.   And if it should so happen that this same frigate by being sent out a fortnight earlier might be employed to carry your Mediterranean despatches so far, I should be strongly tempted to avail myself of the opportunity, and to employ the interval while my packages are making up in a visit to General Don's * dominions.   C. Ellis (who is here with his boys) would go with me.   I am aware that no orders can be given to a captain to take me to Gibraltar, where I have no business, and which certainly is not on my way home.   If the plan be feasible at all, it must be through your management and good nature.   If you should find it so, you will perhaps take the trouble to apprize me beforehand of the time at which I might look for the arrival of the frigate on its way to Gibraltar, in order that I may be prepared not to detain it.

I should not wish to embark my family for Bordeaux before the very end of March.   So I may expect to reach England by the end of the Easter holidays.

Believe me, my dear Sir,

Very sincerely yours,

GEORGE CANNING.

The foregoing letter will not tend to remove from Canning's memory the reproach of having treated his mission to Lisbon as a means of carrying out his own wishes and plans, without much regard for the public service.   Sir H. L. Bulwer— certainly no unfriendly critic—admits that the appointment of Mr. Canning to Lisbon was " considered a job, for an able minister (Mr. Sydenham), on a moderate salary, was recalled, in order to give the eminent orator, whose support the

---

* [Governor of Gibraltar.]

Government wished to obtain, the appointment of ambassador on a much larger salary." And he adds that though Mr. Canning rebutted the specific charges which were brought against him, "it was nevertheless clear that it was because he was going to Lisbon for the health of his son, and that it was more agreeable to him to go in an official position than as a simple individual, that he had been employed, and his predecessor removed." * In the above letter, it will be seen that a pleasure trip to Gibraltar was proposed as a part of the homeward journey, although Mr. Canning admitted that he had "no business" there, and that it was not on his way home. What answer to this letter was returned by Mr. Croker we have no means of judging.

Mr. Croker to Mr. Peel.

August 8th, 1816.

George Cockburn is come back† in good health and spirits ; he gives us no hopes of Buonaparte's dying. He eats, he says, enormously, but he drinks little, takes regular exercise, and is in all respects so very careful of his carcass that he may live twenty years. Cockburn and he parted bad friends but I believe he wishes he had Cockburn back again, for Sir Hudson Lowe is as strict as Cockburn, without any of his liveliness, and little of his activity and talents. I think Buonaparte must feel himself like Don Juan tête-à-tête *avec la statue du Commandeur.* Cockburn says positively that he cannot escape if common vigilance is used, but he (Buonaparte) has had some propositions (mad and wild to be sure) from America on this subject. I ought not to say *has had,* for they were intercepted. You may be sure that his liberation will be attempted from America. His friends there have money, talents, audacity, and despair. What would you have more ? I wish I could have sent you a turtle Cockburn brought me from Ascension. He weighed 300 lbs., but he was in too infirm a state of health to undertake a journey to Ireland.

* 'Historical Characters,' vol. ii. pp. 284–5.
† [From St. Helena, whither he had escorted Buonaparte.]

Some additional information about Napoleon was trans-
mitted later in the year by Mr. Croker to the Père Elysée, who
was attached to the Royal Household of France. " L'homme
de Ste. Hélène," wrote Mr. Croker, " se porte assez bien—je
dois plutôt dire trop bien. Mais il est de très mauvaise
humeur, et quand il ne s'emporte pas il s'ennuye."

The following letters show the impression which was made
upon the mind of the late Sir Robert Peel by his official
residence in Ireland, and they also show how little Ireland
has altered for the better during the last sixty or seventy
years.

Mr. Peel to Mr. Croker.

[Without date.]

My Dear Croker,

The very moment I received your letter respecting the
Irish article,* I sat down and wrote you a very long letter—
about ten sheets of paper. Unfortunately it was very dark
when I wrote the letter, and as it was more than I could do
to read it the next day, I thought you would not have much
chance of benefiting by it. I took it, therefore, to the Park,
with the pious intention of copying it, and in a legible form,
but I never had courage to open the box which contains it—
and there it remains. I remember that I expressed great
delight at your intention, complete acquiescence in your
opinion that Papal superstition is the cause of one-half the
evils of this country, and serious doubts whether the half
would be alleviated by Catholic Emancipation.

I now send you a collection of choice documents consisting
first of *Cox's Magazine*. Cox is of no religion, but would call
himself a Protestant if he were compelled to profess any.
His object in his magazine was to ferment a bitter hatred
against England. His principal assistants in writing were
R. C. priests. Many parts are only suited for and only
intelligible to the lower orders. They relate to the characters
of constables, police magistrates, and persons flogging or
flogged in the rebellion. The work was distributed occasionally gratis, and generally sold at a price which could not

* On the Irish Grand Jury Laws, *Quarterly Review*, April 1815.

defray the expense of printing. It was greatly admired by the common people. Keogh, who was hanged the other day for heading the attack on the barrack at Ballagh, had a box half full of Cox's Magazines, which were found on searching his room after his apprehension. It was quite impossible to subdue Cox by any power which the law gave us. The two last volumes—the worst of the set—were written when he was in Newgate for publishing a seditious libel; he rather preferred a residence in Newgate to any other. He remained in prison a year and a half after the term of his confinement rather than pay a fine of 300*l.*, which I think such a popular character might easily have raised.

The little volume called 'A Sketch of Irish History,' is a more infamous work than *Cox's Magazine*. I have the volumes from which it contains some excerpta. They contain a regular history of Ireland, and on the first page are these words, printed at the bottom, "Intended chiefly for the Young Ladies educated at the Ursuline Convents. By a member of the Ursuline Community at Ash."

This work is written with great care—most mischievous and inflammatory—and yet it is thought to be impossible to convict the printer for libel.

I send also the *Dublin Chronicle*. You know its history. It was established by O'Connell when he and his colleagues had brought the editors of all other papers into Newgate for publishing speeches which they composed and corrected, and afterwards disavowed.

Perhaps the most noteworthy and extraordinary document of all is the letter which I send you. It was written by a priest in Longford to one of his flock, whom he suspected of giving information. He admitted the writing of it to Major Wiles, a police magistrate, but he has not been convicted yet, and therefore names must not be used. Pray read it, it is very curious—an admirable specimen of the purposes for which the priests of Ireland exert their spiritual influence. If I collect anything more I will send it to you, but I will not inflict my letter upon you.

Yours most affectionately,

R. P.

Mr. Peel to Mr. Croker.

Dublin Castle, Sept. 23rd, 1816.

MY DEAR CROKER,

You must give a specimen—one specimen—of the humanity of the poor, suffering, oppressed natives of this country, who are trained up by their priests in the paths of religion and virtue, and are only driven to the commission of outrage by the tyranny of their landlords, or the insulting triumphs of Orangemen. I believe I can furnish you with a more complete specimen—of very recent occurrence—than you could discover in any age, however remote. The murderers of Baker were angels in comparison with the perpetrators of a murder in the county of Limerick.* Inclosed is the evidence on which four persons were convicted and hanged, and on nearly the same evidence have five other wretches suffered capitally. It is a melancholy story, and a most singular fact in the annals of murder, that chiefly on the evidence of the little girl, who is, I believe, 11 and not 14 years of age, have nine men been convicted and hanged—five within the last week. Four are now in custody, and have offered to plead guilty on condition that they may be transported for life. I know not how many more were present at the murder than the 13 above accounted for. What must be the state of morals in a country where thirteen men, after having killed the husband, and when all apprehension of danger was at an end, could kill a woman with an infant in her arms, in the manner in which this unfortunate woman was killed, and where the orphan child of that woman could be told by "all the people in the neighbourhood" to whom she applied for protection, that *"she might go to the devil?"*

All comment would but weaken the unparalleled atrocity of this transaction. The Dillons were Catholics.

Yours most truly,

R. PEEL.

The marriage of the Princess Charlotte—an event regarded with so much interest by the nation—is, strangely enough,

---

* [A man and his wife were butchered on their own hearth, and their little child was stabbed. The child survived, but no one in the neighbourhood would give her food or shelter.]

not referred to in any of Mr. Croker's papers. On the other
hand, there are several letters relating to the bombardment
of Algiers by Lord Exmouth—an achievement which relieved
the Mediterranean, at once and for ever, from the scourge
of piracy, and set free a large number of Christian slaves.
Mr. Croker had always been a great friend of Lord Exmouth's,
and chose his title for him when he was raised to the peerage
as a baron. He now wrote to him on his new successes, and,
while praising him and his men very highly, took the opportunity of discouraging the idea which Lord Exmouth appears
to have entertained of getting a special medal distributed for
Algerian service.

Mr. Croker to Lord Exmouth.

October 23rd, 1816.

MY DEAR LORD,

I never have and never will (I hope) do anything for the
sake of popularity; he that steers by any other compass than
his own sense of duty may be a popular, but cannot be an
honest, and I think not a useful public servant. On the
occasion of a medal for the Algerine exploit I have no hesitation in telling you that I decidedly disapprove of it; and if
my opinion were asked (*which it has not been*) I should say so.
Why should that be done for 5000 men who were at Algiers,
which has not been done for the million of men who have
served in so many glorious actions since 1793? You will
say that the soldiers of Waterloo have had medals, but surely
it is impossible to compare Waterloo with any other battle.
The soldiers of Salamanca, Talavera, Vittoria, Toulouse, and
the Pyrenees, have no medals. In short, my dear Lord, with
the justest sense of the skill and gallantry of your operations
before Algiers, and of the admirable courage displayed by all
ranks, and the wonderful success of your fire, I must say that
I should be sorry to see anything done for it, which should
seem to throw a shade over the 1st June, Camperdown,
St. Vincent's, the Nile, and Trafalgar.

Yours, &c.,

J. W. C.

The purely literary work which occupied Mr. Croker's attention this year appears to have been restricted to his contributions to the *Quarterly Review*, for which he wrote nine articles—among them an enlightened justification of the purchase of the Elgin marbles, and a highly appreciative review of the 'Antiquary,' which had then just taken by storm the entire reading world. Mr. Croker had already written an article upon 'Waverley'—the first of the famous series of novels—full of warm and yet judicious praise.* It was now that Mr. John Murray made his offer of 2500 guineas for a history of the French Revolution by Mr. Croker—a work which he often meditated, but never found leisure to finish. Such portions of the general literary correspondence of this year as are still of interest may be brought together here.

Mr. Murray to Mr. Croker.

Albemarle Street, October 22nd, 1816.

DEAR SIR,

I have been thinking upon your plan of writing 'Annals of the French Revolution' almost ever since you honoured me with a conversation upon the subject, and I can assure you, after much consideration, that my ardour for its prosecution is not in the least abated. It appears to me, however, knowing the immensity of the materials, that it will be almost impossible to comprise any complete account of such extraordinary events in less than *three* volumes in quarto, as there must be a certain quantity of documents (either indispensably necessary, exceedingly curious and interesting, or such as are nowhere else to be found) appended. I presume that your object will be to produce a lively, entertaining, interesting and authentic book, for the instructive amusement of the general reader.

It is not a very easy matter to form a mercantile estimate of what I have not previously seen, but I think I may venture

---

* He reviewed 'Waverley' in the *Quarterly* for July 1814, and there is little doubt that the review of 'Guy Mannering' in the *Quarterly*, Jan. 1815, was also from his pen.

to offer for the copyright 2000 guineas, to be paid in six and twelve months (1000 guineas each) from the day of its publication, and 500 guineas more at six months from the day of publication of a second edition, with such additions and other improvements as you may think necessary, making in the whole 2500 guineas for the copyright. I ought properly to have ascertained your expectations for labours of which you only can be the proper judge, but I have made an offer with my best judgment and feelings, and should it not meet your own estimate, I am sure at least of your kind allowances for my difficulty.

John Gifford, of Pitt memory, has long issued proposals for a history of the French Revolution, for which he has collected a library that would fully occupy all the sides of your office. He has probably made progress in this proportionate only to the little encouragement which it has received, and if his library were worth the purchase, he would gladly sell it to the British Museum.

John Murray.

Mr. Croker to Mr. Murray.

Admiralty, September 18th, 1816.

My dear Murray,

I have read with great pleasure the poem you lent me.* It is written with great vigour, and all the descriptive part is peculiarly to my taste, for I am fond of realities, even to the extent of being fond of localities. A spot of ground a yard square, a rock, a hillock, on which some great achievement has been performed, or to which any recollections of interest attach, excite my feelings more than all the monuments of art. Pictures fade, and statues moulder, and forests decay, and cities perish, but the sod of Marathon is immortal, and he who has had the good fortune to stand on that sacred spot has identified himself with Athenian story in a way which all the historians, painters, and poets of the world could not have accomplished for him. Shakespeare, whom nothing escaped, very justly hints that one of the highest offices of good poetry is to connect our ideas with some "local habitation." It is an old and highly absurd phrase to say that poetry deals in fiction; alas, *history*, I fear, deals in fiction, but good poetry

---

* ['Childe Harold.' Canto III.]

is concerned only with *realities*, either of visible or moral nature; and so much for local poetry. But I did not read with equal pleasure a note or two which reflects on the Bourbon family. What has a poet who writes for immortality, to do with the little temporary passions of political parties? Such notes are like Pope's "flies in amber." I wish you could persuade Lord Byron to leave out these two or three lines of prose, which will make thousands dissatisfied with his glorious poetry. For my own part I am not a man of rank and family, and have not, therefore, such motives for respecting rank and family as Lord Byron has, yet I own (however I may disapprove and lament much of what is going on in France) that I could not bring myself to speak irreverently of the children of St. Louis, of assuredly the most ancient and splendid family of the civilised world, of a house which is connected with the whole system of European policy, European literature, European refinement, and, I will add, European glory. My love of realities comes in here again, and I say to myself, when I see Louis XVIII., overlooking all his personal qualities, here is the lineal descendant of fifty kings, all famous, many illustrious; men who have held in their hands from age to age the destinies of millions; some of whom have been the benefactors of mankind, and others (and this part of the recollection is not the least *interesting*) who have astonished and afflicted the world by their crimes. No; pray use your influence on this point. As to the poem itself, except a word or two suggested by Mr. Giffard, I do not think anything can be altered for the better.

Yours faithfully,

J. W. CROKER.

Walter Scott to Mr. Croker.

[No date.]

I send Murray a review of Lord Byron. I have treated him with the respect his abilities claim, and the sort of attachment which I really feel for his person. But d—— his morals and his politics! What a goodly vessel have they combined to wreck.

*Mr. Croker to the Rev. George Croly.**

November 28th, 1816.

DEAR SIR,

Just as I was about to write to tell you that I had at last found the two volumes I promised you (and they are sent herewith), I received your note, and as you wish for my opinion on one or two points which are connected with the progress of your work, I do not delay to give it, though you will be aware that I shall give it hastily.

I do not think that the fame of Pope, and still less that of Dryden, is on the wane as compared with the taste of fifty years ago. On the contrary, I believe that Dryden rises in the estimation of all good judges. To be sure, every day deprives them more and more of the charm of novelty, and those who read them do not talk about them, because they no longer afford subject for fashionable chit-chat, but I believe they are more read, more profitably, solidly read, than any two of their successors whom you could name. If you mean to say that all our old writers are going out of fashion, it is to a certain degree true, and as must always, to the degree I have mentioned, happen; but surely Dryden and Pope keep their relative situations at least, and if they do stand, when compared with their predecessors or contemporaries, as high or higher than they did, the general depreciation (even if it exist) cannot be said to apply to them particularly.

But I believe there is no real depreciation; for my own part I can say, that though I have little time to read poetry, and notwithstanding all the charms of novelty and fashion, I read more of Pope and Dryden than I do of even Scott and Byron; that is to say, I do not return to Scott and Byron with the same regular appetite that I do to the others. You seem to think that the wildness of the latter poets is their great cause of popularity; and you therefore think that the popular taste is for the irregular, the rambling, and the obscure. I deny your major, and even if it were true, I deny the conclusion. Mr. Scott and Lord Byron have adopted subjects to which their peculiar styles are appropriate. Scott's irregularity is an imitation of the Border minstrelsy which

---

* [Long the Rector of St. Stephen's, Walbrook, London, author of 'Salathiel,' of a poor edition of Pope, and of many other works.]

he has revived and improved, but *he* is never *obscure.* Lord
Byron, on the other hand, in his great work, the 'Childe
Harold,' is *obscure,* because he deals in metaphysics, and in
the internal workings of a dark soul; but *he* is never *irregular.*   So that when you accuse, or rather I should say
when you applaud, the taste of the age for tending towards
the irregular and obscure, you appear to me to commit the
same mistake that one would do who should say that, wonderful to relate, he saw Mr. Jenkins eat salt and sugar to his
dinner, because he ate salt to his mutton, and sugar to his
fruit.   My friend, Mr. Southey, has written several poems;
one at least of them, the 'Curse of Kehama,' unites your
two beauties of irregularity and obscurity in so high a
degree, that it ought to be very popular, and yet no one
reads it, while the 'Roderick,' which is absolutely regular, is
universally read and admired.

But even if there were an epidemic at this hour abroad for
the wild, as there was twenty years ago for the Della Cruscan
style, and as there was somewhat later for the hobgoblin
tribe, ought it to influence a real poet and a sensible
man?   *Decipit exemplar* — the proverb is somewhat musty.
Mr. Scott and Lord Byron are original in their own style,
and their styles therefore become them, but those who imitate
them only catch their faults.   However we bear or even
admire (as we often do) a fault which is original and natural,
we have no such mercy upon faults which are affected and
unappropriate to the wearer.

Add to all this, that the multitude of imitators, good, bad,
and indifferent, has palled the public appetite, and I think
I see that each succeeding poem of even Mr. Scott and
Lord Byron themselves are more coolly received than the
former.

I therefore intreat of you to remember that if you suffer
yourself to be drawn on by what you conceive to be the
taste of the day, you will write a poem which will probably
be but little attended to even at the day, and will more
probably not survive it.   You will write in the same style,
aye, and write as well as Scott and Byron, without sharing
their success; they are originals, and you will be only a
copyist.

But you adduce my example against my argument; let
me concede to you that my example is with you, I should
still say the argument is good, and the example is bad; but

I am not pushed to the *painful* extremity of confessing my
practice to be bad. It is, I think, not irreconcileable with
all I have said. My verses are certainly not obscure (not
intentionally obscure I mean, for that is the question); they
are not even irregular; the recurrence of the rhyme of the
short syllable is at different intervals indeed; but it is all
one metre, and I well remember having taken a good deal of
pains to get rid of a few irregularities, which had escaped me
at first, and, if I recollect rightly, there is but one (and that
so slight as not to be generally perceptible) which has survived my correction. Then there is no attempt at that
misty pomp of language which you appear to think laudable.
I believe there is not one inversion in the whole thing (at
least, I repeat again, not one *intentional* inversion), and
everything goes by its proper name; a spade is a spade; and
a bayonet a bayonet, and if on one or two occasions the
French are the Gauls, I am ashamed of it. I will now, since
I am on the subject, tell you a fact—that 'Talavera' was
written in consequence of a conversation at a literary table,
at which I insisted that poetry ought not to be fiction, and
that so powerful was the charm of simplicity and nature,
that if two poems were to be written on the subject of the
then recent triumph of Talavera, and that one was to deal in
Mars and Bellona, helmets and shields, knights and heroes,
and that the other (ceteris paribus) should call everything by
its proper name, talk of Wellington and Bellona, bayonet
and cap, cavalry and infantry, the latter would be the most
popular. This conversation, added to my regard for Sir
Arthur and my national feeling, set me to work on 'Talavera ;' and whatever success it has had I attribute altogether
to the truth and simplicity, I might say to the matter-of-
factness, with which it is written. One word more on this
point. 'Talavera' was written seven years ago, before the
prolific pen of Mr. Scott and the more prolific pens of a
thousand imitators had hackneyed the eight and six syllable
metre.

You allude to architecture, and say we are come to a new
era of poetical architecture. My good Sir, I should desire
no better theme or allusion. The Athenian Parthenon, the
Roman Pantheon, will attract for ever the admiration of
mankind; they have, as Plutarch said two thousand years
ago of the former, all the grandeur of antiquity and all the
grace of novelty. Not less grand, and little less graceful,

are the miracles of Gothic architecture, miracles of little-
nesses piled together till they become magnificence and
diversity multiplied into sublime regularity. Each style is
admirable in its own way and for its peculiar purposes, but
the mixture of both—I leave you to draw the conclusion.
Excuse the freedom and length of my letter. An anxious
desire to be of use to you is at once my motive and
excuse.

I have, &c.,
J. W. C.

The close of the year 1816 and the beginning of the following year were marked by serious riots in the metropolis
and other parts of the country, provoked chiefly by the want
and misery which prevailed among the poor. It was not
alone the strain of the long war which had impoverished the
community, although that necessarily had been severely felt,
and had left many serious consequences behind it. But 1816
was a disastrous year in all respects. There was no summer;
cold winds and incessant rain prevailed throughout the
months when harvest operations should have been going on,
and in October the grain was still lying rotting upon the
ground all through the midlands and in several of the home
counties. The price of wheat rose to 103*s.* a quarter. Lord
Eldon, who lived in Dorsetshire, (where, in one parish, 419
out of 575 inhabitants, were receiving relief,) declared that
as a farmer he was ruined, and he added, that he looked
forward " to the winter with fear and trembling." Food riots
broke out in almost every direction, and at night the skies
were lit up with incendiary fires. The Ministry adopted a
stern policy of repression, but it was not stern enough to
satisfy many of its supporters or followers, among whom
must be reckoned Walter Scott. " By-the-bye," he wrote
to Mr. Croker, in March, 1817, " we are all shocked at your
giving your mob so much head, and puzzled to account for

H 2

your late acquittals."* At the opening of the session in 1817, missiles were thrown at the Prince Regent's carriage, on its way to Parliament, an incident to which Scott referred in the same letter : " The infamous and unmanly attempt on his Royal Highness makes one's blood boil. I only wish the claymores were walking among the lads, which they would do with right good will." Throughout this stormy era, Mr. Croker kept no journal, and there are very few references in his papers to any of the events then passing. In the subjoined letters a very curious coincidence is referred to, and beyond these there is nothing further relating to the year 1816 :—

Mr. Peel to Mr. Croker.

[No date—evidently December, 1816.]

MY DEAR CROKER,

This moment a most extraordinary (madman I suppose) has left me—a Mr. Davoch, a Roman Catholic priest, officiating, notwithstanding his madness, at St. Paul's Chapel on the Quays. He said he felt it his duty to inform me that he had received information of the latest date from England, that the Royal family were flying for protection to Ireland— of all places in the world—that the populace had possession of London—that the soldiers were in league with them—and so forth. I was relieved a little by his informing me that all this happened in London at three o'clock this day, and that on riding from the Black Rock he saw the indications of these important events in the clouds.

I could only get rid of him by a promise that if on Friday or Saturday next I found his visions confirmed by the more vulgar and common-place intelligence brought by the regular post, I would come to his chapel and hear him preach a sermon on revelations.

I remain yours affectionately,

R. PEEL.

---

* The acquittals of the persons charged with complicity in the Spa-fields riots, which had occurred in the previous December.

Mr. Croker to Mr. Peel.

December 9th, 1816.

DEAR PEEL,

Your letter without date, but which must have been written on Tuesday or Wednesday, relative to the priest of St. Paul's, surprised us exceedingly ("us," I say, for I showed it to Lords Liverpool and Sidmouth). If the priest was not aware of the intention of a riot in London, surely the information he gave you was a very strange coincidence; but I am inclined to think the priest was not mad, but that he was at once willing to let you see he knew something, and unwilling to let you see how he knew it. A nearly similar incident occurred about fifteen years ago, when the king was fired at in Drury Lane. I received a letter two days after, which had been written in Dublin the day of the event, mentioning a report which alluded darkly to an accident happening to the king at a playhouse. This was the more surprising, because there seems no doubt that Hadfield was an insulated madman. Your priest may have been informed of Hunt's and Watson's proceedings; or the very knowledge that a meeting was intended on Monday may have given rise to a suspicion of disturbance. The most curious part of it is that the mob boasted that they had driven the Prince and the Royal family out of London, which your priest seemed to allude to; and to this hour the people believe that the Prince left town on Monday morning, although, in fact, Lord Sidmouth prevailed on his Royal Highness to postpone his journey.

Yours, &c.,

J. W. C.

CHAPTER IV.

1817–1818.

NOTWITHSTANDING the troubled state of the country in 1817, the people occupied themselves to no slight extent with the family affairs of the Prince Regent, whose unpopularity seems to have culminated at the beginning of this year. He was, as it has been stated, pelted on his way to the Houses of Parliament, although he was not subjected to an indignity like that which was inflicted upon him on another occasion, when a man put his head in at the carriage window, and cried out, " Prince, where's your wife ?   Where's your wife ? " The multitude sympathized with the wife, in spite of the many proofs which were daily afforded of her utter want of discretion, to put no worse construction upon her conduct. But it could not be denied even by the Regent's best friends

that he had seriously mismanaged his affairs. The nation
could not be expected to look with entire approval on
the grant by the House of Commons of 650,000*l.* to enable
him to pay his debts. His marriage with the Princess
Caroline of Brunswick had turned out unfortunately; they
were separated immediately after the birth of their child,
the Princess Charlotte, and from that time scandals of all
kinds began to accumulate round the head of the wife.
In 1806, a commission of inquiry was held into one set
of odious charges, and although the Princess of Wales
was pronounced guiltless of the worst of them, it was impossible to hold that she had not committed many grave
offences against propriety. But the public feeling then, as at
a later date, was entirely with the Princess. " All the world
is with her," wrote Sir James Mackintosh in his ' Diary,'
" except the people of fashion at the west end of the town."
By the great body of the nation she was looked upon as an
injured and persecuted woman. " The country," as Sir George
Cornewall Lewis remarked, in his summary of the story,
" regarded his (the Regent's) conduct as the oppression of the
weak by the strong, accompanied with almost every con-
ceivable circumstance of aggravation." *   The time came
when the public did not feel so confident that all the blame
of these miserable brawls rested entirely with the husband,
but for many years they were the means of bringing down
much obloquy upon his head, and of rendering him defiant of
public opinion, which he regarded as obstinately unjust
towards him.

But in the spring of 1817 there was a slight change in the
Regent's favour, in consequence of the marriage of his
daughter, the Princess Charlotte, " the fair haired daughter of
the Isles," as Byron called her in his noble lines. It was

---

* ' Essays on the Administrations of Great Britain,' p. 406.

thought then that the marriage of the Princess afforded the
only prospect of the crown being worn by a descendant of
George the Third, failing the issue of the Duke of Cumberland, who was one of the most unpopular men alive. A
match had been partly arranged for the Princess Charlotte
with the Prince of Orange, but it was broken off, and the
Princess had sunk into a low state of health and spirits. From
this she was roused by the prospect of a much happier union
with one upon whom her affections were securely fixed almost
from the first moment of their acquaintance—Prince Leopold,
afterwards King of the Belgians. The marriage pleased the
nation, as well as the persons who were more directly concerned in it, and there was no objection from any quarter to
the grant of 60,000*l.* voted by Parliament as a wedding
portion for the Princess, or to her annuity of 60,000*l.* At
first the Prince and Princess lived at Marlborough House,
but Claremont was purchased for them, and there they took
up their residence. In the following November the Princess,
whose early life had been so sadly clouded, remarked to one
of her friends, "Certainly I am the happiest woman in the
world. I have not a wish ungratified—surely this is too
much to last."* Her mournful presage was too surely
verified; ten days after she had uttered it, she was dead.
The popular grief was profound, and it found a grand and
lasting echo in Byron's stanzas.†

> "Hark! forth from the abyss a voice proceeds,
> A long low distant murmur of dread sound,
> Such as arises when a nation bleeds
> With some deep and immedicable wound."

The death of the Princess was received by her mother with a
composure which it was hard to distinguish from indifference,

* 'Buckingham Papers,' the 'Regency,' vol. ii. pp. 190–91.
† 'Childe Harold,' Canto IV., 167–172.

but the Prince Regent seems to have felt his daughter's untimely end much more keenly. "He sees nobody," wrote Mr. Croker to Lord Whitworth (14th November, 1817), "but his own attendants, the Royal Family, and such of the Ministers as have business with him, and all his thoughts and conversation turn upon the late sad event. He never stirs out of his room, and goes to bed sometimes at eight or nine o'clock, wearied out, and yet not composed enough for rest." And again on the 18th he writes: "The Prince Regent is better. The necessity of giving orders about the funeral has acted like a blister, and has given employment to his mind." He very soon found other employment for his mind in setting on foot preparatory measures for obtaining a divorce from his wife.

Then followed a sort of race for marriage among the sons of George the Third who were still free to take to themselves wives. The Duke of Cambridge married the Princess Augusta of Hesse Cassel, and the Duke of Clarence the Princess Adelaide of Saxe Meiningen. It was not, indeed, the fault of the latter prince that he had not been married before.* The alliance of the Duke of Kent with the widow of the Prince of Leiningen proved to be by far the most fortunate of these weddings, for it led to all the advantages which the people had vainly anticipated from the union of their favourite princess with Prince Leopold. It is to these events that the next letters refer.

Mr. Croker to Mr. Peel.

MY DEAR PEEL,   November 15th, 1817.

The people continue exceedingly afflicted by the loss of the Princess and her child; but that which was at first mere grief takes, I am sorry to tell you, a very *sour* turn. The Prince's

---

* Memoirs of the Court of England during the Regency ('Buckingham Papers'), i. 146–7.

absence and, above all, the absence of the Queen, are subjects
of very *bitter* regret with all those who do not know that the
Princess would not have the assistance of her Majesty, nor
the attendance of any one but those named by herself, and
who do not recollect that a father is on such occasions worse
than useless.   Fortunate it was for ·the Prince, and for all
who are interested for the popularity of the Royal Family,
that he did come up with such rapidity when the alarming
express reached him ; his anxiety and alacrity in that
moment has preserved him from the most dreadful weight
of unpopularity.   In truth, the conduct with regard to
H.R.H. was very extraordinary ; notice was *not sent to him*
of the beginning of the labour, and he might have been
in London twenty-four hours sooner, if he had been aware
that the Princess had been taken ill.   The Queen's great
experience in such matters points her out to the people as
the person of all others who ought to have been by the
bedside of her grand-daughter, and it must be confessed
that though she could not well have been at Claremont,
she might perhaps have been at Windsor, within call, if
I may use the expression.   It is also said, and I think
with some justice, that no fancy of the poor Princess's nor
any confidence of Dr. Croft's* ought to have induced the
Government to leave her fate in the hands of a single
man at the distance of seventeen miles from any assistance.   So important an affair should not have been left liable
to a little accident.   But even if there were no danger of
an accident to the doctor, there manifestly was to the patient,
and was it right that when the crisis should occur, they
should have to send off to London for another doctor to
consult with ?   To be sure Dr. Sims was sent for, but this
only proves that he ought to have been there, for she had
been twenty-four hours in labour before he was sent for,
and thirty before he arrived.   I am satisfied that nothing
could have saved her, nor even the child, but in an affair of .
such vital importance to herself, to her offspring, to her
family, to the nation, and to Europe, surely precautions
should' have been taken which you or I in our private
families would have thought almost necessary if our wives
were to lie in at a great distance from immediate assistance
or additional advice.

* [Sir R. Croft. He afterwards committed suicide.]

The opening the body has afforded the only melancholy consolation for her loss. It seems she died of exhaustion and external hæmorrhage, and she would probably have soon died after an excruciating illness. If this be true, then her loss was a mercy of heaven to her, and even to us.

Prince Leopold, it is said, endeavoured at first to bear up against the loss with over-fortitude, and he has since been very ill; but I know no particulars, and can easily suspect some little exaggeration in his German physician's account of his present indisposition; but there is no doubt that he is most sincerely and most unaffectedly afflicted.

The shock which the Prince Regent received, added to the effort of so rapid a journey at night, has produced an unpleasant effect upon him, but he was bled and cupped, and thereby relieved. He, however, up to the day before yesterday, was in a state far from comfortable, he harassed himself to death, and when he went to bed at eight or nine o'clock when unable to sit up from fatigue, he was too uneasy to rest. Yesterday, however, he grew more composed, and to-day has (for the first time) seen some of his private friends, but he will not leave his room, and he is really in great need of a little air, exercise, and diversion; I mean of course in the strict sense of the word. He will, however, soon remove to Brighton, when he will ride, and I hope recover his spirits.

At dinner the other day at Yarmouth's, some one said the Duke of York was about to retire from the command of the army, and that the Duke of Kent was to succeed him. The story was laughed at, and yet I think there may be some grounds for the first half of it. Recollect that the Duke of York is now heir presumptive. Is it constitutional, or even proper, that the heir presumptive should have the armed force in his hand? Everybody has the most implicit confidence in the Duke of York, but as a precedent and in theory there is some weight in the objection. I am induced to give some kind of credit to this rumour, because a little circumstance occurred within this day or two to make me think that some proposition has been made that Calvert* should resign and that Torrens† should succeed him. Situated as affairs now are, I cannot conceive the Duke's parting with Torrens, and though he might be, and would be, of the greatest use to a successor, Torrens may not like the prospect, and may be anxious to

* [Adjutant-General.]   † [Military Secretary.]

secure his retreat on good terms.   You have now my speculations, and can judge as well as myself.   I am afraid that
jealousies have already begun to be felt in the Royal Family,
and you may depend upon it they will not diminish.   The
Princess of Wales and the divorce occupy many thoughts,
but nobody speaks about them.   The Prince is anxious for it,
the Ministers strong against it ; the public only waiting to
see the Prince take a part to take one against him.   In short,
my dear Peel, I never looked into a blacker political horizon
than is now around us.   All this is in strict confidence.

Yours, &c.,

J. W. C.

Mr. Peel replied to this letter a few days later, and
incidentally he gave Mr. Croker warning that he had made
another enemy by his pen.   In the *Quarterly Review* for
April 1817 there had appeared an article on a book then but
lately published by Lady Morgan, entitled, "France"—an
article which handled both author and book with much
greater severity than would be deemed justifiable now,
although the work was really open to serious objection.
Reviewers of the present generation, if they wish to convey
the same ideas—as they sometimes do—contrive to wrap
them up with a little more skill.   But these were the days
of plain-speaking, and as a rule the victims did not fail to
prove that they possessed ample powers of retaliation.

Mr. Peel to Mr. Croker.

Dublin Castle, Nov. 22nd, 1817.

My dear Croker,

You are the only man in London who takes compassion on
your friends in foreign parts and enlightens their darkness.

You have not, however, improved in the *caligraphic* art;
and if I had not some skill in deciphering illegible writing,
and had not been disciplined by such writers as Fitzgerald,
I should have lost a part of what was very interesting to me.
I make no apologies to you for quoting from Lady Morgan,

as she vows vengeance against you as the supposed author of the article in the *Quarterly*, in which her atheism, profanity, indecency, and ignorance have been exposed.   You are to be the hero of some novel of which she is about to be delivered. I hope she has not heard of your predilection for angling, and that she will not describe you as she describes one of her heroes, " seated in his *piscatory* corner, intent on the destruction of the finny tribe."   One of her sworn friends was attempting to extract from me whether you were the author of this obnoxious article or not; but I disclaimed all knowledge of the author, and only did not deny that it was to be attributed to you, because I thought you would be very indifferent as to Lady Morgan's hostility.

I was excessively amused by hearing that the female literary circles of Dublin generally attribute the article to Vesey [Fitzgerald].   If he hears this, and hears, too, that Lady Morgan is whetting her tusks, he will deprecate her ire by a formal disclaimer, which she will publish in the preface to the novel.

There was no part of the empire which participated with more sincerity in the general grief on account of the death of the Princess than Dublin.   The shops were voluntarily closed on Wednesday, and more persons attended service at the different places of worship than are generally seen there on Sunday.

Believe me ever, my dear Croker,

Most affectionately yours,

ROB. PEEL.

There was no novel published by Lady Morgan after this of which Mr. Croker was supposed to be the hero, but there was a story, in which he was alleged to have figured as " Counsellor Con," written in 1814; and that was supposed to have been intended as a retaliatory stroke for a review in the first number of the *Quarterly* of an earlier novel by Lady Morgan, entitled, " Woman ; or, Ida of Athens," which also received rough treatment, in a short article of three pages. It seems to have been attributed by Lady Morgan to Mr. Croker; in reality it was written by Mr. Gifford.   This

was not by any means the last occasion on which Mr. Croker
was struck at for causes of offence of which he was wholly
innocent.

Mr. Croker to Mr. Peel.

November 26th, 1817.

My dear Peel,

It is unlucky for you that your only correspondent should
be one who knows so little of what is going forward as I do,
for I never go out, and those who go out do not call upon
me, so that I am but a bad gazetteer.   Such talk, however, as
reaches me you shall have.

Our grief, as you must see, is wearing off, and the public
is in, I think, rather a sulky humour, waiting for any fair or
unfair excuse to fly into a passion, and wreak, like Fag in
the ' Rivals,' their vexation on the first unhappy wight that
may fall in their way.   I am much mistaken if ever there
existed at any former period so much of a bad spirit amongst
the οἱ πολλοί, combined with so much apathy among the
συνετοί; and I expect to see the clouds burst furiously.   If
there should arise any division in the Royal Family, it will
be the match to fire the gunpowder.   *Apropos* of royal
matches, I hear that Ministers have been a little puzzled
how to deal with the avowed readiness of the Duke of Kent
to sacrifice himself and jump into the matrimonial gulf for
the good of his country, but they have hit upon a scheme
which seems politic.   They propose to marry the Duke of
Clarence, as the eldest unmarried Prince, and he who has
a right to the first chance ; and also to marry the Duke of
Cambridge, the youngest unmarried Prince, from whom the
country has the best chance ; and having thus resolved to
burn the candle at both ends, Vansittart discovers that he
cannot afford to burn it in the middle .too, and therefore
Kent and Sussex cannot have the wedding establishments,
&c., suited to their rank.

The ladies who are selected for them are their Electoral
Highnesses, two Princesses of Hesse.   There are seven of
them ; the eldest is forty-four, and the youngest sixteen.   If
the Court of Hesse should imitate our plan, and marry *their*
eldest and their youngest, the Duke of Clarence will be *bit.*

The lady in the Duke of Kent's eye is not ill-chosen for
popular effect.   She is the sister of Prince Leopold.   When

the Duke first thought of her, it could only be in hopes of popular influence. Now he will probably think that any Coburg alliance will be popular.

We have Cabinet meetings every day, chiefly on the Spanish South American affairs. You may judge how unwilling Lord Liverpool must be to interfere; but his phlegm is doubtless corrected by the more magnanimous counsels of Pole,* who, "*though he belongs to every department,*" thinks that measures which have so great an influence on the supply of bullion especially concern the Mint.

You are fond of characteristic traits; here is one. Captain Hall,† of the *Lyra*, who is just come home, and who is mad about certain simple islanders whom he fell in with in the China Seas, touched at St. Helena and saw Buonaparte, and amongst other things told him the story of his interesting inhabitants of Loo-Choo, and happened to mention that such was the primitive innocence of the people, that he could not discover that they had any offensive weapons. "Diable!" exclaimed Buonaparte, "et comment font-ils donc la guerre?" Hall dined some time ago at Vansittart's, and was relating this conversation, and everybody but Vansittart was greatly amused at the natural turn of Buonaparte's wonder. Vansittart, however, took no kind of notice of it, but seemed absorbed in his own contemplations. Hall went on to say that he found Buonaparte quite incredulous upon this fact,‡ and that, in order to persuade him of the extreme simplicity of the islanders, he added another circumstance, which was, that he had not seen amongst them any kind of money. "No money," cried Vansittart, awakened out of his trance, with the greatest vivacity. "Good heavens! Captain Hall, how do they carry on the government!" This is literally true.

Thank you for your information about Lady Morgan. She, it seems, is resolved to make me read one of her novels. I hope I shall feel interested enough to be able to learn the language. I wrote the main part of the article in the *Quarterly*, but, as you know, was called away to Ireland

---

* [Master of the Mint.]

† [Captain Basil Hall, R.N., author of a Voyage to Loo-Choo and numerous other works of travel; died in 1844.]

‡ [Buonaparte was right. Later travellers discovered that the Loo-Choo people had warlike appliances, like other nations.]

when it was in the press; and I am sorry to say that some blunders crept in accidentally, and one or two were premeditatedly added, which, however, I do not think Lady Morgan knows enough either of English, French, or Italian to find out. If she goes on we shall have sport.

Your godson * thrives apace. He has seven teeth, and bites harder than Lady Morgan. Who do you think, of all mankind (if, indeed, he be human), formed an alliance with him at Ryde, who but Lord Nugent! The little fellow was too young to be frightened, and the friendship prospered. Remember me to Vesey, who, I suppose, sometimes solaces himself in your society.

Yours, &c.,

J. W. C.

An acquaintanceship in the field of literature of a far more memorable kind was that with Walter Scott, who frequently applied to Mr. Croker for his help in various ways, but who seems to have taken good care not to divulge the secret of the authorship of the 'Waverley Novels' even to this intimate correspondent. Mr. Croker, in a letter to a friend, written in May 1817, says: "I send you the 'Antiquary' and 'Tales of My Landlord,' by the author of 'Waverley' and 'Guy Mannering.' They are the most popular novels which have been published these many years; they are, indeed, almost histories rather than novels. The author is certainly Walter Scott, or his brother Mr. Thomas Scott. The internal evidence is in favour of the former, but his asseverations, and all external evidence, are for the latter. I cannot decide." Walter Scott had long been anxious to look for the lost regalia of Scotland, under the belief that discoveries of importance would result from his search. He begged Mr. Croker, in 1816, to get the requisite permission from the Prince Regent; and although Mr. Croker felt convinced that

---

* [Mr. Croker's only son, born January 1817.]

the chests contained nothing of material value, he continued to exert himself to gain consent to have the room examined, and at last he succeeded.

Mr. Croker to Walter Scott.

January 9th, 1818.

MY DEAR SCOTT,

I have the pleasure to tell you that at last I have gotten the warrant for searching for the old regalia of the Scottish Crown, which at your suggestion, and by the Prince's command, I have been soliciting so long. It has been two months delayed for the fees, which, however, as soon as I was apprised of the causes of the stoppage, I hastened to advance, and I by this night's post have sent the document to the Lord Advocate. I was not sure to whom I should send it, particularly as I am told that it is uncertain whether you are now in Edinburgh, and I thought I could not be far wrong in addressing it to the Lord Advocate. I shall be, of course, anxious to hear of (though I am not very sanguine as to) the result of your search. I know that both the Regent and yourself have hopes of finding something. I limit my expectations to your ascertaining that there is nothing to be found.

Do you think that such a fellow as Rob Roy would have driven cattle, while there was such a prize at Edinburgh Castle?

Yours, &c.,

J. W. C.

It turned out that Scott was right. In a letter dated 7th February, 1818, and published in 'Lockhart's Life of Scott,' an account is given of the discoveries which were made, which included the Crown, Sceptre, and Sword of State, now shown to the public at Edinburgh Castle. The chest in which they were deposited had never even been seen since 1707, when the room where it was placed was sealed up by the Commissioners.

Although in after years there was a hopeless breach in

the friendship between Sir Robert Peel and Mr. Croker, it is impossible to question the fact, that at this period, and for long afterwards, they seldom took any important step without first consulting one with the other. Mr. Croker was almost the first to detect and appreciate the great powers of the future Prime Minister, and to point out to him the path on which he was destined to reach fame. The following letter seems to have been drawn forth by a report of Peel's intention to retire altogether from public life.

Mr. Croker to Mr. Peel.

July 13th, 1818.

I must now mention to you more seriously (because it has been mentioned more seriously to me) what I have heretofore touched lightly upon, namely, your taking office. I do assure you upon my honour that I have never begun any conversation on the subject, but that in those companies where I have been, composed of very different classes of society, your acceptance of Van's * office, and your ultimate advancement to the highest of all, have been wished for warmly and unanimously. One of these places was Grant's † (of Pall Mall), where, on Friday last, we had Yarmouth, Lowther, Beckett, Lushington, and Berkeley Paget, and on some conversation about the meeting of Parliament, and the state of the Ministry, there was one voice that you were the person whom all the friends of good order would support. Some one had said that our *honest* friend ‡ wanted *eloquence*, and our *eloquent* friend § *honesty*, but that you, uniting both, would unite the confidence of the whole party. There was some more talk of this kind, and considering that of the seven people at table I was the only intimate friend of yours, and that they were all in different interests and feelings, you must allow that their sentiments and feelings must be taken as something more than the mere expression of individual opinion.

* [Mr. Vansittart, Chancellor of the Exchequer.]
† [Sir A. C. Grant.]
‡ [Mr. Huskisson ?]   § [Mr. Canning ?]

I did not, however, think it worth while to relate this circumstance to you, to which I attached no very great importance; but I went yesterday to dine with Yarmouth, * and as I came early I found him alone. After a little talk on general matter, he said to me, "Croker, I have been thinking of what I have twice already mentioned to you, and we must have Peel Minister. Everybody wishes for him, everybody would support him. Lowther, Apsley, and myself, who are three heirs apparent of some weight, in votes at least, would join him heart and hand. I like him personally. I have no other motive than personal liking and public respect, and I should be glad on every account to see him at the head of affairs."

I said a few words of your disinclination from, or rather indifference to, such objects, but I owned that no effort or entreaty of mine should be spared to induce you to abandon the thoughts of a retirement from business, and that I thought I could venture to say, that whatever your private wishes might be, you would still feel it to be your public duty not to flinch from any responsibility which the public service might call you to. People then came and the matter ended.

Now I know as well as you that all this is *en l'air*, and I know that ministers are not made in conversations before or after dinner. But I know also that when the public opinion (which often speaks at such times through organs of the kind I have quoted) designates a man for high station, it is a duty which his friends owe him not to leave him ignorant of the manner in which his name is mentioned. I do what I think to be the duty of friendship and affection towards you in thus telling you what I hear. I shall also do the other duty of friendship, which is to hold my peace, and not commit, by any expression of *mine*, your name in any such conversations. But I do hope that some opportunity may occur of doing the country the double good of rescuing the Exchequer from Van, and of placing you in that office.

Yours, &c.,

J. W. C.

The reply made by Peel has no date, but it enters into his opinions on the question of taking office; and it will be seen

* [Afterwards the third Marquis of Hertford.]

that upon that, as upon other questions, private and public, his views underwent a very thorough change in course of time.

Mr. Peel to Mr. Croker.

[No date.]

My Dear Croker,

To all the latter part of your letter I answer in the emphatic term of a reverend Pastor in the ' Vicar of Wakefield ' —Fudge.

I am thinking of anything but office, and am just as anxious to be emancipated from office as the Papists are to be emancipated into it.

I am for the abolition of slavery, and no men have a right to condemn another to worse than Egyptian bondage, to require him, not to make bricks without straw, which a man of straw might have some chance of doing (as Lord Norbury would certainly say), but to raise money and abolish taxes in the same breath.

"Night cometh when no man can work," said one who could not have foreseen the fate of a man in office and the House of Commons.

A fortnight hence I shall be free as air—free from ten thousand engagements which I cannot fulfil; free from the anxiety of having more to do than it is possible to do well; free from the acknowledgments of that gratitude which consists in a lively sense of future favours; free from the necessity of abstaining from private intimacy that will certainly interfere with public duty; free from Orangemen; free from Ribbonmen; free from Dennis Browne; free from the Lord Mayor and Sheriffs; free from men who pretend to be Protestants on principle and sell Dundalk to ——, the Papist of Cork —free from Catholics who become Protestants to get into Parliament after the manner of ——, and of Protestants who become Catholics, after the manner of old ——; free from perpetual converse about the Harbour of Howth and Dublin Bay haddock; and, lastly, free of the Company of Carvers and Gilders which I became this day in reward of my public services.

Ever most affectionately yours,

Rob. Peel.

Do not venture to say anything about my feelings of public duty, &c., &c. *Say* nothing about me in short.

In the course of the year Mr. Peel relinquished his office of Secretary for Ireland, thoroughly tired of the country as well as of the office, and his feelings of relief at laying down his burden were not greater than those of the Catholic section of the Irish population at seeing his departure. They had long regarded him with hatred, and conferred upon him the nickname of "Orange Peel," which clung to him long after he had ceased to be directly interested in Irish affairs. Mr. Peel, on his part, had no sooner found himself free than he proceeded to give himself the holiday he had so long desired :—

Mr. Peel to Mr. Croker.

[Without date.]

My DEAR CROKER,

Here I am, hoping not much longer to remain here. If I was going to remain, or if I could offer you any inducement to come here, or if I thought you had charity and leisure enough to come here without any, I would beg of you to order your postchaise and repair to Drayton.

I went to Scotland from Ireland, and remained five weeks among the mountains of the Badenoch district of the county of Inverness. Daly, my brother, Col. Yates, and I were of the party. We had one of the best houses in Inverness-shire, a modern castle—tolerably well furnished—as well indeed as we could wish. We had an enormous district of country; plenty of grouse, of which we slew about thirteen hundred; and I took my cook there, to gild the decline of day.

The Scotch expedition succeeded far beyond my expectations. We lived in the midst of a host of Macphersons —terrible Jacobites in the olden time—in a very pretty valley, hemmed in by rocky mountains, with the Spey before our door, and a large woody district of fir behind us. Roes in the wood, and eagles on the mountains, which were rugged and high, and had snow enough on their tops to convince us we were in the "north countrie."

We had supreme dominion, so far as the chase is con-

cerned, over uncounted thousands of acres. Loch Erricht,
and Loch Laggan, and Loch Dhu, and the streams from a
thousand hills, were ours. We had hind and hart, hare and
roe, black game and grouse, partridge and ptarmigan, snipe
and wild duck. We had highlanders for our guides, and
highland ponies without shoes ; and no civilized beings within
ten miles of us.

I really left Clunie with regret : there was so much novelty
in the mode of life—so much wildness and magnificence in
the scenery—so much simplicity and unaffected kindness
among the people.

I came through Yorkshire, and stayed eight or ten days with
Grantham. I shall remain here about a fortnight. I shall
then, I think, either come to town, and go to Oxford from
London for a day or two, or take Oxford in my way to
London.

Lord Erskine could not have said more about himself and
his proceedings, past, present, and future, in so short a space.

Vesey and I talked of going to the continent till the latter
end of January ; but should the Queen die, I suppose we
shall be wanted in Parliament. I shall go to Paris, I think,
for a short time at any rate.

Lord Sidmouth proposed to associate me " with those highly
intelligent and most respectable Bishops and Privy Councillors," who form the unsalaried half of the Education Board,
but I was not so covetous of the honour as I ought to have
been—foreseeing the sacrifice which the Speaker is called
upon to make, both in regard to the society which he loses,
and which he gains.

Remember me to him most kindly, and believe me,

My dear Croker,
Most affectionately yours,
Rob. Peel.

Mr. Croker, however, was full of confidence that Peel
would not be suffered to remain long out of office ; and we
find him writing to Mr. Vesey Fitzgerald, " Mind, I tell you,
whatever may befall your merit or mine, the country will not
suffer Peel's merit to be neglected. It will call for him in a
way that the deafest of the Cabinet will be obliged to hear."

And then he goes on to give some account of the condition of Queen Charlotte, who was now rapidly approaching her end :—

The Queen is very ill and cannot last long. I saw the Prince yesterday, and he seemed to me to apprehend that the conclusion was very near. He is himself looking very well: he had his table covered with papers for perusal and signature, and he *was* signing away in full gallop. I ventured to make a half joke to him on his sinecure office, which was well taken, and he retorted upon mine with a *tu quoque.*

The Duke of Cumberland is gone to *Hanover.* * * He and the *P. R.*, are, I have reason to think, on no very cordial terms. He hardly took leave, and came to the Admiralty to ask for the Royal yacht to convey him, without saying the preparatory word of civility at Carlton House. This is the more to be regretted, for he has got a wig so like the Prince's that on an emergency he might pass for the Regent, if the latter should be confined by the gout from attending any public occasion.

All through the autumn the death of the Queen seems to have been almost daily expected. On the 5th of September Mr. Croker wrote to Lord Melville telling him that her Majesty had not forty-eight hours to live, and giving him a melancholy account of her condition :—" She is not capable of being put to bed. She is blistered in the chest, from which she suffers a good deal, but not so much as from the flutter of her nerves, which makes her very miserable. Her legs are immensely swelled. The bulletin the day before last said ' she had had a better night than was expected.' The fact is, she never slept at all that night, and was expected to expire; so that it was better than expected."

There was no more afflicted household in all England at the time than that of George the Third. Misfortunes had accumulated thickly upon it. The poor old King had been for several years a mere phantom—dead to the world, as the

world was dead to him; deaf, blind, bereft of reason, uncon-
scious of the great events which had taken place in the
nation, and of the changes which time had wrought in his
own family. He was, of course, unaware of the perilous condition of the Queen, to whom he had been devoted, and who
had rewarded his devotion by the most unswerving attachment to him through all his troubles and disasters. It was
the spectacle of the homely simplicity and fidelity of this
aged couple, combined with their domestic sorrows, which
made them so popular with the bulk of the people. Everybody knew that the last and worst blow which fell upon the
King's reason arose from the grief which he felt at seeing
his daughter Amelia gradually sinking into the grave. The
Queen had been thoroughly prostrated by illness during the
inquiry into the conduct of the Duke of York. The hopeless
illness of the King made heavy inroads upon her health and
spirits, and the end came in the month of November.

Mr. Croker to Mr. Peel.

November 19th, 1818,

MY DEAR PEEL,

I presume you see the English papers, or you would have
desired me to send you one; I shall therefore say nothing of
what you will see in them, except that the Queen died about
five minutes before one. The Prince, the Duke of York, the
Duchess of Glo'ster, and Princess Sophia were in the room
when she died; she had been breathing hard and loud for
half an hour as she sat in her chair; suddenly she stopped,
and drawing a long sigh she expired; her hand fell over the
arm of her chair, and her head and body fell towards that
side on which she had not been able to lean during her
illness.

The Prince was extremely affected, and they were obliged
to give him some cordial to prevent his fainting. The will
was, I heard, to be opened yesterday, but I have not since
heard what it contained, nor even if it was opened, but I
presume it was. She had left no money, nor had she any-

thing to leave, except her jewels, which I have heard valued
at 200,000*l.* This is a large sum in jewels.

The Prince held a Council to-day to do the necessary
business; there was a Council without the Prince yesterday,
at which they did little more than resolve not to adopt the
cumbrous precedent of Queen Caroline's funeral. Indeed
it was not possible to follow it; for as the King had repeatedly ordered that he and the Queen should be buried in
Windsor, she is to be there interred; and they do not think
that there is room at Windsor to admit of a *public* funeral.
At a public funeral, you know, all man and womankind walk
each after its rank and species, and though they could walk
in St. George's Chapel, as well as in Henry VIIth's, Windsor
could not hold all their horses and carriages, and lodge
themselves and servants. The funeral, therefore, is to be
private; that is, three or four hundred people only are to
be present.

*Mr. Croker to the Right Hon. Charles Manners Sutton.**

Brighton, Dec. 8th, 1818.

MY DEAR SUTTON,

I have been rather not well than ill for some time past.
My complaint is an uneasiness in the head, Baillie says from
overwork. I myself think from *that* joined with some organic
causes; in short, I am not easy about myself, and make up
my mind to act as if I were in danger. Yarmouth, the most
good-natured man alive, has dragged me down here for a few
days' relaxation and exercise. We live at the inn; he drinks
my health in claret, and I pledge him in table beer. We ride
together, and in the dirty roads splash one another like two
members of your honourable house.

During this visit to Brighton, Mr. Croker kept a journal,
and wrote daily letters to his wife, as he was in the habit of
doing whenever he was absent from her. In the early
part of the year his little boy had been rather ill, and this
had caused both father and mother some anxiety. The
Speaker, Mr. Charles Manners Sutton, had written a note to

* [Speaker of the House of Commons from 1817 till 1835.]

him at that time, in which he said, " I well know the misery
of any apprehension about infants.   It makes cowards of the
stoutest of us.   My boy Charles said, when I told him of
your little one having been ill, ' Oh, I would certainly give
him some magnesia, if the little boy can take it like a man.'
This shows the *materia medica* principally used in my
nursery."   At Brighton, Mr. Croker found the change, if
not the repose, which he sorely needed, and his account of
his visit is written in the light vein which seems, after all,
to have been more natural to him than any other.

Extracts from Journal of 1818.

December 7*th.*—Left Munster House on horseback at 9 for
Cobham, where I was to meet Lord Yarmouth at 11 and
thence proceed to Brighton.   A little beyond Kingston it
came on to rain, and as I happened to overtake a stage coach
I sent back my horse and got into it ; in two minutes after I
got to Cobham, Lord Yarmouth drove up and we set off and
arrived at Brighton a little before 4.   It rained the whole
way, but the roads were so good that we had not a jolt for
fifty miles.   Passed through Leatherhead, Dorking, Horsham,
and Henfield.   Lord Yarmouth had come from Oatlands,
where he had been for two days, and where the Duke of
York had assembled a parliament of dandies.   The Duchess's
life is an odd one ; she seldom has a female companion, she
is read to all night and falls asleep towards morning, and
rises about 3 ; feeds her dozens of dogs and her flocks of
birds, &c., comes down two minutes before dinner, and so
round again.*   She sometimes walks a little, and does some
local charities.   She is now preparing her Christmas presents—
the habitués of Oatlands give her *étrennes* and receive them
in return from her.

The Prince certainly married Mrs. Fitzherbert with the
left hand—the ceremony was performed by parson Johns,
who is still about town.   The Prince had seen her in her
carriage in the Park and was greatly struck with her—
inquired who she was—heard the widow Fitzherbert, con-

---

* [Much the same account is given by Charles Greville—'Greville
Memoirs,' i. 5.]

trived to make her acquaintance and was really *mad* for love. The lady felt or affected reluctance and scruples, which the left-hand marriage and some vague promises of conversion to Popery and resignation of all hopes of royalty silenced. I cannot but wonder at her living here and bearding the Prince in a way so indelicate, vis-à-vis the public, and I should have thought so embarrassing to herself. To her presence is attributed the Prince's never going abroad at Brighton. I have known H.R.H. here seven or eight years, and never saw or heard of his being on foot out of the limits of the Pavilion, and in general he avoids even riding through the principal streets. I cannot conceive how poor old Mrs. Fitzherbert (she is now near 70*) can cause him any uneasiness.

Mr. Horace Seymour and his lady met us as we were going to the warm baths before dinner, and he called in on us while we were at dinner. They are staying at Mrs. Fizherbert's. It was about his sister Mimi † that there arose such a piece of work some time ago. Mrs. Fitzherbert was dotingly fond of her, and when the Seymour family attempted to remove her from Mrs. Fitzherbert's care, she induced the Prince to solicit the interest of Lord Hertford as the head of the family. This brought about the acquaintance with Lady Hertford,‡ and Mrs. Fitzherbert kept the child and lost the Prince.

Beau Brummell is going, or says he is going, to publish an English Journal at Calais, which alarms some great folks, and it is said the French police have been requested to look to it. I hardly think he can dare make such an attempt— he only wants to be bought off, but surely no one will buy him off. I had heard some time ago that he was writing memoirs of his own life; this is likely enough and may have given rise to the other report.

We came to the Castle Inn; the Prince was good enough to offer us lodgings in the Pavilion, but as he is to be down himself to-morrow in the strict incognito of grief, we felt we should be *de trop* there, and have come hither to "take our ease in our inn."

---

* [Mr. Croker, seldom mistaken in an age or a date, was wrong in this. Mrs. Fitzherbert was not more than 62 in 1818. She died at Brighton in 1837, aged 81.]

† [Mrs. Dawson Damer.]

‡ [This was the mother of the 3rd Marquis, Mr. Croker's friend.]

December 8th.—Walked a little about the town, then rode with Mr. and Mrs. Horace Seymour to Shoreham. As we rode up from the sea-side the ground was extremely like the ground of Waterloo, and Horace, who had been Lord Anglesey's aide-de-camp and had greatly distinguished himself there, told me many entertaining particulars. He had been about 2 o'clock sent to the extreme left by the Duke of Wellington with some orders. There he found a report that the Prussians were near—he thought it right to ascertain so important a fact with his own eyes, so he galloped on till he actually met and spoke with the Prussian advance, he then hastened back to tell it to Lord Wellington. Gordon, one of his Grace's aides-de-camp, was so anxious, that he leaned across the Duke to question Seymour. The Duke was, however, much pleased and ordered Seymour to ride back to Bulow with a request to send him 4000 infantry to fill up his lines. Seymour, in crossing the Genappe Chaussée with this message, was taken by the French cavalry. And the Duke, seeing this, sent Fremantle on the errand and sent some dragoons to rescue Seymour, which they did. It was about 3 o'clock that Seymour saw the Prussians, or rather later, perhaps about 4. He was next Lord Anglesey when he was shot; he cried out: "I have got it at last." And the Duke of Wellington only replied: "No? Have you, by God?" Lord Anglesey had himself told me this two years ago. Somebody—"at least we young ones," he said, "thought at 2 o'clock and for hours after that the battle was lost;" he thought that the old ones knew better. He had five horses shot under him that day. One moment when the smoke cleared away, Seymour was riding near the Duke, and he saw the Cuirassiers close to them, and it was only by a very sudden run they avoided being taken. This was while the French cavalry had possession of the Plateau, which afforded a most extraordinary scene. The English squares and the French squadrons seemed almost for a short time hardly taking notice of each other. He never could distinguish Buonaparte, or his staff, *to be sure of them.* "Early in the day we saw a body moving along the French line, which we guessed was him and his staff." While the Cuirassiers had possession of the plateau, Seymour saw one Frenchman place his sabre on one of our cannons, as much as to mark it and say, "this is mine."

Before we went to ride, we went to look at the Pavilion.

It is not so much changed as I had been told, and affords me a new proof how inaccurate people are. I had heard from Bicknell, who had just returned from it, that it was all altered, and even the "round room," which I especially asked about, thinking it unlikely to have been destroyed, he insisted was pulled down.   On the contrary, none of the rooms which the Prince ordinarily uses are altered, that is to say, the low south room (which was the hall, and two sitting-rooms of the original Pavilion, thrown into one many years since), the dome or round room, and the Chinese gallery, are all unchanged.   But in the place of the two rooms which stood at angles of 45° with the rest of the building—one of which I remember, a dining-room and which was also a kind of music-room, and the other, next the Castle Inn, a Chinese drawing-room, which was hardly ever opened—have been erected two immense rooms, sixty feet by forty; one for a music-room and the other for a dining-room.   They both have domes; an immense dragon suspends the lustre of one of them.   The music-room is most splendid, but I think the other handsomer.   They are both too handsome for Brighton, and in an excessive degree too fine for the extent of His Royal Highness's premises.   It is a great pity that the whole of this suite of rooms was not solidly built in or near London.   The outside is said to be taken from the Kremlin at Moscow; it seems to me to be copied from its own stables, which perhaps were borrowed from the Kremlin.   It is, I think, an absurd waste of money, and will be a ruin in half a century or sooner.

December 9th.—The Prince not yet come, nor any reason why not.   I hope he has not got the gout.   A miserable rainy day but for a couple of dry hours before dinner ; walked about, and bought some toys for my children—little darlings !

One reason why Mrs. Fitzherbert may like this place is that she is treated as queen, at least of Brighton.   They don't quite *Highness* her in her domestic circle, but they *Madam* her prodigiously, and stand up longer for her arrival than for ordinary folks, and in short go as near to acknowledging her for *Princess* as they can, without actually giving her the title. When she dines out she expects to be led out to dinner before princesses—mighty foolish all this.   The Duke of York still keeps up a correspondence with her, for Seymour mentioned that she had had a letter from his Royal Highness this morning.   I dare say the Prince would not be much pleased if he knew this.

December 10*th.*—Returned to Munster House.*

December 13*th.*—Rode to Cobham again and met Lord
Yarmouth who had come from Oatlands and arrived at
Brighton at 6.   We were afraid of being obliged to dine at
the Pavilion, so we loitered on the road, and came into
Brighton, and dined quietly and slept at the Castle.

December 14*th.*—After breakfast Blomfield called to scold
us for not going to the Pavilion at once, and to command us
on the part of his Royal Highness to come there.   We went
there and walked through the rooms again and visited the
offices.   The kitchen and larders are admirable—such con-
trivances for roasting, boiling, baking, stewing, frying, steam-
ing and heating; hot plates, hot closets, hot air, and hot
hearths, with all manner of cocks for hot water and cold
water, and warm water and steam, and twenty saucepans all
ticketed and labelled, placed up to their necks in a vapour
bath.

Dined with his Royal Highness, eighteen at table, viz. : The
Prince, Ladies Liddell and Blomfield, and Mrs. Pelham,
Lords Hertford, Arran, Headfort, Carleton and Yarmouth,
Bishop of Exeter, Sirs W. Keppel, B. Blomfield, Ed. Nagle,
Thomas Liddell, Col. Thornton, Mr. Blomberg, Mr. Nash, and
myself.   We dined in the room which was once the hall and
two rooms of the original Pavilion, and the one dining-table
filled what was once the Prince's whole house.   The Prince
was in good spirits—he said, "Lord St. Vincent is gone
abroad only to marry Miss Knight, and to avoide the ridicule
of marrying her at home.   He has disposed of all his landed
and much of his other property to his relations in the way
one might expect, but he has kept a large sum for himself,
which he intends to leave to this intended wife.   She is sixty
past, and he past eighty."   In the evening the new music-room
was lighted and the band played, both magnificent—the band
rather *bruyant,* and the music better heard from the next room
in my opinion.

There was a fine boar's head at the side table at dinner.
The Prince pressed Lord Hertford to eat some of it.   He
refused, and the Prince said it was the only kind of bore that
Lord Hertford was not fond of; this is good, because Lord
Hertford has a real passion for persons whom everybody else
considers as bores.   Got to our bed-rooms at half-past 12.

December 15*th.*—Rode to Rottingdean, a poor little village,

---

* [Mr. Croker's house at Fulham.]

with a couple of good summer lodging-houses. Our dinner
party, twenty, the persons the same, with the omission of Sir
Thomas and Lady Liddell, and the addition of Lady Hertford,
and Lord and Lady Cholmondeley. The dinners are dull
enough, they are too large for society and not quite crowded
enough for freedom, so that one is on a sort of tiresome good
behaviour. How much pleasanter it used to be with a dozen
at a circular table in the old dining-room. His Royal Highness not looking well to-day. The fineness of the weather
does not tempt him abroad; his great size and weight make
him nervous, and he is afraid to ride. I am not surprised at
it. I begin to fear that he never will ride again. He says,
"Why should I? I never had better spirits, appetite, and
health than when I stay within, and I am not so well when I
go abroad." He seems as kind and gracious as usual to
everybody. The etiquette is, that before dinner when he
comes in, he *finds* all the men standing, and the women rise ;
he speaks to everybody, shakes hands with new comers or
particular friends, then desires the ladies to be seated. When
dinner is announced, he leads out a lady of the highest rank
or when the ranks are nearly equal, or when the nominal
rank interferes a little with the real rank, as yesterday, with
Lady Liddell and Mrs. Pelham, he took one on each arm.
After dinner the new dining-room was lighted and he took
the ladies to see it. It is really beautiful, and I like it better
than the other, if I can venture to say that I prefer either.
Everybody was comparing them, and the praise of one was
always, as is usual in such cases, expressed by its superiority
over the other. I ventured to say that this was not a fair
way of judging of them ; that though different they were,
perhaps, both equally beautiful in their respective kinds, like
a " handsome man and a handsome woman." This poor little
phrase had great success. [Note by Mr. Croker, 1821.—
" So great that I heard it this year attributed to Mr. Canning."]
The ceilings of both the rooms are spherical and yet there is
no echo. Nash says that he has avoided it by some new
theory of sound, which he endeavoured to explain, and which
I did not understand, nor I believe he neither. The rooms are
as full of lamps as Hancock's shop. In the evening His Royal
Highness got the plans of the house to show Lady Hertford ;
she made a few criticisms, and I think the Prince was ready
enough to have restored the old entrance if her ladyship had
persisted in her opinion to that effect, but she retracted

hautement, when she saw a tendency to additional expense. I think the tone between his Royal Highness and her ladyship was somewhat *aigre-doux.* She was against all additional expense. Yarmouth seems out of favour with papa and mamma—they are certainly so with him—he is more sensible to attentions than I thought him, and they do not spoil him by too much fondness. From several expressions he has used, I begin to think Lord Hertford would not permit him to continue in Parliament his own master.

December 16*th.*—Before dinner His Royal Highness told me he had been reading Walter Scott's edition of Swift, which, and particularly the correspondence, greatly amused him; and above all he was surprised to find Dr. Sheridan's character to be so exactly that of poor Sheridan. He said he thought the best letters were Lord Bolingbroke's. I ventured to mention Lady Betty Germain. " Oh yes," said the Prince, " excellent, and the Duchess of Queensberry's very natural." I had shown H.R.H. in the morning, a copy of a letter written 40 years ago by Mrs. Delany (widow of the Dr. Swift's friend) giving an account of a visit of the Royal family to Bulstrode, in which H.R.H. was mentioned; he was pleased at this revival of early recollections, and assured me every word of the account was true. After dinner there was music as usual, and H.R.H. made me sit down near him and he repeated to me all that passed in Council on the subject of the men executed yesterday for forgery, in which Lord Liverpool's opinion prevailed (against the new Chief Justice) to pardon two, and to execute the law on the three unfortunates, who died yesterday. The Chief Justice seemed to think the whole equally guilty.

The supper is only a tray with sandwiches, and wine and water handed about. The Prince played a hand or two at Patience, and I was rather amused to hear him exclaim loudly when one of the kings had turned up vexatiously, " Damn the king."

Mr. Croker occasionally made a note of anything he had heard or read which amused him, and the first small collection of this sort is to be found among his papers of 1818. It may fitly be introduced by an extract from one of his own letters to Lord Yarmouth:—

I'll tell you a pleasant piece of Russian diplomacy. When Archduke Michael went to Ireland, he found that the Lord Lieutenant, *Vice Regis*, would not pay him the visit, and he of course had to wait upon him. This was bad enough for a proud stomach, but he was moreover afraid that he would have been obliged *faire l'antichambre* and to avoid this affront, he resolved to follow the *huissier* at once wherever he went, quite sure that it would lead him at once to the Viceroy's presence. They accordingly stuck close to the poor footman, and carthed him in Lady Talbot's dressing-room ; and so the interview took place in her Ladyship's presence, and in the midst of her dressing-box and eau-de-Cologne bottles— and this was considered by the Tartar as a grand coup.

(*From Mr. Croker's Notebook.*)

Mr. Bankes' manners in society are not very easy or agreeable. He has just published a history of Rome, which was pronounced dull, "and yet," said Jekyll, "his Rome is better than his company."*

There is an inscription on the great Spanish mortar in the park in no very classical Latin. Part of the ornaments on the carriage are dogs' heads ; Why *dogs' heads ?* "to account for the Latin," said Jekyll.

The Sun office, in the Strand, was one of the first which exhibited the fashion, since grown so common, of introducing columns ; when it was noticed as a novelty, it was answered that, on the contrary, it was a very ancient fashion—" Atria solis erant sublimibus alta columnis."

Mr. Pepper, a gentleman well known in the Irish sporting world, asked Lord Norbury to suggest a name for a very fine hunter of his ; Lord Norbury, himself a good sportsman, who knew that Mr. Pepper had had a fall or two, advised him to call the horse "*Peppercaster.*"

* [It need scarcely be said that at this period the fashionable pronunciation of the word was "Room." The work here referred to, by Mr. Henry Bankes, M.P., was published in 1818, under the title of "The Civil and Constitutional History of Rome, from the Foundation to the age of Augustus."]

Mr. O'Connell, whose arrest by the civil power as he was proceeding to meet Mr. Peel was supposed not to be quite involuntary on his own part, was soon after arguing a law point in the Common Pleas, and happened to use the phrase, " I fear, my Lords, I do not make myself understood."   " Go on, go on, Mr. O'Connell," replied Lord Norbury, " no one is more easily *apprehended.*"

December, 1818.—We had made a *partie carrée* to go down with Lord Yarmouth to shoot in Suffolk.   After it was formed, Mr. Horace Seymour begged to be admitted as a fifth.   I supported his demand thus—

> " To a party of four t'were unclassic to stint us,
>   Horatius, I think, has some right to be Quintus."

When we went to France immediately after Waterloo, we found great difficulty in landing at Boulogne.   The town major took me almost into custody, and insisted on my going to the Governor's.   As we went along he was very vehement in his assurances that the result of the recent battle had been exaggerated; the flower of the army was saved, and especially the *vieille garde* was still in considerable force.   I observed as we walked along that there was not a regular soldier in the town; and when we came to the Governor's, I found the guard mounted by a party of the national guard of the place, dressed in rags, smock-frocks, great coats, every thing but uniform; and I verily believe the youngest of the squad must have been sixty.   I had hitherto made no answer to my conductor, but I now ventured to take my revenge by saying—" Ce sont apparemment les restes de la vieille garde." He looked as if he had a mind to run me through the body.

CHAPTER V.

1819.

MR. CROKER did not succeed in his first attempt to secure a seat in Parliament for Dublin University, and it became necessary for him, as the Secretary to the Admiralty, to find some other constituency which would be willing to elect him. This proved to be a matter of no great difficulty. With the influence of the Hertford family on his side, he was returned for Yarmouth, and when Grattan brought forward, in May, his motion in favour of the Catholics, Mr. Croker distinguished himself by delivering a speech of remarkable vigour and eloquence. Mr. Spring Rice, afterwards Lord Monteagle, bore emphatic testimony to the excellence of this speech.

Mr. Spring Rice to Mr. Carey.

May 3rd, 1819.

MY DEAR CAREY,

I write to you from the House of Commons to have the pleasure of communicating pleasure to you. I have just

K 2

heard your friend Croker, and you could not wish him or any favourite of yours to have made a stronger or more favourable impression upon the House. His speech was one which was calculated to conciliate at this side of the Channel and to gratify at the other. It was replete with ingenuity and yet free from fanciful refinement. It was characterised by an acuteness of legal deduction, and yet exempt from sophistry or the pedantry of profession. It treated a worn-out subject so as to make it appear a new one. But its principal merit in my eyes lay in its frankness, warmth, and sincerity. It redeemed the pledge and fulfilled the promise of his 'Historical Sketch.' *It showed him to be an honest Irishman no less than an able statesman.* It showed him at this moment to be *disinterested*, and ready to quit the road of fortune under the auspices of his personal friend Peel, if the latter was only to be conciliated by what Oxonians term orthodoxy, and we Cantabs consider as intolerance.

All this pleased me exceedingly, and if it pleased me, it must have delighted others, for you cannot but be aware that I feel strongly and have cause to feel the peculiar unkind-ness, and I will say the unfair unkindness, with which Croker treated me. With all the faults he discovered in my unfortunate 'Primitiæ Literariæ,' he should have seen a dis-position to do right, and he ought to have pardoned the execution for the sake of the motive. I therefore cannot but feel strongly hostile to the official reviewer—but this only gives me an additional pleasure in doing full justice to the talents he has displayed, and I only allude to the circum-stances to give you a yet more favourable scale by which to measure your friend's success. . . . I cannot refuse to myself or to you the pleasure of writing and of hearing the praise of your friend, reserving to myself every right of future hostility whenever it may be my fate to be able to descend into those lists where he is so powerful a champion.

Ever affectionately yours,   .

T. Spring Rice.

Mr. Grattan's motion was lost by a vote of 243 noes to 241 ayes, and this was almost the last occasion upon which the great orator was able to exert himself for the cause which he had so much at heart. In the following year, just as he was about to begin the long battle over again, he was struck down with the illness which proved fatal, but he found strength to declare that the settlement of the question was " essential to the permanent tranquillity and happiness of the country." This was substantially the view which Mr. Croker had always taken. He enters fully into his motive for dealing with the question on the particular occasion now referred to in the following letters :—

Mr. Croker to the Provost of Dublin University.

May 4th, 1819.

My DEAR SIR,

You will perceive by the newspapers that I had last night spoken on the Catholic question, but I fear you will from them form but a very imperfect opinion as to what I said. I cannot conceal from myself that my sentiments on this subject are at variance, at least in some points, with those of some of my best and dearest friends, yourself amongst others ; and I have therefore for many years declined to take any part in the debates. It happened to me, however, as part of my official duty, to have to introduce two years ago the Bill admitting the Catholics to the Army and Navy ; in my researches into the laws while framing that Act, I discovered (or think I did) that the law was already what the Government had consented to make it, and the Bill was in fact brought in and passed at the desire of the Protestant part of the Government, in order, I presume, to avoid any consideration of a wider question. Since that time I pursued my inquiries further, and I really found the whole state of the law to be so strange and anomalous, so contradictory and ineffective, that I could not reconcile it to my conscience nor my honour to keep my discovery, for such I may call it, to myself. I was not, however, hasty in bringing it forward, nor did I bring it forward in a way to entrap or surprise the advocates of the Protestant cause. Mr. Peel, Mr. Leslie Foster, and the Attorney General of Ireland have been long acquainted with my view of this question, and I spoke last night, by arrangement with Mr. Peel and Mr. Foster, before

them, that they might detect any fallacy in my argument.
I was not speaking for victory, nor advocating the claims of
the Catholics ; I was apprising the Protestants of what I
conceive to be the state of the law, and soliciting them to
examine for themselves.   In all I have ever done or said, or
ever shall do or say, my first and greatest object is the
Protestant Church, "the most glorious combination," as I
said last night, "of the goodness of God, and the gratitude
and adoration of man ; of divine wisdom and of human
expediency that ever was exhibited upon earth, and I never
can approve the slightest concession to the Catholics that
can be inconsistent with the glory, the safety, and the ascendency of the Church."   With these sentiments, and
placed under the peculiar circumstances in which I stood,
I trust that you will be of opinion that I could not but
deliver my reasons for thinking that we ought to enter into
a reconsideration of the *existing* state of the laws, and that
my friends, even those who might differ from me as to the
details of the Catholic question, would be pleased at seeing
me take a new and important view of the subject, and communicating to both sides of the House information which it
had not before received.

Believe me, &c.,

J. W. C.

P.S.—Peel and Plunkett were hanging back, each unwilling to speak first, and by accident both were precluded
from speaking, and the debate ended suddenly.

Mr. Croker to the Rev. C. Elrington.

May 21st, 1819.

MY DEAR CHARLES,

I was not blind when I rose to second Grattan's motion to
the difficulties of all kinds to which I was likely to subject
myself, but the Act which I had brought in and passed two
years ago was become so prominent a feature in the discussion, and its real meaning and effect were so little understood,
that I felt obliged in duty and honour to make an exposition
of the existing law, out of which that particular Act had
grown.

Besides, my sentiments had been known for these twenty

years to be in favour of the Catholics, but I was anxious to have
it understood that I supported them, not on their own claims
or merits, but out of my anxiety for the Protestant establishment, which I look upon as more endangered by their exclusion
than it could be by their admission.   I lament from the
bottom of my heart this unhappy question which divides, not
only the Catholic and Protestant, but the Protestants
themselves ; but you may depend upon this, that I should be
so lost in character as to be totally unworthy of your
friendship and support, if, under all the circumstances of the
case, I had endeavoured to evade delivering my opinion.

You may perhaps wonder why I *seconded* Grattan's motion ;
it was an odd circumstance.   I had intended to have moved
an amendment upon his motion, which amendment would
only have gone to appointing a *Select* Committee to inquire
what was the state of the law, and both Peel and Foster
were apprised of my intention ; but when we found Grattan's
motion, which we had not seen beforehand, pointing directly
to the same point of oaths and declarations, Foster thought,
and so did all who sat near me, that instead of moving an
amendment I could do nothing so properly as to second the
motion, particularly as I was desirous of opening to the
House as soon as possible my new view of the law, and of
giving both Peel and Foster, who were aware of what I had
to say, a full opportunity of answering me.   In short, on a
review of the whole case, I am convinced that I could not
have done otherwise, and if you had been sitting by my side
you could not have advised me to any other course.

J. W. C.

Another question of the day, on which Mr. Croker took a
more liberal view than the great majority of his party, was
that of Parliamentary Reform.   He was of opinion that
timely concessions would prevent unreasonable demands and
dangerous agitation at a later period, and moreover he
believed that such concessions were required alike by
considerations of justice and the interests of the country.
The chief manufacturing towns, which were then so rapidly
extending — Manchester and Birmingham, Sheffield and

Leeds—were entirely without representation in Parliament, while numbers of small and corrupt boroughs were allowed to elect two Members.   Manchester at that time (1819) had a population of 112,000 (in 1883, over 400,000).   Birmingham of 97,000 (now about 500,000), Leeds, 54,000 (now 309,000), and Sheffield, 52,000 (now about 290,000).   Mr. Croker saw the necessity of giving to communities such as these their proper representation in Parliament, and he drew up and presented to Lord Liverpool a paper containing a list of all the towns which contained a population of ten thousand and upwards, and which sent no members to the House of Commons.   There were thirty-three towns thus enumerated, many of them in the manufacturing districts, and Mr. Croker urged their claims to one member at least, if not more.   He recommended that the Grampound franchise, then forfeited through bribery, should be "resumed," and given to Leeds and Sheffield, and that the seats for East Retford should be taken away and given to Manchester and Birmingham.   Lord Liverpool received the proposition with indifference, and seems to have taken no steps whatever towards carrying it out, although the forfeited franchise of Grampound might at once have been disposed of.   In 1830, Mr. Croker substantially repeated his recommendations in a letter to Mr. Peel, but afterwards, when much larger measures of Parliamentary Reform were brought forward, he opposed them with an energy which astonished friends and foes alike.   His reasons will clearly appear from his correspondence of a later period ; at present it will suffice to quote a fragment which is found upon the margin of an old proof-sheet of a biographical sketch of Mr. Croker, in which the writer had said that "restlessness" was the great characteristic of the subject of the memoir.   Upon this Mr. Croker writes :—

I cannot presume to gainsay other people's opinion, but I *feel* as if my energy, or rather activity, was not mere "restlessness." I think that of all the men I have lived with, I was, on the whole, the least inclined to mere *change*, even of place—well inclined to be busy, but not, I think, restless. My first feeling, both in public and private, was *quieta non morere*. I was ready and forward to improve the *modus operandi*, but I had a great reluctance to shake any admitted principle—a principle once set in motion seemed to me an avalanche that could not be stopped till it had expended itself, and God would only know what mischief it might do in its course. This was my main and innate objection to the Whig Reform Bill—the reforms which I myself urged on Lord Liverpool and Peel were so limited and guarded that they involved no change, and were in fact a recurrence to existing principles and old constitutional practice.

I refused subsequently to make one of the Duke of Wellington's attempted Cabinet in May 1831, which was to have adopted "a large measure of reform." I thought *that* from Conservatives would have been not only a sacrifice of private and public character, but would hasten and extend the mischief even beyond what the Whigs could venture to do. Peel and I walked out of a meeting at the Duke's together, leaving Lyndhurst, Hardinge, Sutton, and one or two others who were willing to make the experiment. The Duke afterwards sent for me alone and was seriously angry that I was still obstinate, but most unreasonably; for exclusive of my resolution to have nothing to do with *this kind* of reform (I had been an old friend and advocate to the enfranchising *Manchester, Birmingham, Leeds, and Sheffield* with the forfeited franchises of Grampound, Penryn, East Retford, and another delinquent borough, and had proposed and prepared a scheme for doing so in 1820, which the then Cabinet had almost agreed to), I say besides that resolution, I had on our general resignation in November, 1830, apprised both the Duke and Peel that I would never take political office again.

Nothing, then, came of Mr. Croker's attempt to anticipate the inevitable agitation on the Reform question, and there is no evidence that he took any further active part in politics during the remainder of this year. It is once more to literature that he appears to have devoted his leisure hours, and in the autumn he was engaged with his usual ardour in that most dangerous of all experiments — the attempt to establish a new paper. A title which has always been a favourite with projectors of Conservative journals— the " Constitution "—was originally thought of, but it was changed, on Mr. Croker's suggestion, to the " Guardian." The first number was bad, as a matter of course. Mr. Croker explained the whole affair, and supplied incidentally a definition of what he understood by the phrase "Toryism," in letters to Mr. Lockhart and Sir Walter Scott.

Mr. Croker to Mr. J. G. Lockhart.

November 18th, 1819.

SIR,

I trust that the mutual converse of our common friends has so far made us acquainted as to justify me in taking the liberty of writing to you without having had the pleasure of a personal introduction to you. The occasion is this. Some literary gentlemen have determined to set up a weekly paper on principles diametrically opposite to the weekly journals which are now in vogue, that is, principles of morality, loyalty, respect for constituted authorities, &c.—in short, *Toryism.* It is intended that this paper should be not merely a polemical one, but should also be in other respects an entertaining and useful newspaper. Now what I have to request of your kindness is, that you will communicate this design to Mr. Wilson, and that you will both favour this new undertaking with the assistance of your pens. If the principles and conduct of the *Constitution* (the intended name of the paper) shall appear to you and Mr. Wilson to deserve your support, I cannot doubt that the Whigs and Reformers in Scotland will afford you an ample field and plenty of game.

The Rev. Mr. Croly, author of ' Paris,' and some other works, is the editor and joint proprietor; the son of Mr. Street, of the *Courier,* is the other proprietor, and though I cannot at all answer for the talents they may exhibit, I think I can venture to promise that their principles will be such as we can approve.

You will see that for obvious reasons I have not been authorized to mention this matter to Mr. Blackwood, and I

think it will be better that he should not be troubled with it ;
he has quite enough on his shoulders already.   For the same
reasons it has not been communicated to Mr. Murray ; but as
much of the success of the paper will depend upon its advertisements, we must have an agent in Scotland to collect
advertisements and subscriptions; you perhaps would
have the goodness to point out some one to whom the proprietors might address themselves for this purpose.   It would
not be necessary that you should interfere with this person,
but that you should acquaint me through what channel
Mr. Croly might apply for this assistance.

J. W. C.

Walter Scott to Mr. Croker.

[Without date.]

My dear Croker,

I had yours with the Prospectus.   No doubt subscriptions
will be found here, and advertisements will follow circulation.   Circulation, however, will depend on the labour
exerted, and, frankly, you must exert yourself to get support.
What is Canning doing ?   He must not wear the kerchief
now, if possible.   The prospectus is extremely well written.
Support it in the same strain, and it will do.   But as it
requires a strong man to jostle through a crowd, so it demands
a well supported paper to make its way through the scores
that set up pretensions to public favour.   But strength will
conquer in both cases, and though we shall do all that is
possible in Scotland, yet the main impulse must be given
from London.   In the meanwhile, to show we are not quite
idle, I send you a "Vision" * which has made a little noise
amongst us, and which is to be followed by others adapted
to the times.

Our manufacturing districts are in a sad state ; indeed, as
bad as it is possible to be.   But I have no great fear of the
result.   The people of property, by which I mean all who
have anything to lose, however little that may be, are taking
the alarm, and mustering fast.

But I need say the less of these matters as I hope, unless
unforeseen events should keep me at my post, to be in town

---

* [Three essays on certain popular delusions, published in December,
1819, and January, 1820.]

about the New Year, when we will have time to talk over
these as well as over more agreeable subjects.

Ever most truly yours, .

WALTER SCOTT.

Mr. Croker to Walter Scott.

December 13th, 1819.

MY DEAR SCOTT,

Pray don't judge of the *Guardian* by its first silly number.
Our editor, a man of great talents, is, I find, a bad drudge;
but I hope next number to force him into a better course in
spite of his mulishness. *Mon Dieu*, said the French woman,
que les gens d'esprit sont bêtes. Such is our editor.

Your " Vision " I had before, and intended to have inserted
half of it in our first number, but the article on the Duke of
Hamilton was too long to admit the other, and too important
to be omitted. Ours being a weekly paper, must of necessity
deal in short articles. I therefore intend to cut yours in
two, and I do entreat and beg of you that you will send me
some more of the same kind; but if possible don't exceed
half a column at a time; as many half columns as you please,
but always half columns. We find that long articles in
Sunday papers have a bad effect. If you Scots will take up
the *Guardian* and make it your vehicle, it will soon make its
way in Scotland, and with tenfold greater effect than a mere
Scottish publication.

Yours, &c.,

. J. W. C.

Walter Scott to Mr. Croker.

Edinburgh, December 17th, 1819.

MY DEAR CROKER,

Inter arma silent Musæ—I fear the sharp temper of the
times will not be put down by our literary exertions. However, they shall not be wanting. We are gathering and
arming fast here, and I expect to be obliged to go to the
country to bring out those with whom I may hope to have
some influence. They are, high and low, extremely loyal,
and ready to take arms; and if Cumberland and Northumber-

land be but half so bad as you say in London, it is time the
pleasant men of Teviotdale were in motion. If times should
turn worse, I hope that my son Walter may have leave of
absence from his regiment, as he might be of great use with
us. In the meantime there is much distress in my family.
On Monday my mother was struck with a paralytic affection,
from which, at the age of eighty-seven, her recovery is not to
be expected; and what is very extraordinary, her brother
(my uncle, a most respectable and excellent physician) died
suddenly on Tuesday morning. My aunt, the only remaining
member of the family, is dangerously ill; and as we lived on
terms of great affection, we are much distressed. So it may
be some time before I can help the *Guardian* effectually.
I have not seen it yet. Will you hand to the Editor the
subscriptions on the other side?

Yours very truly,
WALTER SCOTT.

Mr. Croker's reputation as a man of letters had grown and
spread every year since his appearance in London, and it is
evident from his correspondence that authors of all degrees of
merit were accustomed to send their productions to him for
an "opinion," and that in many cases he took a great deal of
pains to give it, always with perfect frankness, and yet with
a kindness of heart which was a characteristic of his nature,
although he did not invariably allow this side of his disposition to appear in his published writings. On one
occasion, somebody sent him a long play to read, and
although it seems to have been worthless stuff, Mr. Croker
wrote a careful letter of criticism and good advice to the
author, the criticism on the play being marked by all his
accustomed keenness and sense of humour, while the asperi-
ties of his more formal reviews were mercifully omitted.
The author had, it would appear, appealed in a sort of introduction for "patronage;" and he asked for this, by way of
making more sure of getting it, in two languages, English
and Latin. "But," Mr. Croker tells him, you demand that
which "I cannot give you, which no man can give you. The

public is the only patron nowadays. If you have talents, nothing can keep you down; if you have not, no partiality can raise you." With regard to the play itself—it was a tragedy—he wrote: "Let it not mortify you if I say that if a manager were to ask my advice on a similar piece, I should not advise him to produce it. The first, and the second, and the third requisites in a tragedy are, in my humble judgment, interest, interest, interest. The poetry, and the plan, and the persons are all secondary considerations; the persons may be faultless, the plan regular, the poetry beautiful, and yet there may be no interest; and if there be not, it never can succeed on the stage. . . . Why should all the personages of your play be poets? Why cannot an old Spanish captain see the sun set without comparing him to a bridegroom? Why cannot the general of a besieging army look at a town without talking of 'gilding its towering walls?' Why must one lady invoke memory to 'wear the rugged etchings of despair from a cold heart of rock?' and why must another talk of a warm bath as being 'lassitude divine, that wings the soul for Paradise?'" To sweeten this wholesome but doubtless unpleasant medicine, Mr. Croker offered to pay half the expense of publishing the tragedy, if the author still thought the public were waiting to extend a greeting to him. But he advised him not to place his dependence on literature. "In former days," he wrote, "in which we read so much of the miseries of authors, it would be hard to name a man of talents and good conduct who did not rise to respectability and a competence, if not to affluence. And nowadays, although we never hear of *fortunes made* by literature, we should find, I fear, on inquiry that there is in the lower ranks of authors as much misery as ever." Mr. Croker held the same opinion on this subject as Sir Walter Scott, who was accustomed to say that literature might do well enough as a staff, but was worthless as a crutch.   And yet Scott could make £24,000 by one novel, and he is believed to have realised from his pen no less a sum than £500,000.

One of Mr. Croker's valued correspondents on literary matters was Mr. William Blackwood, the founder of the celebrated magazine, whose list of contributors would be found to include some of the most famous names of the present century.   Mr. Blackwood always invited Mr. Croker to express a frank and free opinion of "Maga," and Mr. Croker generally complied with his wishes.

Mr. Croker to Mr. W. Blackwood

August 24th, 1819.

MY DEAR SIR,

I have received your last number, and in return the best kind of thanks I can give you is my honest opinion of its merits.

As a series of essays, critical and humorous, it is excellent; but in this part of the world we think there is too much criticism and humour for a magazine.   In a work of this kind we expect curious facts and miscellaneous information.

Professed reviews should be left to the professed reviewers; and allow me to say, that the personal and local pleasantry which is so abundant in your magazine, and which, I have no doubt, must be delightful in Edinburgh and Glasgow, is *here* scarcely understood, and in Ireland I have some reason to know that it is a perfect puzzle.   You can best judge the state of your sale, but you may depend upon it that in England we should like your magazine better if it were more magazinish.   The fact is, you are too strong; your contributors are too able; they melt down into a monthly pamphlet the materials which would furnish out perennial volumes. I am, as they are, fond of angling; and I can well imagine the pleasure they have in hooking the huge Whigs, and, in spite of their floundering efforts, dragging them to light and safely basketing them.   But fishing for men, as for fishes, should not be your daily employment but your occasional amusement; and your notices of literary works should be

short, light, and piquant. The last quality you have
at will.

Excuse my presumption in intruding these suggestions.
I make them sincerely, and out of the interest which I take
in the success of your magazine, admiring, as I do, the
principles and talents which support it.

Yours, &c.,
J. W. C.

In the latter part of the year, Lord Byron wrote to
Mr. Murray from Bologna asking him to get a consul's or
vice-consul's appointment for a friend of his at Ravenna—
it is now understood, for the Count Guiccioli. "Will you,"
he said, "get a favour done for me? *You* can, by your
Government friends, Croker, Canning, or my old schoolfellow Peel, and I can't. Here it is. Will you ask them to
appoint (*without salary or emolument*) a noble Italian (whom
I will name afterwards) consul or vice-consul for Ravenna?
He is a man of very large property—noble, too; but he
wishes to have a British protection, in case of changes. . . .
His motive is a British protection in case of new invasions.
Don't you think Croker would do it for us? . . . Perhaps a
brother wit in the Tory line might do a good turn at the
request of so harmless and long absent a Whig, particularly
as there is no salary or burthen of any sort to be annexed
to the office." * Mr. Croker was confined to his house by
some passing ailment when ·Mr. Murray forwarded this
request to him, but it will be seen that the "Tory" lost no
time in endeavouring to serve the "Whig."

Mr. Croker to Mr. Murray.

September 15th, 1819.

Dear Murray,

My illness is neither serious nor painful, and it is quite
a waste of pity to throw it away upon me at present. I am

* [Moore's 'Life of Byron,' vol. ii. pp. 493–94.]

in bed, indeed, but it is only because my apothecary has given me a sudorific.

In spite of my confinement, however, I have had an opportunity of inquiring how Lord Byron's wishes about the *Vice*-Consul can be effected. Consul is out of the question, for we have a Consul-General at Venice; but the Vice-Consular alternative may be achieved without much difficulty. Vice-Consuls are not appointed at home; if they were, I should not have had the least hesitation in asking Lord Castlereagh, even though you had published 'Don Juan' without an erasure. Tories are placable people; and of all Tories, Castlereagh the most so; but as I said, he has nothing to do with the appointments of Vice-Consuls; they are named by the Consuls, and only approved (generally as a matter of course) at the Foreign Office. Now our Venetian Consul is no other than Gifford's *protégé* Hoppner, and a line from the former to the latter will insure the nomination, and a line from you to me, when the said nomination is sent home for approval will insure, I should hope, its final success.

Thank you for the perusal of the letter;* it is not very good, but it will vex these old women of British critics, which perhaps is all the author intended. I told you from the first moment that I read 'Don Juan,' that your fears had exaggerated its danger. I say nothing about what may have been suppressed; but if you had published 'Don Juan' without hesitation or asterisks, nobody would have ever thought worse of it than as a larger Beppo, gay and lively and a little loose. Some persons would have seen a strain of satire running beneath the gay surface, and might have been vexed or pleased according to their temper; but there would have been no outcry either against the publisher or author.

Yours, &c.,

J. W. C.

Mr. Croker to Mr. Murray.

Ryde, July 18th, 1819.

Dear Murray,

I am agreeably disappointed at finding 'Don Juan' very little offensive. It is by no means worse than 'Childe

* [Byron's 'Letter to the Editor of My Grandmother's Review.']

Harold,' which it resembles as comedy does tragedy. There is a prodigious power of versification in it, and a great deal of very good pleasantry. There is also some magnificent poetry, and the shipwreck, though too long, and in parts very disgusting, is on the whole finely described. In short, I think it will not lose him any character as a poet, and, on the score of morality, I confess it seems to me a more innocent production than 'Childe Harold.' What 'Don Juan' may become by-and-bye I cannot foresee, but at present I had rather a son of mine were Don Juan than, I think, any other of Lord Byron's heroes. Heaven grant he may never resemble any of them.

I had Crabbe's tales with me on shipboard, and they were a treasure. I never was so much taken with anything. The tales are in general so well conducted that, in prose, they would be interesting as mere stories; but to this are added such an admirable *ease* and *force* of diction, such good pleasantry, such high principles, such a strain of poetry, such a profundity of observation, and such a gaiety of illustration as I never before, I think, saw collected. He imagines his stories with the humour and truth of Chaucer, and tells them with the copious terseness of Dryden, and the tender and thoughtful simplicity of Cowper. This high commendation does not apply to the whole of the tales, nor, perhaps, to the whole of any one. There are sad exceptions here and there, which might easily be removed, but on the whole it is a delightful book.

Mr. Gifford has set me Leigh Hunt as a *task*. He asks but two or three pages, and I shall see what I can do this evening, but I had rather have let it alone.

Yours ever,

J. W. Croker.

Another application arrived about the same time from Walter Scott, under circumstances which cannot possibly be better told than by Mr. Croker himself in the following letter :—

Mr. Croker to Mr. Goulburn.

September 8th, 1819.

DEAR GOULBURN,

" Accept a miracle instead of wit." I send you a very dull and almost illegible piece of Walter Scott's composition, but . dull and difficult as it is, I hope his name and my request will induce you to wade through the enclosed packet.

The argument of this new 'Tale of my Landlord' is as follows :—

One Pringle, a Scotch Tory, born lame, dedicates himself to literature—sets up a magazine—quarrels with his publisher— is turned off, abused and ridiculed. Sets up a new magazine in opposition to the former, engages with the new publisher for a salary for five years, on the strength of which he marries, computing, as it would seem, that his marriage and all its consequences must be ended before five years. The new publisher as bad as the old—another dismissal—the wife breeds copiously—the little all of the increasing family 100*l.*, which, however, is to last but two years—present difficulties— dreadful prospects—desperate projects—emigration to Canada or the Cape—prefers Canada—changes his mind—prefers the Cape—how to get there ? Applies to Walter Scott, for whom he had done some little literary jobs—and on whose family he had some kind of dependence—sets forth his wishes and his means—the former a grant of land—the latter 500*l.*, and a dozen experienced farmers and their wives, his own relations or servants. Walter Scott receives the proposal, and conveys it to the first Lord of the Admiralty. His Lordship advises Scott to interest Mr. Croker, who can interest Mr. Goulburn, who can interest Lord Bathurst, who can interest Lord Charles Somerset to do something for the interest of the intended colony of the Pringles.

Croker, who was himself bored with reading three long letters and one short one on the subject, writes a longer letter than any of them to Goulburn, and bores him with the whole galimatias. Goulburn in a rage writes a hasty refusal without reading the letters; next day dreadfully wet, can't go abroad; thinks he may as well endeavour to decipher Walter Scott's letter, and wade through Pringle's. Does so in two hours, ten minutes, fifteen seconds. Writes a favourable answer to say the proposals promise reasonably

L 2

well, and that he will do all he can. Croker acquaints Scott—Scott tells Pringle. Pringle in ecstasies of joy runs to tell his wife, big with child,—rapture accelerates her labour. She is brought to bed of a fine boy, who is christened Henry-Scott-Bathurst-Goulburn Pringle.

Finis of the 1st volume.

Yours ever,

J. W. C.

There are, as it has been stated, scarcely any references to political matters or to public affairs of any kind in Mr. Croker's correspondence of this year. He seems to have taken no part in the numerous discussions which arose in the House on financial questions, and he makes no allusion to the appointment of his friend Mr. Peel as Chairman of the Committee to " consider the state of the Bank of England, with reference to the expediency of the resumption of cash payments at the period fixed by law." It was probably supposed that Peel would advocate the continued suspension of cash payments, and Mr. Wynn wrote at the time, " Peel, who is Chairman of the Bank Committee, professes, I find, to have as yet formed no opinion on the subject, but to be *open to conviction;* and the same is the language of the Duke of Wellington."[*] We now know, however, that Peel had very decided opinions, and that they were quite opposite to those which had been attributed to him. He was in favour of cash payments, the rest of the Committee agreed with him, the House adopted its plans, and the Bank resumed specie payments in 1821. This was Peel's first success in the field where he was afterwards to make so great a reputation; and it can only be owing to some accident that no record of it appears in any form among Mr. Croker's papers. He was

[*] The ' Buckingham Papers '—the ' Regency,' vol ii. p. 303.

not idle, as may be seen from his letters dealing with the general topics of the day.

Mr. Croker to Lord Yarmouth.

October 8th, 1819.

MY DEAR Y.,

There is no longer any doubt that the poor Duke of Richmond died of hydrophobia, and as little that it was caused by the bite of a tame fox which had been irritated. The first symptom he showed was on the 23rd of August, when he wished to drink some wine and water, but could not; however, neither he nor any one else minded it; next day he found some difficulty in washing himself, but he dined and drank some wine as usual; he even had company with him; the third day he desired to be placed in a canoe and was rowed on the water, but he soon found the agony greater than he could bear, and was forced to come ashore. On the 26th and 27th the disorder was no longer to be mistaken; the horrible convulsions came on, and during the intervals his mind was quite collected. He dictated messages to his family and friends, but every now and then fresh convulsions disordered his frame and intellect, and at last he died on the 28th, quite exhausted and without a struggle.

This is but a faint sketch of this most melancholy event, which is a new proof of the horrors of this mysterious disease. His attendants doubted whether the disease arose from the bite of the fox, or from his having caressed a favourite dog seven months before, which had been bitten by another dog. I have no doubt the former was the cause.

Yours, &c.,

J. W. C.

Mr. Croker to his Wife.

We talked of the Duke of Richmond's death, and Lady Hamilton told us that she had been bitten at Bruxelles about four years ago by a little dog that was said to have been bitten by a mad dog, and of course you may judge that she was very uneasy; but the poor Duke, who was there, ridiculed her terrors, and said that there was no such thing as hydrophobia, that he had been all his life in kennels and amongst dogs, and bitten a hundred times, and a thousand times had seen people bitten, and that he never saw a case of hydrophobia ; and, in short, he thought it all falsehood and fancy, and he never saw Lady Hamilton after without inquiring jestingly whether she was afraid of water.

I must tell you another anecdote of the poor Duke which Sir Hugh told me, and which is singular of a man of his rank. He died, we know, in a barn—but it seems he was also born in a barn. His mother, Lady Louisa, was taken ill when on a fishing party, and there was only time to carry her to a neighbouring farmyard, where the Duke was born.

Mr. Croker to Lord Yarmouth.

November 6th, 1819.

DEAR Y.,

Here I am once more in England, after an absence of twenty days, fourteen of which in Paris. You are as little interested as I am informed on the subject of French politics, and therefore I shall say nothing on that head ; and on those subjects on which you might desire to know something, I fear I am still more ignorant. I passed my time between book shops and the play-houses, and a few people whom I had business with ; and, in short, I am come back from Paris no wiser than I went. All that I did hear was about ourselves. Rebellion, revolution, what not, at home ; and then her Royal Highness the Princess of Wales made a great figure in the " on dits " of Paris. I myself pay little attention to scandalous stories, and forget them as fast as I hear them, but Stuart told me that she was come to Lyons to meet Brougham ; and that Lord Essex had gone to Lyons to see her, that she thought he was come a deputy from the Whigs, but he undeceived her. She is gone to Marseilles or Montpellier. In truth, she is quite mad, and that will appear one of those days with so much *éclat* as to remove all doubts and difficulties.

The French Government were embarrassed what to do with her, but they at last sent her a message " that she could not be received at Court without the concurrence of the British Ambassador, and as he had stated that he could not present her, the King would see her arrival at Paris with great pain." This, you see, was not a positive refusal, but it was accompanied with a *secret* order to the Préfet to *delay* granting passports. *Before,* however (Stuart says, but I fear not), this message arrived she had already gone off towards Marseilles, so that she is supposed to know nothing of; so much the better; but I cannot but think that it either has reached or will reach her; and that we shall have this added to the list of grievances.

From Mr. Croker's Note-Books.

Dined with the Duke of York at Lord Yarmouth's. It is said in the life of Frederick the Great, that he preserved his health and intellect till within two days of his death (17th August, 1786). His Royal Highness, however, told us that when he was at Berlin in 1785, he dined with the King at a numerous dinner (the late Lord Cornwallis was there). Frederic had never been more lively or entertaining; after dinner he retired as usual, and left his guests to their coffee; but he had hardly left the room, when he dropped down in an apoplectic fit. This, however, was not known at the time. Next morning the Duke was on the parade as usual to meet the King, when the Prince Royal, who was only a Lieutenant-General, asked him whether he had not had an invitation to dine with the King; the Duke said yes; the Prince replied, that he feared they should not have His Majesty's company, as he was ill, but that no notice was to be taken of it. So they sat down—eight—to dinner; and a strange and melancholy dinner it was; everybody knew that the master was dying in the next room, but no one was to take notice of what they were all thinking of. Then the Prince Royal was at table—a secondary kind of person—for as all was regulated by military rank, the old General at the head of the table (I forget his name) commanded him, and every time the door opened they expected to hear their companion saluted King. The King, however, did not die then, nor for some months after; but he never dined in company again.

The Duke said that but one of the peers had a distinct seat in the House of Lords, namely, the *Junior Baron.* His place is fixed, for as in all processions, &c., the Premier goes first, he takes his lowest place (which is on the last bench on the right hand next the gangway), and then all the other lords who appear take their places in succession; and the Duke mentioned occasions on which, by this process, he, coming last, got no seat at all.

The Duke said he had no doubt that he was Earl of Ross in Scotland; Lord Lauderdale thought so too. The claim is that Charles I. (while his brother was alive) and the second son of the King of Great Britain for the time being, was created Earl of Ross. It seems that there were also great estates annexed to this title, a part of which constitutes the wealth of the House of Athol. The Duke consulted Lord Thurlow about prosecuting this claim; but he dissuaded him, as it was likely to be invidious and unpopular. I was surprised to find the Duke of York and Albany and Earl of Ulster, Field Marshal, Commander-in-Chief, Guardian of the King's sacred person, &c., so anxious as he happened to be about the Earldom of Ross, which was, he said, only a *feather*, but a feather which he wished to stick in his cap. I told him that if the estate might be recovered with it, I should think it worth looking after, and that then his Royal Highness would have both the cap and the feather.

We had a very pleasant dinner, but rather too much wine. There were Lord Lauderdale, Colonel Cooke, Mr. Byng, Mr. Luttrell, Mr. Raikes. It was like the dinner at Sans Souci—a dinner of eight—but rather pleasanter.

When Adair, whose father was a surgeon, went as Fox's Ambassador to Russia, Lord Whitworth, then the King's Minister, made a good joke, which tended not a little to lower Adair and to defeat his object. " Est-ce un homme très considérable, ce M. d'Adair ? " asked the Empress. " Pas trop, Madame," replied Lord Whitworth, " quoique son père était *grand seigneur* [*saigneur*]."

Old Languet, the celebrated Curé of St. Sulpice, was remarkable and disagreeable for the importunity with which he solicited subscriptions for finishing his church, which is not yet finished. One day at supper, where Cardinal de Fleury was, he happened to say that he had seen his Eminence's portrait at some painter's. The old Cardinal, who was stingy in private as well as economical in public expenditure, was glad to raise a laugh at the troublesome old curé, and replied, " I dare swear, then, you asked it (the picture) to subscribe;" " Oh, no, my Lord," said Languet, " it was too like ! "

One day an officer came very late to dinner at Talleyrand's, an unusual negligence in France where everybody is exact. He made a kind of impertinent apology, alleging that he had been delayed by a *péquin*, the nickname which

French soldiers give civilians.   M. Talleyrand, himself a *péquin*, asked what a *péquin* was; "Nous appelons péquin," replied the Hector, "tout ce qui n'est pas militaire."   "Ah! ah!" replied Talleyrand, "c'est comme nous, nous appelons *militaire* tout ce qui n'est pas *civile*."   This joke is even better in English than in French.

We were wondering at Lord Stafford's giving up the county as he did, and still more how a canvass of a few days could cost him twenty thousand pounds, which it was said to have done.   "Why," said somebody, "in the first place he secured all the *carriages* in the county"—"including *miscarriage*," added Jekyll.

There have been disputes pending between Baden and Bavaria these two years, which, contemptible as they were compared with the great European system, were yet so serious as to threaten that part of Germany with war.   Some one was lamenting the likelihood of hostilities in presence of M. de Talleyrand.   "Rassurez vous, mon ami," said the Prince, "toutes ces dissensions ne sont que badinage et bavardage."

Lady Warrender told me one day that her alliance with Sir George was a crying proof of the falsehood of the proverb "that marriages were made in heaven."   I ventured, as she had taken a laughing tone about it, to say that, on the contrary, I thought it a strong proof of a providential arrangement, as there would otherwise have been two unhappy couples instead of one.   She laughed very good-humouredly but I believe the joke was plain truth.

CHAPTER VI.

1820.

Mr. Croker's Diary—Death of the Duke of Kent—And of George III.—
Illness of George IV.—The King's domestic Affairs—Scandals con-
cerning the Queen—The Prayers in the Liturgy—Difficulties with the
Cabinet—Funeral of George III.—The Cato Street Conspiracy—
Dinner of the Royal Academy—A Visit to Cornwall—Mr. Croker
elected for Bodmin—Visit of Sir Walter Scott to London—Orator
Hunt—Mr. Peel on the changed Tone of Public Opinion regarding
Parliamentary Reform—Probable Amalgamation of Whigs and Tories
—The Conduct of the Queen—Danger of Riots—Alarms concerning the
Troops—Lady Conyngham, the "Vice-Queen"—The King and his
Ministers—Reported Mutiny of the Guards—Mr. Peel on the Diffi-
culty with the Queen—Death of Mr. Croker's Son.

During the year 1820 Mr. Croker made a few notes from
time to time of certain interesting events, but a great bereavement which befell him drew his mind from public affairs,
and thus there is little or no reference to many incidents
which, as we know, occupied no small share of general
attention—such, for instance, as the disturbed state of the
country, or the growing weakness of the Ministry, which led
one observer of politics to exclaim, "We want another Pitt,
but where is he to be found?" * Mr. Croker's diary deals
very little with public affairs of any description after the
month of May, when he lost his only son, and was obliged to

* Lord Redesdale to Lord Colchester, 'Colchester Diary and Correspondence,' iii. 108.

seek in foreign travel some relief from the poignant distress
which this affliction occasioned him. The very book which
he used for a diary was not favourable to the preservation of
anything but the briefest kind of record of passing events.
It was a copy of ' Richards's Universal Daily Remembrancer,'
with blank spaces for four days on each page. These spaces
were filled in by Mr. Croker at irregular intervals, and his
correspondence does not render the narrative of the year by
any means complete.

The first entry is under the date January 22nd, and relates
to the Duke of Kent, who was seized with an illness two
days previously :—

From Mr. Croker's Diary.

The Duke of Kent is very seriously ill.   Received a note at
Munster House from [Lord] Yarmouth, to say that the Duke
of Kent had rattles in his throat, and was despaired of.   He
could not live a day.   This seems incredible ; so strong a
man to go in so short a space, and from, in its origin, so
trifling an indisposition.*

Mr. Croker to Lord Lowther.

January 24th, 1820.

You will be surprised at the Duke of Kent's death.   He
was the strongest of the strong ; never before ill in all his
life, and now to die of a cold, when half the kingdom had
colds with impunity, is very bad luck indeed.   It reminds
me of Æsop's fable of the Oak and the Reed.

The King too has been very ill these some days ; alarmingly
so, indeed.   The Speaker is kept in town lest he should go off
suddenly, and they won't consent to his going away for
twenty-four hours.

The old King was, in fact, rapidly approaching his end.
He had been suffering from ill health for several months past

* [His illness arose from getting his feet wet while taking a walk.]

and for eight years, with very few intervals, he had been completely dead to the world. His physicians began to see, early in January, that his wonderful powers of vitality were at last failing him; but it was not till towards the middle of the month that all expectation of saving him was abandoned.

From Mr. Croker's Diary.

Jan. 25th.—Heard by letter from Windsor that Dr. Heberden was of opinion that the King had no ailment, and might last several months; so, it is said, is Sir David Dundas; but I learn from Lord Yarmouth that those who know him best think he cannot last one month, perhaps not ten days.

Jan. 27th.—Huskisson, Peel and I were to have gone to-day to shoot at Sudbourne with Lord Yarmouth, who was to have had a battue for the Duke of York, but the Duke of Kent's death prevented the latter, and the imminent danger of the King dissuades the rest of us, as if he dies Parliament must meet immediately, and we should have to hasten back to town. We have therefore given it up.

Jan. 30th.—Early in the morning had a note from Melville to say the King was dead. Came immediately to town from Munster House. He died about the very instant when I received the account last night. Made immediate preparations for the official measures to be taken on this occasion. Followed the precedent of the Queen as to the mourning, for, strange to say, no other precedent is to be found; and indeed I have ascertained that, on the demise of George II., no orders were given from this office [the Admiralty] except the notice of the officers' mourning.

Received a note from Lord Sidmouth to attend at Carlton House at two to proclaim the new King. Privy Councillors were summoned at one. About 50 people attended. We all signed the proclamation, and then the Privy Councillors went up stairs to be sworn in. The King [George IV.] has been very unwell with an inflammation of the chest, but he got up to receive the Council. He was very gracious and even affectionate to all, except the Duke of Sussex, who was not admitted into his bed chamber, as the rest of the royal family were, but stood in the outward room with the other Privy

Councillors (none of whom spoke to him), looking very sullen and ashamed, and reminding one, as I was told, of *Frankenstein's man.*

The new King was now seized with a disorder which, for a time threatened to carry him off, and in the course of a few days he became so much worse, that his own medical advisers grew seriously alarmed. It has been stated that 130 ounces of blood were taken from him,* and this is confirmed by Mr. Croker, who was in constant communication with the principal physician, Sir William Knighton.

From Mr. Croker's Diary.

Jan. 31*st.*—The hurry and agitation of all these great affairs has made the King worse. He was proclaimed exactly at 12 o'clock at Carlton House inside the screen,† with a good deal of applause of the people, but more of the soldiers. A very fine day.

Feb. 1*st.*—The King is much worse, alarmingly worse. They are bleeding him profusely. *Evening.* The King is in imminent danger. Went down to the House and took the oaths and made the declaration, all except the qualification oath. Not more than 40 or 50 were sworn to-day, and I believe not so many yesterday. We are to adjourn over the King's funeral, which will take place about the 16th.

Feb. 2*nd.*—The King is a shade better, but not at all out of danger. Wrote to Dr. Boyd and my other friends at the University to say that Lord Liverpool felt so strongly against disturbing Mr. Plunkett's ‡ election that I could not but accede to his wishes. This is a great sacrifice, and one which Lord Liverpool had certainly no right to expect from me; and I should not have consented but that I did not wish to commit my friends against the Government.

Feb. 5*th.*—The King would be better but that his anxiety about the Queen agitates him terribly.

* 'Colchester Diary and Correspondence,' iii. 111.

† [The Ionic screen, added to Carlton House by Henry Holland, and removed with the rest of the building in 1827.]

‡ [The Right Hon. W. C. Plunkett, who had been successful in the contest for the representation of Dublin University against Mr. Croker.]

The miserable state of the King's domestic affairs was now occasioning him more vexation than ever, for the Princess of Wales had caused her friends to understand that she would insist upon sharing the throne, while the King was fixed in his determination that she should never again be received under his roof. She had been absent from England ever since 1814, travelling from place to place, oftentimes in very dubious company. She had made her valet, the notorious Bergami, a Knight of a new order created by herself, the order of "Saint Caroline of Jerusalem," and had procured for him several titles, including that of a Baron, from foreign powers. He was very seldom absent from her side. " The Princess of Wales," wrote Lord Colchester, "changed horses to-day at Genoa . . . . Her travelling party consisted of herself, with the Baron courier and a Frenchwoman in one carriage ; and the Baron's brother and sister, and William Austin, and another female in a second carriage, both battered old German calèches." *   The " Baron's " sister was the Princess's waiting-woman, and his brother was her equerry. The whole of the Bergami family had, in fact, been saddled upon the Princess—with the somewhat important exception of his wife, who was kept out of sight. A plentiful crop of scandals was continually brought to the notice of the Prince of Wales, and there is no reason to doubt that he strongly believed his wife's guilt, and had perhaps done so ever since 1805, when the first serious charges against her were brought forward. Upon his accession to the throne, he was obliged to take a definite course in regard to her. Down to that time, "their Royal Highnesses George, Prince of Wales, and the Princess of Wales," had been prayed for in the Liturgy, and the Prince could scarcely help this, although he had been separated from his wife since 1796. But now it

* 'Colchester Diary and Correspondence,' iii. 111.

was necessary to alter the prayer in the Liturgy, and the King felt an invincible repugnance to the thought of his wife's name being once more coupled with his own as Queen. It is to this situation of affairs that Mr. Croker's next entries refer :—

From Mr. Croker's Diary.

Feb. 6th, Sunday.—The King was better, but unluckily last night he recollected that the prayers to be used to-day were not yet altered. He immediately ordered up all the Prayer-books in the House of old and new dates, and spent the evening in very serious agitation on this subject, which has taken a wonderful hold of his mind. In some churches I understand the clergy prayed for " our most gracious Queen " ; in others, and I believe in general, they prayed for " all the Royal Family."

Feb. 10th.—Came in [to town] to breakfast with Lowther. We talked over the difficulty about praying for the Queen. It struck me that if she is to be prayed for, it will be, in fact, a final settlement of all questions in her favour. If she is fit to be introduced to the Almighty, she is fit to be received by men, and if we are to *pray* for her in Church we may surely bow to her at Court. The praying for her will throw a sanctity round her which the good and pious people of this country will never afterwards bear to have withdrawn. Lowther said that in all the discussions he had never heard the matter argued from this religious point of view, and he advised me to communicate my opinions to the King. We accordingly went over to Carlton House, and saw Blomfield,* and, strange to say, this view of the subject was as new to him as to Lowther. It made a great impression upon him. He said it never had occurred to the King to argue the question in that way ; that it had been discussed as a mere matter of civil propriety and expediency, but that this was a new and clear view, and quite decisive. " If she was fit to be introduced as Queen to God she was fit to introduce to

---

* [Sir B. Blomfield, Keeper of the Privy Purse, and Private Secretary to George IV., afterwards raised to the peerage. The name is spelt "Bloomfield" in the Peerage and elsewhere, but in Sir Benjamin's own letters there is clearly but one o in the signature. The Editor has followed these letters as the best authority.]

men. Yes, yes; the King is to see the Ministers to-day on it, and he shall in half an hour be in possession of this unanswerable argument." On my return I repeated this line of reasoning to Lord Melville, and, wonderful to say, it appeared that the religious and moral effect of the prayer had been overlooked by the Cabinet also. They had considered it only as to its legal consequences. Three or four of the Cabinet are for praying for her as Queen, but they will be outvoted. This question is of great importance, and I do not see the end of it.

Feb. 12*th.*—A Council held to-day, and it is finally settled not to pray for the Queen by name. An order to this effect will appear in to-night's Gazette. The Archbishop* was for praying for the Queen.

Stayed in town, and dined *tête-à-tête* with the Speaker.† He, of course, thinks with the Archbishop, and, on the whole, does not approve the course which the Ministers seem to have adopted. He thinks they ought to have taken one line or the other—Queen or no Queen.

Feb. 13*th.*—A new and most serious difficulty has arisen. The King wants the Ministers to pledge themselves to a divorce, which they will not do. They offer to assist to keep the Queen out of the country by the best mode, namely, giving her no money if she will not stay abroad; but this will not satisfy the King. He is furious, and says they have deceived him; that they led him on to hope that they would concur in the measure, and that now they leave him in the lurch. It looks like a very serious breach. Sir John Leach,‡ who has a mind to be Chancellor, suggests, it is said, a new administration, and it is reported has authority to sound Lord Wellesley, if not the Opposition. The Cabinet offer all but a divorce; the King will have a divorce or nothing. His agitation is extreme and alarming; it not only retards his recovery, but threatens a relapse. He eats hardly anything—a bit of dry toast and a little claret and water. This affair becomes very serious on a more important account than the plans of the Ministers, but the King has certainly

* [The Archbishop of Canterbury, Dr. Manners Sutton.]
† [Charles Manners Sutton, son of the Archbishop.]
‡ [Sir John Leach had been one of the Prince's Whig friends in the Regency days, and was now the Vice-Chancellor, having succeeded Sir Thomas Plumer, appointed Master of the Rolls.]

intimated intentions of looking for new and more useful servants.

Feb. 14th.—Reports that Leach is trying to enlist an Administration. Lord Castlereagh had a conference of several hours to endeavour to soothe the King's mind. I went to tell Blomfield, as a friend of the King's, that the plan of a new Government was madness; that if the present men were turned out on *this point*, the whole clergy, gentry, &c., would go with them; that the Whigs, with the sincerest intentions, must fail; that their own followers would desert them; and that I knew of no question but this one upon which a Tory Opposition would be formidable. I had before mentioned this view to some of the Cabinet. And as they knew I had been sometimes honoured with some personal notice from the King, they thought it right that I should state my opinion in a way that it might reach his Majesty, to which I could have no objection, seeing, as I think I do, the King about to take a false step, which will not only expose him to great vexation, but will ultimately defeat his object. Castlereagh is charged by the King to ask the Cabinet for explanations on some points, suggested, I believe, by Leach. He is to give him their answer to-morrow.

Feb. 15th.—The Cabinet's explanation is not likely to be satisfactory, but they defend themselves from the charge of surprise by saying that in June last they explained their present views in a Cabinet minute, which was laid before the Regent. Castlereagh seems to think His Majesty was more placable at this last interview. There is a blunder about the prayer after all. The Act of Uniformity authorizes only the change and not the omission of names.

Feb. 16th.—Went to Windsor with Lords Melville and Binning to attend the late King's funeral. Dined and slept at Mr. Locker's. Having no official place in the procession, Sir George Naylor made me one of the supporters to the Crown of Hanover, but, by some error in the heralds in placing me, I luckily never got near the Crown, and walked between Lords Roden and Breadalbane, who carried the banners of Ireland and Scotland, and Lords Grenville and Howard, who carried the Union and St. George. I could not help admiring the felicity of the heralds (who are by profession typifiers) in making Lord Grenville bear the Union banner. The night was very cold, and the whole ceremony unaffecting, though I suppose it looked splendid. The music

tiresome, and too long.   All that I saw or heard worth notice
were, first, the Yeomen of the Guard, in black in a black
room, not half lighted, which preceded the apartment in
which the body lay.   The haze and hangings of the room
made a kind of palpable gloom which was very striking, and,
through the mist, these fellows looked like black giants;
secondly, as the procession moved round the edge of the
Castle walks, the dismal and monotonous sounds of trumpets
from the park below had a very solemn effect ; and, thirdly,
the death-like appearance of old Lord Hertford's fine but
feeble figure tottering in before the coffin, and looking almost
as if he was going to his own grave, was very melancholy.
It was over by 20 minutes past 11.

Feb. 18th.—Yesterday the King wished to postpone the
message for a few days.   This shows that he has still some
design not quite in consonance with the Ministers.   They
merely replied that, according to all precedents, the message
must be brought down, and they did so, which gives them an
additional hold of the King.   But what could H.M. do ?   No
men could undertake [to accomplish] his object, nor, if they
did, could [they] carry it.   Dined at Peel's with the Speaker,
Grant, Lowther, Huskisson.

The wretched squabbles about the Queen were for a time
cast into the background by the singular affair which afterwards became known as the Cato Street Conspiracy.   The
prime mover in it was Arthur Thistlewood, who had previously taken a leading part in the Spafields riots.   The
plan resolved upon was to assassinate the entire Cabinet, and
to get possession of London by means of an armed mob.
The news that the Ministers would all meet on the 23rd of
February, to dine together at the house of Lord Harrowby in
Grosvenor Square, was received by the conspirators with
great exultation, for they entertained no doubt that a most
favourable opportunity was at hand for carrying out all their
plans.   But, as in so many other conspiracies before and
since, the informer was early at work; Lord Harrowby was
apprised of all that was going on, and so was Lord Sidmouth.

The police were sent to arrest the ringleaders before they could strike a blow, and the whole plot ignominiously collapsed. In the following May, Thistlewood and four of his confederates were hanged.

(*From Mr. Croker's Diary.*)

February 23rd.—The Cabinet which was to have dined at Lord Harrowby's, dined at Fife House, having traced an intention of which Thistlewood was the head to assassinate them by attacking Lord H——'s house at half-past 8. Mr. Birnie, the magistrate, came to the place of meeting of the conspirators before 8, and after a kind of action in which one man—a constable—was killed and several wounded, he took nine of them; but Thistlewood escaped. Mr. Fitzclarence, who commanded the guard, mistook his post, else they would have been all taken. Personally, Fitzclarence behaved perfectly well.

February 24th.—Thistlewood is taken. I saw him twice at Lord Sidmouth's office, looking mean, squalid, and miserable, but I dare say if he was dressed, and above all at the head of 10,000 men, he would be called a good-looking man. Long, who saw him on his trial two years ago, and saw him now with me, would not have known him again. Having had occasion to go two or three times to the Home Office, I saw three or four more of these wretches; they looked so intensely miserable that I pitied them. I went afterwards and called on Yarmouth, where I found the Duke of York, who knew no more of the whole affair than the newspapers told him. When I informed him that the Ministers had *not* dined at Lord Harrowby's, he was at first incredulous and afterwards almost indignant. It seems odd that he has not been called to the council, for Lord Sidmouth told me that the Cabinet felt so much like *parties* in the affair that they wished for a few other Privy Councillors; and I accordingly sent Long* and Peel. I never saw the Duke looking gayer or better.

The mob exclaimed that Thistlewood ought to be hanged. A poor man gave Harrowby in the Park a note addressed to Castlereagh, or as he spelled it Castellroy, warning him of the danger. This was on Tuesday. The Cabinet had been before

* [Right Hon. Sir C. Long, M.P. for Haslemere; Paymaster-General of the Forces.]

apprised of the danger, and this was the confirmation; the letter is so badly written and spelled as to be almost unintelligible.

February 25th.—All the world talking and wondering about the conspiracy. I believe that it is not directly and immediately connected with any larger design, but is a kind of episode in the great plot against the whole establishment, made by a few individuals under the excitement of particular feelings. Almost all great conspiracies have had their underplots created by, but not necessarily connected with, the main design, and this I think will be found to be such a one.

February 26th.—Dined at Robinson's * with our ladies and Miss Temple, Lords Ancrum, Sandon, the Speaker, Warrender, Richard Wellesley, Planta, Perceval, Grant, Huskisson. A very agreeable day; Lady Sarah complained much that she knew nothing of the conspiracy; none of the women were trusted with the secret but Lady Harrowby, whom, and her daughter, it was necessary to get out of the house.

April 29th.—Dinner of the Royal Academy; a picture by Phillips, of Lord Grey, which Lauderdale took for me and told me it was a fine likeness. So it seems several others thought too. I sat at a small table with Messrs. Bankes, Phillips, Campbell, Mulready, Turner, Sir Wm. Elford, and Sir Thos. Heathcote. Bankes, by some mistake in reading the catalogue, thought Lord Grey was by some one else, and praised it to Phillips. The Duke of Sussex speechifying—I never heard anything so bad. In one speech he got into certain ramifications out of which he could not extricate himself. It is the first time I ever heard him, and with my good will should be the last. A bad exhibition; there are but two good pictures in it to my taste; Sir Wm. Grant, by Lawrence, and Two Boys, by Mulready; all the rest is common-place, except Fuseli, who is madder than ever.

There had been, of course, a dissolution of Parliament on the death of George the Third, and Mr. Croker was prevailed upon to stand for Bodmin, where it was tolerably certain that he would succeed in securing a seat in the new House. He went to see his proposed constituents in the early part of March.

* [Right Honourable Frederick John Robinson, created Viscount Goderich, 1827; Earl of Ripon, 1833. Married in 1814 Sarah, daughter of the fourth Earl of Buckinghamshire.]

(*From Mr. Croker's Diary.*)

Arrived at Bodmin and canvassed the borough. Thirty-six corporators, one-third in the rank of gentlemen, the rest trades-people. Their patron is rather their agent than their master; he has no other hold over them than good offices and good will; they jealously elect their own fellow-corporators who must be residents, so that the patron can never get his own private friends into the corporation. Sir John Morshead, a former Lord Warden, was their patron, and on his death or resignation, they placed themselves under the Pitts, Lords Camelford, who had some property in the borough. On Lord Camelford's death, Lord Grenville wished to be patron, but some kind of demur took place, and Mr. C. Rashleigh, who was an attorney and a chief manager in the borough, advised them to invite Lord de Dunstanville, which they did; he does them favours, and I believe may lend money occasionally to some of the inferior corporators. After the canvass we went on and slept at Truro, Prince's Hotel, a large good inn.

March 5th.—Had a visit from Mr. Polwhele,* the poet and historian of Devon and Cornwall; he is in a peck of troubles about his church which he began to repair without proper authority, and his parishioners are now threatening him with law. He appears, like most of the old race of poets, to have very little worldly wisdom. Our modern bards understand the " main chance," as it is called.

Went to church—a fine country church, good organ, very good organist; an indifferent reader; a tolerable preacher; a very crowded and respectable congregation; and the most ridiculous (in voice, manner, and appearance) clerk I ever heard. Absurd epitaph on Mrs. Vivian, mother of Sir H. Went on to Tehidy Park to dinner. A miserable mining country. Lord de Dunstanville has planted a good many pines and firs about his place, but it is cold and dreary; the house is a tolerable *corps de logis,* with four pavilions, but it is neither lighted nor warmed as it ought to be; we were perished with cold.

March 6th.—Went in Lord D——'s carriage to see the great copper mine of Dalcoath, between Redruth and Cam-

---

* [The Rev: Richard Polwhele, a voluminous writer (1760–1838). He was the author of Histories of Devonshire and Cornwall, Anecdotes of Methodism, and other works.]

borne. The mines here are always worked by adventurers, as they are called, who give the Lord of the soil a portion, say one-sixth of the ore produced. Sometimes the Lord has a share in the adventure. The annual expenses of Dalcoath are now about 60,000*l.*, and its produce not more than 10,000*l.* above that sum, and this is considered very prosperous ; in general they little more than clear themselves ; the greatest depth is, I think, 268 fathoms. I was much pleased with the maps and sections of the mines ; all the rest I had seen before elsewhere.

March 8th.—Breakfasted at Truro, and went across the passage to see Tregothnan. Lord Falmouth has spent all his money on the exterior of his house, which he has disfigured with pinnacles or minarets which look like pepper boxes ; the house itself will be but a small one after all. As we returned we thought it right to leave our names for Lord Falmouth who was residing at the vicarage, but on opening the front door we found it led into a parlour where he and Lord Fitzroy Somerset were at breakfast. He was good humoured, even on the subject of the election, though he told me he had made up his mind to the loss of one seat. Returned to Bodmin and dined with Mr. Wallis, who asked Lord Yarmouth, who happened to be at the inn, to dine with us, to the visible and ridiculous annoyance of Gilbert.

March 9th.—The election—proposed by Mr. Raleigh Gilbert, and seconded by Mr. Edyvean ; a good and decent dinner at 3 ; tumultuous and merry ball in the evening. I danced, by order, with Miss Wallis and Miss Stone, the young female representatives, it seems, of two parties in the town. They happened also, luckily for me, to be two of the prettiest damsels in the room, so I was obliged to dance regularly through thirty-six couples four times over. Upon the whole, the affair was at once tiresome and foolish.

March 10th.—Called on all the corporation to return thanks. Mr. Phillips, a clergyman, and Mr. Watkins, an upholsterer—two of what are thought to be a discontented party —were forward in offering their services on a future occasion. Some ladies and gentlemen of the county came to the ball last night in what they call a double horse, *i.c.* the lady riding on a pillion behind the gentleman. At 1 P.M., Lord Yarmouth, who had been also elected at Camelford yesterday, came over to pick me up on our way to town. *Faute de chevaux*, we left our servant in my carriage and came on together in his. Crossed at Torpoint in the dark, and got to the hotel at Plymouth about 9.

March 11th.—Went to breakfast with Lord Exmouth—there I found Lord Clinton; walked through the dockyard and went out in a rowing-boat to the breakwater with Lord Exmouth. We could not proceed many yards from the landing place, as a S.W. wind was breaking the sea over the Breakwater. Returned in a tender in a few minutes—though we had been two hours rowing out—went two miles out of our road to the southward to see Lineham, the seat of my ancestors—a delightful place; slept at Totnes; Seven Stars Inn, better than it looks.

March 12th.—Passed through Exeter and Sidmouth, where we dined, to Crewkerne, where we slept at the "George," a slovenly place. I saw at Sidmouth the *Vale of Tears*, a little cottage where the Duke of Kent died. There is a little stream running through its little lawn. It is at the west side of the Esplanade. Sidmouth is a very agreeable wateringplace, except that the neighbouring roads are hilly, and that there is no sand. The hotel is a good inn with an excellent view of the sea and of the walk or parade which runs along in front of the town.

The patronage of Bodmin is quite personal, and I suspect from his superabundant caution and punctilious manœuvres, that Mr. Davies Gilbert has a mind to succeed Lord de Dunstanville in that office. He took care to assure me that Lord D—— left the whole management to him, and indeed he acted the manager all through with some degree of ostentation, which, perhaps, occasioned Lord D—— to hint, and Mr. and Mrs. Wallis to say plainly, that though he was a Cornish man, and had sat two or three times for Bodmin, he was no more connected with the borough and no more on his own ground than myself. I, however, thought it right to indulge Mr. Gilbert by doing whatever he wished, and by appearing to defer to him. His importance was innocent, amusing, and not unfriendly; his dread of Lord Yarmouth quite laughable.

March 13th.—Passed through Sherborne, and went to see Lord Digby's place; the ruins of the castle are finely situated, but ill taken care of, and no evergreen planted about them. The house was a lodge to the castle; it is a small odd old English house, and when repaired or modernised, has been done in the poorest and most parsimonious way; the staircase is hardly as good as that of the inn where I write. A few pictures, one or two by D. Mytens, probably; called Vandyke. One called Lord Mornington, with the Star of the Bath, and one prodigiously like Lord Wellesley, called the late Lord Digby. The grounds fine; the made water natural, except the head of it near the entrance-gate which ought to be hid with bushes. Went to Wardour, the old castle beautiful, at once sheltered and commanding; the grounds and water fine and natural. We were too late to see the new house, which is large and ugly and would not be a good county hospital. Pent Hill and Wootton, which we intended to see, not shown. Slept at Deptford Inn, very comfortable; stopped at Stonehenge. At a little distance it makes no effect. When you approach and consider it, it rises in height and grandeur. I feel before it as if I were in presence of twenty centuries. I still think, as I always thought, that in its rudeness it exhibits something of the proportion and grandeur mixed with beauty of the Greek Doric, particularly the two triads of stone which are perfect, and which probably backed the altar.

To-day is the chairing of the county members at Wilton, and the road is full of carriages and horsemen proceeding to the show. Most have cockades on both sides of their hats, but of different colours. A gentleman who attended some ladies in a chariot and four, and four servants, drank at 9 in the morning, at Deptford Inn door, a dram of raspberry brandy, and pressed the ladies in the carriage to do the same. They, to be sure, refused, but a clergyman who was of the same party accepted the offer as far as *half a glass*. When they had driven off, the servants on horseback lingered behind and had full glasses, of which, however, they drank but half. All this looks like a state of society which I thought was quite obsolete. Arrived at home (Munster House) at 8 o'clock P.M., and found all well.

March 23rd.—Walter Scott came to town and called upon me; he looks older and not so well as I had hoped to find him, but his spirits are excellent, and he had not been ten minutes with me when he repeated some stanzas of a ballad made on some laird or laird's steward in the west of Scotland, who is represented as sending out the tenants to catch a mermaid which was rumoured to be on the coast. I recollected but one stanza:—

> " Some they fished with long lines,
>   And some they fished with sma',
>   And they caught him plenty of whitings,
>   But the devil a mermaid at a'."

March 25th.—Scott and his son dined at Munster House with Palmerston and Miss Temple, Mr. and Mrs. Arbuthnot, Yarmouth, Torrens, &c. Speaker sent an apology. We had a very agreeable day.

March 27th.—Dined at Lord Anglesey's to meet the Duke of York, Duke of Montrose, Lord Chancellor, Lord Camden, Earl of Lauderdale, Yarmouth, Congreve, Jekyll. A pleasant day. Great apprehensions of the acquittal of Hunt * and his fellows at York, through the time-serving misdirection of the judge.

The belief at that time was very general, as the last entry suggests, that Hunt would not be punished. " Hunt's conviction," wrote Lord Grenville,† " is beyond my hope. . . . It would have been a dreadful thing indeed if it had been established by the result of that trial that the Manchester meeting was, under all its circumstances, a legal assembly." About this time Mr. Peel wrote to Mr. Croker requesting some news, and asking, " Will Hunt and Burdett be acquitted; and if they are, will not their acquittal make a great and lasting impression upon the country ? " In the same letter, the future Prime Minister enters more largely into the field of politics, and reveals the nature of the questions which were evidently then occupying his mind. He seems to foreshadow, in one or two remarkable passages, the change which was destined to take place in public opinion, as well as in his own future policy.

* ["Orator Hunt," arrested in 1819 for being concerned in the "Peterloo" agitation, which had such disastrous consequences; he was sentenced, the following year, to two and a half years' imprisonment.]

† To the Marquis of Buckingham. 'Memoirs of the Court of George IV.,' i. 15.

Mr. Peel to Mr. Croker.   Extract.

Bognor, March 23rd.

Do not you think that the tone of England—of that great compound of folly, weakness, prejudice, wrong feeling, right feeling, obstinacy, and newspaper paragraphs, which is called public opinion—is more liberal—to use an odious but intelligible phrase—than the policy of the Government? Do not you think that there is a feeling, becoming daily more general and more confirmed—that is, independent of the pressure of taxation, or any immediate cause—in favour of some undefined change in the mode of governing the country? It seems to me a curious crisis—when public opinion never had such influence on public measures, and yet never was so dissatisfied with the share which it possessed. It is growing too large for the channels that it has been accustomed to run through. God knows, it is very difficult to widen them exactly in proportion to the size and force of the current which they have to convey, but the engineers that made them never dreamt of various streams that are now struggling for a vent.

Will the Government act on the principles on which, without being very certain, I suppose they have hitherto professed to act? Or will they carry into execution moderate Whig measures of reform? Or will they give up the government to the Whigs, and let them carry those measures into effect? Or will they coalesce with the Whigs, and oppose the united phalanx to the Hobhouses, and Burdetts, and Radicalism? I should not be surprised to see such an union. Can we resist—I mean, not next session or the session after that—but can we resist for seven years Reform in Parliament? Will not, remote as is the scene—will not recent events in Spain diminish the probability of such resistance? And if reform cannot be resisted, is it not more probable that Whigs and Tories will unite, and carry through moderate reform, than remain opposed to each other?

This was not the solution which time and circumstances worked out, but it is evident that Peel—like Croker himself —clearly perceived that the question of Parliamentary Reform could not be perpetually kept upon the shelf, and that the Government of the day, or some other Government, would soon be called upon to deal honestly with it.

There was now, however, but one topic of conversation in London—the conduct of the Queen. From this time till the end of the year, her name and her cause were continually before the country, and discussions upon her guilt or inno-cence raged violently in every grade of society. The populace generally took her side, while the well-to-do classes were unanimously against her. All sorts of apprehensions were entertained as to the results of the commotion in her favour. Mr. Plumer Ward records that one day he met a noble lord in the park, who told him that she was a bold, dangerous, impudent woman, "full of revenge as careless of crime, and that if we did not take care might play the part of Catherine the Second, who by means of the guards murdered her husband, and usurped the throne." * There were, indeed, very serious doubts at one stage of the dispute concerning the fidelity of the troops, and it was known that in London the guards were much more disposed to sympa-thise with the Queen than with the King. "The City is completely with her," wrote Mr. Fremantle to the Duke of Buckingham †—"not the Common Council, but the shop-keepers and merchants—and I have great doubts if the troops are not infected. The press is paid for her abun-dantly, and there are some alehouses open where the soldiers may go and drink and eat for nothing, provided they will drink prosperity and health to the Queen." The truth was that the bulk of the people did not find the life of the King so irreproachable as to give him any right to act the part of a censor of morals. They had heard of Mrs. Fitzherbert, of Lady Conyngham, and of other associates of George the

* 'Memoirs of Mr. Plumer Ward,' ii. 56.
† 'The Court of George IV.,' vol. i. p. 51.

Fourth, and in the popular literature of the day the scandals
of the Court were magnified rather than underrated. Moreover, the people did not believe the stories of the Queen's
misconduct. They were convinced—and perhaps they were
right—that some, at least, of the foreign witnesses had
perjured themselves; and they received with ridicule the
statements made by the Italians, caricatures of whom, with
a label coming out of their mouths, inscribed "Non mi
ricordo," lingered in the shop windows even down to the
youth of the present generation. There were times when
the popular feeling ran so high in favour of the Queen, that
serious riots were anticipated, the Ministry were in a state of
great alarm, and even the Duke of Wellington is said to have
been "earnest for disbanding one of the regiments of
Guards." * Several of the reasons which existed for regarding a portion of the army with distrust are explained in
Mr. Croker's letters.

All that is of any interest on this and kindred subjects in
his diary and correspondence is brought together below,
in the form most convenient for reference.

From Mr. Croker's Diary.

April 12th.—Brougham, it is said, *grossly, has sold the
Queen.* There is no doubt that he has withdrawn himself a
good deal from her, and I believe has been for some time in
underground communication with Carlton House. Certainly
none but madmen could think of making common cause with
her a measure of party; but at the same time there will be
something very revolting in Brougham's taking up the King's
cudgels against her. Caring little as I do for her or B., I
should still be sorry for the sake of public character.

April 15th.—I hear that Leach has been again sent to by
the King, who is still as agitated and anxious as ever about
the Queen. It is said the Cabinet have stated to him that,

* Buckingham Papers—'George IV.,' i. 54, 55.

whatever else may be done hereafter, *Queen* she is, and Queen she must be officially called. Lords Donoughmore and Hutchinson; Congreve, Kinnaird, and Warrender dined with me at Munster House. Kinnaird and Congreve want to pay off the National Debt by confiscation.

April 16th.—Last night's Gazette appoints Lord F. Conyngham Master of the Robes to the King. Lord Hutchinson, talking of the Queen to me yesterday, said, " All the accounts which *we* have received make us fear that her arrival would make a great sensation among the lower and middling orders." He is again in favour and confidence at Carlton House. The King could not have an honester or more judicious friend. It is a pity that he is so deeply committed with the Whigs, for he is in truth a very moderate man in politics, and a very good kind of man in every other respect.

April 19th.—The King came to town from Brighton. Lady C., whom they call the *Vice Queen*, is gone, they say, to her brother's (Denison) * to appease his indignant virtue by the offer of a peerage. It is also said that Legh, the traveller, is to be created a peer on marrying Lady Elizabeth.† This must be nonsense. I remember two years ago the King telling me after dinner that he wished to make Legh a baronet. This was, I since heard, because he was then flirting with Miss Aston, one of Lady H.'s ‡ cousins.

April 22nd.—Brougham and Denman sworn in the day before yesterday as Attorney and Solicitor General to the Queen. Brougham, I hear, wished to secure the profits without the inconveniences of this appointment, and offered not to assume it if Government would give him a patent of precedence, but the Chancellor refused. Dined yesterday at the Comptroller's ; an Admiral Wilson dined there who was a midshipman with Lord St. Vincent when a captain. They have now the same flag at the same masthead; odd enough.

April 27th.—The King went to Parliament ; little applause

* [Lady Conyngham was the eldest daughter of Mr. J. Denison, of the Denbies, near Dorking. She outlived all the famous " Pavilion set," dying in 1861, aged ninety-two.]

† [The daughter of Lady Conyngham. Mr. Thomas Legh, M.P., was the author of a ' Narrative of a Journey in Egypt and the Country beyond the Cataracts," published in 1816.]

‡ [Probably Lady Harriet, second daughter of Lady Conyngham.]

and no great crowd, except of carts and waggons, which blocked up Whitehall for 3 hours after the King had repassed. His Majesty's equipages were very handsome. He came down through Charing Cross; hitherto his father and he had come from St. James's through the park.

June 5th.—The Queen is embarked for England. Lord Hutchinson and Brougham have mismanaged their negotiations sadly.

June 6th.—Queen landed yesterday. People at Brooks's said that Brougham has acted most basely by her. I can hardly believe it; but, at all events, if he finds that her arrival here succeeds, he will back out and rejoin her. Queen came to town at half-past five.

June 7th.—The mob obliged some people near Alderman Wood's (in Audley Street) to put candles in their windows last night. Lord Sidmouth, going home from Cabinet with the Duke of Wellington, could not get into his own house, and the mob broke the windows of the Duke's carriage. I think the Ministers wrong, that is, injudicious in proposing a secret Committee.

June 8th.—A strange debate last night. I was not there, and I find that I cannot even command my attention to read the speeches; but they told me that Castlereagh's was long and vague; Brougham's clever, and particularly so as holding a door open for himself either way; Canning's highly complimentary to the Queen's person and manners.

Nov. 13th.—The Speaker called and sat an hour with me. He thinks that Lord Liverpool ought to go out, conditioning with the King to take Lords Grey and Lansdowne, who would be in such difficulties with all their pledges that they could not hold six months. I think if the King could be persuaded to take the opposition, it would relieve him from a deal of present unpopularity; but he will not, I think, consent to do so, and if he will not, Lord Liverpool, as a man of honour, must stick to him. If the Queen has political courage, and will stand her ground, the trouble is only beginning; but I suspect Lord L. must have some kind of hope that she will not.

Nov. 14th.—The King and the Ministers are again at variance, the King wearied and worn out with this horrid affair; wants to have it ended, and that Ministers should meet Parliament on the 23rd and settle the Queen's allowance, &c. The Ministers wish for delay till the meeting in spring. Lord Donoughmore tells me that the Queen yesterday pledged herself to her friends not to go away, as she had some thoughts of doing ten days ago. If she has strength and courage to push her advantage, she must turn out the Ministers, and may overturn the country, but then she must have a Whig ministry to assist her.

Dec. 15th.—The King sent to desire to see me at one o'clock. He talked to me very freely and fully of public affairs; told me all the details of his communication with Canning, his resignation, and the King's acceptance of it, and finally his commands to Lord Liverpool to propose to Peel. I called on Peel in the evening, as I was going to dine at Yarmouth's, to warn him of what was coming. He had as yet heard nothing, and seems disinclined to accept.

Mr. Croker to Lord Yarmouth.

June 6th, 1820.

DEAR Y.

I came to town last night. The Queen landed yesterday at Dover. The populace drew her to her inn, and pelted away a guard of honour which Colonel Ford foolishly sent to attend her. He also fired a royal salute, for which I think he will be sorry, for it was *almost* against orders, he having been ordered *not* to salute on her birthday. She had not passed Rochester at two this day. Lord Hutchinson and Brougham seem to mismanage the affair, and to have misunderstood one another sadly; for after travelling together, when they got to St. Omer they took up their quarters in different places, and began to fire off *notes* at each other. Hutchinson is thought to have acted, if not wisely, at least honestly and honourably; as much is not said of the other. In short, they have a difference by way of episode in the great piece.

Yours, &c.,

J. W. C.

Mr. Croker to Lord Melville.

June 16th, 1820.

MY DEAR LORD,

We were very much alarmed yesterday evening with a report that the Guards (the 3rd regiment) had mutinied, and

you may judge that at this moment such a rumour *was* very
alarming.   The truth, however, is that this regiment (which
it seems its Royal Colonel the Duke of Glo'ster, has been
endeavouring to manage upon principles of what he thinks
rational and philanthropic discipline), has been long in an
unsatisfactory state; and that they have been lately removed
into temporary barracks in the mews; this removal from
quarters and a good deal of duty are supposed to have dis-
gusted them; and the lower orders of the people knew
on Wednesday and yesterday morning that the regiment intended to strike work, as the tradesmen would say.   The
adjutant and non-commissioned officers either did not know
of the intention or did not report it (and either case seems
very serious).   As soon as the thing was known, measures
were taken to get their ammunition, and some ten or dozen
of the men refused to give it up.   It is not very clear to
what extent of insubordination they went, certainly not a
great way, far enough, however, to render their immediate
departure from town necessary, and orders were given for
them to march at three this morning; all last night they
individually talked of not marching, and several of them removed their *kits* from the barracks and seemed inclined to
disband themselves, but all this came to nothing; and at four
this morning one division was paraded and marched, *one man*
only having dared to refuse to shoulder arms.   They are
now quartered about Hounslow, and the reports of their conduct are satisfactory.   The second division is to march to-
morrow, and in the meanwhile is kept in the mews with the
gates locked.   They are said to express shame and contrition
for their offence.   The people, who assembled in very small
numbers about the gates, seemed to take no part with the
soldiers, but rather ridiculed them.   The business is now I
hope over.

Mr. Peel to Mr. Croker.   Extract.

Mickleham, near Leatherhead, August 10th, 1820.

I do think the Queen's affair very formidable.   It is a
famous ingredient in the cauldron which has been bubbling
a long time, and upon which, as it always seemed to me, the
Government never could discern the least simmering.   They
applied a blow-pipe, however, when they omitted the Queen's

name in the Liturgy: when they established a precedent of
dethronement for imputed personal misconduct.   Surely
this was not the time for robbing Royalty of the exterior
marks of respect, and for preaching up the anti-divine right
doctrines.   If she be worse than Messalina, nothing but the
· united voice of King, Lords, and Commons should have degraded her.   I certainly would have tried her the moment
she set her foot in England, but I would have prayed for her
as Queen till she had been tried.   What is to be the end of
it ?   What mean all the compliments to Colonel Bosanquet
and 143 City light horse men ?   Did you read them ?   Is the
army suspected ?   I *saw* the Queen the other day pass the
barracks in Hyde Park, and at the moment of her passing
there was an immense shout.   I did not see whether the
soldiers joined in it or not.   The 'Morning Chronicle' says
they did.

Ever most affectionately, I am,

My dear Croker,

ROBERT PEEL.

Mr. Croker to Mr. Peel.   Extract.

September 1st, 1820.

MY DEAR PEEL,

As to the Queen's affair, I can only tell you that all the
disgusting details proved against her seem to make no change
in the minds or numbers of her partisans.   This is natural—
they adopted her because she was in opposition to the King
and the Government, and her personal conduct, if it only
continues impudent and violent enough, is of no kind of
importance to the mob.   What the opinion of the sober
middle classes may be, I do not know, but I have never met
any one of any kind who believes her to be innocent;
and if the country believes her to be guilty, I cannot
but think that they must approve of the proceedings substantially, and that there will be no difficulty in passing
the Bill—although the Whigs with their usual half-sided
wisdom will oppose the *form* without venturing to impugn
the *substance.*

In fact, I now think the whole of the Queen's chance is
narrowed to a point.   She had two lieutenants of the English
Navy with her in the polacre, and through most of her

journeys. Now if she does not produce them, as they are both on the spot, she is undone ; and all that Majocchi and Dumont, &c., have sworn must receive universal credit. I myself am persuaded that she will examine them ; and I believe it for this reason, that Hownam, one of the lieutenants, is married in France, and was obliged to go thither lately to his wife's lying in ; now this was as good an opportunity and excuse as could be desired for his absence, but he is come back. I therefore conclude that they intend to produce him. Now can they be mad enough to produce him unless he will contradict* the whole of what all the other witnesses have said ? and if he does contradict them, I am afraid, as he is a man of hitherto good character, that he will be believed against the whole host of Italians. This consideration excites the only doubt I have on the case.

There was a report yesterday in the Lords that Brougham did not intend to ask for any delay. If Hownam and Flynn will deny the facts stated, he is quite right to go on directly, and take advantage of the present ferment, which would by the evidence of these two English officers be blown up into a conflagration that would reduce the whole proceeding to ashes, and might involve the Government, the Throne, and the constitution in the destruction. In this case we ought all to be at our posts on the 17th, because the case is nearly closed against her, and the examination of the two lieutenants could not take two days. But all this you will see is mere conjecture upon which you can form your opinion as well as I, from the premises which I have stated to you.

Yours ever,

J. W. C.

Mr. Croker to Mr. Peel.   Extract.

November 3rd, 1820.

Dear Peel,

The debate still goes on. Grosvenor violent against the Bill ; Harewood, hare-hearted, thought the Queen guilty, but the Bill impolitic. Donoughmore for the Bill exposed Harewood's inconsistency. Grey in a long and laboured speech introduced his conscientious verdict of *not guilty*. At half-

* [He attempted to contradict, but broke down on his cross-examination.]

past three Liverpool got up to answer him, and will probably speak till seven. Some people think that they will divide to-night. I think not—but what you will stare at is that I believe after carrying the second reading and voting that the *preamble is proved* they will drop the bill.*

Mr. Croker to Lord Yarmouth.

November 14th, 1820.

Dear Y.,

It is hard to find the truth of anything. I told you that the King and his Ministers were agreed, and *mutually* satisfied ; such *was* the tone of Blomfield's room. To-day I learn that Fife House and Carlton House *are*, or at least *were*, two hours ago at variance, and what do you think the variance is ? The King wants to have the Queen's allowance, palace, &c., &c., *immediately* settled by Parliament, while the Ministers wish to postpone it to the next year. I leave you to meditate upon so wonderful a change of sentiments as this seems to imply. In fact, the poor K. is weary of the whole affair, and only anxious for a little peace and quiet. The Ministers are resolved not to replace her in the Liturgy, and to go out if necessary upon that, but not else. The Queen has been for the last fortnight upon the point of what the Scotch call flitting ; but her quite unexpected triumph has given her new life and courage, and she yesterday pledged herself to her friends not to go.

Yours,

J. W. C.

Before the close of the year everybody was becoming tired of the Queen and her case. The tone of the public mind was cleverly expressed in an epigram written by some one on the *malapropos* passage which concluded Mr. Denman's speech for the Queen, and in which he begged the House to tell her to " go and sin no more " :—

* [" The bill was carried by a majority of 28, 123 voting for and 95 against it. This majority, however, dwindled down to 9 upon the third reading, four days afterwards, upon which Lord Liverpool at once intimated that he would proceed no further with the measure."—Martin's ' Life of Lyndhurst,' p. 182.]

N 2

> " Most gracious Queen, we thee implore
> To go away and sin no more ;
> But, if that effort be too great,
> To go away at any rate." *

The Queen herself now saw that her cause had been taken up by the Whigs chiefly to suit their own purposes. " No one, in fact, care for me," she wrote, in her broken English, " and this business has been more cared for as a political affair, dan as de cause of a poor forlorn woman." After the Bill against her had been withdrawn, she sank comparatively out of sight, and the public became more and more indifferent to her until, happily for herself, she died in the following year.

The event of 1820, which was of profound and lasting moment to Mr. Croker personally, was the death of his only child, a son still of tender years, but old enough to have engaged the deepest affections of his father's heart. From this time he appears to have relinquished all ambition, and to have studiously avoided the opportunities of political advancement which presented themselves to him. " I look upon office," he wrote at the end of 1821, " as Hamlet did on life, and would not be displeased with him who should take it from me. Indeed, since the death of my poor child, I have been meditating a retreat, and would have executed it but that I am afraid of my own powers of bearing solitude and *désœuvrement*. However, I conveyed lately to Lord Liverpool my readiness, if my office could facilitate his arrangements, to place it at his disposal. My poor wife is still worse than I am, and reverberates all my griefs upon me with double intensity. She is bodily ill and mentally miserable, and spends her time between pain and sorrow. She has not been able to walk across the room these six months."

---

* [' Diary and Correspondence of Lord Colchester,' iii. 181.]

The child was taken ill, as it appears from Mr. Croker's diary, on the 25th of April. "His illness," he writes five days later, "is the same as he had last year—fits of sickness and dulness, with intervals in which he is lively and well. Sent for Sir William Knighton. He thinks nothing of it." But the sufferer continued to grow worse, and his father records on the 6th of May that the torpor had increased— "he takes nothing; he has an odd kind of nervous sighing or groaning, very frequent." The doctors—Dr. Baillie now with Sir William Knighton — again assured the anxious parents that there was no occasion for alarm. But they appear to have had a sad presentiment of the truth. Mr. Croker, during these days and nights of suspense, rarely left his child's bedside. There are five days on which he made no entry in his diary. At last there are three entries, one made some months after the date :—

May 15th.—My child departed this life at exactly nineteen minutes after five in the morning. God be merciful to us and enable us to support this loss. I write this the 16th.

May 16th.—The head of our child was opened by Dr. Baillie, Mr. White, and Mr. Jackson. It appears that water on the brain was the cause of our misfortune. (I write this nine months after, and feel this dreadful loss as keenly as I did at the first moment. My poor, pretty boy !)

May 22nd.—An anniversary which we had intended to keep, and of which our poor child was to be the ornament. Alas ! this day week he died.

"My poor wife is heart-broken," he writes to Robert Peel ; "heaven preserve you from such a calamity as has beaten us down." "I am almost unwilling," Peel wrote to him in reply, "to break in by any allusion upon the sacred subject of your grief, for I know how futile every attempt must be to offer any other consolations to you than those to which your own mind has already had recourse. I most deeply and sincerely sympathise with you, and earnestly pray for every alleviation of misery that it is possible for you and the partner of your woes to receive."

This grief tinged the whole of Mr. Croker's subsequent life. On the anniversary of the dark day he never ceased to visit the spot in the churchyard at Wimbledon where his lost child was buried, and almost his last thoughts turned upon his desire to make arrangements by which they might both rest in the same grave. Mrs. Croker's affliction was still more distressing; she could not be persuaded to revisit any of the houses where she had lived with her son, and it was necessary to take her abroad in the hope of diverting her mind from what proved to be a hopeless grief. Some consolation the bereaved couple derived from the society and companionship of a sister of Mrs. Croker, who was adopted by Mr. Croker as his own daughter before his son was born, and who became, as it has been stated, Lady Barrow. But there are many evidences throughout Mr. Croker's writings that to his own last hour, the old wound reopened and bled whenever he realised that the one great hope of his life had been taken from him.

The following lines were written by Mr. Croker, and placed over the child's grave at Wimbledon :—

> " Oh pity us who lost when Spencer died,
>   Our joy, our hope, our pleasure, and our pride.
>   In him we saw, or fancied, all such youth
>   Could show of talents, tenderness, and truth ;
>   And hoped to other eyes his ripened powers
>   Would keep the promise they had made to ours.
>   But God a different, better growth has given,
>   The seed he planted here now blooms in heaven."

CHAPTER VII.

1821.

MR. CROKER'S private sorrows, and the redoubled attention
which he wisely paid to the duties of his office and to the
literary work he had taken in hand, prevented him from
making any record of the political events of the early part of
the year. There is thus no direct reference in his papers to
Canning's resignation of his office as President of the Board
of Control, to the continued wrangles in Parliament over
the question what was to be done with the Queen, or to
Mr. Plunkett's motion in favour of the removal of Catholic
disabilities — upon which, for the first time, a majority
was gained for the cause of Catholic emancipation. Nor
is there any allusion to the expectation, which was so
generally entertained at the time, that Mr. Peel would be
induced to take office in the place of Mr. Canning, who had

retired from office that he might not have occasion to vote against the Queen. Mr. Croker, it has been said, was one of the first to perceive Peel's great powers, and he was certainly not blind to the growing opinion that a distinguished career lay before the ex-Secretary for Ireland. In the closing month of the previous year he had written the following letter :

Mr. Croker to Lord Yarmouth.

December 20th, 1820.
DEAR Y.

There seems to be no doubt that Peel has been or will be offered office, and as little that he had declined or will decline it. I confess that I myself would do so ; and with a great fortune and domestic habits like his, I think the stormy sea of politics can have little temptation for him. But then, what is the Government to do ? I cannot tell ; they have not one man in the house who can speak so as to command attention, and though good speeches do not perhaps get many votes, they prevent many shy votes going away.

In short a Government cannot go on without the gift of the gab. Suppose Lord Liverpool were to make Brougham an offer ?

Seriously, I think they will move Pole or Robinson to Canning's place, and will appoint a successor to the vacated office not in the Cabinet. This is the best thing they can do. I hear that the country gentlemen are favourable, and that if we had but a spokesman or two we should shuffle through the session.

Yours,

J. W. C.

Mr. Peel, however, did not take office at that time. He was not anxious to become involved in the unpopularity which Ministers had brought upon themselves by the Queen's trial—for as such it was regarded—nor had he any ambition to assist them to " shuffle through the session." He therefore kept aloof from public life till January, 1822, when he succeeded Lord Sidmouth as Home Secretary.*

Mr. Croker, anxious to find some distraction for his thoughts, threw himself with greater ardour than ever into the affairs of his office, and in his hours of leisure he worked hard at the letters of Lady Hervey, an edition of which he had undertaken to prepare for the press, at Mr. Murray's desire. As usual, when he had engaged to perform any task of this kind, he threw out his net far and wide for information, and thought no pains too great to ensure accuracy in small things as well as in great. Before arranging his plans, he wrote as follows to a descendant of Lady Hervey :—

Mr. Croker to the Earl of Mulgrave.

Mr. Murray has just put into my hands a volume of letters of Mary Lepell, Lady Hervey, your grandmother, which he is now publishing. I have always taken an interest in Lady Hervey, to whom Horace Walpole introduced me (though she was dead twenty years before I was born) ; and as well for her sake as out of regard to her descendants, I am anxious that the forthcoming publication should do credit and justice to this agreeable and amiable lady. The letters in Mr. Murray's possession he knows little or nothing about, not even to whom they are addressed. They are evidently not originals but copies carefully made. I enclose you one sheet which contains part of three letters. You will observe in the third page a Mrs. P——ps mentioned with great regard, but with so much formality, that it can hardly mean her own daughter, married to your lordship's father about three months preceding the date of this letter. Can your lordship form any guess to whom the letters were addressed, and who Mrs. P——ps can be ?†   I believe your father had a

---

* " Peel has declined accepting office, but whether it is because he likes to live retired with his pretty wife, or that he thinks the Ministry will not stand, I know not."—Mr. Wilbraham to Lord Colchester, 'Colchester Correspondence,' iii. 202.

[† These letters were addressed to the Rev. E. Morris. The lady was Mrs. Phipps.]

sister who died unmarried; she might in the fashion of that day be called " Mrs."

The whole collection of these letters is large enough to make a couple of volumes; but though they are all full of good sense and good taste, they want variety; they are all addressed to one person, and are almost all of a grave turn. Now I think it is a pity that so very *narrow* a view of Lady Hervey's talents should be exhibited, and I cannot but wish that her family would enable me to enliven, or rather to diversify, the publication with some letters of a different class, and if, as I should guess, she has left any little original pieces of her own composition, I should be exceedingly glad to have them. I intend to give Mr. Murray a little *sketch* of her life, and if you could help me to any original materials, I need hardly say what an advantage it would be; and I suppose also I need hardly say, that as my share in the publication will be anonymous ·and of a very humble character, I can have neither any object of reputation or profit from it.

Ever, my dear lord,

Yours affectionately,

J. W. C.

This work was brought out in May, 1821, and was the first of several collections of the kind which Mr. Croker was the means of giving to the public.

There are no entries in the diary of this year until the end of May, when we find the following :—

May 31*st.*—Lord Melville * informs me that he is about to be *kicked upstairs* (his expression) to be Secretary of State for the Home Department. He does not wish it, but Lord Liverpool and the King insist upon it. The fact I take to be that Lord Sidmouth is tired of so laborious an office, and indeed unequal to its duties, and that Lord Liverpool is anxious to bring in Canning again; but as the King could be hardly expected to like to have Canning in an office of such close and constant personal intercourse as the Home Department, Lord Melville must go there, and Canning come to the Admiralty,

---

* [The second Lord Melville.]

for which he was designed in 1807. He (Melville) intimates to me that Peel has been offered, and declined to come. It is not quite clear *what* Peel was offered; but it is clear that Lord Melville understands him to decline everything. Lord M. said that Wilmot and Twiss had been mentioned to him as Under Secretary. I advise Wilmot;* Twiss has not yet weight enough with the House. I suggested Spencer Perceval,† but without any expectation that he could be seriously thought of yet; his late unsteady conduct is not forgotten. A place at one of the Boards would suit him better.

June 1st.—Lord Melville and I saw Peel and the Speaker walking on the Parade under our windows in deep converse. Lord Melville said, " I have not lost all hope that Peel may be persuaded to join. I am sure the Speaker will give him good advice."

Lord Melville thinks, and I agree with him, that Canning, *for his own sake,* ought not to take office *just now;* and I go on to say, that he ought not to take a *better* office than that which he has left. He has so many enemies, and so many imputations, false and groundless, but general and credited, are made against him, that he ought to be more cautious than another man of what he does.

June 2nd.—Met Peel in Pall Mall; he was coming to me, so I turned back with him. He told me that Lord Liverpool had sent for him, and made him an offer of Cabinet office, but that it was done in a strange, shuffling, hesitating sort of way, that nothing specific was offered, but that he conjectured, from the style and the expressions, that Lord Liverpool referred, in his own mind, to the Board of Control. Peel gave an answer as vague as the application. He is now inclined to write to Lord Liverpool, to understand him as distinctly offering the India Board, and to refuse it. His reasons are, first, he refused it before when the Government was in danger, and he thinks it might look shabby to take it now when the vessel has righted, but he would not care for mere appearances or misrepresentation of his motives; but, secondly, he

* [Mr. R. Wilmot, M.P. for Newcastle, Staffordshire.]

† [The late minister's son. His " late unsteady conduct " was doubtless a reference to his enthusiasm in behalf of the Queen. It was he who suggested to Brougham at her trial the effective quotation from Milton—
" What seemed his head
The likeness of a kingly crown had on."]

does not think he could be of use in that office. He has no
taste or turn for debate unless when obliged by his office to
take part in it, &c.   Neither of these motives satisfy me, and
I begged him not to write a final answer, or, if he did, at
least to limit his refusal to the office in question. He seems
generally disinclined to official life, but *haud credo*.

June 3rd.—Paid my usual visit to [Lord] Yarmouth. He
told me that Lord Sidmouth was going out and Canning
coming in, and Lord Melville shifting, and that Sturges
Bourne was to be Secretary of the Admiralty. But not
a word of Peel. I of course said nothing of what I knew
from Lord M. or from Peel, but answered that I thought
all the rest probable, except as to Bourne, which could
hardly be without my knowledge.

Yarmouth had betted General Gascoyne twenty guineas
that Canning would be in office before the 25th of June, and
he is now quite sure of winning. I tell him that I doubt it,
and so I do; for even if he chooses to accept Lord Liverpool's
offer, it can hardly be accomplished before the 25th; but the
Speaker tells Yarmouth that we shall adjourn on that day,
and of course the writs must be previously moved. Called at
Carlton House, and was just beginning to have some talk
with Blomfield, when the King sent for him.

I fancy that I see Lord Liverpool's game. He wants,
à toute force, to have Canning in. Canning, I presume, feels
reluctant to return to the India Board; therefore Lord Sidmouth must ask for *otium cum dignitate* in the Duchy or
presidency of the Council. Then Lord Melville is to be persuaded that Peel would not consent to succeed Sidmouth,
and that *he* must; he reluctantly consents, and then Canning
may have the Admiralty, and Peel may be distinctly offered
the India Board. But, as there may be some hitch in the
arrangement, Lord Liverpool keeps Peel open to have him at
hand to put into any gap which he may not be otherwise
able to fill up, in the Admiralty if Canning should refuse, or
in the Home Department, if that should be more convenient.
In short, he wishes to have Peel under his lee; he was
obliged to say *something* to him lest Peel should be offended
if he heard of these changes first from other quarters ; but he
could not speak plain as he does not yet quite know what he
has to give.

June 4th.—Saw Blomfield: quite clear that the King
does not wish for Canning's return; insists upon the Admi-

ralty's being an office of much personal intercourse, not quite so much as the Home Department, but enough so to require confidence and cordiality. B. talked as if the King did not know of Peel's *refusal* of the India Board in the spring, which is next to impossible; "but if he *did* refuse then, how can they expect him to accept the *same* office now?" It seems, therefore, that the King will suggest Peel either for the Admiralty or the Home Office, if for no other purpose than to keep Canning out.

Peel called on me, and says he is going to Lord Liverpool to refuse the *India Board*. I cannot blame him, for certainly his accepting now what he before refused would be liable to misinterpretation, and as he dislikes office, and is really above all little motives, it would be hard to expect him to subject himself to the imputation of acting from such. I endeavoured to convince Peel that, if not in Government, he would soon be in Opposition.

June 5th.—Goulburn called on me. As he seldom comes, and as he began immediately to talk about the changes, I think he rather wished to find out how Peel was disposed through me. Peel had spoken to him last night, and had stated Lord Liverpool's offer of the India Board as much more distinct than I had understood it; and it seems that, after leaving me yesterday, Peel went to Lord Liverpool and verbally and positively refused it. Goulburn regretted this, and when I rather justified it, dropped that Peel could hardly expect to have a higher office than Canning, which is true. Goulburn, I have no doubt, loves Peel and has no particular regard for Canning, but wishes that we should keep all together. We laughed about his refusing to go to Ireland on account of the expense, and Charles Grant laying by 4000*l.* a-year out of it. He agrees with me that Wilmot would make a better Under Secretary than Twiss; indeed he is very anxious for Wilmot. Twiss he thinks highly of, but would advise him to stick to his law. I spoke to him of Spencer Perceval, and suggested a place at one of the Boards for him.

June 6th.—The negotiations are all at a stand. The King holds out against Canning, and last evening Lord Sidmouth told Lord Melville that he had consented to stay a little longer; but I do not think the King will long resist; he is too good-natured to bear personal grudge for any length of time.

Yarmouth called to tell me "that Peel was *yesterday* offered the India Board to reconcile the King to Canning's appointment." This is erroneous in fact, and I do not see how it could be just in reasoning, even if the fact were true; but Y. insisted he had it from a *good quarter*, which only shows me that at Carlton House Peel is set up against Canning. Yarmouth says that he supposes the Ministers will now use the *droit du plus fort* with the King, since they have discovered H.M.'s attempt some months ago to bring in the Opposition through Donoughmore, who had, he says, authority to speak to Lord Lansdowne, but came back to represent that he could not in honour make any proposition to Lord L. that should not include Lord Grey; that the King hesitated for some while, but at last gave authority to include Lord Grey. I can hardly believe all this; it must have been before Donoughmore's wishing me to bring him and Lord Liverpool together. In short, I do not believe it.

June 7th.—Peel and I walked down to the Court of Claims. As we went he told me of his interview of Monday with Lord Liverpool, and he now agrees that Lord L. was playing a game, and, he thinks, not quite a fair one. When Peel said that he came to decline the offer of the India Board, Lord L. said hastily, "And *anything else* I should offer?" Peel begged to say that, when anything else should be offered, it would be time enough to decide on it, as he could not presume to refuse what perhaps never would be tendered for his acceptance. He thought Lord L. was peevish and embarrassed. I am sure that, what between his fear of having Peel as his Chancellor of the Exchequer and his desire of forcing Canning on the King, he would be glad to have a general refusal from Peel, who would have been but too ready to give one if he had not suspected that Lord L. wished for one, which piques him a little.

June 8th.—Canning arrived the night before last. Lord Melville says the King is angry with Peel. This can hardly be for Peel's refusal of the India Board, as he himself anticipated it.

The King is gone to-day to Windsor. What a wonderful constitution! He has had a fit of the gout this last fortnight which would have reduced any other man to helplessness. He was in bed the day before yesterday, and, for aught I know, yesterday, and to-day he has frisked off to Windsor.

The great Derby race at Epsom to-day. The Queen was

there, little noticed, less applauded. They say that on her return she was *hissed*—this seems doubtful.

The King has sent out cards for a children's ball for the 13th inst. He has honoured my little girl with his recollection and an invitation; he was greatly taken with her at Brighton.

June 9th.—The Speaker spent an hour and a half with me. We talked over Peel's affair, and, as Peel before told me, we agree nearly in our view of it. We both wish him to be in office, and both would have *rather* advised him to accept the India Board, but neither feel that he has done wrong in acting upon his own view of the awkwardness in which he thinks an office without Parliamentary business would place him. I think, however, we both agree in thinking that it is perhaps looking a little too high at first, because, in fact, except the Chancellor of the Exchequer, and occasionally the Secretaries of State, no one has *ex-officio* any distinct share of House of Commons business; the argument which applies to the India Board applies equally to the First Lord of the Admiralty. The upset, however, is that all is at a stand, and that the King will not have Canning. I know the King's placability, and do not think this obstacle likely to last long.

June 10th.—The King is not quite so well as he was; the jaunt to Windsor was too much for him. He is resolved to go to Ireland by long sea. I am sorry for it, and do not think he will accomplish it.

Had a talk with Blomfield, chiefly with a wish to explain Peel's refusal not to have been general, but limited to the Board of Control; but this without any authority from him, and indeed without any opinion of my own whether he would or would not refuse other offers if made. The King is by no means dissatisfied with Peel, as had been stated to me; and his refusal was, it seems, put to His Majesty upon the score of health. The King still disinclined to admit Canning. I advised him to consent to Canning, on condition that Peel should be Chancellor of the Exchequer. This would *at once* cool Liverpool, Castlereagh, and Canning, and the failure of the negotiation would then lie with them and not with the King, who, of course, is averse to giving a decided exclusion to Canning.

June 11th.—They tell me that the Chancellor says that he will resign if Sidmouth does. This must be the King's mode of excluding Canning. Poor Lady Liverpool died at

half-past five this morning. An amiable creature ; she has
been long wasting away, and if grief was not selfish, we
should have no reason to grieve for her. I am really sorry
for her. She felt for our sorrows this time last year, and
I have not seen her since. She was the only Hervey I ever
knew in whom one could not perceive some little *travers.*

June 12*th.*—Yarmouth, Lowther, Shawe, Watson, Smith,
and the two Hooks dined with me. Much punning, none
very good.

The *Courier* to-night publishes a correspondence between
Canning and Burdett * ; the latter comes shabbily off, for he
denies a meaning which his words have, if they have any.

June 13*th.*—Took my little girl † in the evening to the
King's ball. We arrived at five minutes after the appointed
hour, half-past 8, and His Majesty was already in the room.
In spite of his gout he walked about for full two hours without sitting down. He was very gracious to Nony, and kissed
her at her departure. Princess Augusta also took great notice
of her. I really believe that of the nobility present the
majority were persons who had voted for the Queen. There
were the Duke of Devonshire, Lords Lansdowne, Grey,
Grantham, &c. Nay, there were even some ladies who had
visited the Queen.

None but the children danced, and they only sat down to
supper ; it was a very pretty *fête.* We got home a little
after 12. Lady Conyngham was, I think, a little too much
en évidence.

The King took me aside in the beginning of the evening,
and said, in allusion to the proposed changes, that " they
were madmen (meaning the Ministers) not to let well alone."
After a few words more of disapprobation, he asked *me* how
I should like the change proposed for the Admiralty. I
replied that it was *my duty* to like anything which should be
settled. " Ah ! " he replied, " but it's not mine." I thought
he received Lord Grey as coldly as he well could in his own
house, and Lord Lansdowne much less formally.

---

* [In a letter on Parliamentary Reform, Burdett had called Canning
the champion of a system by the hocus pocus tricks of which he and his
family received public money.]

† [This allusion in Mr. Croker's letters or diaries always refers to Miss
Rosamond Croker, his adopted daughter, afterwards Lady Barrow. Her
pet name was Nony.]

June 14*th.*—The King dined with the Duke of Devonshire.

June 15*th.*—I hear the dinner yesterday was not as magnificent as might have been expected; no gold plate and no fine china. There was an assembly in the evening. Lord Wm. Bentinck was at the dinner with his ribband of the Bath over the wrong shoulder.

June 17*th.*—A curious story going about that the King gave Princess Charlotte a remarkably fine sapphire on her marriage, and that after her death he asked it back as being a royal jewel, that Prince Leopold returned it reluctantly, but that, lo! Lady Darnley has recognized it on Lady Conyngham's neck. Another story now a-going I know to be false; they say that at the ball Princess Augusta asked leave of the King to place the Princess Feodore* in a quadrille, and that his Majesty answered, "You must ask Lady Conyngham; I have left it all to her." I had myself the honour of assisting Princess Augusta in making some quadrilles of the little folks, and she certainly never asked the King or the lady about them; and, after the first one or two dances, the King and she went and sat behind a door in the ante-room and danced *qui voudrait.* If there be any kind of colour for this story, it must be that Princess Feodore might have been thought too old for the rest of the dancers. I happened to be present when she and the Duchess of Kent came in, and the King kissed her and received her with great kindness and even affection. I saw this, for there were few come at the time.

June 18*th.*—Went to the House of Commons to vote for 6000*l.* to the Duke of Clarence. It had been voted in 1817, but he was then advised to decline it. Three divisions, 144 to 18, 167 to 30, 131 to 81. The last was on a strong point, whether H.R.H. should have the arrears since 1817. Sir James Graham, as H.R.H.'s friend, made a most absurd speech, in which he said that the Duke was very unwilling to decline the allowance in 1817, but had been over-persuaded by wiser heads, meaning the Ministers.

June 19*th.*—I hear that public report gives me Huskisson's place in the Woods and Forests, and sends him to the India Board. The latter is probable, the other absurd. I presume no one would take the trouble to advance me (as such a

---

* [Feodore, Princess of Hohenlohe Langenburg, was a daughter of the Duchess of Kent by her first marriage, and consequently half-sister of Queen Victoria.]

change would be considered) without my consent, and I would much rather stay where I am; as long as I am able to hold office, I do not wish to change.

They talk of a correspondence between the Duke of Devonshire and Lady Jersey, because the Duke had (at the King's desire *s'entend*) put her off from coming to his assembly the other night. She rates him soundly for pusillanimity and want of gallantry, &c.

June 20*th.*—Rode a little with the Speaker. He is vexed that, in consequence of the prorogation, he cannot walk as *Speaker*, and is more vexed that he must walk, as he says 5 degrees below his rank as a Privy Councillor. The King is to occupy his house for the night before and the night after the Coronation. I hear that Lady Spencer has also written angrily to the Duke of Devonshire because she and Lord Spencer were not invited to his dinner to the King. Lady Jersey's correspondence is, they say, handed about, but I have not seen it or any one who has.

June 21*st.*—Grant tells me that he hears of my going to the Woods and Forests from the Opposition. *Grand Merci!* Canning made an excellent speech last night on the subject of the self-sacrifice of the Hindostanee widows.

Lowther is gone down to the Cottage at Windsor, where the King has been ever since Monday on account of Ascot races.

The Queen was at Astley's last night, and received as one would suppose *such* a person would be by *such* company as is ordinarily found at *such* a place.

June 22*nd.*—I hear the Duke of Devonshire is gone down to the Cottage. It is clear that the King is playing the game of softening, if not conciliating, the Opposition. He thinks he will obtain domestic quiet by that line of conduct, and so he may for a time, but, in the long run, I do not think it can succeed. Party is in England a stronger passion than love, avarice, or ambition; it is often compounded of them, but is stronger than any of them individually.

The King was twice on the course at Ascot, Tuesday and yesterday, looking ill the first day, but well and lively the second.

June 23*rd.*—I find that the Queen's reception at Astley's was not at all so flattering as I had heard. Orby Hunter, who was there, and who is an impartial witness, assured me that it was quite the contrary. She took an odd mode of procuring applause. At one moment there happened to be a

profound silence in the house, of which she took advantage
to stand up and curtsey all round. This was answered by
some applause, but the majority was against her.

In the month of July, there was celebrated the Coronation
of the King, amid every circumstance of splendour—and as
some said of extravagance—that the heralds and other officials
could devise. The new crown alone had cost £54,000, and
£24,000 was spent upon robes. At a later period there
was a great outcry, in Parliament and out of it, concerning
this expenditure.

July 18th.—The King sent at 10 A.M. to desire me to come
to him. I did so. He told me that he had heard that I did
not mean to see the coronation (it was settled that I should
stay at the Admiralty to be at hand to give directions in case
of any confusion), that he knew the reason, and was obliged
to me for it, and that, to make me what amends he could, he
begged me to accept a gold snuff-box, which he pulled out
from under his pillow, with a fine medallion of himself. He
also sent a gold coronation medal to my wife, and one to
"*the darling little girl,*" as he was pleased to call her. He
complains of Lord Liverpool's temper and manners. The
king went at night to sleep at the Speaker's; some ill-
disposed persons, not half a dozen, I am told, cried "Queen!"
as he went along.

July 19th.—I went to the Speaker's house in the morning
to see Knighton, who is attending my wife. I sat an hour
with Blomfield and his son, who were dressing in their silks
and satins; the boy's dress as falconer was pretty. The
King heard I was there, and sent for me. He was waiting,
dressed in his underclothes, for the public officers to proceed.
Even after he had put on his robes and hat, most cumbrous
and heavy, he had to wait full half an hour for the Great
Chamberlain, Lord Gwydir, who, it seems, had torn his robes,
and was obliged to wait to have them mended. I dare say
the public lays the blame of the delay on the King, who was
ready long before anybody else. His Majesty told me the
story of the Queen's various attacks on the lines of circum-
vallation and her several repulses.

She had passed by the Admiralty on her retreat, attended

by a thin and shabby mob. She pointed to "God save the
King!" which was over the screen for the evening illumin-
ations, and her mob hooted.

We had rumours all day of mobs and riots. I went myself to see what had happened; it turned out that half a
dozen windows were broken in half a dozen places, and that
was all. There was no more crowd opposite the Queen's
door than served to fill the pavements; the centre of the
street was quite clear.

The shoals of people that crowded the streets and parks all
this day and all night are incomprehensible. The day indeed
was remarkably fine, and I should really believe that there
were full a million of people out of doors.

The suggestion relative to the canopy was adopted.

How fortunate my suggestion about a *fête* in the parks has
been, and hardly less fortunate the change from the *Green* to
Hyde Park. I am confident that 500,000 people were par-
takers of this beautiful *fête*.*

The King was bled *profusely* last night. Knighton was
very uneasy in the morning as to H.M.'s getting through the
day. This mode of bleeding is a strange kind of tonic, but
the King finds that it does him good.

Mr. Croker to Mr. Peel. Extracts.

July 24th, 1821.

My dear Peel,

You can have no idea either of the splendour of the
pageant or of the good order and good luck which accompanied the ceremony of the coronation . . . . I assure you it
was not only worth seeing, but, according to Dr. Johnson's
distinction, worth going to see, particularly the procession on
the platform and the fête in Hyde Park. Lord Gwydir had
too much to do and yet did it pretty well. One little mortification he suffered. He *abused*, some say *struck* with his
wand, one of the heralds for some supposed breach of duty.
The herald, with great good sense, took the blow as a mere
mistake and said, "My lord, you do not know our functions,
characters, or duties; we are not servants—my family were

---

* [Chinese bridges had been thrown over the ornamental water in St.
James's Park, and fireworks exhibited from temporary platforms, at Mr.
Croker's suggestion.]

gentlemen five hundred years before a Burrell was heard of."
Lord Gwydir was in fact in the wrong, and had treated the
herald by mistake as if he were one of the attendants.

The Queen and Wood were hooted by the spectators. She
went off in a rage of disappointment. She, no doubt, came
down not to get in, for she took care to have but one ticket,
and that one irregular, although she might have had fifty good
ones, and would have been let in if she had produced a
proper ticket. The attempt to get admission was therefore
only a pretence for the parade through the streets, and that I
firmly believe was *calculated* to try her strength, and it only
proved her weakness. And from eight o'clock on Thursday
morning we heard not a word more of her till about the same
hour yesterday morning when the ' Morning Post ' and all the
town had it she had fled, some said to Italy, and others to
Scotland. In fact she was in the dumps at Brandenburgh
House, and we hear to-day intends, like the Duke of
Monmouth of old, to make a progress in the West.

The King and his Ministers are, I hear, worse and worse ;
this vacancy of the Chamberlain's office is unlucky for both
parties. I myself do not think that a change was ever so
likely—certainly Lord Liverpool never was worse with His
Majesty than at this moment, when it would require the
greatest cordiality and good understanding to enable them to
agree on a fit Lord Chamberlain.

The King talks of leaving town for Brighton on Monday,
and embarking next day for Dublin, I, if Mrs. Croker be
tolerably well, will go by land, and, after spending a few
days about my own private concerns in the country, will go
to Dublin to pay my duty.

Yours ever, &c.,

J. W. C.

The King's visit to Ireland, which was then supposed to be
the beginning of a " new era " of reconciliation ; his subsequent journey to the Continent ; the Queen's death ; the
difficulties between the King and his Ministers—all these
topics are touched upon in Mr. Croker's diary or correspondence for the remainder of this year.

(From the Diary.)

July 29th.—Dined at Yarmouth's with the Duke of York. We had also the Speaker, Shaftesbury, Huskisson, Beckett, Greenwood, Watson Taylor, Col. Armstrong, Mr. Dent and Chin Grant.* Before he came, Yarmouth and the Speaker said the Duke was greatly out of spirits, vexed at *all* that was going on, with the King, and with the Ministers, and with the reductions in the army. When he came, however, I could not think I had ever seen him in much better spirits. The truth is, the Speaker is vexed, and he fancies other people are so too.

July 30th.—I was to have set out for Dublin to-morrow, but Mrs. Croker continues so ill that I cannot leave her. I was to have had an audience of the King to receive his last commands for Ireland, and I saw H.M. at two o'clock; but I was obliged to ask leave to stay, which he granted with many expressions of regret, and he desired that, if Mrs. C. grew better, I should hasten after him. He is as well as I ever saw him; he was a *little warm;* Lord Liverpool had been just with him, and, after I had said "my little say," he began to complain of Lord Liverpool. He says he cannot go on with him, and that he will not; that he likes all the rest of his Cabinet, nobody, for instance, better than Castlereagh; that if the Cabinet chose to stand or fall with Lord Liverpool, they must fall; if not, he does not wish for any further change. The Cabinet, he says, is too large, and people are in it who have no title to be there. He asked how it could be suspected that he wished to get rid of his Ministry, he who had made them himself. But Lord Liverpool was captious, jealous, and impracticable; he objects to everything, and even when he gives way, which is nine times in ten, he does it with so bad a grace that it is worse than an absolute refusal. Even fo his own personal comfort the King cannot get the smallest things done; for instance, two rooms of one story to his cottage are positively refused him. When he is refused such a *misère* as that, what must it be with greater matters? But

---

* [Sir Alexander Grant. He sat in Parliament from 1812 to 1843, and was Chairman of Ways and Means in the House of Commons from 1826 to 1832. He was also a member of the Board of Control in Sir R. Peel's Administration, 1834–35, and was so much attached to Peel that he wore mourning for him long after his death.]

he would bear it no longer; he is *rex Dei gratiâ*, and *Dei gratiâ rex* he would be.

There was a great deal more of this kind. It is quite impossible that Lord Liverpool can stay in with such feelings existing towards him; the King described him with one happy, and though exaggerated, not on the whole unjust trait : " *he is in the highest degree irritable, without having any feeling.*"

There was no great *reciprocity* in our conversation, for I said little or nothing, only of Castlereagh. When he spoke of him, I said that, though he was not popular with the mob, he was highly so in Parliament.

July 31*st.*—The King left town at half-past eleven, and Mrs. Croker is so much better that Sir William Knighton has told the *King* that I *may* go, and *me* that I *must* go, to Ireland.

August 1*st.*—Slept at Oswestry.   Lord Beresford and Lord George had passed me on the road, and I have rejoined and supped with them.

The road and scenery through Wales delightful.

Our supper whimsically served ; the first dish being *green peas* alone, and when we asked for the mutton chops we were told they would be ready by the time we should have *done with the peas.*

Dublin, August 4*th.*—The King's tables begin to-morrow, the Lords and Grooms at the first, the equerries and the rest at the second.   As I have no character but as the King's guest, they gave me my choice at which table I should dine ; but I need not make a formal choice, as I shall dine little at either. I must dine once or twice with both, which is as much as I shall be able to do.   Visits and invitations shower upon one with a most embarrassing and overwhelming profusion.

August 5*th.*—We have an account of the Queen's being dangerously ill of an inflammation in the bowels.   This unexpected event throws all the preparations here into a state of indecision, as it is impossible, if the disease should end fatally, that the King should come hither for some time at least.   Sir M. Tierney thinks ill of her from the bulletins, but he can know no more than we all do.

August 6*th.*—The Queen's disorder is said to be unabated ; but I cannot think she is in such extreme danger as is supposed.   Some people think it is all a hoax, and others not more charitable say that she is poisoned.   Certainly her death at this moment would be a most extraordinary occurrence.   I suppose they will have sent expresses to meet the King off the Land's End.

August 8th.—The King arrived at Holyhead yesterday, and received there the first accounts of the Queen s illness. He went immediately to Plâs Newydd, and Lord Sidmouth sailed at nine this morning to advise His Majesty to postpone his public entry till something more decisive should be known as to the Queen's state. Lord S—— reached Holyhead in six hours, saw the King, and took the steam-packet again about six in the evening, and was in Dublin in about eleven hours, blowing a gale of wind the whole time. The steam-packet returned immediately to Holyhead with the mail of the preceding evening.

The bulletins give expectation of the Queen's recovery.

August 9th.—Dined with the Archbishop of Dublin, with the Lord Lieutenant, Duke of Montrose, Lord Graham, Lord Winchester, Lords Meath, Longford, Belmore, Sidmouth, Castlemain, Lovaine, Howden, and Beresford, Lord George Beresford, Capt. Anson, and the Attorney-General : grave enough. Lord Sidmouth tells me that the King had not a line of communication from his Ministers in London either as to the Queen's illness or as to his own course upon it—nay, Lord Sidmouth had not a syllable on the subject himself, except a note from Hobhouse to say that, if she died, the event should be announced in the Gazette without the usual expression of regret, and that a short mourning should be ordered ; but not a word from Lord Liverpool himself as to what the King was to do in such an event. This seems incredible, but it is true. Lord Sidmouth, however, advised the King, if the next mail should bring fatal accounts, to retire to Plâs Newydd ; if the accounts should be doubtful, to come over and land privately and proceed without ceremony to the Park to wait the result ; but if all was looking well, then to make his public entrance as originally intended. Lord Sidmouth expressed the greatest surprise at Lord Liverpool's most unaccountable neglect both of the King and of his colleagues.

It blows very hard to-night in squalls.

August 10th.—A mail arrived in the night with an account that the Queen was " suddenly much worse." We had also a copy of a private note to the same effect from Doctor Morton to Watson. The result is that the King will land *incognito* at Howth and go to the Park—a great disappointment to expectations *here*, and yet perhaps more than will be approved in England.

August 11*th*.—The Queen died on Tuesday evening. Her will is tolerably expressive of her feelings. She mentions neither Brougham, Denman, nor Wood, and leaves Billy Austin residuary legatee. She desires that on her coffin may be inscribed " Caroline, the *injured* Queen of England." Lord Liverpool writes to Lord Sidmouth that this inscription no authority can place, but that her servants may do as they like. It is observed that she says *injured*, not *innocent*, and that no clergyman attended her in her last moments.

August 12*th*.—The King came over in the steam-packet, and landed at Howth at about half-past four. His birthday. Dined with the equerries. The King was uncommonly well during his passage, and gayer than it might be proper to tell; but he did not appear upon deck after he heard of the Queen's death, and, though it would be absurd to think that he was afflicted, he certainly was affected at the first accounts of this event. He walked about the cabin the greater part of the night on which the news reached him.

In conversation on Friday, which began on other matters, Lord S. told me all the details of his breach with Pitt. I never doubted that the latter was in the wrong as regards Lord Sidmouth.[*] He did not act either fairly or even politely by him. I thought so at the time, and have always continued to think so; that Lord Sidmouth's account only confirms a " foregone conclusion."

August 13*th*.—The King remains in seclusion in the Park; his family and friends dine together at the Castle. To celebrate his birthday we were 33 at table, very hot and very dull.

Blomfield tells me that the King intends to wear mourning at his private *levée*, which is to take place in a day or two, and crape round his arm for the rest of the time. It was not easy, I learn, to persuade him to this.

August 14*th*.—I learned a curious fact. In the absence of letters from Lord Liverpool or any other Minister, Lord Londonderry, at Holyhead, thought himself justified in opening a letter from Hobhouse to Lord Sidmouth, with a view of obtaining some information as to the Queen. He did so in the King's presence, and began to read till he came to " *The Duke of York*—" when he looked horrorstruck and stopped

---

[*] [In 1803, on the question of admitting the Grenvilles and Mr. Windham into the Cabinet.]

short. "Come, come!" said the King, "you must now go on
with it, or I shall think it worse than I daresay it will turn
out to be." Castlereagh was then obliged to stammer on,
"*The Duke of York is in despair at an event which so much
diminishes his chance of the Crown.*" The King, however,
laughed very good-humouredly at it, and afterwards repeated
the story with equal good humour.

August 15th.—The King had a private *levée* in the park in
deep mourning. I dined with Mr. F. Hutchinson, where we
had, beside Lord Hutchinson and the sons of Frank and Kit,
the Archbishop of Tuam, Lords Roden, Luton, Powerscourt,
Monck, and Hawarden, Mr. Lefroy, and Mr. Bernard. The
best dinner and wines I have seen at any house in Ireland,
but it must be confessed that the tone of conversation, of
Lords Powerscourt and Hawarden, for instance, is not very
refined. Lord Hutchinson whispered me to sit near him, and
he made me remark that we had fallen into a company of the
over-righteous. His brother, he said, was beginning to tend that
way. The Archbishop of Tuam is the patriarch of this sect.

August 17th.—As early as six the people began to assemble
for the King's public entry. I walked about for two or three
hours to see the preparations, which are not costly, but to
which the dimensions of the streets and buildings impart
some of their magnificence. The entry was fine and the procession had more carriages and horsemen than I thought
Dublin could have afforded. They said there were 500
carriages and 3000 gentlemen on horseback; probably half
the number would be nearer the truth : 100 carriages make
a great train. One fact I saw. The train of carriages which
preceded the King had passed the College, where I stood, and
had gone through Dame Street, Cork Hill, both Castle yards,
and by the back streets and Grafton Street back again into
College Green before the King had arrived at Carlisle Bridge,
so that there must have been, I should think, at least an Irish
mile of carriages. The people *shouted.* The Irish, it seems,
do not know how to *hurrah* or *cheer;* they have not had much
practice in the expression of public joy. After the King had
received the addresses on the throne, he sent for me into his
private room. He was walking about greatly agitated between
pleasure at his reception in Ireland and dissatisfaction at
what has occurred in London. He renewed all his complaints
against Lord Liverpool, and said roundly that he would not
go on any longer with him. He kept me full half an hour,
and talked the whole time, alternately of the triumph of Dublin

and the horrors of London.* B. tells me that the King sat up
the greater part of the night fretting about this latter affair ;
it affects him certainly more deeply than I should have
expected.

The day was, in my opinion, not very favourable for the
procession : it was hazy. The King, however, said " it was
just the day he wished for ; no sun, no wet, no dust." A
triumphal arch was erected at the upper end of Sackville
Street *near* (not *at*) the bounds of the city, where the Lord
Mayor offered the keys. I gave the architect the inscriptions
for it. On the face towards the King I proposed " Regi
Cives," and on the other next the city this from the 6th
Æneid :—

> " Hic est, tibi quem promitti sæpius audis
> Augustus."

The latter only was used. The other side had " *An hundred
thousand Welcomes* " in Irish. Better than mine.

August 18*th*.—A review in the park ; the day was wonderfully fine, and the scene was delightful. I went in one of the
King's carriages with Lords Winchester and Charles Bentinck, and Sir Ed. Nagle. Most of the others went on horseback. The prettiest part of the show was the children of the
Soldiers' Orphan School marching past ; their tiny discipline
was very exact, and their appearance singularly touching ;
they brought recollections into my mind and tears, which I
could not check, into my eyes.

In the evening I dined with my old friend the Master of
the Rolls.† When I went my first circuit I found MacMahon
in a kind of Coventry, and was warned not to continue my
acquaintance with him. As I had never known anything of
him that was not kind and honourable, I rejected the advice,
and had the pleasure to see MacMahon rising every day to
wealth and honours. We had at dinner Lords Roden, Donoughmore, Aylmer, and Gort, the Bishop of Ferns, Mr. Barnard, Mr. Doherty, and some ladies and others.

August 19*th*.—The King went to church, where, what with
chaunting long Te Deums and anthems, they kept him exactly
three hours. After he returned to the Castle, His Majesty

---

* [Referring, no doubt, to the disgraceful scenes which occurred at the
Queen's funeral.]

† [Sir William MacMahon.]

sent for me, and I saw him for a few minutes; he was tired, and anxious to get to the Park. When I was going out Sir Matthew Tierney came in, but the King said, laughingly, "Tierney, I do not want to see you; I never was better in my life." Yet I know he had not been well in the morning, and Tierney had been desired to wait upon him on his return from church.

August 20th.—The King held a *levée,* and previous to it received the addresses of the Synod of Presbyterians, the Quakers, and the Catholic bishops in the closet. He also had an investiture of St. Patrick and the Bath. Lord Graves, proxy for the Duke of Cumberland, and Lords Donegal, Ormond, Meath, Roden, Fingal, and Courtown, were invested.

The address of the Catholic bishops was in bad taste : it talked too much politics, and said that they were four-fifths of the population. Everybody observed how unseemly this tone was at this time. Some days after, Lord Donoughmore told me that he had written this address, and he took great credit for having inserted these very passages. He told me that the address which the Catholic prelates themselves had prepared was mere milk and water, welcome and adulation, but that he wished to give their address political substance and weight, and to register the fact of Catholic importance and preponderance in Ireland in an address to the throne, where, if not contradicted from the throne, it would remain an indisputable admission of the fact which he wanted to prove. I thought all this wrong, and I told him so, and that if I had been Secretary of State for the Home Department, I should have rejected these passages of his address. I cannot conceive how a man can be so blinded by vanity or party as not to see that his address is at least a thing not to boast of.

The *levée* which ensued was wonderfully crowded. I reckoned 1500 names, and was told there were 2000. I know not how many guineas were offered for the loan of a dress sword, and I know two people who were kept away by the want of this article of court dress. Some who came had most incongruous swords, and there were many ludicrous figures, but they were lost in the immense crowd, and many passed the King without seeing or recognising him.

August 21st.—I dined at the Lords' table. I had promised to dine there one day, and thought this a good opportunity to go. Dressed for the drawing-room. By opening a large suite of rooms, and by publishing the King's desire that no gentlemen should come except in attendance on ladies, the crowd was not so inconvenient as at the *levée*, though the numbers were greater. I should suppose that above 1000 ladies were presented, and really they were (with a very few and very inconsiderable exceptions), all ladies who might have very properly appeared at St. James's, and their dresses were both rich and in good taste. When the rooms began to thin, about twelve o'clock, I walked about with Lord Lovaine, making our observations, and we both agreed that it was a drawing-room quite equal, except as to jewels and titles, to any we had seen at St. James's. By some interruption, about one-third of the company were cut off and prevented coming up with the stream. The attendants thought there were no more to be presented, so the door of the presence chamber was shut, and the King made his bows and retired. In a few minutes it was found that the ante-rooms were again full (the interruption in the train of carriages having been obviated). What was to be done? The King had retired and was undressed. On the other hand, the ladies were dressed and had no mind to retire; after a good deal of *pourparlers*, the King was told of the circumstance, and with great good nature he put on his fine coat, came back to the presence chamber, and went through the ceremony of kissing about 300 ladies more.

August 23rd.—The City dinner, extremely splendid and, what is more wonderful, good and well regulated and well served. About 400 dined. The room built for the occasion in less than six weeks, and for less than 5000*l.*, represented the interior circular court of a Moorish palace open to the sky; the battlements were a gallery filled with ladies, music, and a company of halberdiers, in Spanish dresses of light blue silk as a guard of honour to the King. It was lighted by a vast circle of light, hung by invisible wires, which had a wonderfully fine and curious effect. Foster pleasantly and forcibly called it *Saturn's ring*. The whole was gay, graceful, and grand, and went off *à souhait*, except the music, which was bad—poor and scattered. The finest incident was that after the loud cheers of the company on drinking the King's health had subsided, the distant cheering of the people from the surrounding streets burst in (from the invisible windows of the ceiling), and gave an air of reality to the whole pageant.

August 24th.—A beautiful *déjeûner* on the lawn of the

Dublin Society—a splendid and profuse breakfast in a royal pavilion and in about thirty other tents. There were about 1200 persons present, and *scats* at table (as I was told and believe from what I saw) for 900.

The King went minutely through the museum and other parts of the interior. Whether this tired him or that he was too impatient to get to Slane,* I cannot tell—perhaps both; but he did not appear on the lawn for above four minutes. He walked a little way down, bowed on each side, and returned, as every one supposed, to take, or appear to take, some of the refreshments which had been prepared for him; but no, before anyone would have guessed it, he was already in his travelling carriage and on the road to Slane. Great disappointment and some criticism, which five minutes more would have prevented.

August 25th.—My sister and aunt arrived in town last night. I spent this day in showing them what I could of the shows, and dined with them and Mr. and Mrs. A. Hutchinson at Dean Bond's. I am commanded to Slane to-morrow, which I regret on several accounts. The Duke of Montrose, who went yesterday, is returned enchanted with Slane : " the finest place he ever saw in England or Scotland. Dunkeld, the best Scotch place, is a *bagatelle* to it." Slane *is* a fine place, but it is narrow and owes nearly half its beauties to its neighbours; but these defects are not visible unless one is apprised of them, and it is really, in both senses of the word, a very imposing place. The King went to see the scene of the battle of the Boyne; it seemed, from what he afterwards said to me, that they had not explained the matter clearly to him.

August 26th.—Went to Slane with Col. Thornton. Called at Sir M. Somerville's for Sir Andrew Barnard. Sad rainy weather, so that I never went outside the doors of Slane. At dinner, besides the King and the Conynghams, old and young, we had the Esterhazys, Fagel, the Blomfields, and the Attorney and Solicitor-General. The pleasantest dinner I almost ever was at; the King in excellent tone and spirits, and the Attorney and Solicitor delighted with him. He pleasantly asked Saurin's† legal opinion whether he might not stay where he was, and send Lord Talbot, as Lord Lieutenant,

---

* [Slane Castle, the seat of the Marquis of Conyngham.]
† [William Saurin, Attorney-General for Ireland.]

to England. A round Gothic room at Slane, very handsome and handsomely lighted. In the evening the King conversed a good deal with the two lawyers. He had been at Slane Church in the morning; great crowds and some oppressive loyalty.

At Slane they showed me a musical instrument, very like, I suppose, an ancient lyre, which a neighbouring gentleman had sent as a present to the King; the testudo, or shell, was formed of the skull of a horse, and of the horse—so ran the inscription—which Duke Schomberg rode at the battle of the Boyne.

August 27th.—I left my carriage at Slane for Barnard and Thornton, and, as I wanted to be in town early, I came in with the Attorney and Solicitor. We had an agreeable drive, and the Solicitor (Bushe)* was very amusing. Still heavy rain.

The College dinner went off very well; the library was the reception room, and the theatre the dining room, both fitted up with great splendour and taste. The dinner was handsome and good, the wines very good, and the music excellent. The King seemed much pleased, but he retired half an hour too soon. The young men at the gates took leave to express their approbation, and in some instances their disapprobation, of the guests as they passed to their carriages. Bad taste, although I had the honour of being amongst the applauded.

August 28th.—Left Dublin, intending to proceed from Howth to Holyhead by the steam-packet; but an accident had occurred to the packet, and there was none but a sailing-packet going; so, as the wind was high and adverse, I did not embark. Lord and Lady Manners were in the same predicament, and we agreed to stop at Howth instead of going back to the festivities of Dublin. Baron Fagel, the Dutch Ambassador, was also there, and we spent a very stormy day agreeably enough by the fireside. Went out for a moment to the hill to see the steamboat arriving—a very sublime and almost alarming sight; she rolled tremendously.

August 29th.—Sailed in the steam-packet, the wind quite against us, very strong, and a good deal of sea. We had a rolling and disagreeable passage of ten hours and fifty minutes. The sailing-packet, which had sailed twenty-four

---

* [Charles Kendal Bushe, the Irish Solicitor-General.]

hours before us, we passed at sea, and she cannot arrive for twelve hours after us. If she has any passengers on board, they must have passed a miserable time. I sat in my carriage on deck ; everybody was deadly sick. I was not at all incommoded ; I fancy the motion of my carriage on its own springs—a motion to which one is accustomed—prevented my feeling the motion of the vessel as much as I should otherwise have done; but Lord Manners and Baron Fagel, who tried the same plan, were both horribly sick.

August 30th.—Breakfasted at Bangor Ferry ; then spent an hour fishing in one or two spots where the road goes by lakes and rivers, with a little, and but a little, swamp.

Dined at the King's Arms, Llangollen, a new inn in a beautiful situation, where I found Herries stopping on his way to Ireland, where he is going as one of the Commissioners of Inquiry. Travelled all night.

Sept. 1st.—I find London more quiet, *in fact*, than it looks in *the newspapers.* The strange inquest on the man killed at the Queen's funeral still going on, with a violence on the part of the prosecutors and rabble and a partiality on the part of the jury which disgusts all right-minded men of all parties, and must after all do good. It is, indeed, now of no kind of consequence what verdict they bring in.

Sept. 2nd.—Cockburn explains to me his motives for advising the Queen's funeral not to go by water, and I am satisfied that he was right; but I think that she should have been sent to Portsmouth, where the ship was which was to convey her. To this I can also see objections, but it was, on the whole, the easiest way of proceeding, and the least likely to produce mischief.

Sept. 3rd.—I had a letter from Arbuthnot, complaining that I had talked of the King's being dissatisfied and the Government in danger. As I had not been out of the Boardroom, I knew that this came from Osborne to Lord Liverpool. I answered that Osborne was a little mistaken in some details, but that the facts were true enough, and, as I was not delighted at this kind of *aigre doux* remonstrance, I stated that no one meddled with such things less than I did, not because I wanted opportunities, which H.M.'s favour sometimes offered me, nor because I did not think myself *as well entitled to push myself into their confidences as another*, but simply because I did not like the pursuit ; and little as I ever had liked what is called political intrigue, I now had every day less and less reason to dabble in such troubled waters, for that all my ambition, which never was very great, was now buried with my poor child, and that I did not want and would not accept change of office or of rank as any favour. I continue in office not because it gratifies me, but because I am advised, and indeed feel, that having spent my life from twenty-seven to forty in office, I should be *désœuvré* out of it, and that, under my present feelings, I could not answer for my own strength of mind.

I observe that my nerves, as they are called, grow every day weaker and more irritable, above all when I think of my poor boy.

Sept. 8th.—I had a letter from Lord Liverpool at Walmer, saying that he was very anxious to see the King as soon as possible, and begging me to inform him of His Majesty's movements. He added that as the affair of the Queen's funeral was the *great sin* of which the King now accused the ministers, he begged Sir Geo. Cockburn and me to draw up a *mémoire justificatif* of the arrangement made on that occasion.

I wrote to him in reply that the Queen's funeral would not be considered as the true cause of the dissatisfaction, and that, since he did me the honour of opening the subject to me, I should venture to say that I looked upon that as a trivial point of difference, and that the real quarrel was old, and lay deeper, and should be treated accordingly.

In the evening I had a note from his lordship, to say he was come to town, and would be glad to see me next morning before church.

Sept. 9th.—I called on Lord Liverpool. We talked over all the details of the Queen's funeral, and we both agreed that the reasoning for not going down the Thames was conclusive; and I promised to get Cockburn to draw up a statement of his nautical view of the subject, to which I would add a summary of the more general reasons. At the same time I repeated that I thought this case ought not to be argued with the King in any hope that convincing His Majesty on this head would satisfy him on many others, and I hinted that Lord Liverpool had perhaps some personal excuses to make on one or two points. He agreed to all I said, but quoted the fable of the wolf and the lamb. I did all I could to soften Lord L.'s feeling, and to induce him to meet the King, not argumentatively, but kindly and frankly.

He is undoubtedly in the wrong towards the King on some points, and for these he ought to offer something like apology. Lord Liverpool talked of the refusal of the Chamberlain's place to Lord Conyngham, and of the King's desire to make young Mr. Sumner* (Lord FitzCharles's tutor) at once a Canon of Windsor. He talked a good deal and freely about Lady Conyngham and her designs against the Government. I said that I had seen no marks of it, that a change of Government would place her husband and son in rather awkward circumstances, and that I hardly thought that she was ready to run all the risks of throwing the King and herself into the arms of the Opposition, and I asked, would the Opposition, with all their boasted public virtue, dare to receive the Government from a female intrigue? He said, yes, no doubt that Lord Grey paid great court to Lady C. What Lord Lansdowne might do was more doubtful, as he was a cautious and reserved man, whose sentiments were not so easily discoverable. He talked also of the difficulties arising from the ladies of the Ministers, and mainly Lady Londonderry not associating with Lady C.

Sept. 10*th.*—I brought Lord Liverpool Cockburn's statement and my summary, which he highly approved of. I have renewed to him my advice not to treat this matter as a pure logical argumentation, for, convinced or unconvinced on this point, the King's feelings towards him will not be softened, though they may be rendered more adverse by debate.

I took the liberty of telling Lord Liverpool that I gave this advice for no object but peace sake; that I was in a situation which would render it highly irksome to me that the King, who honoured me with his private favour, should be dissatisfied with those under whom I held a public office, but that I was above or below the reach of royal or ministerial favour; that I wanted nothing, and would take nothing,

---

* [The Duke of Wellington to Lord Liverpool, October 26th, 1821:— " As I told you at Walmer, the King has never forgiven your opposition to his wishes in the case of Mr. Sumner. The feeling has influenced every action of his life in relation to his Government from that moment; and I believe to more than one of us he avowed that his objection to Mr. Canning was that his accession to the Government was peculiarly desirable to you." —'Wellington Despatches,' New Series I. 195. Mr. Sumner afterwards became Bishop of Winchester.]

and, in fact, had no object but to prevent, as far as my humble advice would go, dissatisfaction and dissension.

Sept. 11*th.*—A severe gale of wind from the S. and S.S.W. It is impossible that the King's squadron can make head against it. I hope they were not at sea.

The whole Cabinet is summoned to town to meet the King; they seem to think that he is inclined to make an immediate change. I cannot think this; he must postpone anything of that kind till after his journey to Hanover, or postpone his journey to Hanover to another year.

Sept. 14*th.*—No account of the King. I do not think he can have got round the Land's End, and, as he has not returned to Milford Haven, he must have gone for Cork. I wonder at his perseverance.

Sept. 15*th.*—The King was obliged to return to Milford Haven on the 12th, and on the 13th he landed and pursued his journey to town. They say the yacht was taken aback in a squall in the night between the 11th and 12th, and might have gone down but for the presence of mind of Lieut. Maingay, who was on deck. He had returned to Milford time enough for us to have heard it yesterday; but, I know not why, nobody wrote, and our daily office reports did not arrive.

The King slept at Chapel House * last night, and Blomfield happened, by a very curious chance, to fall in with His Majesty, he being on his way from Dublin, where he had stayed after the King. A still more curious chance had almost brought H.M. in contact with his old friends Lord and Lady Hertford, who sleep at Chapel House to-night, on their way from Ragley to Sudbourne. In the days of their favour, Chapel House was the favourite meeting place on the road to Ragley.

Sept. 16*th.*—Lords Melville, Lovaine, Yarmouth, Beresford and Lowther, Sir Hudson Lowe, Mr. Robinson, Hamilton, and Watson dined with me.

Yarmouth is just returned from a tour which took him as far as Milan and Venice.

Lord Liverpool wrote to me early this morning, or indeed I should rather say last night, to ask some further explanations, as the *lamb* was to be in presence of the *wolf* to-day at

* [A posting-house, ten miles beyond Woodstock, on the Birmingham road.]

eleven. At eleven accordingly he went to Carlton House, but the King would not see him. His Majesty saw the Chancellor, and desired him to tell Lord Liverpool that, if his lordship would abstain from speaking about *political arrangements*, he would receive him to-morrow. This seems to me a mortification to which I wonder Lord L. can submit, particularly as the King has seen Lords Londonderry and Bathurst ; and, by the way, he is not much pleased with the latter, for, although he knew that he was the only Secretary of State in *England*, neither the Queen's illness nor HER DEATH brought him up from Gloucestershire, where, in any circumstances, he ought not to have been when there was no other Secretary of State who could attend in London. It must be confessed that, whether it be the King's own popular manners, or the habits into which the Regency has led his Minister, or the levelling temper of the times, the Royal authority and the King's person are treated with a striking degree of levity, and no reformers, if they knew the whole secret, would wish to reduce the monarch lower in real and effective state and power than his Ministers place him.

Sept. 20th.—The intention of the King's going to Vienna is quite given up, and his going to Paris is doubtful. The reasons stated are the necessity in such a tour of also going to Berlin and the late season of the year. I have heard, in private, that the expense of *sovereign visits* to these continental courts, and particularly to Vienna, is so enormous as to terrify the nerves of the Privy purse. I forget what they say that the Emperor of Russia's visits cost him. All this was in discussion when I went to Brighton ; on my return I found it had been so finally arranged.

Sept. 23rd.—I dined with Lord Melville, and in the evening we looked over some papers of his father's correspondence with the late King and with his colleagues, particularly Mr. Pitt, and Lords Spencer and Grenville ; the former particularly curious. The King's notes show a great deal of shrewdness of thought and terseness of expression. They are not very important, because the King saw his Ministers on regular days, and these notes were only occasional communications *pro re natâ*. Some epigrammatic remarks upon the Duke of Richmond and his brother, the late Duke, whom H.M. appears to have much disliked ; great tenderness for and a high opinion of the Duke of York ; considerable knowledge of detail of the army, and other branches of the public service ;

aversion to a peace with the French Republic, and a great inclination to colonial aggrandisement.

He everywhere evinces reluctance to *expeditions*—that to Ferrol was forced upon him by Pitt and Dundas declaring that they must resign if they were thwarted in it.* One of the King's notes, in answer to Dundas, was so sharp upon him that the latter had written a letter of resignation, which, however, Pitt induced him not to send.

The King's note, declaring his resolution not to accede to the Catholic claims, is well written and dignified, and his subsequent acceptance of the Minister's resignation is cool and formal.

In the earlier notes particularly the King's observations are shrewd, and sometimes satirical.

Sept. 24*th.*—The King set out for Hanover at ten minutes before 1 P.M. I was waiting in the hall to make my bow to him as he passed. He took me into one of the rooms and made me sit down. He told me that he was not well, and that he was tired of his journey before he began it. He then went on to speak of his ministry, complaining that Lord Liverpool had thrown the weight of rejecting Mr. Canning on his shoulders. As it was more likely that some one of thirteen should have dissented, he should have first communicated with his colleagues, and then come to him with their joint or their divided opinions, but, without taking the pains of ascertaining whether, after all, the Cabinet would admit him, Lord Liverpool threw the odium of the decision on the King in the first instance. He said he had postponed his determination on the subject of his Government, but he hoped in the meanwhile they would be true to their own interests and his honour by resisting Canning and making some arrangement with Mr. Peel. He was told, he said, that Mr. Canning would become his irreconcilable personal enemy; that was the fault of Lord Liverpool's unconstitutional pro-

---

* ["Ferrol was the scene of one of our greatest military blunders. In 1800, a squadron, under command of General Pulteney, made an attack upon the town. Just as the inhabitants were preparing to surrender, the cowardly Pulteney—scared by the rapidly falling barometer, and beaten (it is said) at the game of brag, ordered the re-embarkment of his almost mutinous troops, amidst the jeers of the sailors of the English fleet, and to the astonishment of the Spaniards themselves."—Vide Ford's Spanish Handbook.]

ceeding, which had brought him into direct contact with Mr. Canning's claims, and therefore the Government was bound to support him against that personal enmity, which, after all, he valued very little, and only alluded to it as it was a threat brought forward in the shape of an argument. During all this *conversation*, or rather during this *speech*, he seemed very fixed and very determined, not talking at random, but with a deliberate design. He seemed to avoid mentioning Lord Liverpool's or Mr. Canning's name, but pointed them out by descriptions and allusions not always flattering. Peel's name he mentioned just as I have written it.

Lord Conyngham and Sir B. Blomfield went in the coach with his Majesty; Sir Andrew Barnard, Lord Francis Conyngham, and Sir William Knighton followed in a second coach. It was observed to me by a friend in Carlton House that Blomfield would be in a sad *minority*.* Knighton himself thinks the King not very well, and it is now clear that this journey is made rather to keep the promise than from any great desire on H.M.'s part to go abroad.

Sept. 25th.—The King sailed from Ramsgate at half-past eleven, and arrived at Calais between four and five; it was low water, and not only could no yacht get in, but his own barge drew too much water, and he was obliged to take to a French fishing boat; but even that struck on the bar, and was in considerable danger. She fortunately, however, bumped over it, but half filled with water, and all the passengers drenched. The King's coolness and presence of mind in this danger were very conspicuous. It was altogether an awkward affair; the wind was so strong as to render the vessel's lying in Calais roads till the tide made, impossible.

Mr. Croker to Mr. Peel.

September 14th, 1821.

MY DEAR PEEL,

The King's visit to Ireland has done good. It has for a moment assuaged the *violence*, and for some time removed the

---

* [This is probably an allusion to the fact that the King and Lord Conyngham were strongly against Lord Liverpool, whereas Blomfield was an equally strong partisan of the Prime Minister's. As it is explained later on, he was the means of making peace between the King and Lord Liverpool.]

rancour of party. Human passions will break out again, but Sir Edward Stanley cannot call O'Gorman *rebel*, nor O'Gorman call him *bloodthirsty bigot* again.

I agree with you that there was a considerable condescension in the King, and something like meanness in his Ministers, in the course adopted with regard to Alderman Darley;* but you will agree with me that the case was a little hard to deal with. The offence was not the drinking a toast, which in itself is loyal, constitutional, and such as Lord Fingal and every other honest man would drink if it had no meaning but what it professes; but in Ireland it has been considered as a *watchword*, as a party-cry, without any reference to its original meaning (for, in fact, William and the Stuarts are equally extinguished). The King had desired that party feelings should be as much as possible suppressed, and that party expressions should be altogether avoided during his residence in Ireland. Under all these circumstances, it was, I say, very hard to know what to do with the Chief Police Magistrate, who, at a dinner given to the King, presumed to violate his commands, and to give a toast which was at once offensive to the King and to the majority of the people. I cannot but say that I should respect Darley's boldness, steadiness, and consistency, if I thought he was sober and deliberate when he did it, and in any case I like the generous impulse which prompted him; but I confess that I hardly think the King could have let the thing pass without some expression of disapprobation. You know enough of Ireland to know that if he had done so every man, Protestant and Catholic, would have believed that the Alderman had acted under Castle influence, and that his conduct was agreeable to the King, which would have been to raise an imputation against His Majesty of meanness and duplicity, under which no gentleman, much less the Sovereign, could have consented to lie.

My own opinion is, that if *you* had been there you would have conveyed a *direct and open reprimand* to Darley; and you would have told him that if His Majesty had not been unwilling to mark his visit in Ireland with any instance of rigour, he would have taken a more serious notice of this want of respect to his known wishes, if not to his positive

---

* [Who proposed at a public dinner the famous Orange toast "The glorious memory of King William."]

commands; and you would have allowed that reprimand to have made its own way. The erecting Lord Fingal into a fourth estate in these realms appears to me, as to you, highly improper, not to say dangerous; for the *principle and admission* which are deduceable from such a recognition may have most perilous consequences. Lord Fingal is a very good man, but I do not like any political Confessor for an English King.

I shall visit you some of these days; but we are all at this moment at our posts like an army drawn up in its position to receive the attack of an enemy. The whole Cabinet is in town to meet the King, who is certainly highly displeased with Lord Liverpool, and I believe desirous of just so much change as would get *him* out. I do not think he *now* looks further, but I am architect enough to know how much the removing a main wall shakes a house, and how little any one can tell where such alterations may end.

For my own part, in the whole round of the political compass there is no point to which I look with any interest but yourself. I myself remain in office only because I doubt my own strength of mind, and am afraid of the consequences of idleness and of a change in that mode of life in which I have spent all my best days; but ambitious hope or wish I have not; and there is really nothing that royal or ministerial partiality could do for me that I would accept as a favour; and, moreover, there is not, in public life, any one man in whose fortunes I feel that kind of interest which gives a zest to political existence—for I do not look upon you as now a public man. I confess I should like to see you in high and *effective* office, for a hundred reasons which I have before told you, and for some which I have not told you and need not tell you; but if I looked only to your own comfort and happiness, I should never wish to see you within the walls of Pandemonium.

Yours affectionately,

J. W. C.

To Mr. Peel.

November 12th, 1821.

DEAR PEEL,

We have no public news that is *public*, but the Ministerial negotiations with the King are, I understand, to commence·

to-day. Lord Liverpool has consented to give up Canning for the present, and Canning has consented to wait for Lord Moira's old shoes as Governor General, and the Grenvilles are to have the Board of Control and the Irish Secretaryship. I have reason to believe that the King intends to propose, perhaps to insist, that the Home Office should be offered to you. One thing seems certain, that the King and Lord Liverpool will come to an understanding.

Yours affectionately,
J. W. C.

To Mr. Peel.

November 13th, 1821.

MY DEAR PEEL,

Castlereagh saw the King yesterday, and found that some seeds of accommodation sown at Hanover (I believe by Blomfield) had fructified, and that all differences were likely to be arranged. Lord Liverpool saw His Majesty to-day, and the reconciliation was complete and cordial. Canning is not to be pressed into the Cabinet, and Lord Conyngham will probably be Lord Steward, vice Cholmondeley, but I believe no details were entered upon, nor have I heard your name mentioned. I only know that before Castlereagh saw the King His Majesty expressed his opinion that you were by a great variety of qualifications suited to the Home department. I should not be surprised if you were by this post to hear from Lord Liverpool.

Yours affectionately,
J. W. C.

To Mr. Peel.

November 26th, 1821.

DEAR PEEL,

Lord Liverpool is gone down to Brighton to submit to-day to the King his arrangements, and yet I do not find that the arrangements are supposed to be *finally* made. I believe you will find that I was right in my former information, and I reckon that to-morrow or the next day Lord Liverpool will write to you. My belief is, as before, that he will offer you the Home Department, all the formerly existing reasons for

which are increased by the alarming state of affairs in Ireland.
Grant is certainly to be recalled, and I believe Lord Liverpool
will again apply to Goulburn (or has already) to succeed him.
Some think that Charles Wynn would be still better, and
others think Fremantle would be better than Wynn! You
and I will not be of these opinions. I have not heard *distinctly* what Plunket is to have, but I hear Attorney-General;
Saurin being promoted to be a Chief Justice. I learn also
that old Norbury has been asked to retire, and that he has
declined—I daresay not without a jest. With all these
things unsettled, it seems odd that Lord Liverpool should be
prepared to lay his *arrangements* before the King. Oh! I
forgot to say that Canning had accepted the *reversion* of India
when he thought that old Moira was *not* coming home; that
is, as it would seem, he wished to hold on with the Government and take the chance of the chapter of accidents, but lo!
a letter arrives by the last ships stating that Lord Hastings
has had the misfortune to *rupture* himself, and therefore
wishes to return forthwith. Upon this they say that Canning
turns round, and is no longer ready to be the great Mogul—
he alleges some letter which he wrote to Lord Hastings, and
which he says would look as if he had wished to supplant
him, if he were now to accept his place. I know not the
rights of all this, but I tell you what I hear. The result,
however, is that Lord Liverpool has told Canning that he
may take it or leave it, for that he cannot now do anything
else for him and that Canning is supposed to have left town
again very sulky.

Yours ever,

J. W. C.

Mr. Croker to Mr. Vesey Fitzgerald.   Extracts.

December 20th, 1821.

Canning has been shuffling about India, yes, no—no, yes.
The King *will not* have him at home. Canning hopes this
disgust is, like all the King's dislikes, placable and temporary,
and he therefore accepted India when it was *not* vacant, as a
kind of rope *to hold on to* the Administration by, but *unluckily* old Moira has had a double rupture, and is perhaps
already on his way home: this would clench Canning for
Indian exile, and he is now therefore punctilious about accept-

ing poor Lord Moira's place, before he knows that it is
vacant—so folks talk; and there is, I believe, some truth in
their talk. I am sorry to be obliged to confess that all
Canning's conduct gives a handle to this sort of imputation.
His genius is a bright flame, but it is

> "Brillant comme le feu que les villageois font
> Pendant l'obscure nuit, sur le sommet d'un mont."

It is liable to every gust of wind and every change of
weather; it flares, and it flickers, and it blazes, now climbing
the heavens, now stifled in its own smoke, and of no use but
to raise the wonder of distant spectators, and to warm the
very narrow circle that immediately surrounds it. If he does
not take care the Canning bonfire will soon burn itself out.

Londonderry goes on as usual, and to continue my similes,
like Mont Blanc continues to gather all the sunshine upon
his icy head. He is *better* than ever; that is, colder, steadier,
more *pococurante*, and withal more amiable and respected.
It is a splendid summit of bright and polished frost which,
like the travellers in Switzerland, we all admire; but no one,
can hope, and few would wish to reach.

The Conynghams carry, I think, their favour meekly and
good-naturedly, and really excite no observation, but with
those who would observe ill-naturedly upon anything. You
will have heard of "their intrigues" and so forth for "station
and office"—all false. I know and can assure you they
asked for, wished for, nothing—and the King's kindness
towards Lord Conyngham, natural as it was, was not only
spontaneous upon His Majesty's part, but, I might almost
say, *imposed* upon him.

CHAPTER VIII.

1822.

Peel and Canning enter the Cabinet—Mr. Croker's Belief in Peel—The King's Objections to Canning—Assumed Rivalry between Peel and Canning—Suicide of Lord Londonderry—His Funeral—Reconstruction of the Ministry—Political Rumours of the Day—"Prosperity" Robinson and Huskisson—Peel as a Sportsman—The third Marquis of Hertford—Mr. Croker's Intimacy with him—Lord Hertford's Character—His Dependence for Political Information on Mr. Croker—His Marriage with Maria Fagniani—Supposed Portraits of Lord Hertford in "Vanity Fair" and "Coningsby"—And of "Mr. Rigby"—True Nature of the Relations between Lord Hertford and Mr. Croker—The Hertford Estates—Character of the second Marquis—Examples of Lord Hertford's Letters—Sir B. Blomfield—The "Court" at Brighton —Lady Conyngham and the King—A Children's Ball at Carlton House—The "Master of the Robes."

MR. CROKER'S confident expectation that Peel would not long be allowed to indulge his preference for private life was this year fulfilled, and he also saw, though with perhaps a less lively degree of satisfaction, the appointment of Canning as Foreign Secretary. His admiration for the abilities of Peel, and his faith in his firmness of character and steadfastness of principle, were at this time unbounded; nor was his confidence ever shaken until Peel took that course which necessarily severed him from the great bulk of his party. The resentment which was felt towards Sir Robert Peel by reason of the sudden reversal of his opinions in connection with the Protectionist policy and the Corn-laws,

was assuredly not confined to Mr. Croker. " That those
who had followed him," said Lord John Russell in 1846,
" when they found he had changed his opinions, and proposed measures different from those on the faith of which
they had followed him ; that they should exhibit warmth
and resentment, was not only natural, but I should have
been surprised if they had not displayed it." There was
never any personal bitterness in Mr. Croker's feelings
towards his old friend. He defended him warmly, long
after he had lost the confidence of most of the Tory
party ; and even when political differences had produced a
hopeless estrangement between them, he remained on friendly
terms with the members of Sir Robert's family, and indirect
messages of kindly interest were occasionally still exchanged.
In 1822, however, the separation was still far distant. There
was no one in whom Mr. Croker believed more firmly than
in Mr. Peel ; there was no one in whose judgment Peel had
greater confidence than in Mr. Croker's. He seldom took an
important step without first soliciting the opinion of his
friend at the Admiralty. Mr. Croker was under the impression that Peel was a man of an unambitious and retiring
disposition, and thought that he needed a great deal of persuasion to force him into public life. This was not the view
which many of his contemporaries took of his character.
Charles Greville, for instance, records in his diary,[*] that
Peel was seen to be preparing to throw over the Tories, and
seeking to gain popularity with the country at large. " He, in
fact," writes Greville, " means to open a house to all comers,
and make himself necessary and indispensable. Under that
placid exterior he conceals, I believe, a boundless ambition ;
and hatred and jealousy lurk under his professions of esteem
and political attachment." Repeatedly after Peel had taken

---

[*] February 14th, 1833, vol. ii., p. 354.

office, he talked much of retiring into private life for ever. Mr. Croker evidently took all this quite seriously, as probably it was meant to be taken at the time; and it will therefore be found that he constantly uses arguments to dissuade Peel from an intention which seems, after all, never to have held more than a temporary lodgment in his mind.

There was no obstacle to Peel's appointment to office as Home Secretary, in 1822. But there was a difficulty with regard to Canning which appeared likely to prove serious. The King had then an invincible repugnance to him, founded upon the sympathy and friendship which he had always shown for the Queen. It had been arranged that he should become Governor-General of India, and the King was not only willing, but anxious, to see him undertake the duties of that post, for he would then be out of the way of interfering any further in English politics. But Lord Liverpool, who had parted with Canning very reluctantly on a former occasion, and who had always been greatly under the spell of his genius, now much desired to secure his services at home, and many attempts were made to overcome the King's objections. The Duke of Wellington essayed to make the conversion; but His Majesty told him that he had pledged his honour as a gentleman never to receive Mr. Canning again as one of his Ministers. "You hear, Arthur, 'On my honour as a gentleman!'" The Duke, as Sir H. Bulwer relates,* told the King that he was not a gentleman; and upon His Majesty starting back in surprise, the Duke added, that he was "not a gentleman, but the Sovereign of England, with duties to his people, and that those duties rendered it imperative to call in the services of Mr. Canning." The King

---

* The story, however, must be received with doubt. The Duke, as it appears from the 'Wellington Despatches,' did not have any interview with the King at this time, though the conversation may have taken place on some other occasion.

drew a long breath, and said, "Well, if I must, I must." *
But although Canning was thus admitted to the Cabinet as
Foreign Secretary, he was not taken into favour by the King
until five years afterwards, when the Minister had found
out the short way to win the good graces of George the
Fourth. It was not very long before Canning's motives for
accepting office were represented in a distorted light to his
constituents; and he had not yet won that popularity with
the masses which came to him in so great a measure before
his death in 1827. Efforts were made in 1822 to foster a
rivalry between Peel and Canning; but they never met with
much success. Mr. Canning makes the following reference
to this point in a letter to Mr. Croker of April 3rd, 1822:
"As to the two great names whom you mention in your last
note,† be assured that my feelings towards both are exactly
what you wish them to me [*sic* in original, but doubtless *be*]. To P. especially I feel it quite impossible to
do justice, for a frankness and straightforwardness beyond
example, and for feelings for which I own I did not before
give him credit, but which I hope I know how to value and
to return. The other has this moment left me, after a conversation of two hours, which has cleared away a world of
misapprehension, and left all well."

The circumstance which placed it within the power of
Lord Liverpool to offer the Foreign Secretaryship to Mr. Canning was the death of Lord Londonderry (Castlereagh), who
had outlived his popularity and usefulness alike. The facts
were described by Mr. Croker in a letter to Sir B. Blomfield,
who was then in disgrace with the King, but to whom
Mr. Croker never swerved in his fidelity. The ex-private

* Sir H. Bulwer's 'Historical Characters,' ii. 324.
† There is no note of Mr. Croker's to be found. The other "great name"
referred to was most probably that of the Duke of Wellington.

Secretary was almost completely deserted by his old friends, for the sufficient reason that he was out of favour at Court. But Mr. Croker did not run with the fickle crowd, and among other little services that he had it in his power to render his friend, he kept him constantly informed as to all that was going on.

Mr. Croker to Sir B. Blomfield.

August 12th, 1822.

Dear B.,

With what horror and surprise will you hear that Lord Londonderry is no more, and, alas! dead by his own hand! That such a mind should break down! I will endeavour, as well as grief and astonishment will allow, to tell you this lamentable, this distracting story.

On Friday he had his parting audience with the King, and his conversation towards the close became so incoherent and unhappy, that the King that evening wrote to Lord Liverpool at Coombe to come to him *directly*, but not to tell any one that he was coming, and not to see any soul till he should see him. You may judge of Lord Liverpool's surprise at receiving such a note, and with what strange thoughts he must have hastened to the King. His Majesty told him that Londonderry's mind was gone, and that when so strong and well-regulated an intellect was shaken, the consequences were likely to be proportionably serious. What more passed, or what Lord Liverpool did upon this, I cannot tell, probably nothing; as he certainly did not suspect the *extent* of the danger. He found that Londonderry had left town with Lady Londonderry for Cray, and had before he went appointed to meet Lord Liverpool in town on Monday or Tuesday. I understand that the Duke of Wellington, who left town on Friday, had also observed something wrong, and had sent Dr. Bankhead, Londonderry's favourite physician, to him. Dr. Bankhead saw him in St. James's Square on Friday evening, and now I shall give you *his* story. He found him labouring under a strong mental delusion, accompanied with fever. He had him cupped, which relieved him, and in the quiet of the evening it was thought he might go down to Cray with Lady Londonderry, Bankhead promising to follow next morning and stay till his Lordship was quite well.

He remained in bed all Saturday, and was kept as tranquil as possible. On Sunday (yesterday) he was much worse, a good deal of fever, heat, thirst, and an increase of delusion and wretchedness. He, however, grew less uncomfortable towards night, and it would seem that his state was not such as to prevent his sleeping as usual in Lady Londonderry's chamber. Doctor Bankhead took leave of him about midnight, and retired to his own room, which was close to theirs. About seven this morning Dr. Bankhead was called by Lady Londonderry's maid, who said my Lord wished to see him. The Doctor immediately rose and went into the bedroom, when he found Lord Londonderry had just gone into the dressing-room. He followed him, and saw him standing with his face to the window (and of course his back towards the Doctor) in his dressing-gown, with his head leaned back, and his eyes fixed on the ceiling. "My dear Lord," said he, "why do you stand so?" "O Bankhead," he said, "I am glad you are there, let me fall into your arms; it is all over:" and he fell back into Bankhead's arms, who then, for the first time, saw clenched in his right hand a small-bladed pen-knife, with which our unhappy friend had just divided by a deep cut the carotid artery, and with a sudden effusion of blood the body fell forward on the face, and Castlereagh expired without a struggle.

Precautions had been taken to remove his pistols and razors from his dressing-room, but with a little nail-knife which he carried in his pocket-book, and which had escaped their vigilance, he executed his fatal purpose with, they tell me, anatomical accuracy.

We had all dined with him the other day at Cray, and so happy did he appear, so amiable, so contented with all about him, that we all congratulated him on having so well recovered from the fatigues of the session, which had evidently pressed heavily upon him for the last weeks of our sittings. Little could any of us see in that placid countenance, in that playful smile, in those outstretched hands spread to welcome us, the dreadful change that a few days were to make. Good God! what weak and wretched creatures are the wisest and best of us! I write, I fear, very incoherently. God bless you.

Yours affectionately,

J. W. C.

Lord Londonderry had long been an unpopular man, and his friends dreaded that at his funeral there would be some manifestation of the ill-feeling with which he was regarded. These anticipations proved to be not altogether unfounded.

Mr. Croker to Sir William Knighton.

August 20th, 1822.

I am just come from poor Lord Londonderry's funeral. The Foreign Ministers and all the members of the Government (except the Cabinet and his lordship's more immediate connexions) assembled in the Jerusalem Chamber, near the Abbey. As I was in this situation, I did not see the procession; but I have been told that the people behaved very well. There were one or two observations made by individuals, such as 'Why did you not do as much for the Queen?" which Lord Maryborough heard; but in general there was no ill-disposition shown along the streets; but I am grieved and ashamed to say, that at the abbey door, when the coffin was taken out of the hearse, there was a *loud cheer*, a hurrah of triumph! In tone it was little different from the applause with which Lord Londonderry was last year received in the same place, when that which is now a corpse was the second figure in the most splendid ceremony that this country ever saw.* I had been all along apprehensive of some insults, and had used my little endeavour to persuade the friends to have an earlier and more private funeral; but I confess I apprehended only a *scattered* disapprobation, groans, or perhaps hisses; but the loud acclamation of joy from a considerable body of people I was totally unprepared for; and some persons within the abbey, deceived by the sound, thought it was a shout for the Duke of Wellington.

Ever yours,

J. W. C.

A reconstruction of Lord Liverpool's Ministry was now rendered necessary, but there was an interval of some days, during which nothing could be done in consequence of the

* [The Coronation.]

absence of the King, who had sailed for Scotland, two days before Londonderry's death. The history of the subsequent negotiations is contained in Mr. Croker's letters :—

Mr. Croker to Mr. Peel.

August 14th, 1822.

I happened to meet Huskisson to-day, and as he and I have had naturally a good deal of talk about Canning's going to India, he began to allude to the possibility of that voyage being defeated by *employment* at home. I need not attempt to detail our conversation—or rather his, for I had little to say. He seemed to think that the King's determination was likely to be most influenced by you, the more particularly as you were now the only House of Commons Minister, and must have a powerful voice in deciding who was to be your assistant; and this brings me to the real motive of my writing to you, which is to say that Huskisson dropped, in the most natural and unhesitating way possible, that there could be no doubt as to your being the *leader*, the only question being whether Canning was or was not necessary to *second* you, to enable you to carry on the public business. It would be too tedious to explain to you the slight but sincere and unaffected way in which this fell from Huskisson, as if it had been already settled. Willing to ascertain whether this was spoken in the very confiding way it appeared, I at the end of our conversation asked the question *direct*, but in an idle gossiping tone, whether Canning would give you the lead, to which he answered, with plain frankness, that he had no doubt of it, and the mode he answered my point-blank question satisfied me that the first insinuation was what it appeared, a casual hint of an opinion already formed.

Affectionately yours,

J. W. C.

To Mr. Peel.   Extract.

August 16th, 1822.

Dear Peel,

I have now to tell you that I find that Huskisson's anticipation of Canning's opinion was not correct. Canning came to town the day before yesterday, and yesterday Huskisson saw him for two or three hours; the result was, as H. told me to-day, that "if it were fairly and frankly offered to Canning to *fill Londonderry's place* both in office and the House he would accept it; but if there was to be any higgling or anything that showed suspicion of him, he owed it to himself to reject it with scorn." I use the words, though not *all* the words used to me. "He (C.) added that he had been five-and-twenty years before you in the House, that you would probably not have long to wait before he himself, who was now fifty-three, would leave you the career open; that he thought he could not with honour take an inferior station in the House, and if *that* were the alternative he must go to India." In the meanwhile he is to go to Liverpool to visit his constituents, and take leave, as if irrevocably destined for India. I leave you to form your own judgment upon all this. I only repeat (now, as in my last letter) what was said to me, and of which I could not justify to myself the leaving you ignorant.

I took care to-day to remind Huskisson of how much mistaken he had been as to Canning's real sentiments, but I did not do so in any way to imply that I had given any more weight to what he had said than to a common conversation between two friends. What followed I think is equally important. Huskisson laughed and said yes, but he might *also* be mistaken in another point. He was sure Canning liked India; he always had looked at it as a great object; he had acquired parliamentary reputation enough, and thought the station and consequent advantages of Governor-General extremely suited to his political feelings and private fortune, but Mrs. Canning was *furious* against it; that her opposition made him very uncomfortable (this I know is quite true, and existed before the late catastrophe); that she and several of his nearest friends always opposed his going, and would do so now with ten times more violence and with some colour of reason. He (H.) still thought he would go, if not detained by the offer already stated, "but what are the odds that in either case (viz. of the offer or no offer) he will stay at home?" I think the meaning of this clear; for my own part I have all along doubted that he would go; judge how much that opinion must be strengthened by the late event.

Huskisson, both to-day and before, alluded to Van [Van-

sittart], and said that he was the real *blot* and *sin* of the
Government. I said frankly that Van, though not a very
creditable Chancellor of the Exchequer, was a very useful
one. "For instance," I said, "if *you* had been in his office
this last year, we should have been all turned out, for you
neither would nor could have eaten your words and given
up principles in the way he did."

Affectionately yours,

J. W. C.

To Mr. Peel. Extract.

August 25th, 1822.

MY DEAR PEEL,

Every one agrees that if the present Government is to go
on, you or Canning must lead the House of Commons.
Canning has stated that he must have that duty or the
Foreign Seals, or that he will not come in at all. The best
informed think that the objection to him for any Cabinet
Office, and particularly for one of so much intercourse, is
insuperable. I do not believe in the insuperability of objections of that class; but it is certain there is strong disinclination, and *that* disinclination is likely to be reinforced by
some other minor circumstances, such as the feeling of the
Chancellor, &c. Those who build upon this foundation believe
further that Canning will go to India, and there are many good
reasons for such a supposition : yet I confess I incline to the
other opinion. Let us now look at the various alternatives.

If Canning is to come in on his own terms, with the consent of the present Cabinet—all is said; it will excite a good
deal of dissatisfaction amongst the subordinate office men,
and probably amongst some of the country gentlemen; but
this will not break out into any flame, unless Canning shall
mismanage his power either by indiscretion or by intrigue.
But all this is futurity.

If Canning does not come in, can you carry on the business
of the country in the House of Commons—1st, without him ;
2nd, against him ? Everybody says "Yes" to the former,
and *almost* everybody to the latter.

In the first case, you will be the only man of our party in
the House who has as yet shown himself equal to take the
great line of general debate, and even you are new in it.

If you were ever so practised, it could not be expected that human talents, health, spirits, could bear the whole weight of such sessions as we are likely to have. You must therefore have assistants. Who are they to be?

I shall put out of the question in this particular view Vansittart and Bragge Bathurst, because they are both inefficient for general debate. There remain Robinson * and Charles Wynn. Our friends say that Robinson must work, and some even are of opinion that he would, with a little practice, become an excellent and powerful debater. I myself believe that the minds and talents of men are more generally equal than is supposed and that most men are found, or at least become, equal to what is expected from them. Therefore if Robinson will boldly throw himself into the stormy current of debate, I think he may possibly be found to swim very well; but I doubt his making the effort. On this point, however, you, I suppose, would see your way, for, although it would be a delicate topic either of inquiry or convention, it is one which ought to be understood.

From Plunkett, except on Irish affairs, I do not think much could be expected. I do not think he has either the versatility, information, or boldness necessary for a general debater. Besides, I hear he is dissatisfied; and if he be sulky, nobody is so sulky. In short, if he and Goulburn manage Ireland and keep Spring Rice, Lord Wellesley, and Kit. Hutchinson† in check, it is as much as can be expected; but I ought to add that some of our friends here, and particularly the peers, talk sanguinely of Plunkett's assistance.

As none of those I have mentioned, except Robinson, are looked to even to play second fiddle, many persons have turned their thoughts to Palmerston, who they think as powerful in intellect as Robinson, and much more to be relied on in readiness and nerve. I agree in the latter part of this opinion, but not in the former. He himself was yesterday expressing great expectations from Robinson's acuteness of mind and great natural eloquence of expression, if he could be induced to take heartily to the work. I think

* ["Prosperity" Robinson, afterwards, as stated in a previous note, created Viscount Goderich and Earl of Ripon. He became Chancellor of the Exchequer in 1823.]

† [The Hon. Christopher Hutchinson, M.P. for Cork, son of Lord Donoughmore.]

Palmerston's deficiency is exactly that which we are now considering how to supply—that *flow* of ideas and language which can run on for a couple of hours without, on the one hand, committing the Government, or, on the other, lowering by commonplaces or inanities the station of a Cabinet Minister.   No Government, I believe, was ever better manned in the subordinate departments than ours.   There are, as Lord Londonderry often said to me, in each office, persons able to repel any assailant on the details of the particular office; and of these Palmerston was the very ablest, but is he fit to be a lieutenant-general, and command the right wing of the army?   If he be, and that His Excellency General Bordotradovitz * will undertake the responsibility of the left, *vous voilà au complet!*

Finally, and I have reserved this for the last, Huskisson's claims to the Cabinet are by his acquaintances much insisted upon.†   He must feel that if Canning comes in on this *peculiar* vacancy he cannot, and in honour need not, make any stipulation for him.   If Canning goes to India, Huskisson may think that you can hardly do without *him;* and if Canning stays, he probably foresees that he, H., will be eventually dragged into opposition, which on every account he would dislike.   I believe public men are more often candid and disinterested than people give them credit for, and I believe H. is really anxious for Canning's success in his object, on the score of friendship, as well as from his belief that Canning's peculiar quality of Parliamentary eloquence ought not to be exported to India like the skates and warming-pans to Buenos Ayres.   But if that fails, he will, I dare say, have no objection to come himself into the Cabinet, and is likely to be very much dissatisfied if he be passed over; though if Canning go to India, he will not venture to throw up and go into opposition alone.   At the same time it must be recollected that all that Huskisson can do for the Government he can do best in his present rank. He is not a good debater, and is still worse at those great speeches which I have before spoken of.   He is *au fait* in all official and financial details, and has a great deal of what the French call *administrative* experience.   But the defects of

* [A nickname for Robinson, who was President of the Board of Trade.]

† [Among all these changes, Huskisson was made President of the Board of Trade.]

his manner and voice prevent his being a useful speaker, for
no one is useful whom the House merely tolerates—who, on
the contrary, does not force them to attend to him. From
what I have before written to you, you will conclude that he
hankers after Van's gold gown ; but great as may be the
difference between the men, I almost doubt whether Van
is not as safe and as work-withable a Chancellor of the
Exchequer as Huskisson would be, and I think I may say
that the general opinion seems to leave Van in the quiet
possession of his dead weight and his small remnant of
sinking fund.

Mr. Croker to the Marquis of Hertford.

September 2nd, 1822.

DEAR H.,

Peel arrived yesterday about fifteen minutes before the
King. I had half an hour's conversation with His Majesty,
and an hour's with Peel. Neither knows any more of L.'s *
intention than you or I. K. [the King] is evidently averse
from Canning, and has made up *his* mind on that point ;
reste à voir whether he can hold his intention. Peel has
never opened his lips on the subject to King or Minister.
Even I do not know what he will do, though I can guess
what he would wish. In truth, no one can any more tell
what he may in the course of a negotiation be brought to do
than one can foretell what will happen in a battle to be
fought to-morrow. One thing I am sure of, he would not
be very sorry if, with honour, he was out of his office.

The King asked me whether Lord L. was in a good
humour, almost as a boy after holidays asks in what temper
Dr. Busby may be.

Yours,

J. W. C.

While all these speculations as to the future of the Cabinet
were going on so actively in London, Mr. Peel appears to have
been intent chiefly upon the enjoyment of his country life.
He had written to Croker from Edinburgh in August, giving

* [Lord Liverpool.]

some account of the King's reception, and making a passing remark only in reference to Lord Londonderry's death: "There are some subjects on which one does injustice to one's feelings by saying anything, and our departed friend's death is one of them. I bitterly deplore it." In October, Mr. Croker wrote to Lord Hertford: "I hear from Peel that he shot in one day to his own gun—pheasant, 1; rabbits, 8; hares, 11; partridges, 41."

It will be observed that the last letter given above is addressed to the "Marquis of Hertford," who has hitherto appeared in this correspondence under the title of the Earl of Yarmouth. In the year now under consideration, he succeeded to his father's title and estates. From this time, down to about the year 1840, it will be found that some of Mr. Croker's most interesting letters were written to Lord Hertford; and there are various other circumstances which tended to make his intimacy with this nobleman somewhat remarkable. It will therefore be desirable to say a few words upon that intimacy before going any further.

The Earl of Yarmouth had been one of the first to recognise the undoubted abilities which Mr. Croker displayed at the outset of his parliamentary career, and when he became personally acquainted with the young member he was struck, as was everybody else who knew him, with his great gift of discretion, and his unfailing stock of common sense. These may seem to be but homely qualities, after all, and yet it falls to the lot of comparatively few persons to possess them in an eminent degree. Moreover, Mr. Croker was a man of great quickness of spirit and acuteness; his intellectual powers were keen, and they were rapidly brought into play when they were needed; his range of information on political and literary subjects was wide; his tact in dealing with other men was always to be trusted; and in private society, no one could be more amusing or more gay. All who knew him concur in giving substantially this account of him—modified, of course, by personal likes or dislikes, but not varying in any essential point. That he won the confidence of everybody to whom he was attached is, however, the best proof that could be afforded of Mr. Croker's superiority to the common run of men in all the qualities just mentioned.

The Earl of Yarmouth, then, became a great friend of Mr. Croker's. He was himself a man of superior ability, and probably had he chosen to devote serious attention to political life, he would have made a distinguished figure in it. But he was essentially a man of pleasure, and no one has ever yet succeeded in acquiring political distinction who devoted the greater part of his time and ingenuity to the indulgence of his own whims or propensities. Fox can scarcely be called an exception to this rule, for, although he was undoubtedly fond of pleasure, he always found ways and means of bestowing an adequate degree of attention upon political business. But Lord Yarmouth—or Lord Hertford—studied nothing but his own desires. He lived the life of a voluptuary, and was satisfied with it. Yet he always took a lively interest in public affairs, and for many years he depended almost exclusively upon Mr. Croker for giving him the means of understanding that which was going on—for he spent no small part of his time abroad, and very rarely read any papers. He sought Mr. Croker's opinion on the management of his estates, and gradually he came to place entire reliance upon his judgment, and was more than once saved from very great embarrassments by following the suggestions of his prudent counsellor. Mr. Croker, in fact, exercised a kind of practical superintendence over the property, just as Mr. James Loch, M.P., did over the estates of the Duke of Sutherland and Lord Ellesmere—with this important difference, that Mr.

Croker received no salary.   Frequently he was urgently
pressed to accept some compensation for his services, for they
involved the sacrifice of no small amount of time and attention ; but these offers were invariably declined.   Lord Hertford
always declared that he would compel Mr. Croker to receive
part of the wealth which he had helped to preserve, under
the provisions of his will; and that he was sincere in this
intention we shall hereafter have occasion to see.

In the year with which we are now dealing, Lord Hertford
was forty-five.   In 1798 he had contracted a marriage which
did not turn out very happily, although there is no reason
to suppose that the fault rested with any one but himself.
His wife was Maria Fagniani, a young lady whom the
well-known George Selwyn had adopted as his daughter,
although his claims to this privilege were not entirely undis-
puted.   It was said that the Duke of Queensberry, "Old Q.,"
was equally willing to acknowledge Maria Fagniani as his
own child.   According to Horace Walpole,* she was eight
years of age in 1779, and therefore at the time of her marriage
with the Earl of Yarmouth, she must have been twenty-
seven—six years older than her husband.   Walpole makes
two other allusions to her.   In 1789, he writes:—" I have
such a passion for dogs that a favourite one is a greater
misery than pleasure, and to give me one is to sow me with
anxiety.   I would as soon adopt Mademoiselle Fagniani."
In 1791, he tells us that George Selwyn had left his adopted
daughter thirty thousand pounds, the Duke of Queensberry
to be residuary legatee—a droll concession, apparently, to the
peculiar claims which the Duke felt himself entitled to make
at an earlier period.   The Duke of Queensberry left her

---

* " La Signorina I have not seen, and, in truth, did not not ask to see
her.   I love David too well not to be peevish at an Abishag of eight
years old."   (Letter to the Countess of Ossory, November 21, 1779.)

150,000*l*., and three houses, making her husband, Lord
Hertford, residuary legatee.*   Then there was her other father
—or, at any rate, the husband of her mother—the Marquis
Fagniani.   How much he left her is nowhere stated.   Never
before did a lady have so many fathers, or derive so,much
profit from them.

By this lady, the third Marquis of Hertford had two sons
and one daughter; the elder of the sons lived to become
the fourth marquis, and died in 1870.   It does not appear
that after the birth of the third child, Lord Hertford lived
with or saw much of his wife, and his occasional references
to her in his letters are not of a particularly affectionate or
cordial description.   She survived him fourteen years—dying
in 1856 (one year before Mr. Croker) at the age of eighty-
five.   Lord Hertford himself died in 1842, at the age of
sixty-five.   In the chapter dealing with the events of 1842 it
will be necessary to review certain circumstances which
arose out of his death.

In a reference to Lord Hertford, however brief, it would
be vain to ignore the fact that he has usually been
identified with the "Marquis of Steyne" of 'Vanity Fair,'
and with the "Lord Monmouth" of 'Coningsby'—not to
enumerate many less celebrated and less vitriolic sketches.
These portraits, if such they really were intended to be,
extenuated nothing in the original; in one case, indeed,
personal animosity towards Mr. Croker alone prompted
the introduction of Lord Monmouth, in order that there
might be linked with him an abject wretch named "Rigby,"
one of the most repulsive objects in the whole range of
modern fiction.   Why Mr. Disraeli hated Mr. Croker so bitterly

* "In 1810 he succeeded to the greatest part of the disposable property
of the rich and eccentric Duke of Queensberry—the putative father of his
wife." *Annual Register*, 1842, p. 255.

it would scarcely be worth while now to discuss; enough that
there were reasons for it, although they were not good reasons;
and we need not the evidence of Mr. Croker's case to attest
that Mr. Disraeli paid off his personal grudges with no niggard
hand. In the first part of his life, especially, Mr. Disraeli
was a relentless, and it may almost be said, an unscrupulous
antagonist. It may be doubted whether any man was ever
so base as the Rigby of 'Coningsby' is depicted; it is a
conception which must inspire in the mind of every reader
contempt and detestation. And yet this vile creature is
supposed to have been Mr. Disraeli's portrait of Mr. Croker.

Whether the satire was just or unjust, every impartial
reader will be able to decide when he has come to the end of
the records of Mr. Croker's life. Before Mr. Disraeli's own
position became assured, he pursued all who seemed to cross
his path with the vindictiveness of a Red Indian. Mr. Croker,
he believed, had once or twice stood in the way of his projects,
at a time when politics were less important to him than
literature. It has also been stated that Mr. Croker provoked
Mr. Disraeli's resentment by attacking him in the *Quarterly
Review* and elsewhere; but in reality Mr. Croker had never
written a single line against or about him. With Isaac
Disraeli he had always been on most friendly terms, and
when the 'Commentaries on Charles the First' appeared,
it was found that the author had referred in grateful and
eulogistic language to the object of Benjamin Disraeli's vin-
dictive lampoons. "To my ever kind and valued friend,
the Right Hon. John Wilson Croker"—so wrote the elder
Disraeli—"whose luminous and acute intelligence is as remarkable in his love of literature and art, as it has been in
the course of a long, an honourable, and distinguished public
life, I stand deeply indebted." The son did not share this
admiration for Mr. Croker's "acute intelligence." Apparently

it was too acute, and had been exercised with too much good
faith, to satisfy him. How deep was his resentment he showed
by a scurrilous attack upon Mr. Croker immediately after his
death, published in a newspaper which was known to be his
mouthpiece—the *Press*. This attack provoked an indignant
remonstrance even from *Punch*. "What," it exclaimed,
"the man who served the Conservatives before he gave them
that delicate name—when they were Tories—and was serving
them from his bed of sickness and pain until within a few
hours of his death ? The ablest advocate with tongue and
pen whom they have had during half a century ? The man
dies, and before he is laid in the tomb, the paper sacred to
his party and to their plebeian chief issues this spiteful and
ungrateful picture ? " So it was ; and the animosity and
injustice which Mr. Disraeli thus exhibited will always remain a blemish on his literary reputation.

What Lord Hertford's morals may have been is a different
question. Mr. Croker, it is to be presumed, was not responsible
for them. He did not make them, and he could not unmake
them. To suppose even that he had any influence over them
is preposterous, for Lord Hertford passed much of his life
in Paris, Naples, or Milan, and his amusements, such as they
were, could scarcely have been selected for him in England.
The strictest moralist will scarcely contend that it was Mr.
Croker's duty to decline any further acquaintance with Lord
Hertford, on account of his irregular habits ; if that principle
were generally enforced, it is to be presumed that many men
would have to cut off one or more of their friends. The
Duke of Wellington, Sir Robert Peel, Sir Walter Scott, Lord
Carnarvon, and other eminent men of the time were intimate
with Lord Hertford, and no one thought the worse of them on
that account. In Lord Hertford's letters there are a few free
expressions here and there ; men used rather free expressions

to each other—and not to each other only, but to women—
in the days of the Regency; but there is no evidence in
these letters that the writer was a desperately immoral man.
There is other evidence which tells heavily against him; the
evidence of his own acts which became only too notorious
in the end must be deemed absolutely ruinous. All sense of
decency and shame must at last have departed from him.
The probability seems to be, as we shall see hereafter, that in
his last and worst days his mind was disordered. But on
points of morals, he never dreamt of consulting Mr. Croker,
and it is not very likely that he would have been guided by
his good counsel, had it been offered. The question which concerns us is, what were the relations existing between Lord
Hertford and Mr. Croker? Were they those which prevailed
between "Mr. Rigby" and "Lord Monmouth," or such as
might exist between honourable men? The correspondence
will enable any one who considers it fairly to arrive at a just
decision.

The father of the Lord Hertford with whom these pages
have to do, died in June 1822. The following letter explains
all the circumstances.

Mr. Croker to Sir B. Blomfield.   Extract.

June 21st, 1822.

My DEAR B.,

Poor old Lord Hertford is gone at last. The will is not yet
opened, but it is known by the report of his attorney that he
has tied up his real estates as tight as he could, and has left
all his personals to Lady Hertford. It cannot be denied
that he judged wisely and kindly in making Lady Hertford
an object of future attention from his family, and it was but
just that he should *share* with her accumulations to which
her great property no doubt contributed; but on the other
hand it seems hard, considering that she has between thirty
and forty thousand a year, that she should have *all* the
personals, and that Yarmouth should not have even £20,000

for his " mise en campagne." After all, however, it is said
that the accumulation does not exceed £200,000, and the
best part of the other personals, such as plate, pictures, &c.,
&c., are old family property and belong of right to Yarmouth.
The landed estate is said to be about £85,000 per annum.
viz : — Ireland, £57,000 ; Scotland, £3000 ; Warwickshire,
£15,000 ; and Sudbourne, £10,000 ; and Lord Hertford having
died a few days before *Midsummer*, the half year's rent now
falling due is his, and will, of course, give him £40,000 to
start with. As I dare say he will not begin, all at once, to
increase his expenses, he may enter upon the next year with
a clear income (including his own separate property) of at
least £90,000 per annum. The old lord is to be buried on
Monday next at Ragley. Beauchamp * is here, and I hope
Yarmouth, who felt the inconvenience of a narrow and jealous
system himself, will act handsomely by him. I have no
doubt that he will do what he thinks just and liberal, for in
all my life I never knew a man so fixed upon doing what he
considered his duty, but he has a little of a " neither more
nor less " disposition, which makes him sometimes appear
unamiable when he considers himself as doing all that can
possibly be expected of him. It was this temper which got
him the character of avarice in the world, although we who
know him well, know him to be one of the most generous
and most friendly of men, but he always stickled about *right*,
and while he was giving away hundreds as *bounty* and *favour*,
he would resist a *claim* of *two-pence*. I once saw an amusing
instance of this disposition. One day when he was out of
Parliament, he came all the way from Seymour Place to the
Admiralty for a *frank* to his servant in the country ; it was
the depth of autumn, and there were no Peers or Members
in town, so that he was obliged to come to me, and the
object of his letter was to give orders for the reception of a
party of friends which cost him at least £500—here he saved
sixpence, and if he had been tired would have got into a
hackney coach and paid half a crown fare in order to get
this said frank. His real character is, however, beginning to
be understood ; the world now sees that although he is
minute and strict in trifles, and though he has shades of his
family oddities, he is one of the highest minded, most

* [Horace Beauchamp Seymour, nephew of the old Earl of Hertford,
and M.P. for Orford ; afterwards Sir Horace Seymour.]

generous of men—"a bitter foe but an unbounded friend" as his relation, Horace Walpole, said of himself; and indeed, after all, Yarmouth's friendships are much more warm than his enmities.   What a chapter of La Bruyère I have written, and to *you*, too, who know the man as well as I do.

In a subsequent letter to Sir B. Blomfield, Mr. Croker somewhat reduces the amounts given above—the total income from the land and other sources being, he thinks, about 80,000*l.*—and he says of the heir, "with his houses and gardens and preserves, his wife, and his sons and his daughter, and all other claims upon him, I doubt whether he will be really a richer man than he was, and I am sure not so happy a one."   Sir B. Blomfield, in his reply, remarks: "I know acts of his bounty to a considerable amount, and which he never willingly allowed to meet the light."

Mr. Peel to Mr. Croker.   Extract.

September, 1822.

I was really pleased at Lord Hertford getting the Garter. I was pleased very disinterestedly, and for his own sake merely, for I like him.   He is a gentleman, and not an every-day one.

We call him Lord Hertford now.   He was Yarmouth with his familiars.   I dare say he has no curiosity to know what he would have been with his brothers and sisters.

Lord Hertford's letters to Mr. Croker were generally in a light and playful vein; and his comments on passing events were often marked by much shrewdness and discernment. Few of them bear any date, superscription, or signature.*

* There are not many of Lord Hertford's letters among Mr. Croker's papers.   Probably most of them were returned to the writer before his death.

Lord Yarmouth to Mr. Croker.

[No date, but marked by Mr. Croker " 1820."]

DEAR CROKER,

I delight in your notes; they are always musical to my ears, though to me your language never has either of two very essential harmonic sounds—the *sharp* and the *flat*.

I thought you were quite *en garçon*, or would have sent you game. My father writes me word he sends me a *buck* for my numerous party, and so as I have no party, I pray you eat a *haunch*, the Orbys will eat another, and the skinny apothecary shall fatten *his* on its *sides*. And so God bless you.

[Same period.]

DEAR C.,

Verily I have forgotten to tell you that a garret in my stable contains several pheasants for Munster House. I hope they are alive, pray take them away; and so no more at present.

Aldborough, October, 1821.

DEAR CROKER,

How do you do? What's going on in town? I came to Sudbourne the day after you all honoured me at dinner, and stayed till my seat at table between my father and Lady William Gordon reminded me too plainly of my hereditary right to a cell in Bedlam;* and then I went to Rendlesham, where there was a pleasant party, with Scappa, the opera band leader, to make musical noises, and I return to Rendlesham next Sunday to meet the Duke of York; meanwhile I am come to eat shrimps, and look at the sea.

Tell me whether Peel's woods are near his castle or far off—meaning whether I ought to send my cavalry or trust to my legs, now in very good walking trim. I sent you some sherry, which Colonel Hare got from some great friend somewhere in Spain; I hope it will be good, but I have no hope it will (of its kind) be equal to what you sent me.

The scene here is now gay—*quia triste*—wreck picking up, and seven anchors fished out of the mighty deep, besides a

* [This allusion derives a deeper significance from the events preceding his death. See Vol. II. Chapter XXII., pp. 415–419.]

Memel timber ship knocked ashore. I wish you were to be at Rendlesham to meet the Duke on Sunday, and then, perhaps, you would come here for a day or two first, and breathe fresh air. And so God bless you.

March, 1822.

All London saith B. B.* is restored—that Ministers objected to the Lady's † nomination, and that the K [ing] said, "If I cannot please you by·dismissing an old and faithful servant, let me have him back."

And she answered, and said, " Yea."

The allusion in the last letter is to the downfall of Sir B. Blomfield, which was ascribed to the influence of the person then paramount at court—Lady Conyngham. On the other hand, Sir B. Blomfield's administration of the king's private purse does not appear to have been guided by very strict principles of economy, and the King's suspicions were aroused. But the deposed private secretary was soon consoled by obtaining employment in the diplomatic service, and eventually by receiving a peerage.

Mr. Croker did not believe that Lady Conyngham's hand was in this intrigue; but of her great power over the King, he, like all the world, was fully assured. Some curious glimpses of the inner life of the Court are given in a diary of this year, and in certain parts of the correspondence.

From Mr. Croker's Diary.

January 11*th*, 1822.—Left town at 12 and arrived at Brighton at 6. On our arrival the servants told us that we were late and should have barely time to dress, as the King's dinner-hour was *six*. We therefore made all possible haste, and were accordingly the first of the *inmates* in the saloon, except Lord St. Helens, the Lord-in-waiting. Mr. and Lady

---

* [Sir B. Blomfield.]   † [Lady Conyngham.]

Anne Becket were also there.   The King came in about 20 minutes after 6, and dinner was served about half-past.

Lady Blomfield came in just before Lady Conyngham and Lady Eliz., and was, I thought, to all appearance on the same footing as heretofore.   Sir B. himself came in after the King, and no one could [fail to] see in his quiet and reserved manner a difference from the kind of *factotum bustle* in which we used to see him.

The King was looking remarkably well and stout on his legs ; he went round the circle as usual.   I thought—perhaps it was fancy—but I thought that his manner was somewhat more *hasty* than usual, and that he expressed himself to his family with more pettishness than I had ever seen, in public, or, I should rather say, in his circle, where he was always, to all persons and under all circumstances, particularly gracious. To-day he had quite the air of scolding Paget.

Our dinner-party were the King, who sate between the two Ladies Conyngham, in the centre of one side ; Lord Conyngham and Lady Anne Becket, at the upper end ; Lord Francis and Andrew Barnard at the other ; Blomfield exactly opposite his Majesty, and Lady Blomfield, Lords Lowther and St. Helens, Sirs William Keppel, Charles Paget, Edmund Nagle and Hilgrove Turner, Col. Thornton, Mark Singleton and myself, rather too close, round the table.

The dinner was, I think, rather shorter than usual.   I thought the cuisine a shade inferior to what it used to be. The King made us all eat some roast wild boar from Hanover. It was very good, like pork with a game flavour ; he asked me what I thought of it.   I said it was to pork what pheasant was to fowl.   "There I differ from you," said the King, "nothing is so good as a fowl ; if they were as scarce as pheasants, and pheasants as plenty as fowls, no one would eat a pheasant."

When H.M. took a glass of wine with Lady C., he *touched glasses* with her in the old-fashioned way.

I suppose I ought not to omit that she and Lady Eliz. were dressed in rich cashmeres ; Lady C.'s a white, and Lady E.'s a scarlet ; the wide borders of the shawls making the flounce of the gown.   They are very *costly*, as Conyngham told us, but they make no great show, and are not, I think, very becoming.

At dinner some conversation arose about the King's being expected to go to the play one of those evenings, and of the

manager's having announced it.   He seems a good deal
annoyed; he said that he had consented to give the poor man
" his patronage, but that meant a hundred pounds and not his
company."   Lady C. insisted that the *public* expected him;
that it would be a great disappointment; that 10 guineas
had been given for a box; that whether by mistake or otherwise, the royal word was *engaged*, and so forth.   The King
warmly denied the *engagement* and appealed to Blomfield,
who quietly and determinately said, " I not only *told* him,
but *wrote* to him that the King *would not go*;" but still
the ladies insisted, and at last Lady C. applied to Lord
Francis, who said that the man had told him that he did not
expect the King, " but nevertheless his *placard* gave out that
the play was by command, and everybody expected the King,
and that ten guineas had been given for a box."   This went
on for some time, the King still on the defensive, and appealing to Blomfield's statement.

This brought him to the play at Calais, of which he gave
us an account, enlivened by Sir Ed. Nagle's admiration of one
of the opera dancers, who as Sir Ed. expressed it, " held her
leg up *square with her shoulder* in a wonderful manner;" but
the best of all was the king's mimicry of the old Duc de la
Chatre, explaining to him that these actors and dancers at
Calais were second-rate performers.   I never heard anything
so perfect in the way of imitation of voice, matter, and
manner, as his representation of the old mumbling Duke.

He talked of Tickell, the author of 'Anticipation,' and
praised his talents highly.*   He said that Sheridan, his
brother-in-law, was a little " *refroidi* " towards Tickell after
the great success of 'Anticipation.'   Tickell was in great
distress and committed suicide by throwing himself out of a
window of his apartments at Hampton Court; the same Lord
George Seymour now has: " the fall was so violent, that
there was a hole *a foot deep* made by his head in the gravel
walk."   The King did not, he said, know much of Tickell,
personally, but if he had known he was in distress he would
have, at least, saved him from the necessity of such a
catastrophe.

This led him to speak of 'Anticipation,' which he did *con
amore* and quoted some of the speeches: by the way, it was

---

* [Richard Tickell, died in 1793. 'Anticipation' appeared in 1778.
He was a contributor to the ' Rolliad.']

this which introduced the mention of Tickell. The King quoted from 'Anticipation' Lord Lansdowne's ridiculous quotation, and this brought on the rest of the conversation. Lady Conyngham had never read 'Anticipation;' the King said he would have it looked out for her. The events and the piece were gone by, he said, but the wit and pleasantry of it never could fade. I, myself, doubt whether Lady C. will find either wit or pleasantry in it. She will read it like an old parliamentary debate.

This led him to *John Bull,* which, he said, was the only thing in political writing which rivalled ' Anticipation' and the 'Rolliad.' I admitted that *Bull* had force and sometimes pleasantry, but that I thought *he* wanted *taste,* which the others possessed in an eminent degree; the King would not agree in this, and went off into a dissertation on *taste* and *genius.* Very clever but rambling. He made some really just and critical distinctions, but then he, in some passages, involved himself to a degree to be hardly intelligible.

He ended, however, by saying that neither *he,* nor his ministers, nor his parliament, nor his courts of justice all together, had done so much good as *John Bull;* he stated this in a way which surprised me from its force and vehemence and, let me add, exaggeration.

He then fell upon Judge Bayley, for his sentence on the editors of this paper,* and for his conduct at Nottingham two years ago. Whereon, he said, they were obliged to recall him. The King now intimated that Lord Liverpool agreed that Bayley ought not to be left in the King's Bench, and that on an expected vacancy in the Exchequer, Bayley would be removed thither, where he could do much less mischief. Both Becket and I attempted to say a word in mitigation, but he would not hear a syllable; indeed, I never saw His Majesty so very impatient of anything that looked like contradiction as he now was.

In the beginning of dinner he again alluded to my not having come down earlier, and was particularly kind in lamenting that I had not brought down " that dear little girl

---

* [The proprietors of the *John Bull* newspaper were defendants in three cases in 1821. First for a libel on Lady Jersey, when they obtained a verdict of not guilty on a technical point, and subsequently for libels on the Queen and on Alderman Waithman, in both of which cases they were cast in heavy damages.]

of mine" to his child's ball last Monday. He was very good-natured and condescending on this topic, and desired me to tell the little girl how angry he was with me on her account.

When we had had our coffee we followed His Majesty, and found the company increased by old Lord Eardley and Lady Say and Sele and her daughter, Lord and Lady Ravensworth and two daughters, Lady Ongley, Lady Wm. Bentinck, Prince Ladoria, Count St. Antonio's brother, Lord Newburgh and his brother, and some other young man whom I did not know (Lord Ongley, I believe); the King was at the forte piano with the two Misses Liddell, and sang with them "Life's a Bumper," "The Friar of Orders Grey," and two or three Italian trios. They are pretty girls and sing well.

While all this music was going on, Lady C. and Lady Elizabeth sat apart. I thought that they did not much like it.

Afterwards the King took Barnard's arm and walked about with him, treating him with marked affection; after which he sat down to a card-table with Barnard and Lady C. and played at *patience* the whole night. Blomfield, never spoken to nor taking any part in what was going forward, made a party of whist with Lords Conyngham and St. Helens, and Sir William.

The band was in the long gallery, and there, on a sofa, sat old Michael Kelly,* whom the King once went out to speak to. Blomfield introduced me to the old man, who, but for his gout, would not look so *old*. About half-past eleven sandwiches were handed round, and the King wished us good night.

He had for the last hour missed his snuff-box, and there was quite a tumult about it, and a search *high and low;* everywhere, in short, except in the King's own pocket; it was quite a scene in a farce, all the actors in it looking wonderfully grave. At last, as the King was going away, after a vain hunt, which, as Lowther said, was like "hunt the slipper," he turned severely to Blomfield and said, "re-

---

* [This incident is mentioned with great pride in Michael Kelly's memoirs, published in 1826. Kelly was a well-known singer and actor. At this period he suffered much from the gout, but, he says, "the chief and dearest comfort remaining to me in this life, is the proud consciousness that I am honoured by the patronage of my beloved monarch."]

member it *must* be found to-morrow," and this he repeated, even *sternly*. When he was out of hearing, I called out to Blomfield, "Blomfield, which of the Ladies have the *King's box* for this evening?" This put us into good humour again, and in a quarter of an hour one of the pages came to tell us that the King had found the box himself. The King would not say *where*, but we all knew from the page that it was, as I expected, in his own pocket.

July 12th.—I walked about town with Lady Anne Becket. There is quite an *émeute* about the King's not going to the play; I cannot guess how it will end, but I see it is very unlucky and indecent that the King's name should be used to swindle people to take play-house tickets. It is whispered that Lady C. had engaged to persuade the King to go, and that she will be mortified if she fails. Lady Anne, who sat near Lord C. at dinner yesterday, says that he whispered her, that Lady C. was going to propose the King's going. · "Oh," said his Lordship, "*she will make him go.*"

The Beckets think that Lady C.'s favour is, if not on the decline, at least not at such a height as it has been. If it were what it was a year ago, they think that the King would not have hesitated to have gone to this play. I do not think much of this circumstance, but I think there may be some reason for their notion that the *fever* of affection is gone by. *Nous verrons*. Lady Anne told me of a little passage at dinner yesterday which I had not observed. The King was recommending some kind of toddy, or negus, as being very good. Becket said heedlessly, "O yes, sir, there can be no doubt of its being good, for it was introduced here *about four years ago and it has held its ground*." Lady Anne says that Lady C. gave Becket an angry scowl for thus celebrating the glories of the *last reign*.

I am surprised to find the Royal *Chapels* in the Lord Steward's department. Lord Conyngham, to whom I expressed my wonder, says it is because the choir must *eat*, and that as he furnishes the table for the singing men, they and the chapels are "de son ressort." The reason does not seem satisfactory; for all men eat as well as the singing men, yet all things are not in the kitchen department. However it may be, Conyngham was all day busy in preparing the new Chapel for to-morrow's service. It is only fitted up in a very temporary manner, and even its more permanent ornaments are plain even to a fault. The ceiling, for instance, has not one bit of stucco, except a paltry little rose for the screw that is to hold the lustre. Their chief care seems to be how to make and to keep it warm enough. Two great fire-places in the body of the room and a Russian stove in the King's own tribune seemed not enough; but in the midst of all their debates and consultations I happened to ask to what heat they had brought it; and lo! there was no thermometer, nor had they thought of measuring the heat that way.

What an atmosphere the King lives in! He never, since he has been at Brighton, has left his own room, except to walk *across* at half-past three or four to Lady C.'s house, and at six to walk back, he then dresses and comes down to dinner, and that is the whole of his air and exercise. By-the-bye, all the world, if they chose, might see this daily visit; for the King goes out at the south gate of the inclosure and has a few yards of the common street to walk to reach the steps of Lady C.'s house.

Dinner to-day was half an hour later than usual; the King, it seemed afterwards, was trying on some new coats, and he had sent for Sir Edmund Nagle to give him one in which His Majesty did not feel uncomfortable. The King amused himself with Nagle's attributing this " trouvaille " to his being a *well-made man*, but while His Majesty laughed at Nagle's pretence, *he* took care to let us know how ridiculously ill the coat fitted Nagle; and Nagle who blunders "certâ ratione modoque," paid his court by sending the coat, which, he said, fitted him so well, to London *to be altered.*

At dinner the King quoted one of Sir Charles Hanbury Williams's odes.* He attributed too much of the darkness of Sir Charles's latter life to his poltroonery as to Hussey; in fact, the most brilliant part of his public life was after that scandal. They now began to talk of Lady Hervey's letters, and I owned to the King that I was the editor of them,†

---

* [Sir Chas. Hanbury Williams (1709–1759) wrote an insulting poem called ' The Conquered Duchess,' addressed to his friend Mr. Fox, on the marriage of the Duchess of Manchester with Mr. Hussey, an Irishman. Sir C. H. Williams, whose courage was not equal to his wit, fled into Wales to avoid a hostile meeting with Hussey, and was glad to leave the country and accept the office of Envoy at Dresden in 1746. For an account of his poems see *Quarterly Review*, xxviii. 46.]

† [See *supra*, p. 185.]

so far as adding a short life of her Ladyship and a few
notes, in one or two of which I said His Majesty would
see that I had ventured to use some anecdotal information
which I had heretofore received from him. He was very
gracious on this point, and said that if I had consulted
him and let him into my secret, he would have afforded me
still more. He was, he said, a great *reservoir* of anecdote, for
he had lived not only with all the eminent persons of the last
fifty years, but he had had an early acquaintance with several
eminent persons of the preceding half century.

He spoke very highly of Mr. Bayle Walsingham, the son
of Sir C. Hanbury's second daughter. He said he had more
wit and talents, and as much good sense and good nature as
any man he ever had known, and if he had not died early
would have been one of the most considerable men that
England had produced.

Our dinner party had been the same as the day before,
minus the Beckets; they were now in the saloon with Lord
and Lady Ravensworth and the two musical daughters, and
Knyvett, Sale, and Hawes, with two of the boys of the Chapel
Royal, and the sub-dean Mr. Holmes. These latter ones came
to sing in the Chapel to-morrow, so the King takes advantage
of their being here to have a musical night. He never left
the pianoforte; he sang in 'Glorious Apollo,' 'Mighty Conqueror,' 'Lord Mornington's Waterfall' (encored), 'Non
nobis, Domine,' and several other glees and catches. His
voice, a bass, is not good, and he does not sing so much from
the notes as from recollection. He is, therefore, as a musician
merely, far from good, but he gave, I think, the force, gaiety,
and spirit of the glees in a superior style to the professional
men. Attwood was at the instrument.

The two Misses Liddell also joined in the concert, and old
Michael Kelly was wheeled in, in a gouty chair, and sang the
solo of " Sleep you or wake you," with all the force of a broken
voice, in which, however, there were the remains of better
than the other men could now produce.

Lady Conyngham and Lady Elizabeth did not conceal their
dissatisfaction at all this music, and particularly at the
Liddells. Lady Elizabeth asked me what title Mr. Knyvett,
the singer, claimed. I told her. " I suppose," said she, " he
begins to hope to get it now that he sees that one *musical*
family has got the peerage."

The King, indeed, left his music but one moment the whole
evening, and we had the unmusical ladies all to ourselves.

At six o'clock I heard that the King had sent to have the fire lighted in his box at the play-house; so that I suspected that Lady C. had accomplished her object. However, His Majesty did not go, and the Conyngham and Blomfield *children* and their governesses filled the box. Lowther, Blomfield, and one or two others looked in ; the audience was very loyal, and, I was told, applauded Blomfield.

The King expressed great satisfaction at Lord Wellesley's conduct in Ireland. He told us that Lord Wellesley on accepting the office, had made a kind of apology for his former secession and expressed his gratitude to the King for re-admitting him into favour and his devotion to his service ; "in short," said the King, " I could not help exclaiming to him, ' RICHARD'S *himself again.'* "

Mr. Croker to Sir B. Blomfield.   Extract.

May 29th, 1822.

I suppose you have heard about the *tracasseries* on the subject of the Irish ball. It was sillily mismanaged, and almost became a crying scandal. The Duchess of Richmond and Lady Hertford,* I hear, set the thing afoot, and named a committee. Lady Conyngham (and in her situation I do not think she could have done more or less) sent to beg her name might be added to the list. This the other ladies were so ill-judging as to refuse. The consequence was, that the King interfered with the Duke of York, stopped the first ball, and patronized another, which is to take place to-morrow, under the auspices of a *new* set of ladies, that is, the old set, with the omission of the Duchess of Richmond and Lady Hertford, and the addition of Lady Conyngham. The young men who are the managers of the ball are doing a very foolish and I think indecent thing, they are going to introduce the opera-girls to dance quadrilles, in other words, as part of the company at the ball, and lest this should not be indecent enough each happy man selects his fair one, and furnishes her, at his own expense, with a dress for the occasion. Yarmouth tricks out Roland ; Lowther, I believe, Varenne ; Fife, of course, Noblet, and perhaps in his magnificence, Mercandotti.

---

* [The mother of the Lord Yarmouth who became, as previously stated, Marquis of Hertford in this year. There was an old scandal afloat about the relations between this Lady Hertford and the King.]

To Sir B. Blomfield.   Extract.

June 21st, 1822.

I was last night with my little girl at a child's ball at
Carlton House.   We arrived at the appointed moment (half-
past eight) and in two seconds after (there not being a dozen
people in the room) His Majesty entered, accompanied by
Sir William Knighton, who, I presume, had dined with him,
and dined alone, as they came in *par les derrières*, and there
was no other attendant.   The King was gracious, as usual,
and appeared in excellent health and spirits, and much
amused with the children.   He walked about, except for
about an hour and a half that he sat in the conservatory with
Lady Conyngham and Madame de Lieven, while the children
danced before him and the company stood around him.   There
was no *chuchoterie*, like what we have formerly seen.
Lady Conyngham took little interest in the arrangement of
the ball, and Lady Elizabeth none at all.   Graves and Lady
Morley were master and mistress of the ceremony.   The
company was not numerous, and as usual rather a preponderance of Whigs and Whiggesses, Dukes of Devon and Portland,
the latter in a *full* dress of deep mourning, every one else
being in frocks, looked quizzical even beyond Bentinck
uncouthness.   Lord Lansdowne, the Jerseys, Cowpers,
Gwydyrs, Morpeths, Harrowbys, Bathursts, Morleys, Grenvilles, Maryboroughs, Cholmondeleys, were, I think, all of
note, except the *Court* itself, in which I include the Duke
and Duchess of Wellington.   The King retired as soon as he
had seen them all at supper, which was about a quarter past
twelve.   Knighton *s'éclipsa* very early ; indeed he walked in
with the King and walked out again, without, I think,
speaking to any one.   I ought not to have omitted the Princess Augusta, and the Duchess of Kent and her daughter ;
the latter danced all night, and the royal ladies seemed to be
in high good humour, though they held their court *apart*.

They have talked about gout in the elbow, but there is no
such thing.   Paget saw him this morning in bed, in the old
style, with his papers, &c., about ; but, what is not quite in
the old style, Frank Conyngham was in attendance *en robe
de chambre.*   This is being Master of the Robes with a
vengeance !   F. C. is a good-natured, well-meaning young
fellow, and the King is as fond of him as if he were his
son—probably a good deal more so ; for kings are not the
fondest fathers in the world, nor heirs apparent the most
dutiful sons.

CHAPTER IX.

1823–4.

A PROJECT had long been in Mr. Croker's mind which he
now endeavoured to bring into some practical shape. This
was the foundation of a club especially designed for men of
letters and artists. "I thought of it," he says, in a note
written on the margin of a biographical sketch before referred
to, "because the University Club, the Travellers', the United
Service, and other such clubs, had superseded and destroyed
the old coffee-houses, and I considered that literary men and
artists required a place of rendezvous also. Many have got
in who would have been more eligible for other clubs, but
still the predominant character of the club is literary."
Having once thoroughly understood what he meant to do, he
lost no time in setting about doing it. The first person

whom he approached on the subject was Sir Humphry Davy, then the President of the Royal Society. " We must lay down clearly and positively as our first rule," he wrote,[*] "that no one shall be eligible except gentlemen who have either published some literary or professional work, or a paper in the ' Philosophical Transactions '; members of the Royal Academy; Trustees (not official) of the British Museum; hereditary and life governors of the British Institution. The latter will open our doors to the patrons of the arts. I do not see any other classes which could be admitted, unless bishops and judges, who are *par état* literary men, although they may not have published any work." He went on to suggest the appointment of a Committee to invite certain gentlemen to join the club, and he proposed that there should be an entrance fee of ten guineas, and an annual subscription of five, " which would' enable us to provide a tolerable house until we grow rich enough to build one."

Such was the origin of the "Athenæum" Club, an institution in which Mr. Croker took the greatest interest down to the last day of his life, and which he had the satisfaction of seeing reach a height of prosperity and distinction he could scarcely have anticipated in 1823. No doubt the express object of the club, as defined in Mr. Croker's words, and in the declaration which is still prefixed to the rules, has been found capable of considerable expansion; but if the " Athenæum " is no longer a purely literary and artistic association, it remains, what it has always been, one of the most famous clubs in the world. Its excellent library would alone cause admission to it to be much sought after and highly valued. It is understood, indeed, that so great is the throng of applicants for membership, that an interval of nearly twenty years has now to elapse between the entry

---

* November 23rd, 1823.

of a candidate's name in the books and the decision of his fate at the ballot-box. But even from the first, the honour of belonging to the "Athenæum" was much coveted. Among Mr. Croker's papers there are scores of letters desiring his support for various candidates, and it is evident from his answers to some of them that he was very chary about promising this support. He selected the original Committee, and it does not appear that his first plan was materially altered, although perhaps it was somewhat extended, by the suggestions of those whose co-operation he invited. Sir Humphry Davy took up the idea with enthusiasm, and it will be seen that he recommended the admission of Members of Parliament, for a reason which must strike many legislators of the present day as rather quaint, namely, that their duties could not properly be performed without "a competent knowledge of literature."

Sir Humphry Davy to Mr. Croker.

November 23rd, 1823.

My dear Sir,

We should lose no time in drawing up the "Prospectus." I think members of the Royal and Antiquarian Society, and of the Linnean, ought to be admitted by ballot; for my idea is that it should be a scientific as well as a literary club. Lord Aberdeen, with whom I have had a good deal of conversation on the subject, has taken it up warmly.

I know already more than 100 persons who wish to belong to it, and many, most of their names will be attractive— Mr. Heber and Mr. Hallam, Mr. Colebrooke, Dr. Young, Mr. Chantrey, Mr. Hatchett, Mr. Brande, Mr. Herschel, and a number of other men of science, will give their names.

When I talked to Lord Spencer on the subject, he did not seem to take an interest in it; and Dr. Wollaston says he is not a man of clubs. But we are certain of success. The difficulty will be in a short name, and one not liable to any Shandean objections. We can talk of this when I have the pleasure of seeing you to-morrow.

I do not think it would be going too far to make members of the corporate scientific and literary bodies eligible by ballot. I see no reason for excluding Judges, Bishops, and Members of both Houses, none of whom can perform their high duties without a competent knowledge of literature.

Very sincerely yours,

H. Davy.

In less than a month, Mr. Croker had provided the club with a name, had produced a prospectus, and had circulated it among the persons whom he desired to bring together. He objected to the reception of one gentleman as a member, on the ground that he was "so notorious a bore;" but this principle, like the rule relating to authors and artists, may possibly have been found difficult of rigid application since the early days of the club. Mr. Croker also writes, on the 9th of February, 1824: "I have ventured to add Lord Palmerston's name; he is a patron of the arts, and to my knowledge a person of literary powers." A letter from Mr. Jekyll seems to show that when Mr. Croker was absent from any of the Committee meetings, not a great deal of business was done:

Mr. Croker to Sir Humphry Davy.

December 13th, 1823.

DEAR SIR HUMPHRY,

I enclose you a few prospectuses of our new Club. I have written the names that I should wish to see of the Committee. In all cases *founders*, as you and I are, must decide who are to be on the Committee; and this is a matter of so great ultimate importance that I would beg of you not to decide on any new name without a consultation. My experience in these matters is considerable, and I assure you that all depends on having a Committee with a great *many* good *names* and a *few* working *hands*.

I am going out of town for one week, but your list of Committee-men may be sent to the Admiralty, and it will reach me in time. I have applied to no one but to Lord

Lansdowne, Sir Walter Scott, and Thomas Moore. I wish you would apply to any persons who are in my list whom you may know; but to avoid mistakes, I shall not apply to anybody else till I hear from you. My list contains about twenty-eight names; the Committee should be of about thirty-six; and we should have four or five practical and practicable people who would attend and help the business. Perhaps a few more artists and a musician should be on the Committee; and what do you say to Charles Kemble? I shall be at home till four.

Yours ever,

J. W. C.

Mr. Jekyll to Mr. Croker.

Spring Gardens, Wednesday, April 28th. [1824.]

DEAR CROKER,

We did as much yesterday at the Committee as could be done in the absence of such a *primum mobile* as yourself. Elections and nominations were expedited. We have now, I should think, 380 members, and above 100 invitations remain unanswered. Verging so closely on our 400, we suspended 50 invitations suggested by a list sent in by Heber, and containing many eligible names.

Saturday next, many of us dine with the Royal Academicians, so the Committee will meet again on Monday, May 3rd.

If our candidates overflow, Davy said the Society might extend its numbers to 600.

Burton said the house might be ready in a fortnight. By Heber's direction Chalié sent in a wine estimate. Wine and servants seem at present the principal desiderata; and except yourself, I think we have no active member for those details. Chalié's wines are high priced. If you desire to inspect his paper before Monday, I will send it to you.

Yours ever,

JOSEPH JEKYLL.

The members met at first in temporary quarters, but by the month of October, 1824, the new club seems to have been pretty well established.* Mr. Croker is able to report of it to Lord Hertford that "it is said to shine in Irish stews and pancakes." From that time the reputation of the club steadily increased, and many of the most famous names in literature and art have been inscribed upon its roll of members. While the permanent building was in course of construction, Mr. Croker continued to watch vigilantly over the interests of the members, as may be seen from the following letter—one of many—to the architect.

Mr. Croker to Mr. Decimus Burton.

August 12th, 1829.

My dear Mr. Burton,

Excuse the liberty I take—prompted entirely by my regard for you—of requesting your serious attention to the excess of the expenses of the Athenæum over the estimates. You are a young man, just making your way in your profession. You have many rivals, and, I dare say, a few whom I might almost call enemies. They will all watch with critical care your proceedings in this your first great work in town; and I need hardly tell you that in public opinion the worst character an architect can get is that he exceeds his estimates. All the excess may be not only *excusable,* but *proper* and right to have been incurred; but the world will not enter into details, and you will be generally spoken of by the thousand mouths of the Athenæum, and by the ten thousand mouths that will echo them, as "one who *exceeds his estimates*"—a reputation, I repeat, the most likely of all others to be injurious to a young architect.

I therefore implore you to exert all your ingenuity and influence in curtailing all possible expenses, not merely for the Club's sake, but for your own.

Yours truly,

J. W. C.

---

* The club, when opened, consisted of 506 members, of whom one only, Mr. John Lettsom Elliot, still survives. (1884.)

There were two other matters in which Mr. Croker exerted himself at this period—one was an attempt to extricate Theodore Hook from the difficulties in which he had become entangled; the other was an earnest effort to turn Benjamin Haydon, the painter, from the course upon which he had entered, and which ended in the tragedy of 1846. With regard to Theodore Hook, it need only be said briefly that he was arrested in 1823 for a debt of 12,000*l*. due to the Government on account of defalcations which had been discovered in his accounts as Treasurer and Accountant-General of the Mauritius. A part at least of these defalcations seems to have been owing to the misconduct of a person employed by Mr. Hook. The system of filling offices of this kind by deputy was not a great success, either in Hook's hands or Thomas Moore's. Both appealed to Mr. Croker for advice or help, and neither went to him in vain. Throughout his life, indeed, Theodore Hook was indebted for a thousand acts of kindness to Mr. Croker. He lent him money; he induced others to subscribe for the relief of his necessities; the brilliant humourist repaired to him in trouble, as a weak nature will always fly, if it can, to a strong one. Mr. Croker has been accused of ill-nature, but his good-natured acts seem to have exposed him to more malicious misrepresentation than those of the other kind. One of his most recent assailants, who declares that Mr. Croker's "chief pleasure in life" was "to cause mental suffering to his fellows," insinuates that he was guilty of some unkindness towards Hook's family.* The fact is that but for Mr. Croker, Hook's family would very often have been in a sorrowful

---

* The assailant in question is Mrs. Houstoun, a daughter of Mr. Edward Jesse, who was an old friend of Mr. Croker's. Mr. Croker had shown many kindnesses to the Jesse family, and even obtained a situation in the Admiralty for one of Mrs. Houstoun's brothers. Hence, perhaps, her resentment.

s 2

plight. The following is one of the appeals which he made for Hook at this period :—

*Mr. Croker to Mr. R. Lushington.**   *Extract.*

January 2nd, 1823.

Dear Lushington,

Read the enclosed note.†

Excuse this trouble, for I assure you I am as unwilling as possible to give it you, but common charity and compassion obliged me to endeavour to do something for a poor persecuted fellow, whom I believe to be quite innocent of the charge made against him, and whom it is sought to punish for *other reasons*—to be sure, as he says, when it is recollected how other and greater defaulters have been treated, he does seem to receive severe measure. I well know that it cannot be helped. I well know that the Treasury *dare* not do for him what they would do for a Whig, and I am aware of the delicacy of your position, but as I believe in my soul that he is persecuted because he is suspected of being the writer of 'John Bull,' that alone is with me a sufficient motive to do all I can to defeat the unjust persecution. If you are in town pray let me see you on Friday or Saturday, if not write me a line.

Yours,

J. W. C.

The appeal was at this time unsuccessful; but, as we shall see, Mr. Croker never desisted from his kindly interference until he had rescued Theodore Hook from gaol. Some years afterwards, when he was in one of the financial straits which were of periodical occurrence in his affairs, Mr. Croker again hastened to assist him. These were among the incidents which writers who complain of Mr. Croker's "asperity" have been pleased to torture into evidences of his mean and envious spirit. Not thus, apparently, were they regarded by Mr. Hook or his family.

---

* [One of the Secretaries to the Treasury.]

† [Letter from Theodore Hook.]

From the Rev. W. F. Hook * *to Mr. Croker.*

Vicarage, Leeds, August 27th, 1841.

MY DEAR SIR,

Although you have been duly informed of my poor uncle Theodore's death, I cannot refrain, as the eldest of his surviving relatives, from writing to you to say that I remember with gratitude that he was indebted to you for almost everything in life. When he was under circumstances of the deepest depression, you were the person who helped him; and when all the world was frowning upon him, in you he found a patron and a friend. Many years have passed since these things occurred, but my grateful admiration of your conduct was strongly excited in my youth, and I have not forgotten those feelings now that I am past my meridian. Your name is sometimes remembered in my prayers as the benefactor of one most dear to me.

Although of late years my uncle shrunk from our society, still I am sure he loved me, and I know he loved you; and you will be glad to hear that he died penitent and praying. I hope, I think, he was awakened. My very dear brother acted with the pious wisdom of a most judicious Divine, and perhaps my uncle listened to him the more readily, as he is a layman.

If you would like to read the affecting details of his last days, I will forward to you the confidential letters of my brother to me. With kindest respects to Mrs. Croker,

I remain, my dear Sir,
Your grateful friend and servant,
W. F. HOOK.

With reference to Haydon, it is clear, from the correspondence, that the unfortunate artist had written to Mr. Croker in reference to his peculiar craze of "historical painting," and in reply he received a letter suggesting the important question whether it might not be possible that he was on the wrong tack altogether? No one can now doubt that it

---

* [Afterwards the well-known Dean of Chichester.]

would have been well for Haydon if he had pondered this more carefully.

Mr. Croker to Benjamin Haydon.

July 7th, 1823.

Sir,

I regret that your opinion of the relative value of portrait and poetical painting seems to differ so much from mine, and I regret it the more because I fear that your difficulties may in some degree be owing to the view you have taken of this subject.   But it would be an idle waste of time to enter into a discussion of who may be right or wrong.   One thing we should probably be all agreed in, that the *excellent* in any class of the fine arts is better than *mediocrity* in any other, and that a Dutch kitchen from the hand of Teniers is in every respect preferable to a whole Olympus of the Gods and Goddesses of Verrio.   I therefore candidly confess that I think you would do well to consider whether it be not possible that the neglect of historical painting may in some instances arise from the failure of the artists themselves, and whether in aspiring after objects which they consider of more dignity young men do not often neglect the (*humbler* in their opinion, though not in mine) walks in which they might have attained a respectable degree of success.

I am, Sir, your most obedient humble servant,

J. W. C.

While dealing with the correspondence of this character, it may be as well to introduce here a couple of letters concerning a mechanical device of which a good deal was heard some years ago, but which never answered to the expectations that were formed of it—Babbage's " Calculating Machine."

Mr. Peel to Mr. Croker.

Whitehall, March 8th, 1823.

My dear Croker,

You recollect that a very worthy seafaring man declared that he had been intimate in his youth with Gulliver, and that he resided (I believe) in the neighbourhood of Blackwall. Davies Gilbert has produced another man who seems to be able to vouch at least for Laputa. Gilbert proposes that I should refer the enclosed to the Council of the Royal Society, with the view of their making such a report as shall induce the House of Commons to construct at the public charge a scientific automaton, which, if it can calculate what Mr. Babbage says it can, may be employed to the destruction of Hume. I presume you must at the Admiralty have heard of this proposal—

> " Aut hæc in vestros fabricata est machina muros,
>   Aut aliquis latet error."

I should like a little previous consideration before I move in a thin house of country gentlemen, a large vote for the creation of a wooden man to calculate tables from the formula $x^2 + x + 41$. I fancy Lethbridge's face on being called on to contribute.

Ever affectionately,

ROB. PEEL.

Mr. Croker to Mr. Peel.

March 21st, 1823.

MY DEAR PEEL,

Mr. Babbage's invention is at first sight incredible, but if you will recollect those little numeral locks which one has seen in France, in which a series of numbers are written on a succession of wheels, you will have some idea of the first principles of this machine, which is very curious and ingenious, and which not only will calculate all regular series, but also arranges the types for printing all the figures. At present indeed it is a matter more of curiosity than use, and I believe some good judges doubt whether it ever can be of any. But when I consider what has been already done by what were called Napier's bones and Gunter's scale, and the infinite and undiscovered variety of what may be called the *mechanical powers* of numbers, I cannot but admit the possibility, nay the probability, that important consequences may be ultimately derived from Mr. Babbage's principle. As to Mr. Gilbert's proposition of having a new machine constructed, I am rather inclined (with deference to his very superior judgment in such matters) to doubt whether that would be the most useful application of public money towards this object at present.

I apprehend that Mr. Babbage's present machine, which however I have not seen, answers the purposes which it is intended for sufficiently well, and I rather think that a sum of money given to Mr. Babbage to reward his ingenuity, encourage his zeal, and repay his expenses would tend eventually to the perfection of his machine. It was proposed at the Board of Longitude to give him 500*l.* out of the sum placed at our disposal for the reward of inventions tending to facilitate the ascertaining the Longitude. But the Board doubted that the invention was likely to be practically useful to a degree to justify a grant of this nature.

I think you can have no difficulty in referring the matter to the Council of the Royal Society (of which, although unworthy, I have the honour to be one), which by the assistance of its scientific members will give you the best opinion as to the value of the invention, and when that is obtained, it may be considered whether another machine should be made at the public expense, or whether Mr. Babbage should receive a reward either from Parliament or the Board of Longitude.

Yours faithfully,
J. W. C.

It is now necessary to compile a selection from the general correspondence of these two years.

Mr. Croker to Sir B. Blomfield.   Extracts.

March 21st, 1823.

My dear Blomfield,

The King has had two or three relapses of gout and is, I hear, much weakened by them—naturally—but as he told me, laughingly, eleven years ago at Brighton that he was *going down hill fast,* such repeated attacks cannot but alarm those who love him, as we do. I believe his *intérieur* is very comfortable; he sees fewer strangers than ever, and even of old friends, those only who are about him.

The Duke of Clarence, you see, is General of the Marines, £5 per diem, but as he had a half pay of £3 per diem as

Admiral of the Fleet, which is not receivable with the full pay of the Marines, he gets but £700 a year by the change. I doubt whether he was aware of this. If he expected to have the whole £8 per diem it will be a great disappointment. His R.H.'s chance of being *King* begins to mend—do you remember my little discussion with him at Brighton eight years ago, when he told me that when *he* became King, *I* should not be Secretary of the Admiralty ? I told him "a bird in the hand was worth two in the bush." He had just before told me that he would in that event declare himself Lord High Admiral, and asked me "what objection I could start to that." I replied, with a low bow, "none ; that there was a case in point—James II. had done the same." This was a little bold, to say no worse, on my part, but he had been, for half an hour before, giving me provocation beyond all endurance, such as abusing Lord Melville, Sir Geo. Hope, and the rest of the Board, and though I begged of him to recollect my situation with them and spare me the mortification of hearing such attacks made on my friends and colleagues, he went on with still more violence. By the time he comes to be King, however, he will be a good deal more quiet and reasonable than he was eight years ago.

I must take a scrap of paper to tell you a joke attributed to the King, and I think a good one. You know Wm. Peel married *Lady Jane* Moore, and his younger brother has lately married *Lady Jane* Lennox. " The Peels," said H.M., " have still a hankering after the *Jennies.*"

Mr. Croker to Sir B. Blomfield.

May 10th, 1824.

Politics look fair and smooth; but the old knowing ones mutter something about " *ignes suppositos cineri doloso.*" Their hints lead one to think that they suspect Canning of a design to get rid of some of his colleagues, and they dwell upon the compliments bandied backwards and forwards between him and the Opposition. Such a suspicion is, of itself, likely to accomplish its own prophecy, and although I am slow to believe the existence of *intrigues*, I think it not unlikely that if anything was to induce Lord Liverpool to retire we should have what is vulgarly called a blow-up, and Lord Liverpool is certainly far from well. His pulse is so low as 50 and they cannot raise it, and this state, even if it has no worse effect, must, if it lasts, incapacitate him from exertion of any kind. If he were to go now, I think the King would be inclined to send for the Duke of Wellington ; but he, too, is far from well— he looks very ill, and really before the recess looked extremely ill, withering and drying up; but he is better. In any case, however, no doubt Canning would try for the first place, and it is not impossible that Lord Lansdowne, Mackintosh, and the more moderate part of the Opposition, might join him ; but that could only be on a resolution to carry the Catholic question, and what the effect of such a coalition for such a purpose might be who can tell ? Canning's going to Lord Mayor Waithman's dinner excited a good deal of surprise in the world, but still more in the Ministerial circles who knew that the Cabinet had come to an understanding not to go. This event was rendered more important by Waithman's not being invited to Peel's birthday dinner, which took place some time after. As Lord Mayors have been, I understand, invariably invited by the Home Secretary on such occasions, the omission, following Mr. Canning's visit to the Mansion House, was supposed to be a strong and not a well-judged expression of Mr. Peel's dissent from the conduct of his colleague, and I, for one, was not a little surprised at it. But I have since heard that although the fact proves a difference of opinion, it does so in a way which nobody suspected. It turns out that Peel's resolution to exclude Waithman was taken and communicated to his colleagues *before* the dinner at the Mansion House, and it is surmised that this determined Canning to go to the dinner whither he might not otherwise have gone. This *dessous des cartes* is not known, or at least has attracted no attention, and it was probably some disapprobation of Peel's exclusion which induced Lord Liverpool to authorize Canning to say that he would also have dined at the Mansion House had he been in town—certain it is that Lord Liverpool had previously deter- mined with the rest of the Cabinet not to attend.*

* [The King wrote to the Duke of Wellington, May 1, 1824, with reference to these incidents : "The public life of the individual filling the office of the chief magistrate of the City of London has been marked by a series of insults to the Government, to the monarchy, and, above all, personally to the King himself," &c. &c. Wellington Desp., N. S., ii. 251.]

To these circumstances are to be added Canning's uncalled for eulogy on Sir Robert Wilson in his speech on the Spanish question, and several other panegyrics pronounced by him on individuals of the Opposition which were repaid by the Opposition in the same coin—all this is indicative of anything but cordiality amongst the Ministers, and their union is, in my opinion, precarious. Canning has never been averse to coalitions of this nature—he has twice or thrice been on the point of junctions with the Opposition ; but whenever he accomplishes such an union he will find, if I am not much mistaken, not strength but weakness. The public never has liked these combinations, and Canning has (whether justly or not) a character for intrigue and insincerity which will expose whatever he does to peculiar suspicion. In all this I give you no opinion of my own, but I lay before you the *data* on which you may form yours ; and, situated as you are, these visions, if even visions they be, cannot fail to be interesting to you. Perhaps, so variable is the political sky, that my next letter may tell you that all these clouds are dissipated and that some unexpected tornado has sprung up from another quarter of the heavens.

You will see in the papers a story of Lord Londonderry's having fought Battier, but the papers have not the whole truth.* After Battier had declared himself satisfied, Hardinge addressed him and said, " now that *you* are satisfied, I am desired by Lord Londonderry to say that your published letters contain two *falsehoods*, and his lordship is here ready to support that assertion." After some hemming and hawing, Mr. Battier declared that he was *still satisfied*, and with this exquisite satisfaction left the ground. To sum up the whole, it seems that when Sir Henry Hardinge wanted to find Mr. Battier to arrange the final meeting he was obliged to follow him to the ' Swan with two Necks ' in Lad Lane, where this worthy lodged.

Canning was now beginning to be regarded with distrust by his old political associates, and his visit to Ireland, in September, 1824, was made the occasion of a thousand

---

* [The Earl of Londonderry had succeeded his half-brother, the late Foreign Secretary. In consequence of some dispute in the mess-room in Dublin in Nov. 1823, he fought a duel with Lieutenant Battier. See ' Wellington Despatches,' N. S., ii. 247, 265, *seq.*]

conjectures. Some supposed that he had gone there to concert measures with the Roman Catholic leaders; others that he was preparing himself for a dissolution of Parliament. He was rising so rapidly in the public favour that all his acts were watched, and whether deservedly or not, many of them were watched with suspicion. Mr. Croker, however, never believed that the visit to Ireland was anything more than a pleasure trip. "It is Canning's misfortune," he wrote to Mr. Goulburn, in October, "that nobody will believe that he can take the most indifferent step without an ulterior object, nor take his tea without a stratagem." Affairs in Ireland were then, as they have been ever since, in a more or less disturbed state, but it is clear now that Mr. Canning's visit had no special reference to them. In December, Mr. Croker wrote to Sir B. Blomfield, "Parliament will meet on the 1st February and if things remain in their present state, we never met under better auspices. Everything seems prosperous but Ireland." England was perhaps a little too prosperous; a passion for wild speculation set in, the whole country seemed to be smitten with it, and the train was laid for the great commercial panic of the following year.

One element in England which excited alarm was the Catholic Association, "a lever," as Mr. Croker said in a letter to Mr. Goulburn, "by which the disaffected hope to overthrow the Government itself. Out of the proceedings of one meeting of this body at Dublin, an unwise prosecution of Daniel O'Connell was instituted by the Government. O'Connell had used the words, 'If Parliament will not attend to the Roman Catholic claims, I hope that some Bolivar will arise to vindicate their rights.'" Mr. Croker was strongly opposed to the prosecution, and its utter failure proved the justice of his views.

Mr. Croker to Mr. Peel.

Kensington, December 24th, 1824.

DEAR PEEL,

I have seen in the *Courier* the accounts from the Irish papers of O'Connell's affair. I must say to you in confidence they alter my first impression; the words, as given, are guarded by conditions "your *if* is an excellent peace-maker." Would not you or I say that "IF Ireland were, which God forbid, to be persecuted and oppressed, we hoped she might find a Hampden, a Paoli, a Washington, and why not a Bolivar?" Nay, Bolivar is the innocentest name of all, for he is not what can be called a rebel.

But the words are *denied.* Who will prove them? Who of the gentlemen of the press will, when urged, negative the possibility of some slight error, of the omission of an "if," a "but," a "let us suppose," a "for argument sake."

Distant as we are, and ignorant of their proofs, can we at present give the Irish Government more than a vote of confidence? If the Law Officers of Ireland thought the words seditious, if the Government thought the words provable, they have done right in prosecuting. But I doubt both. I admit, however, that their intentions are right, and deserve support and approbation so far; but, I own, I should hesitate before I gave unqualified approval, and I should be reluctant to embark myself, *toto corpore,* with what looks to me a little like the haste which often follows an undue supineness. When a sentinel has fallen asleep on his post, and is suddenly awakened, he always fires his musket, but with so much haste and want of thought that if he wounds any one, it is probably himself or his friends.

Your affectionate

J. W. C.

Towards the close of this year, Mr. Croker resolved to publish Horace Walpole's letters to Lord Hertford, and he wrote to Lord Liverpool requesting his opinion and advice. Lord Liverpool's father was Secretary of the Treasury about the period comprised in Walpole's letters. This request led to the following correspondence.

Lord Liverpool to Mr. Croker.

Walmer Castle, August 23rd, 1824.

My dear Sir,

I am very much obliged to you for the specimen which you have sent me of Horace Walpole's letters to Lord Hertford, which I return. I have been much amused by it, but I own I look at most things which come from this quarter with great prejudice. I believe Horace Walpole to have been as bad a man as ever lived; I cannot call him a violent party man, he had not virtue enough to be so; he was the most sensuous and selfish of mortals. If there could have been any doubt about this, the last publication of what was left to Lord Waldegrave would prove it. I do not therefore look to any publication of any letters of his as likely to be of much service to history, and think they will rather mislead than instruct the rising generation. The works of Burke with his letters (if a good collection of them should be made) will contain the whole strength and secret of the Whig cause during the last reign. You see I am not uncandid; I differ with him on many points, but I look to him as one of the great oracles of my country. I wish the Tory cause had found as good an expositor. Dr. Johnson is admirable as far as he goes. It would do you good to take down his volume of political pamphlets (they are all in one volume of his works), and read them *de suite*, but he stopped at a most important period. I regret Lord Glenbervie * did not begin his 'Life of Lord North' sooner; he had all the late King's original letters, and he would have executed his purpose temperately and respectably. The American War having been a losing cause, it is not likely to find now even an apologist; all that will be written will be written with a strong bias the other way; Glenbervie's work would have been, therefore, a desideratum for the cause of truth.

Who is Mr. Prior? I have read his 'Life of Burke' with the greatest satisfaction, and have told Payne that he may recommend it, if he pleases, on my authority. There are very few things in it which I should wish to alter, and it is a most important addition to our literature.

With respect to Lord Camden,† his object was to set him-

* [Son-in-law of Lord North.]

† [Mr. Croker had asked in his letter, "What disappointment made Lord Camden such a patriot?"]

self up against Lord Mansfield under the shield of Lord
Chatham; he became, therefore, the *patriot lawyer* of the
day. They both got into a scrape afterwards upon the Corn
Embargo, of which Lord Mansfield very successfully availed
himself. Lord Camden's conduct was very bad upon the
Middlesex election; you will see the particulars in the Parliamentary history.

The real cause of the continued agitated state of men's
minds for the first few years of the late King's reign, was
that the Government was changed almost every year, and
perpetual changes had the effect naturally of destroying all
confidence. No one knew on what he had to rely. This
continued till Lord North came to the head of Government. Lord North, though a man of very considerable
talents, was by no means qualified for the situation, and
never wished to have been in it; yet he had a very strong
Government when the American War began in 1774, and it
continued so for several years.

It is a curious historical fact, that Queen Elizabeth, who
bears the character of a capricious woman, was the most
steady Sovereign in her politics that ever filled a throne; she
knew when she was well served, and kept the same Minister
for more than forty years.

I have been led on further than I intended.

> Believe me to be, my dear Sir,
>> Very sincerely yours,
>>> LIVERPOOL.

Mr. Croker to Lord Liverpool.

October 13th, 1824.

MY DEAR LORD,

I entirely agree in your lordship's opinion of Horace
Walpole—there never lived a more selfish man; a more
factious politician, a more calumnious writer. It is because
I think him so, that I am anxious to prevent as far as I can
his poisoning the sources of history. His descent, his name,
his station, the force and vivacity of his style, his perpetual
professions of disinterestedness, his apparent carelessness for
office, have all contributed to give him considerable authority,
and I have no hesitation in saying that his 'Memoirs' and

letters, already voluminous, and of which I know that a great deal more is forthcoming, have given and will give a most false colour to the transactions and characters of his day. With regard to his ' Memoirs ' published two years ago, I think I may flatter myself that I did something, by a review in the *Quarterly*,* towards exposing his errors and defeating his personal malevolence; and I am glad that the possessor of the letters, now about to be published, has permitted me to add such notes as I may think necessary to sift his truth from his falsehood, and to mix some grains of doubt and allowance into the mixture which his partiality has brewed, and which without some such corrective will poison the minds of posterity. I may be told, then why publish these letters at all ? I answer that it does not depend upon me. Walpole seems to have taken care that all his remains shall be published, and I am confident that Lord Waldegrave's whole collection will (and that in obedience to Walpole's own wishes) be successively produced, and be probably edited (as the ' Memoirs ' were by Lord Holland) without one word to explain or correct the grossest errors and injustice.

I also perfectly agree with your lordship as to the causes of the otherwise unaccountable unpopularity of the early years of George III., and this judgment will be forcibly strengthened by some avowals made by Walpole in the very letters before me. Nothing can be more different than two modes of conducting Government affairs in this country, which are often confounded—I mean *party* and *faction*. Godolphin, Harley, Walpole, and latterly Mr. Pitt and his Tory successors and his Whig opponents, all proceeded on the principles of *party*. Newcastle, the elder Pitt, and Fox, the Grenvilles, Lord Bute, and all their underlings, the Doddingtons, Rigbys, Sandwiches, Ellises, Legges, &c., &c., conducted their administration by a balance of *factions*, and the alternate purchase and dismissal of little political coteries. The fate of the Coalition was the deathblow of that system. A long peace and great internal prosperity, by not affording great rallying points on which *parties* may be formed, will perhaps revive *factions*, and whenever that happens we shall see played over again all the lamentable scenes of the last years of George II. and the early ones of George III. If to these causes be added, a rapid succession of sovereigns and a minority

* [*Quarterly Review*, No. 53, July, 1822.]

or two, those who live to see such events will find subjects for a new 'Doddington's Diary ' and ' Junius's Letters.'

I will just state here, *en passant*, that I have strong reason to suspect that Lord George Sackville was the author of 'Junius.' He *may* have had a literary assistant, but I am convinced by a great variety of reasons, that *he* was substantially Junius : as I have also little doubt that Walpole found the sarcasm and libel, and Mason the poetry of the celebrated ' Heroic Epistle.'

Mr. Prior, in his ' Life of Burke,' of which your lordship thinks so highly, takes on all the subjects (which, of course, Mr. Burke did not) the same view as the author of the ' Sketch,' though I do not think he had seen this pamphlet. In reply to your inquiry, I am sorry not to be able to give you any account of Mr. Prior. I am not acquainted with him, nor did I ever hear of him till his book appeared. He is evidently an Irishman ; and perhaps may be some connexion of Mr. Burke's, though I doubt this ; because my family was closely connected with Mr. Burke, and I never heard of any relationship with any one of the name of Prior. His book, in spite of many and great errors, I had almost said barbarisms of language, is all you say of it, and in some of his *characters* and *parallels* he is very able in his views and happy in his expressions. I shall endeavour to make his acquaintance ; he resides in one of the villages in Surrey, near town.

J. W. C.

*Lord Liverpool to Mr. Croker.**

Walmer Castle, October 21st, 1824.

MY DEAR SIR,

I shall be happy to receive and look over the sheets of Walpole's Letters, as it may be convenient to you to send them.

I am surprised, after the dedication, that you have no personal knowledge of Mr. Prior. I agree with you, that his style is in many respects full of errors, and even of barbarisms, but I think it a most valuable addition to our biography ; and every person to whom I have recommended

---

* [This letter appears in Yonge's 'Life of Lord Liverpool,' but it is printed here from the original, to render Mr. Croker's own letters more intelligible.]

it, concurs in this opinion.   There is real *mind* in the book,
and some originality of thinking.   Now, any drayman could
have written as good a life of a public man, with the advantage of the letters and the parliamentary debates, as my
old friend the Bishop of Winchester has written of Mr. Pitt.
The only defects in Prior's work, as a piece of history, are
the following:

He makes Burke more the leader of a party in the House
of Commons than he ever was.   He was undoubtedly the
oracle of the Marquis of Rockingham, and of all the *pure
Rockingham party*, but the House of Commons never did, nor
ever would, have submitted to him as a leader of any party;
and this his best friends knew.   Prior has likewise too much
overlooked his defects.   Why, it may be asked, being gifted
with acquirements beyond all other men perhaps, living or
dead, and surpassing all his cotemporaries in the *highest flights*
of eloquence, was he not the leader of his party?   First, because
he wanted taste; and secondly, because he was the most impracticable of men.   He never knew when not to speak; he
never knew when to speak short.   He never consulted the
feelings and prejudices of his audience.   I remember hearing
Lord Thurlow say of him and Fox that the difference between
them during the American controversy was, that Fox always
spoke to the House, and Burke spoke as if he was speaking to
himself.

I cannot agree with you in the opinion that Lord George
Sackville was the author of 'Junius.'   I am quite satisfied
that he was incapable of being so; and even his political life
does not correspond at all with the real opinions of Junius.

The only *clear fact* as to 'Junius,' is, that he must have
been a friend of Mr. Grenville, and under some considerable
obligation to him or to his family.   Mr. Grenville is the only
public man whom Junius really protects.   If he had not had
some particular or mysterious connection with him, he would
have been one of those whom he would have most abused.   I
have heard Lord Grenville say, more than once, that he knew
a great deal about it, but that he never could tell what he
knew.

Lord George Sackville was in decided opposition to
Mr. Grenville's Government,   The party that took him up
after his disgrace was the Rockinghams.   They restored him
to the Privy Council upon their coming into office in 1765.
He continued in opposition after they went out in the fol-

ing years, till the troubles in America took a serious turn. He then took a line of his own, and threw out some ideas respecting America which happened to hit the feelings of the House; and it is a most singular fact, that this very individual, who had been condemned by a court-martial for cowardice, and struck out of the Privy Council, was appointed War Secretary of State to conduct the American War, with the acclamation of the great majority of the House of Commons. I have heard persons who remembered the transactions of both times say, that his station in the House of Commons in 1774 and 1775 was very much the same as Wyndham's was in 1792 and 1793, at the beginning of the French Revolutionary War.

Believe me to be, my dear Sir,

Very sincerely yours,

LIVERPOOL.

The great interest taken by Mr. Croker in the preservation of ancient works of art, and his anxiety to secure as many of them as possible for his own country, were shown by his successful exertions to induce the Government to buy the Elgin marbles. He was always on the watch for treasures of a like kind. In 1822 reports arrived in England that the Turks were destroying part of the Parthenon. Mr. Croker wrote at once to the admiral commanding the station: "If this be so," he said, "I would entreat of you to write to any captain who is likely to go near Athens, to endeavour to save all that he can of sculpture that these barbarians may have pulled down; and any expense he may be at in purchasing or moving the fragments, I shall most cheerfully pay, and he may draw upon me for the amount." In 1824, he endeavoured to get Cleopatra's Needle moved to England, and he proposed to do it by means very similar to those which were actually employed in 1877.

Mr. Croker to Sir B. Martin, K.C.B.

December 16th, 1824.

MY DEAR SIR BYAM,

In reference to our former communications, public and private, on the subject of the transport to England of Cleopatra's Needle, I wish to call your attention to an idea which has struck me on the subject.

The difficulties which formerly deterred us were principally the expense of moving the Needle into the *ship*, and the necessity of building a pier out into the deep water, where the ship must lie to receive it, to say nothing of the preparation of the ship itself to receive so cumbrous a freight.

Now it occurs to me that as you bring home a large quantity of Adriatic timber, it might be possible, and would not be any great increase of expense, to have a *raft* composed of the timber which else would come home as freight; on this raft the Needle would be placed with comparative facility, and the raft being roughly shaped into the best sailing form that the circumstances will admit might be towed by a steam vessel, during a favourable season. I suppose the formation of the raft would cost less than the freight of the timber, and if so the expense would be little more than the expense of the steam vessel for the two or three months she might be employed on this service.

Believe me to be, my dear Sir Byam,

Yours faithfully,

J. W. C.

The following letter, on a very different theme, was written early in the ensuing year:—

Mr. Croker to Robert Southey. Extract.

January 3rd, 1825.

MY DEAR SOUTHEY,

I am delighted at your idea of a ' Book of the State.' If you execute it with the same spirit and success as the ' Book of the Church,' you will have created the two most valuable standard works in our language—works which will become

(and it is the greatest praise and prognostication of usefulness which I can give) school books, and will lead future
generations to good principles and right feelings in matters of
Church and State.   Do you remember my once saying to you
that " Westminster Abbey was part of the British Constitution "—that vague metaphor expresses more vividly, than
perhaps more distinct explanation could do, my feelings on
this subject, and as I know that they are in accordance with
yours, you may judge how glad I am that you are inclined
to contribute another tie to that union.   I do not mean the
mere *political* connexion of Church and State; but that
mixture of veneration and love, of enthusiasm and good
taste, of public liberty and self-control, of pride of our
ancestors and hopes for our posterity, which affects every
patriot and Christian mind at the contemplation of that
glorious system, which unites in such beautiful association
and such profitable combination our civil and ecclesiastical
constitutions, our ambition and our faith; the one thing
needful and the all things ornamental; our wellbeing in
this world and our salvation in the next.   I am as satisfied
that no political State can exist without some connexion with
religion as I am that the *body* cannot be kept in heat and
motion without the *soul.*   Civil sanctions which cannot reach
the body will never sufficiently affect the mind, so as to
regulate the conduct of that complex machine, man; there
must be a higher and more sacred influence to operate upon
that ethereal portion which seems as if it aspired above all
human laws, as fire while consuming its earthly materials
and fenced in on five sides by human guards, escapes on
the sixth towards Heaven.   But I am losing myself in
metaphors and metaphysics, and shall return to imploring
you to go on with the good work you have promised me.

CHAPTER X.

1825.

The Roman Catholic Claims—Proposed Provision for the Irish Clergy—
Mr. Canning's Opinions—Mr. Croker on the "Emancipation" Policy
—View taken by the Duke of Wellington—Mr. Peel's Opposition—
Mr. Henry Drummond—The Irish Problem—Theodore Hook—Mr.
Croker procures his Release from Gaol—Moore's Life of Sheridan—
Misstatements in the Work—Annoyance of George IV.—Narrative
dictated by the King to Mr. Croker—His Intercourse with Sheridan
—His Course on the Catholic Question—The reported Marriage with
Mrs. Fitzherbert—The Regency Question—Sheridan's Extravagance—
Receives £20,000 from George IV.—Moore's Conduct towards his
"Patrons"—The alleged Neglect of Sheridan—The Story of Sheridan's
Last Days—Notes of Conversations with the Duke of Wellington—
Anecdotes of Talleyrand, Bonaparte, &c.

IT must have been evident in 1825 to every shrewd observer
that a final settlement of the Roman Catholic claims could
not be much longer postponed. In some form or other, the
question had been a cause of excitement and agitation ever
since 1778, and successive statesmen had been anxious to clear
it out of their path ; but the resistance of the King was fatal
to every effort they made. It has long been admitted that the
proposal made by Mr. Pitt in 1801 would have prevented
much bitterness and many serious misfortunes, and his ideas
were cordially adopted by Mr. Croker, who, until the subject
was disposed of once for all in 1829, never swerved in his
support of every well-directed measure for Catholic relief.
He saw clearly that violent controversies, and the lawless-

ness to which they so frequently gave rise, could not be brought to an end by such measures as the suppression of the Catholic Association or by prosecutions of O'Connell. In this respect, as it has already been pointed out, he was heartily in accord with Canning. There is a rough draft in Canning's handwriting of a resolution in favour of making provisions for the priests, but it was probably put aside for the time on account of the introduction of Sir Francis Burdett's Bill. At a later period of the session, however, Lord Francis Leveson Gower proposed to provide a State endowment of the Roman Catholic clergy to the amount of 250,000l. a year. Canning's resolution mentioned no sum, but merely declared the wisdom of " making provision for the maintenance and support of the Roman Catholic clergy of Ireland." Mr. Croker wrote to him about the same time—namely, in the month of February—avowing that he would, if he could, "pass to-night the Bill we carried some years ago, with the addition of a take-it or leave-it provision for their clergy." In the following letters he adheres to the same opinions :—

Mr. Croker to the Bishop of Ferns.

March 2nd, 1825.

I was glad last night to have an opportunity of bringing on the tapis my favourite topic of paying the popish clergy. I forget whether you approve of that plan. I am convinced that if it be not adopted a rebellion and massacre will go near to pull the *establishment* about our ears. I am a high churchman, and think the best assistance that ever can be given to the Church of Ireland is the making a provision for the Catholic clergy out of the general funds of the State. I do not say that this will altogether quiet them, and wholly tranquillize Ireland, but you may depend upon it it will go a great way towards it; and what is of great importance, if they afterwards stir a finger we shall know their real object, and the universal and undivided voice of England will put them down. Now, they assist the Church under cover of poverty and grievances, but let us take away that pretence, and instead of 247 Members voting for them they will not have 7. I was delighted to find that Plunket and Brougham both considered the plan as practicable, and likely to be accepted by the priests; nor was I much less pleased to find that the laity who are here Catholic Associators, and others, look upon it with great jealousy—to be sure it would spoil their trade.

Mr. Croker to the Right Hon. W. Plunkett.

March 12th, 1825.

My dear Plunkett,

After the best consideration which I have been able to give to your suggestion of getting my proposition relative to a provision for the Roman Catholic clergy into an ostensible shape immediately, I find that the forms of the House oppose difficulties which are, I fear, insuperable. It cannot be done without the consent of the Crown, and I do not think until the Emancipation Bill shall have been read a second time, we could ask the Government to give the King's consent even *pro formâ.* It seemed to me on the former occasion, and I am still inclined to be of the same opinion, that the proposition for the provision of the clergy will not have fair play if it be moved before the *principle* of the Emancipation Bill be decided by the second reading; this might have excited a doubt on the expediency of any immediate step, but the insuperable technical objection renders any consideration of the former point unnecessary.

What I therefore would, with your concurrence, propose would be, the day after the second reading (which I take for granted will be carried) to move resolutions for a provision for the clergy; and in the meanwhile we may be bringing our measures into such form as to be enabled to produce them on the instant, if the House should agree in the resolutions.

The Relief Bill passed the Commons, but was thrown out by the Lords, the Duke of York making a speech against it, in presenting a petition, which added much to the anger and irritation then prevailing. He ascribed his father's "severe illness" to the pain and annoyance the Catholic agitation had caused him, and he declared, with an oath, that he would never relax his opposition to the Bill. The measure was, as is well known, so unpopular out of doors that its rejection by the Peers caused great rejoicings, and Lord Liverpool was strongly urged to seize the propitious moment and dissolve Parliament. The Duke of Wellington was earnestly in favour of this course, and he expressed his opinions freely in a conversation with Mr. Croker, of which some account is given in a letter written in the midst of the events.

Mr. Croker to Lord Hertford.   Extract.

September 22nd, 1825.

We then talked of the dissolution. He is decidedly for it, the most so of all the Government. He thinks it would strengthen the Ministry, by weakening, in some degree, the Catholic interest, and by damping the ardour of the Catholic majorities in our House—for he says, "the Government cannot go on, in its present frame, if there are decided and active majorities on different sides in the two houses. The Duke of York may say, 'so much the better, form a Protestant Government,' but those who know the case are well aware that a Protestant Government could *not* be formed, nor could a Catholic one. In short, all that can be done is to get over this crisis, and by-and-by look at the question at large, and with great deliberation." To this end he thinks a dissolution this year will tend. "Not," said he, "that I would raise a No-Popery cry, nor that I should refuse Mr. Huskisson all the influence of Government at Liverpool, or Mr. Canning wherever he may go, but if I were First Lord of the Treasury I should take care that none of the boroughs in my disposal should be given by these gentlemen to their followers, and that all the Government seats should be filled by good men and true. This would make a sufficient alteration in the House to damp, if it did not break down, the Catholic majority."

The Cabinet is at this moment sitting on the question. I

have heard the opinions of such as are guessed at stated to be, Canning, Huskisson, Melville, Bexley, against; Wellington, Bathurst, Westmoreland for — Liverpool, Peel, and Harrowby I have not heard classed either way, and Robinson is of both opinions.

The Duke asked me about your shooting, as if he should like to see a little of it. He told me that there never was seen such a day's shooting as he had had with the King of France—they killed upwards of 1700 head to 4 guns; the King, the Dauphin, the Duke, and the Captain of the Guard. The King walked like a tiger and shot amazingly well. The Duke killed 280 pieces to his own share, I cannot say to his own gun, for he had ten guns and ten Swiss soldiers to load them—his shoulder was all contused, and his hand and fingers cut, and he says the force of practice was so great that latterly he *could not* miss a shot.

It must be remembered that a large portion of the public firmly believed that the cry for "Emancipation" was a mere pretext, intended to conceal designs of a much more formidable and far-reaching character. Most persons, in England at least, held that the removal of political disabilities would never satisfy the Catholics or give peace to Ireland. That view was entertained by Peel,[*] who voted against Mr. Canning's resolution in 1812, against Grattan's Bill in 1813, and against Sir F. Burdett's Bill in 1825. On the last occasion he threatened to resign because the House of Commons had passed the Bill, and with difficulty he was induced to change his decision. He had little idea at that time that this was to be among the questions on which he was destined to undergo a series of the most remarkable conversions recorded in political history, and that his would be the hand which would at last render that justice to the Catholics which he had done so much to withhold from them.

Among the friends with whom Mr. Croker corresponded at this time, and for many years afterwards, was Mr. Henry

---

[*] 'Memoirs by the Right Hon. Sir Robert Peel,' vol. i. p. 4 *et seq.*

Drummond, whose support of the Irvingite sect caused him to be regarded by many persons as a man remarkable chiefly for his eccentricities, whereas there can be no doubt that he possessed an unusually large fund of common sense. The church which he built on his estate at Albury for the followers of Mr. Irving cost him 16,000*l.*, and it is well attended to this day. Mr. Drummond always took a profound interest in politics, and his letters to Mr. Croker are written in a dry humorous vein which sufficiently accounts for his popularity among the friends who were delighted to meet in his house at Albury. "He had eyes," as Sir Henry Holland said of him, "and understanding peculiar to himself for all he saw, and language and manner as original as his thoughts." Another of his acquaintance has told us that his " conversation, always rich, animated, sparkling, suggestive, and desultory, resembled a kaleidoscope in the brilliancy and heterogeneous character of the materials ; whilst his perfect breeding and exquisite refinement of tone gave the last finish to its charm."* It is to be regretted that the letters of this original and interesting man are few and far between in Mr. Croker's papers ; but care has been taken to preserve all that could be found of the slightest public interest. In a short letter, containing a reference to the Catholic question, there is a passage which shows that Mr. Drummond substantially held the same view as Mr. Peel, together with some opinions which are more familiar to modern Radicalism.

Mr. Henry Drummond to Mr. Croker.   Extract.

February 26th, 1825.

What madness it is to think that the miseries of the Irish people will be alleviated by emancipation.   Carry over there

* *Quarterly Review*, Vol. cxxxii. p. 184.

the English Poor Laws, and abolish the Lord Lieutenancy (not [that] this last affects the potato-eaters) and you will do more to give happiness to the many than all the toleration that can be devised. I much err if the enemies to the happiness of the Irish people are not the Irish gentlemen and nobility: but this [is] a truth that well-conditioned people like you dare not utter.

Mr. Croker to Mr. Drummond. Extract.

March 4th, 1825.

Alas, poor Ireland! But I think we shall carry the Catholic question, which I look upon as the best chance for her. While that question affords a furnace to heat the people, and to light the firebrands of demagogues, there will be no peace; but I look upon the measure only as a sedative under the influence of which other and more effective machines may have opportunity of operating.

Irish affairs, however, by no means occupied the whole of Mr. Croker's attention during this year. In the first place, he found time to intercede once more for Theodore Hook. On this occasion he wrote to the Chancellor of the Exchequer, begging him most earnestly to release the prisoner from confinement.

Mr. Croker to the Right Hon. F. Robinson. Extracts.

March 26th, 1825.

My dear Robinson,

If I believed Mr. Hook to be guilty of *peculation*, I should never have interested myself for him. *I* believe him *wholly innocent*; but, if he were guilty, I doubt whether he has not been sufficiently punished.

Twice over has he surrendered all he had in the world, even to his dressing-case; and the second time the value of accumulated riches was under 60*l.*

Six-and-twenty months has he been in confinement: ten months under circumstances of great misery and danger, and the last sixteen months under circumstances of discredit and disgrace.

For many, the best, *years* of his life he has been prevented following any business or providing in any other way for present or *future* subsistence by the cruel occupation of endeavouring to explain to those who, he says, have as assiduously endeavoured not to understand.

He has lost a valuable office; and with it all hopes of an establishment in the line of life he had adopted, and he is too old to begin anew.

If he be a *criminal*, show me a criminal of his class who has been more punished! but if, as I believe the fact is, his imprisonment is not, and cannot legally be, meant for punishment, then, I ask you, have you a doubt that you have twice over gotten all that he had? Have you an expectation that, by breaking his spirit and destroying his health by protracted confinement, he will become better able to discharge his debt.

Look at *other* defaulters; think of the sums they have abused! Have they pined in prison? Have they been deprived of the necessaries of life even down to a razor case? and why this savage virtue against Mr. Hook alone? I can tell you; like a blockhead (which many a man of talent is) he mixed himself with politics, and what between low people on our side, wishing to curry favour with opposition, and high people on our side, not wishing to be attacked for favouring a person politically odious to their antagonists, he is visited with a severity which, if he had not been suspected of being a Tory writer, would never have been dreamt of, and which, if he had been an avowed Whig, would not have been tolerated.

He interested me in his case before he ever was suspected of writing a word of politics, and what he may have done in that way has been without my knowledge, and knowing his position, I should if I had known or suspected it anxiously have dissuaded him from doing anything to mix himself in politics. He neither asked my advice nor gave me any opportunity of offering it, and I therefore speak without any personal prejudice when I say that what he has been suspected of doing has been done in general (I speak not of individual passages or topics) with good intentions and with great ability, and that he has been (though not always with the weapons we could have wished employed for us) a strenuous and a powerful supporter of His Majesty's present Government; and this is the cause, I will venture to assert, the sole cause, of his receiving from the hands of that Government a measure of severity of which there is, I believe, no other instance.

If the Government mean to keep him still longer in prison, I beg of you *in mercy* to say so, and to affix what time, one, two, three, or four years is deemed necessary to his expiation of his peculiar offences and his singular misfortune —a certainty, though so cruel, would be less so to his spirits and infinitely so to his pocket (he supports himself solely by his pen) than the state of agitation and deferred hope in which he is now perplexed. Follow the dictates of your own judgment, but *decide*. If you are disposed to think he ought to be enlarged, enlarge him in the name of God, and let not another Easter pass over him in prison;' if you think he ought still to be *kept in gaol*—pray *say so*. He will then know his fate, and will bear it better, I hope, than you or I should probably do in like circumstances.

Yours ever,
J. W. C.

This appeal accomplished its purpose. It took some weeks to complete the business, but in the month of May, Theodore Hook was set free.* Mr. Croker's kindly services to him were called into requisition more than once at a later period.

In the course of this year, Moore published his 'Life of Sheridan,' and a very warm controversy was immediately stirred up over many passages in which the author of the 'Irish Melodies' had displayed a remarkable lack of discretion, in reference alike to the dead and the living. It was scarcely probable that the public estimation of Sheridan's character would be improved by the revelations made by his friend and biographer. His amours, his debts, the miserable expedients to which he was reduced to raise money, his utter disregard of all the conditions which go to make up a well-regulated, or even what the world would consider a decent, life: all these failings were brought out into full relief by

---

* See Dean Hook's letter, *supra*, p. 261.

Moore. One of his statements attracted particular attention
in the inner circles of society at that time. It was to the
effect that Sheridan had been allowed to linger in want for
weeks together, although his dreadful situation was well
known to the King, who, when Prince Regent, was never tired
of associating with the wit. Some money, it appeared, had
been sent to Sheridan, through a Mr. Vaughan, then known
as "Hat" Vaughan, and it was said to come from the King;
but Moore affected to disbelieve this story. It would
be difficult to suppose, he pretended, "that so scanty and
reluctant a benefaction was the sole mark of attention
accorded by a gracious Prince and master to the last death-
bed wants of one of the most accomplished and faithful servants that royalty ever yet raised or ruined by its smiles."

This insinuation at the expense of the King was promptly
met and disposed of at the time in the *Quarterly Review,*
but it continued to cause a great deal of discussion in the
press and in private circles. In November, Mr. Croker was
sent for to dine with the King at Windsor, and he very soon
found that Moore's accusations were rankling deeply in His
Majesty's mind. What occurred at this interview was
placed upon record by Mr. Croker, and it is quite obvious,
from his preliminary statement, that the King intended it to
be made public at some future time. The record touches
upon many topics of greater interest and importance than
those which relate to Sheridan's affairs, and therefore, it is
here printed in its entirety. It will be observed that the
King once more treated his reported marriage with Mrs.
Fitzherbert as an idle story. The portion of this curious
narrative which relates to Catholic Emancipation presents the
conduct of the King when Prince Regent in a somewhat new
light; and it seems to dispose in a very effectual manner of

* Vol. xxxi. pp. 588–591.

Moore's charge against George the Fourth of treating Sheridan with a want of generosity.

From Mr. Croker's Note Book.

On the 25th November, 1825, I went by His Majesty's invitation to dine and sleep at the Royal Lodge in Windsor Park. His Majesty had intended to have shown me his plantations and improvements made during the autumn, but it snowed heavily in the night, and next morning the weather was so exceedingly bad that there was no possibility of stirring out, and His Majesty admitted me to his dressing-room, and conversed with me for a considerable time—indeed all the morning. Mr. Moore's 'Life of Sheridan' was lying on the table, and in allusion to the variety of misstatements made in that work with regard to His Majesty's conduct, he took up the book to point out to me particularly some of these errors.

After some desultory remarks of this kind on this or that passage, he entered into a more extensive and regular history of some circumstances of his political life, and seeing that I listened with great interest to what he related, he guessed the desire which certainly I should not have ventured to express, and he handed me a sheet of paper, and successively others, and permitted me to make notes of what he said, and he even moderated the flow of his narration when he saw that I had any difficulty in following him. These notes I that evening and the next morning transcribed into the following statement, in which I have, as nearly as I was able, preserved everything that fell from His Majesty in his own words and order of statement, and I have occasionally under-lined expressions to which he gave peculiar emphasis. Some incidental topics which, however interesting and agreeably narrated, did not appear necessary to the historical course of the statement, I omitted to note at the time, and I have not thought fit to supply them from my unassisted recollection. Much, no doubt, that fell from his Majesty in so long a con-versation I must, even with the assistance of my notes, have lost; but I can be quite confident of not having written one statement and hardly an expression which did not come from his Majesty's lips.

His Majesty narrated, or I may almost say *dictated*, to me

for some hours without interruption (except by a few inter-
locutory observations on my part and several anecdotical
episodes on his), and with a clearness, grace, and vivacity of
which my notes can supply but a very inadequate idea.   The
quotations of the sentiments of the several persons mentioned
were generally enforced and illustrated by a slight degree of
mimicry of *their* voices and manner, while his Majesty's own
narration was at once fluent and precise in recollection, and
accurate in expression, to a degree which I never had before
witnessed in any similar statement, and for which, notwithstanding my long acquaintance with his Majesty's readiness
in conversation, I confess I was not entirely prepared.

Rex Loquitur.

I must begin by telling you some anecdotes of the first
Regency question.

The quarrel between Mr. Burke and Sheridan was not what
Mr. Moore represents it to be; it arose out of the celebrated
letter to Pitt which Mr. Burke wrote for me, and which I
think one of the most beautiful and noble compositions that
ever was penned, but in the original draft there were some
passages of great violence.   I showed the draft to Sheridan,
who made a few alterations *in pencil*, some of which I
adopted, and others I did not; those that I adopted I wrote
in with my own hand, the others I erased.

I know not how Burke knew that Sheridan had thus
revised this work of which he was proud, and very justly;
but he never forgave him.   I believe that Burke guessed it
from the warmth with which, at a meeting at the Duke of
Portland's, Sheridan supported my amendments of the original
draft, and I even believe that they had some warm discussion
on that point, which was rendered more offensive to Burke by
Fox's agreeing with Sheridan.

When my father's recovery put an end to this affair, Burke
was so inveterate that he would not let it die away, and he
insisted that we ought to draw up a kind of manifesto to be
addressed to the King, to put his Majesty in possession of the
real conduct of the Queen and of the Ministers as contrasted
with that of me and my brother* and our friends.

At that period we had a kind of Cabinet, with whom I

* [The Duke of York.]

used to consult. They were the Dukes of York, Portland, Devonshire, and Northumberland, Lord Guilford (that was Lord North), Lord Stormont, Lords Moira and Fitzwilliam, and Charles Fox. Burke's proposition having been communicated to us, the Duke of Portland summoned us for a certain evening at nine o'clock to hear Burke's paper read. We met at nine—no Burke; ten, eleven—no Burke; till, at last, near twelve, he wrote to say that the paper was not finished, and that with all his diligence it could not be done that night, and he begged the meeting to adjourn till next day; which we did, to Carlton House at one o'clock; but before we broke up I proposed that we should consider, while Burke was absent, the prudence of presenting any such paper at all.

This I stated to be, in my opinion, a very doubtful policy, as we certainly had great prejudices against us, that the King's mind was in a very delicate state, and that if he had anything like a relapse, the fault would be laid on us and our paper.

Lord Stormont supported this view, even more decidedly than I had advanced it, and expatiated on the danger to the King; but it was finally settled that we should meet next day to hear Burke's paper, and that until we had heard it, it would be premature to discuss it.

Accordingly we met next day, with the addition of Burke and Sir Gilbert Elliot, who, at Burke's request, was admitted to read the paper, which I believe he had copied out from Burke's rough drafts.

The paper took two hours in reading, it was exceedingly eloquent and violent. I have strong in my mind's eye the effect it made on the audience. The Duke of Portland looked more stupid than usual. [Here the King interjected, " Not that he was at all as stupid as he looked—he had very good sense."] He was really in *a maze!* Lord North kept up a perpetual noise between a cough and a growl;* and Fox kept digging his fingers into the corner of his eye, a trick he had when anything perplexed him.

After it was read, there was a silence for some moments;

---

* [*Note by Mr. Croker.*—Here the King acted all this, and actually made himself look like the parties. So he did all along, and there were a hundred little touches which showed how vividly he remembered what he was relating.]

at last Lord Stormont repeated what he had said the night before; adding that he saw nothing in the temper and expressions of the paper to remove the disinclination which he had the night before avowed to any paper at all.   The paper was drawn up, he admitted, with great force and effect, but was, he thought, for that very reason the less proper to be laid before the King, who would be forced by it to one of two alternatives (both, he thought, equally disastrous), viz., either to take the Queen's part and to banish me and my brother from his presence for ever, or else to separate himself publicly from the Queen!   There would be, he said, no possible medium.

Burke answered all this with his usual ability and violence, and at last we were actually driven to divide upon it. Burke, however, and one other person only, were for this perilous proceeding—I and the rest were against it. Who do you think of all our Cabinet was the person who divided with Burke? why [laughing heartily] my brother, the Duke of York.   A fact, upon my honour—strange, considering his subsequent conduct, you will say—but a fact!

Out of deference to him and Burke, the negative upon the paper was softened down to a statement that it was not to be acted upon *at present*, and it was delivered to me " en dépôt," to be reserved for any occasion, if any such should occur, when we might find ourselves driven to make use of it.

When this meeting was over, Fox told Sheridan what had passed, and described the paper as having, I remember the words as Sheridan repeated them to me, "all Burke's bitterness."   He also told Sheridan that he quite approved the part I had taken, and the manner in which I had conducted the discussion, and that the Duke of Devonshire (as was natural for his quiet good sense and easy temper) perfectly agreed in the suppression of Burke's passionate invective.   Sheridan came to me with this statement of Fox's opinion, and his (Fox's) desire that Sheridan might read the paper.   He did so in my presence—every now and then exclaiming, "fine, very fine, mad, furious, admirable," and so on; and when he had done he gave it to me, saying that, if it were to get to the public, people in future, instead of saying of anything violent that it *out-Heroded Herod*, would say that it *out-Burked Burke!*

The paper was then given into the custody of Jack Payne, who at that time kept all my papers.

After some time, Sheridan came to me one day and begged to read the paper again ; he was writing, he said, something that would be extremely useful to us, and that he thought he could pick something valuable out of the paper. I told him carelessly enough, and not believing that he *was* writing (in which I am sure I was right) that he might go to Jack Payne and *read* the paper.

He, however, with an inaccuracy not unusual to him, poor fellow, told Payne that he had my authority to take away the paper, which he did. Of course he never wrote anything, and when I heard accidentally that he had taken the paper, I desired him to return it. This he postponed and delayed year after year, on a thousand pretences, and at last, a couple of years before his death, he fairly confessed that he had either absolutely lost the paper, or that it was buried in what he called the "chaos of his papers," which he had no hope of being ever able to arrange.

This is the paper which Mr. Moore mentions in his 'Life of Sheridan,' and which I must try to regain possession of; I dare say that they will have made copies of it, and that it will become public, which I should be sorry for, particularly out of the respect I feel towards my mother's memory, who is certainly not favourably represented in the paper ; but under any circumstance Mrs. Sheridan's friends can have no right to it, for it is mine, and, even if it had been fairly lent to him, ought to be returned to me.

On the subject of my supposed marriage with Mrs. Fitzherbert, and the debate upon Mr. Rolle's observations, some false statements have been made. When Fox mentioned it to me, I contradicted the supposition at once, with " *pooh*," " *nonsense*," " *ridiculous*," &c., upon which Fox, in the heat of debate, and piqued by Rolle, was induced, not merely to contradict the report, which was right enough, but to go a little further and to use some slighting expressions which, when Mrs. Fitzherbert read them in the paper next morning, deeply afflicted her, and made her furious against Fox. Mr. Moore states that I applied to Mr. Grey to set the matter right, and that when he refused, I said, " Then we must bring Sheridan into play." There is not a word of truth in this. I had no kind of communication with Mr. Grey on the subject, and Sheridan's interference was, so far as I was concerned, perfectly accidental.

Calling that morning at Mrs. Fitzherbert's he found her in

an agony of tears. Her beauty, her deep affliction affected him ; he was also, as he afterwards said, afraid that the great power she had over me would be turned to make a breach between me and Fox, against whom she was exasperated, and he (Sheridan) therefore endeavoured to conciliate and console her, and, amongst other topics, he assured her that Mr. Fox was misreported, and that he (Sheridan) would take the earliest opportunity of correcting any impression which might be made to her prejudice, by saying in his place what he, as well as Mr. Fox, and every one else must feel towards her.

He accordingly made that celebrated eulogium on Mrs. Fitzherbert, in which, however, I never could discover, what other folks fancied they found there, any confirmation of that absurd story of my supposed marriage. I looked upon it as gallantry to the lady, and as an effort to keep Fox and her on good terms, which no doubt was my feeling also.

When the Whigs came into the Government after the death of Mr. Pitt, I, of course, saw a great deal of Mr. Fox, and was consulted by him on all public affairs ; indeed I may say that I was the only person to whom he could unburthen his mind. He had not even a private secretary* whom he could trust, concerning which I will tell you a curious anecdote, which perhaps you may know, for it got wind.

Fox had intended Adair for that office—he was a person in whom he had great .confidence, as indeed he showed in the Russian affairs, but he was prevented from appointing Adair by a very singular circumstance.

Adair had married a French woman, with whom Andreossy, when here as Buonaparte's Minister, intrigued. This, I suppose, led to what I am going to tell you.

I happened to call one morning on the Duchess of Devonshire, whom I found evidently discomposed and agitated. As I knew that she had pecuniary difficulties and a good deal of vexation about her own affairs, I fancied that this was some trouble of that nature, but I soon saw that it was something of a different character. She exclaimed two or three times that the most shocking, the most cruel thing had just happened to her, and at last she told me that Mrs. Adair had been with her, and had offered her a bribe !—a bribe of 10,000*l.* down, and as much more whenever she might want it—if she would

---

* [*Note by Mr. Croker.*—His Majesty said private secretary; I suspect he meant *Under-Secretary* of State.]

communicate the Cabinet secrets with which the French thought she could not fail to be acquainted, through her intimacy with all the leaders of the Government. She said that she had dismissed the negotiatrix abruptly, and had sent off instantly for Mr. Fox to tell him of the circumstance, which indeed seemed to overwhelm her with shame and vexation. I, of course, could only say that she had taken the best possible course in sending for Mr. Fox.

Mr. Fox was equally astonished and vexed at a discovery which, besides its other effects, placed him in great personal difficulty with respect to Adair. He could not think of placing him in the station of confidence he had intended for him, and yet how was he to excuse his not doing so? He could not clear himself without telling Adair not only that his wife was a spy, but also that she was something worse. He was obliged at last to tell Adair that an obstacle which he could neither reveal nor overcome, but which did not affect or alter Fox's personal regard for him, prevented his appointment, and with this mysterious excuse Adair was obliged to content himself till he was sent abroad.

This accident left Fox without one personal friend to whom he could open himself, and contributed I dare say to increase the confidence which existed between us.

Soon after the change of Government (perhaps six weeks), Fox came to talk to me on their general position, and to consult me as to the public measures of the new Administration.

We discussed the three principal points which pressed for the earliest consideration, and I gave him my opinion on each.

First, as to the Abolition of the Slave Trade, I said that the King, my father, had a strong opinion of the impolicy and inefficacy of that measure, and that I owned that I a good deal agreed with His Majesty, and had never given it my support; but that as it was a case of public interest in which the Ministers were not only the responsible advisers, but really perhaps the best judges, I hoped that this question might, by a little moderation and prudent management, be arranged to their satisfaction.

Second, as to an attempt to make a peace with France, I knew the Ministers were pledged to it, and neither the King nor I could possibly have any other objection to it than our conviction that the attempt would fail. Fox replied that he feared so too—that he had no hopes from Buonaparte [to whom he applied a very harsh term—indeed, he always hated him] ; but that it was indispensable to make the experiment.

The third point was the Catholic Question. Upon that I was convinced that the King would not listen to *any* overture whatsoever, that my own sentiments coincided with my father's, but that, even if they had not, I should equally have deprecated the stirring of a question which had already once disturbed the King's mind, and might endanger his life. " You may call," I said, " his Majesty's sentiments what you please, whether, as I think it is, a sense of duty ; or whether, as others may term it, obstinacy, prejudice, bigotry—*insanity even*—call it what you will, the feeling cannot be denied to exist ; and, after all the calumny which you and I have suffered in the former regency question, would it not be madness on our part as well as a gross want of duty, to sanction any proceeding which might renew the King's malady ? The world would accuse *me*, and not unjustly I must say according to appearances, of having sacrificed my father's feelings in order to get the regency into my hands—possibly, even the crown on my head. But even supposing the thing to take a less lamentable turn, the best that could happen would be that the Ministers would be turned out in a week."

All these topics I urged upon Fox, and I entreated him to repeat them to the Cabinet, and to endeavour to persuade them, for my sake, for the King's sake, and even for their own, to drop all intention of moving this question—that as to this year, they had quite excuse enough, as they were hardly warm in their seats, but that even next year it could not be brought forward with propriety or any hope of success ; and that, in fact, it should be put off *sine die,* or at least during the King's life. I was convinced, I added, that whenever it should be proposed to the King, the first result would be to break up the Government.

Fox admitted that there was a great deal of weight in these considerations, and told me that he would mention them to the Cabinet that night. Next morning he called upon me in high spirits, and said he had brought over the Cabinet to my view of the question, but that there still remained the minor difficulty of the mode in which the postponement was to be brought before the public. I said I thought he had nothing to do but to collect those who were considered as more particularly the heads of the Catholic party, and explain to *them* the real state of the case—the King's immovable resolution, my disinclination, the certainty of breaking up the Government if the question was persisted in, and then appeal to them whether they would force on a question big with such disastrous consequences.

Fox shook his head. They were, he said, the proper arguments, but it would not *do* that the *Government* should use them. Who then? I asked. Why *you*, he replied; *you* have really suggested them, *we* adopt them on your suggestion, and we think we have some right to claim the assistance of your influence to make them go down with others.

To this I had no answer, and I consented, provided that His Majesty, to whom I should mention my intentions, did not object.

I accordingly wrote to the King that letter which Mr. Moore says that Sheridan wrote for me; which is false— I wrote it myself! After I had written it, indeed, I showed it to Sheridan as I also did to Fox. Sheridan suggested the alteration of a word or two, and of the turn of one sentence, but these alterations were in no way substantial, and I have to this hour my rough draft on which you would see these alterations. The letter itself was to state to the King the advice I had given to Mr. Fox—its success, and my willingness, though otherwise reluctant, to make the proposed communication to the heads of the Catholic party, if it would at all contribute to His Majesty's ease and comfort.

To this letter I received a very cold answer—very cold indeed—expressing a great and general distaste to the question, or any stirring of it. But as His Majesty did not disapprove of my proposal (though it was plain he did not like the thing in any shape) I determined to avail myself of his silence, and to do him what I considered an essential service, in spite of his teeth!

Accordingly, I assembled in the bow room of my little red house in Pall Mall, the Duke of Bedford, who was going as Lord Lieutenant to Ireland, Lord Moira, Lord Hutchinson, and I think his brother Kit, the late Lord Ponsonby, Mr. George Ponsonby, the Irish Chancellor, Mr. Grattan, and I believe some others, and I stated to them the view of the subject which I had already opened to Mr. Fox.

In this they all acquiesced; and on this footing matters stood till Mr. Fox's death, when I determined to retire from the prominent situation which I occupied with the Ministers. I was a kind of sleeping partner, but a sleeping partner who unluckily had a great deal of the business to do, and ultimately much of the risk to run.   I had no longer any friend in the Government except Lord Holland, perhaps I ought to add Lord Ellenborough.   Lord Moira, to be sure, was still in office, but he was dissatisfied, had little weight, and thought, I believe justly, that he was not treated with confidence.

As to my own personal position, I foresaw that one or other of two things would happen—either that I must submit to the Grenvilles' nomination of the persons who were to come in, and so connect myself subordinately with persons and a party I did not like, or else place myself at once at the head of the general party, liable to all its chances, accidents, and variations.   I did not like either alternative, and resolved to retire as civilly as possible.   I therefore wrote to Lord Grenville to state that I should retire from any direct participation in the management of affairs, but that I wished well to his Majesty's existing Government, and as a proof of doing so I made some suggestions as to the pending arrangements.   This letter of mine crossed, as I believe, one from Lord Grenville, stating the arrangements which he had made, and with which he stated that everybody concerned was satisfied.   I, in reply, expressed also my satisfaction, and begged that the suggestions which I had made in my former letter might be considered as *non avenus.*

[Here his Majesty told me something of a visit he made to the King at Windsor on some occasion, but the note is so imperfect (having been accidentally rubbed and blotted, as well as being originally short and straggling) that I do not venture to make any use of it.   The visit itself could hardly have occurred about this period, as the Prince does not seem to have seen the King between his two visits to the north.*—J. W. C.]

I was at this time on a tour in the north, and I came to town for the purpose of attending Fox's funeral, but the King sent me a message through Lord Grenville to forbid my doing so.

I therefore returned to the north, and made a long round of visits, and came late to town.

About the month of March in that year, Lauderdale, whom I had not seen since Fox's death (indeed, he had been at Paris) sent to offer to wait upon me; I appointed him the next morning at eight o'clock.   He came and breakfasted

* [October, 1806.]

with me; of course we talked about his late negotiations and
generally on public affairs. At last, he said that he did not
much like *that bill*. "What bill?" I asked. "Why," he
said, "the alteration in the Mutiny Bill, which, after all, will
not satisfy the Catholics, though it cannot but embarrass the
Ministers, for I hear that the bishops and the King's friends
will all come down to oppose it."

I, who had never before heard a syllable of the matter,
expressed, as I well might, the greatest surprise at this. I
said it was directly contrary to the pledge which I was authorised to give to the King, and I expressed my indignation at
the scandal that would be created, if the King should be
obliged to send down his personal friends to vote against his
Ministers. "Depend upon it," I told him, "if they thus
break faith with his · Majesty and me they will not be
Ministers a week."

Lauderdale undertook to see the Ministers that forenoon,
and requested to see me again in the course of the day; but,
"as the Grenvilles are already inclined to be jealous," he wished
to avoid coming to Carlton House, and begged that I would
meet him at the Duke of York's at one o'clock.

I accordingly went at one to my brother's (who, of course,
was absent; he knew nothing of my conversation with Lauderdale, and was indeed fixed against the question in any shape or
way).

Lauderdale came and told me that he had seen Grenville
and Grey, that they told him that all was right and smooth,
that Grey had seen the King, and had his Majesty's consent
to the bill; but I don't know how it is, continued Lauderdale, I do not like the state of the affair; as to the Ministers
themselves, they are so *pig-headed* (that was his very phrase)
that there is no managing them.

All this surprised and a little alarmed me, and I desired
Lauderdale to come to me with Lord Holland and Lord Grey
at eight o'clock next morning—Lauderdale and Lord Holland
came at eight, Lord Grey not till nine.

When he came I stated how contrary this measure was to
the pledge which I had conveyed to the King. Lord Grey,
in his high and mighty way, was proceeding to make light
of all this, and to pooh-pooh his Majesty's objections. I interrupted him, and said that I did not want to hear his
reasons, which could have no effect with me, after a promise
made; that I wished, on the other hand, to make him aware

of my fixed opinions. I appealed to Lord Holland that these opinions were not new, that the course I had pursued had had not merely the sanction of Mr. Fox, but was taken by his advice and request; that I was convinced that they were utterly mistaken if they thought the King indifferent to the question, and equally so if they thought his opposition was to be disregarded; that I was satisfied that they would be turned out, and that I must state distinctly that if they were, they were not to expect that I was to follow them into opposition to my father's and to my own opinion; that I would do no such thing; and that, therefore, I thought their first and indeed only endeavour now should be to prevent a rupture, and *that*, I thought, could only be accomplished by respecting the King's feelings.

This declaration on my part seemed to startle Lord Grey, who undertook to see Lord Grenville and convey my sentiments to him.

That evening I had intended to go to the play, and had ordered an early dinner with Tyrwhitt and Blomfield.

We dined in the little room on the left hand as you enter Carlton House, where you have sometimes dined with me, and during dinner I saw the gate open and a carriage drive in. I knew the black and white liveries, and said, "Here's Moira coming to join us, lay a cover for him."

In came Moira and Erskine; I invited them to sit down, and take share of my dinner, and then come with me to the play.

Moira said no, that the Cabinet were to dine with him that day, and that he and Erskine had come to speak to me about some very particular business before they met the Cabinet; upon this Tyrwhitt and Blomfield walked out into the hall with their napkins in their hands, and Moira began by congratulating me on the good service I had done—that Grey had been in to the King—that the bill was to be withdrawn, and that all was settled on the footing which I had recommended.

Erskine repeated the same story in great glee and highly delighted. He expatiated on the ruin that must have befallen the country if this lucky conciliation had not been accomplished. It was amusing, I remember, to hear him describing the *national calamity* which would have inevitably followed a rupture, it being quite evident that the *national calamity* which he deprecated was no other than his ceasing to be Lord Chancellor!

They left me to go to the Cabinet dinner, and Moira begged leave to call on me in the morning to enter with me into the details of what had passed. I appointed him at seven o'clock next morning.

Accordingly next day at seven he came. I was in bed in that great bedchamber which I had on the lower floor at Carlton House. When he came in he made no great haste to commence his history. I soon observed that he was uneasy; he went over to the chimney and rearranged the cards, and handled the china which was on it; in short, it was clear that he had something to say which he did not like to begin upon.

At last, he told me that the Cabinet had sat at his house till three o'clock that morning; that they had all signed a paper, to be presented to the King, saying that in obedience to his Majesty's scruples the bill was withdrawn, but that the consequence would be that the Catholic question would be brought forward, and in that case they must, in consistency with their declared opinions, support it.

"Then," said I, "you are out; and have *you* signed it ?"

"Why," replied he, "I certainly do not approve it, and I did all I could to prevent their doing so. I think it both foolish and wrong, but I was persuaded to add my name, by this consideration that it would have been considered dishonourable to have separated myself from them at the moment they were going out."

I said that I could see no such thing, when they were going out on a point on which I differed from them, and that I must own that I thought it tasted a little of the *potato* that he should sign a paper which he disapproved of, with no better reason for doing so than that the evils which he attributed to it were likely to be realised; however, the thing was done, and I could only repeat that, as I was no party to it, so neither should I be to the consequences of it.

All this while, the investigation about the Princess had been lingering on without coming to a conclusion, in spite of all I could do to have a decision one way or the other, and the attempts of Moira, Erskine, and Ellenborough to get the Cabinet to dispose of the matter. However, the matter was now ripe for the final decision, but the very day after they had sent their papers to the King, they resolved to throw on their successors, for they saw that they were gone, the difficulty of that case.

Mr. Perceval now saw the King, and received his commands for a new Ministry, but he made the reception of the Princess a *sine quâ non* of his undertaking the negotiations. The King was obliged to acquiesce, and his acquiescence was communicated to me. I thought it rather hard that while I was doing all I could to keep the King easy, and had decided not to oppose his new Government, that my peace and honour were to be the first sacrifice to that new Adminstration. I therefore requested an audience of the King, which was appointed for the next day at Buckingham House at ten o'clock. His Majesty came to me out of my mother's dressing-room, he was a good deal flurried, and began in a way that showed that he would not suffer himself to be interrupted.

He began upon the Catholic question and the conduct of the late Ministers. He reminded me of the letter I had written him, of my interview with the Ministers, and that with the Catholic leaders in Pall Mall, and finally of my pledge that the question should not be pressed upon him, and that if the Ministers were to go out on it, or any part of it, that I was not to follow them into opposition. He said that if Mr. Fox had lived, this, he was sure, never could have happened. I must here observe that my father was perfectly satisfied, and was pleased, I may say, with Mr. Fox, in all their intercourse after he came into office.

I got an opportunity of just saying that I would keep my pledge, and that I would *not* go into opposition. His Majesty was greatly struck; he took me in his arms, said I was a good son, and a man of honour; that we had had enemies who kept us asunder; that they were, he found, more *his* enemies even than *mine*, but that this conduct on my part wiped away all past misunderstandings, and established us on that footing of confidence and affection which was natural to both of us.

While he was going on in this way I interposed to say that I had heard that he was to see the Princess.

He replied, hastily, "Yes, I have seen that infamous woman, but what could I do? I consulted Lord Hawksbury what I was to do in the circumstances in which the Ministers had placed me. He sent Mr. Perceval to me. Mr. Perceval stated that the first step must be the reception of the Princess; I answered," continued His Majesty, "that it was a cruel alternative, that I had early reason to be dissatified with the

Princess, that she was a firebrand in the family, and that besides she had a disposition to be, the thing I most hated in the world, a female politician."

Mr. Perceval, however, was steady. He told me plainly that without this point there would be no adminstration. My situation was in the last degree perplexing—on one side the Catholic question, on the other side the vain ceremony of a Court reception—the latter, disagreeable as it was, I thought it my duty to adopt as the less of two evils. I told Mr. Perceval, therefore, that I would receive her for form's sake any public day, but that I should forbid the Queen and my daughters to have any intercourse whatsoever with her except on that one occasion, " and now," he said, " go up to your mother, and see if she does not confirm what I have told you."

I went accordingly to the Queen, and found that everything had passed just as his Majesty had stated it, and she repeated to me her resolution that neither herself nor my sisters should ever hold any manner of communication with the Princess, except the single reception at the Drawing-room.

And this promise their Majesties religiously kept, for although the Duchess of Brunswick contrived on two occasions to get her into the house, the King would not speak to her, and both times sent to apprise me of the circumstance, that no rumour might lead me for a moment to believe that he had forgotten his engagement to me.

A few days after this, Moira and MacMahon came to report to me that Mr. Tierney was taking great freedoms with my name, and that he had *in terms* accused me of *betraying* the late Government, and of having sold myself to Mr. Perceval, and that the Princess was to be sent off. Upon this I thought it due to myself to write a letter to Moira, which I begged of him to show to every member of the late Cabinet. Mr. Tierney had not been of the Cabinet, and I certainly did not mean to offer *him* any explanation.

This is the letter which Mr. Moore says Sheridan wrote for me. Mr. Sheridan never saw it. I wrote it with my own hands, and I have the rough draft which I can show you.

This letter states that I could not go into opposition as the Ministers had broken the pledge, that I respected several of them, and that I had a strong individual friendship for some, &c., &c.

Mr. Moore says that he read this letter, but was not allowed to take a copy. Now Moira states to me that he does not believe that he ever showed the letter to Moore. Indeed, it seems to me extraordinary conduct on his part if he did. I therefore do not believe it, and must think he has had his information in some other way.

With regard to Mr. Moore himself, he got acquainted with me through Lord Moira and the Harringtons.

The Harringtons have a passion for tea drinking. Whether it be taste or insanity I cannot say, but the drinking of tea in that house was most extraordinary. It began naturally enough at breakfast, but it extended very *un*naturally through the whole day and night. I have seen them drink tea just before dinner, I have even seen them drink tea after supper, and the whole family, old and young, were possessed with this slipslop propensity.

A consequence of this system was that they never could find tea enough abroad, and that the old lady used to spend her evenings at home and at tea, and it was a custom that, come *qui voudrait* to her evening parties, whatever else they might or might not find, they were at least sure of *tea*.

Sometimes in spring they opened the doors into St. James's Gardens, and made a little kind of *al fresco* of it, and after the opera Lady Harrington was very glad to have the young men about town drop in to amuse her daughters. In such a society as this Mr. Moore was very welcome; he talked small talk, and sang little madrigals and love songs, and made himself very agreeable.

I used to go sometimes to Lady Harrington's, and there I saw him, but he had also some special acquaintance with Moira, and had been recommended as a countryman to MacMahon, who took a good deal of notice of him, and was anxious that *I* should take some notice of him also. I shall here only say that the return he made was to libel both of us, for immediately after this change of Government, MacMahon observed some things in the newspapers which he had traced to his guardian [quondam?] friend Moore, who, I know not why,* chose to take a great interest in the Catholic question. Afterwards it became worse, and he wrote that series of libels called the ' Penny Post Bag,' in which he introduced in the

* [It is odd, but certain, that the King did not know, or, at least, did not recollect, that Moore was himself a Roman Catholic.—J. W. C.]

most ungentlemanlike, and, I will even say, *unmanly* way, the names of Lady Hertford and other ladies.

While he was employed in this way, MacMahon, indignant at his duplicity and ingratitude, told Moira of it. (I forgot to say that we had amongst us got him a place.*) Moira, equally indignant, sent for him, and began to reproach him with this scandalous conduct. Moore swore to him, as Moira told me, that he had not written a line of these libels, and that he was too much indebted to him, to MacMahon, and to me to be guilty of any ill-natured observations on us, much less such atrocious libels. I believe he persuaded Moira—I knew little of the man or his libels, and took the thing as they represented it to me ; but *now,* I am told, that he avows all those things that he *then* swore were not his.

When I withdrew myself from the opposition, Sheridan certainly became less forward in that party, but not solely out of any deference to me ; he had been on bad terms with them from the very formation of their Government, and had increased their ill-humour towards him by those sentiments, which he afterwards condensed into the celebrated joke that he had known men knock their heads against walls by accident, but that these Ministers were the first persons he ever had heard of who *built* the wall to knock their heads against. Moreover, Lord Grey and Mr. Whitbread were become the leaders of the party, and he did not like either; of Mr. Whitbread he had an actual hatred ; even before Drury Lane affairs had brought them into almost personal conflicts. He therefore naturally, and for every reason, disapproved of Mr. Whitbread's taking up the cause of the Princess, and they had warm words about it ; and Sheridan always thought that Whitbread wished afterwards to keep him down, and above all out of Parliament, lest he should interfere with the scheme of ambition which he had begun to build on the Princess. I remember Sheridan's telling me with great satisfaction that Whitbread having alluded to Sir John Douglas in some injurious way, Sir John had required an explanation which Whitbread thought fit to make to this officer, who was supposed to be a very determined man, and whose conduct in the breach of Acre under Sir Sidney Smith has gained him a reputation for courage which Whitbread knew was not to be trifled with.

* [This was the office at the Bermudas, which Moore filled by deputy.]

I don't like mentioning such things, but I must now tell you in confidence that all through our intercourse I had aided Sheridan to an enormous amount. I can venture to say that he has had above 20,000*l.* from me. I gave 1000*l.* to him the day before he failed.

I need not tell *you* all the circumstances of the last regency question, nor the motives that made me keep my father's Ministers. You knew it all at the time as well as any one. In fact, there was little or nothing, either first or last, that was not pretty publicly known, and I believed printed; at least stated in Parliament. But you recollect the strange figure Sheridan made in the debate when it appeared that he had concealed from his party the fact that my household were ready to resign. This completed the coolness, I might say breach, between them, though he still affected to belong to them.

At last the Parliament was dissolved in, I think, 1812 * or 1813, and Sheridan was left without a seat, unless he could get once more returned for Westminster, which there was no chance of, unless he could have the support of the Government. When he mentioned this to me, I saw at once the difficulty of applying the Government interest to the success of a person who had held the principles which Sheridan had formerly professed; but as I knew that he was anything but a Jacobin or democrat, and that in general he agreed in my politics, I thought that if he professed generally Mr. Fox's principles, and abstained from pledging himself to the new questions of the day, of which he thought as I did, he might keep most of his old friends; and that friends of the Government might, without inconsistency, prefer him to those who were going great lengths to which it was notorious that Mr. Sheridan was really adverse, and would give him their second votes. In truth, I saw no objection to Sheridan and Moira's both coming into office, and was desirous that they should do so.

On the subject of the Westminster election I desired Sheridan to see Arbuthnot, who was prepared to give him all the assistance he could on the fair grounds that I had stated.

But Sheridan's natural indolence and procrastination, added perhaps to some feeling that he might risk his popularity, prevented his taking any decisive step. He also had some hopes of Stafford, but there he failed at last, and found him-

* [It was in 1812.]

self, as I had feared, out of Parliament, without any chance of getting in.

He came to explain to me his failure at Stafford,* of which he had laid all the blame upon Whitbread, of whom he spoke with perfect fury, and called him, I well recollect, *a scoundrel !* He said that Whitbread was already building a scheme of ambition on the Princess; that he was afraid of Sheridan in Parliament on that point; and had determined to keep him out. This induced him, Sheridan said, to refuse to pay him 2000*l.* which Sheridan had a clear right to, and, as he told me the story, I thought he had.

Some time after this, just before Moira went to India,† he came to me and said that it was a pity that poor Sheridan at the close of such a life as his had been, should be out of Parliament.

I told him that Sheridan's own indolence and indecision, and his being neither on one side nor the other, were the causes of his being thus left out, but that I had always been ready, and was still, to do all that I could to bring him into Parliament; and *that*, without exacting any dependence on one or any allegiance to the Ministers.

Moira said that he so understood my intentions, or he should not now have approached me with the proposition he had to make, which certainly went rather to place Sheridan again in opposition.

The Duke of Norfolk had a seat to dispose of, for which he expected 4000*l.*, but he consented, as he called it, to subscribe 1000*l.* towards bringing Sheridan into Parliament; or, in other words, to accept from Sheridan 3000*l.* for the seat. As even the payment of this sum was not to leave Sheridan perfectly independent, the Duke expecting that he should vote with him, I did not consider the offer quite so noble as the offer of subscribing 1000*l.* towards bringing Sheridan in seemed to affect to be; but I nevertheless told Moira that I should find some way to get 3000*l.*, and that Sheridan should have it.

This affair, however, did not proceed, from I forget what misunderstanding. Sheridan, however, soon came with a new plan; he had found, he said, a young gentleman who had bought a seat with a right of vacating for another,‡ and

* [In October 1812.]
† [Lord Moira was appointed Governor-General, December 18th, 1812.]
‡ [Mr. Attersoll; the borough was Wootton Bassett.]

that he had settled with this gentleman (whose name he told us, though I forget) to be elected in his room on payment of the 3000*l.*

It happened that Moira had 3000*l.* of MacMahon's in his hand as a trustee, and it was agreed that this should be advanced to Sheridan, and that Moira and I should be responsible for it, and in the event I had, as might have been expected, to pay the whole sum.

Not that we advanced the sum to Sheridan himself; we knew him too well for that; but the money was lodged in the hands of Mr. Cocker, a respectable solicitor named by Sheridan, who was to pay it over to the young man in question when the transfer of the seat should be made. Sheridan took a world of trouble to convince MacMahon that all this transaction was *bonâ fide.* The day before he was to go, he called and took leave of MacMahon, saying he was going to set out early next morning. Late that evening he wrote a note to MacMahon to say that he had forgotten to say something to him, and that as he was to set out at nine next day, he would call in Pall Mall at eight, and begged to have some breakfast. MacMahon laughed at the notion of Sheridan's calling on him at eight; but he came. What he had to say to him I forget, but it ended in urging MacMahon to deposit the money with Mr. Cocker, which MacMahon promised should be done. At last Sheridan said "Come, it is time to be off. My carriage is at the door, and Mr. (whatever his name was) is waiting for me."

I do not know whether by invitation from Sheridan or from some lurking suspicion of his own, but MacMahon walked up with him to where he lived, George Street or Savile Row, or that neighbourhood; where, to be sure, there was a travelling carriage at the door, and servants packing it. Sheridan asked where the horses were. The servants said they were put up till he was ready. "Very well," said he, "put them to as soon as Mr. —— arrives." But Sheridan was quite on the fidget. MacMahon went into the house, and found breakfast laid, and after a little, Sheridan still very fussy; a message came from Mr. —— to say that he was detained a few minutes, but would be with him in a quarter of an hour. Then appeared Mrs. Sheridan, and MacMahon feeling he was *de trop*, took his leave, and left the carriage at the door ready to set off when Mr. —— should arrive.

The money, of course, was deposited, and he expected that

X 2

Sheridan, as he promised, would write us an account of his reception and his success. The borough, I think, was in Wiltshire, and about eighty or ninety miles from town. Three days after I was on horseback in Oxford Road, and I thought I saw Sheridan at a distance. The person, whoever he was, turned down into Poland Street, or one of those streets, as if to avoid me.

When I came home I sent for MacMahon, and asked him if he had heard of Sheridan. "No," said MacMahon, "not since I saw him *off*," for he had seen him so *nearly off* that he looked on it as the same thing.

"Damn me," I said, "if I believe he is gone!" "Not gone?" "No. I believe I saw him to-day in town." "Impossible!" "I will not be too confident, but I am almost sure that I saw him in Oxford Road this evening."

MacMahon was thunderstruck. Next morning, however, came a note to him from Sheridan to say that he was still in town, and would come to explain why, and soon after another note to say that he was coming immediately.

He was this time as good as his word—he came; laid all the blame on the man, Mr. ——, whom however, he only accused of a mistake. He had gone to a coffee house when Sheridan had written to his lodgings, and the note of appointment followed him to his lodgings when he had come back to the coffee house. Sheridan, on the other hand, having written the note which was to say he was waiting for him, thought he might as well look after some business which he had, so he walked out, leaving word that if Mr. —— came or sent an answer, it was to be brought to him at Brooks's, or at Drury Lane. If he ever wrote such a note at all, he took good care never to receive any answer; "but," he continued to MacMahon, "all these *malentendus* are rectified, and we are to set out to-morrow at the dawn of day."

Next day, or the day after, a new note from Sheridan; sorry to say that the negotiations had failed, but he had the pleasure to assure us that a still more satisfactory arrangement was on foot.

MacMahon, however, now became seriously alarmed about the money, and he wrote to Mr. Cocker to say that the plan for which the money had been advanced was at an end, and he desired that it might be returned.

Cocker answered that this question of a seat in Parliament was quite new to him; that Mr. Sheridan when he desired him to receive the money never hinted at any such object, that it was paid to him on Mr. Sheridan's account, and that he had disposed of it according to Mr. Sheridan's directions; viz., to pay certain pressing debts, and particularly a debt to himself, Cocker, which he was obliged to press Mr. Sheridan for, and which Mr. Sheridan directed him to take out of the sum so lodged.

I was, as I told you, obliged to repay this money, but I never saw Sheridan (to speak to) after; not that it was much worse in principle than other things of his, nor that I had given orders to exclude him, but it was felt by Sheridan himself to be so gross a violation of confidence—such a want of respect and such a series of lies and fraud, that he did not venture to approach me, and, in fact, he never came near me again.

He, however, came to MacMahon, and again endeavoured to lay all the blame on Whitbread, who, he said, had got him into all the difficulty; first, by refusing to pay him his 2000l., and afterwards by paying it upon a hard condition which he forced upon Sheridan.   "In short," said Sheridan, throwing off the air of shame and contrition with which he began the conversation, and taking up a kind of theatrical tone and manner; "in short," said he, "I went to see that scoundrel Whitbread, and it was like the scene of Peachum and Lockit. I told him that I came to tell him that I did not want his assistance, that I retracted the intreaties which my necessities had obliged me to make to him, that I could wait for the 2000l. which he had refused to let me have to get into Parliament, for that I had got 3000l. without being under any obligation to him, and that I should be in Parliament next week. 'My dear Sheridan,' replied Whitbread, 'it is true that I would not give you 2000l. to get into Parliament, and in your circumstances I am sure I acted the part of a true friend, but did I ever refuse you 2000l. *to stay out* of Parliament?'   In short, he paid me my 2000l. on condition I should *not come in*, and when I came to ask for the 3000l. which you, my dear friend, had advanced, for the purpose of returning it to you I found that that fellow Cocker had chosen to apply it to his own debt, and that it was not forthcoming."

MacMahon listened to all this, but with no good-will towards Sheridan, and came immediately to report it to me, but after that Sheridan never came near either of us.

I sometimes, however, heard of him, and I once saw him by accident, as I shall tell you presently.   He now took to live in a very low and obscure way, and all he looked for in the company he kept was brandy and water.   He lived a good deal with some low acquaintance he had made—a harness-maker; I forget his name, but he had a house near Leatherhead. In that neighbourhood I saw him for the last time, on the 17th August, 1815.* I know the day from this circumstance, that I had gone to pay my brother a visit at Oatlands on his birthday, and next day as I was crossing over to Brighton, I saw in the road near Leatherhead old Sheridan coming along the pathway. I see him now in the black stockings and blue coat with metal buttons. I said to Blomfield, "There is Sheridan;" but, as I spoke, he turned off into a lane when we were within about thirty yards of him, and walked off without looking behind him. That was the last time I ever saw Sheridan, nor did I hear of or from him for some months, but one morning MacMahon came up to my room, and after a little hesitation and apology for speaking to me about a person who had lately swindled me and him so shamelessly, he told me that Mr. Vaughan, Hat Vaughan they used to call him, had called to say that Sheridan was dangerously ill, and really in great distress and want. I think no one who ever knew me will doubt that I immediately said that his illness and want made me forget his faults, and that he must be taken care of, and that any money that was necessary I desired he would immediately advance. He asked me to name a sum, as a general order of that nature was not one on which he would venture to act, and whether *I* named or *he* suggested 500*l.* I do not remember; but I do remember that the 500*l.* was to be advanced at once to Mr. Vaughan, and that he was to be told that when that was gone he should have more. I set no limit to the sum, nor did I say nor hear a word about the mode in which it was to be applied, except only that I desired that it should not appear to come from me.

I was induced to this reserve by several reasons. I thought that Sheridan's debts were, as the French say, "la mer à boire," and unless I was prepared to drink the sea, I had better not be known to interfere, as I should only have brought more pressing embarrassments on him; but I will also confess that I did not know how ill he was, and after the gross fraud he had so lately practised upon me, I was not inclined to forgive and forget so suddenly, and without any colour of apology or explanation; for the pretended explanation to MacMahon was more disrespectful and offensive to me than the original

---

* [He died July 7th, 1816.]

transaction, for he had before told me *why* Whitbread wished to keep him out of Parliament, namely, lest he should serve me in the object nearest my heart, and yet he had suffered Whitbread to bribe him out of my service with his own money, and had then swindled me out of mine.

And, finally, there is not only bad taste but inconvenience in letting it be known what pecuniary favours a person in my situation confers, and I therefore, on a consideration of all these reasons, forbid my name being mentioned at present, but I repeated my directions that he should want for nothing that money could procure him.

MacMahon went down to Mr. Vaughan's and told him what I had said, and that he had my directions to place 500*l.* in his hands. Mr. Vaughan, with some expression of surprise, declared that no such sum was wanted at present, and it was not without some pressing that he took 200*l.*, and said that if he found it insufficient he would return for more. He did come back, but not for more; for he told MacMahon that he had spent only 130*l.* or 140*l.*, and he gave the most appalling account of the misery which he had relieved with it.

He said that he found him and Mrs. Sheridan both in their beds, both apparently dying and both starving. It is stated in Mr. Moore's book that Mrs. Sheridan attended her husband in his last illness. It is not true; she was too ill to leave her own bed, and was, in fact, already suffering from the disease (cancer of the womb) of which she died in a couple of years after. They had hardly a servant left. Mrs. Sheridan's maid she was about to send away, but they could not collect a guinea or two to pay the woman her wages.

When he entered the house he found all the reception rooms bare, and the whole house in a state of filth and stench that was quite intolerable. Sheridan himself he found in a truckle bed in a garret, with a coarse blue and red coverlid, such as one sees used as horsecloths, over him; out of this bed he had not moved for a week, not even for the occasions of nature, and in this state the unhappy man had been allowed to wallow, nor could Vaughan discover that any one had taken any notice of him, except one old female friend—whose name I hardly know whether I am authorised to repeat—Lady Bessborough, who sent 20*l.* Some ice and currant water were sent from Holland House—an odd contribution; for if it was known that he wanted these little matters, which might have been had at the confectioner's, it might have been suspected that he was in want of more essential things.

Yet, notwithstanding all this misery, Sheridan on seeing Mr. Vaughan appeared to revive ; he said he was quite well, talked of paying off all his debts, and though he had not eaten a morsel for a week, and had not had a morsel to eat, he spoke with a certain degree of alacrity and hope.

Mr. Vaughan, however, saw that this was a kind of bravado, and that he was in a fainting state, and he immediately procured him a little spiced wine and toast, which was the first thing (except brandy) that he had tasted for some days.

Mr. Vaughan lost no time in next buying a bed and bed clothes, half-a-dozen shirts, some basons, towels, &c., &c. He had Sheridan taken up, and washed, and put into the new bed. He had the rooms cleaned and fumigated. He discharged, I believe, some immediately pressing demands, and, in short, provided as well as circumstances would admit for the ease and comfort, not only of Sheridan, but of Mrs. Sheridan also.

I sent the next day (it was not till next day that Mac-Mahon repeated this melancholy history to me) to inquire after Sheridan, and the answer was that he was better, and more comfortable, and I had the satisfaction to think that he wanted nothing that money and the care and kindness of so judicious a friend as Mr. Vaughan could procure him ; but the next day, that is two days after Mr. Vaughan had done all this, and actually expended near 150*l.*, as I have stated, he came to MacMahon with an air of mortification, and stated that he was come to return the 200*l.* 'The 200*l.*," said Mac-Mahon, with surprise. Why, you had spent three-fourths of it the day before yesterday ! " " True," returned Vaughan, " but some of those who left these poor people in misery have now insisted on their returning this money, which they suspect has come from the Prince. Where they got the money, I know not, but they have given me the amount, with a message that *Mrs.* Sheridan's friends had taken care that Mr. Sheridan wanted for nothing. I," added Mr. Vaughan, " can only say that this assistance came rather late, for that three days ago I was enabled by his Royal Highness's bounty to relieve him and her from the lowest state of misery and debasement in which I had ever seen human beings."

[Here His Majesty concluded.—J. W. C.]

CHAPTER XI.

1826.

In the autumn of 1825, even the Catholic question and
Ireland were forgotten in the presence of a danger which
threatened to entail severe misfortunes on all classes of the
community. There had been a period of wonderful prosperity
after the great wars, and it led to a rage for public gambling,
by which " promoters " and stock-jobbers reaped a rich harvest.
It prepared the way for the inevitable crash which overtook so many country banks and commercial houses towards
the close of the year. Mining shares, on which small sums
of money had been paid, were run up to four, five, or even
thirteen hundred pounds each. When the blow fell, it ruined
thousands of men all over the country, and among the most

memorable of the sufferers was Sir Walter Scott. When the
worst of the panic was over, Mr. Croker sent to the Duke of
Wellington, who was then travelling on the Continent, an
account of the proceedings of the Ministry, and of the excitement which broke out in Scotland when the circulation of
bank notes below the value of 5*l.* was prohibited. The
proposal was denounced by Sir Walter Scott in the "Letters
of Malachi Malagrowther," to which replies were hastily
written by Mr. Croker in the *Courier* newspaper, also under
an assumed name. In the end, the Ministry withdrew its
scheme, so far as it applied to Scotland, and the victory
rested with the author of 'Waverley;' but after 1826, one
pound notes were no more heard of in England.

Mr. Croker to the Duke of Wellington.   Extract.

March 20th, 1826.

I dare say you have heard the whole story from day to day
by better informants, yet you may like to see my view of it.
I need not tell *you* all the reasons (very good ones) why the
Government did not like to undertake an issue of Exchequer
Bills, but as soon as the whole mercantile body, as soon as
Tierney at the head of the opposition, and as soon as every
man of the old Pitt party expressed a unanimous concurrence
in that measure, we all thought that it would do no great
harm to adopt it as a special remedy in a special case.* But
Lord Liverpool, influenced as the world said by his pledge
and prophecy of last year relative to the evils of overtrading,
would not listen to it, and on the evening on which the
petition of the London merchants for the advance of Exchequer Bills was to be presented, he at half-past four sent
for Canning, and told him, as Canning himself told me, that
he would resign if such a measure was forced upon the
Administration, and he not only authorized, but desired
Canning to say so.

Canning, a good deal surprised, and taken on the sudden,

* [In 1793 Pitt had issued Exchequer Bills, and so had Mr. Perceval in
1811.]

still felt that he could not leave Lord Liverpool in the lurch, and he accordingly came down resolved to pledge, as I suppose he was authorized to do, the whole Government to make common cause with Lord Liverpool. I heard in the House that the Government was resolved to abide by its decision, though I did not know that they intended to place the existence of the Administration on that narrow question, and during the debate on the Petition I went up to Canning and said, " For God's sake take care what you say about this issue of Exchequer Bills, for the whole House is against us, and our best friends are mutinying at our backs." He replied with considerable nervous excitement, "So much the better ; it will bring matters to a point sooner." I really at the moment did not understand the whole meaning of this phrase, but he soon cleared it up by declaring on his legs, in a very bold and uncompromising tone, that if the House chose to adopt the proposed measure they must also be prepared to find Ministers to execute it, for that they *would not ;* and this he repeated very steadily, and to the ears of some of the country gentlemen, offensively.

I know not why or how the Opposition failed to take advantage of this pledge, for if they had driven us to a vote on the point that night (which they might easily, and even fairly have done), they would have beaten us by about 140 to 80 ; or if the whole numbers were smaller (as they probably would have been, as people would have slunk off on one side, and rallied on the other), in a still greater proportion. Canning has since told me that he acted in this matter under Lord Liverpool's immediate impulse, and from a sense of a colleague's duty towards him. I could not help saying that the difference between the advance of the money from the Exchequer and from the Bank guaranteed by the Exchequer, was so trivial that if we went out upon *that*, we should be like the poor lady shown in Westminster Abbey who died of pricking her finger with a needle. This device of calling in the Bank was, Canning told me, his own. Liverpool was pledged not to advance the money directly, but he was not pledged, it seems, to prevent the Bank's doing it ; and an obsolete clause of their Charter being discovered which afforded a pretence for this arrangement, a negotiation was commenced, which, after a deal of squabbling both in private and in public between the Bank and the Government, was arranged, and we all keep our places a little longer.

This was altogether the most ridiculous political intrigue, if it may be so called, I ever saw, and indeed all that is visible of it to me is so very absurd that I cannot but suspect that there were some better, or at least more important, reasons at bottom.   There was a moment, I am convinced, in which the Government was on the point of dissolution, and I could collect that Mr. Canning, as certainly was very natural, was considering how it could be recomposed. If you had been here this could not have happened.   Whatever Cabinet secrets there may be at the bottom of the affair, which of course I do not pretend to guess, I can assure you that the Government was only saved by the supineness, connivance, or ignorance (I know not which) of the Opposition, and finally by the reluctance of the Bank to go to extremities with us, and take on themselves the responsibility of turning out the Ministers.   It is not very comfortable to think, nor very creditable to have it known, that the Administration was for four or five days at the mere mercy of the Opposition and the Bank.

We had hardly got out of our scrape with the Bank when all Scotland, with the spirit of the ancient Caledonians, rose upon us in defence of their *One pound Notes.*   Walter Scott, who, poor fellow, was ruined by dealings with his booksellers, and who had received courtesy and indulgence from the Scotch bankers, thought himself bound in gratitude to take the field for them, which he did in a series of clever but violent and mischievous letters, as he attacked with great violence and injustice the administration of Lord Melville, and indeed of our party in general.   I was easily induced to take up my pen against him, and I scribbled away a reply to Sir Walter in the same style (as far as I could imitate so superior a genius), which he had used.

That matter is, however, fast subsiding, and I will only add that from the best information I can collect I am led to fear that my suspicions of the *hollowness* of the Scotch banks are but too well founded.   It is thought that they were already in difficulties before they began this discussion, and such a discussion was certainly not likely to make their position more comfortable.   It would not surprise me if you were to find us in very serious financial difficulties on your return, and though I have fought the Government battle against Walter Scott, and though I honestly believe that whatever is done in England must be ultimately done in Scotland, yet I have very serious doubts whether we are quite right here. We have a debt, and of course a fictitious income so much greater than we had, when we had cash payments before, that I cannot think that the same quantity of gold currency will suffice for the transaction of business. For every purpose of life we now carry about twice as much cash as we used to do thirty or forty years ago, and of course I think that we shall require twice as much circulating medium, and if so, I doubt whether we shall be able at any expense to keep a sufficient quantity of gold for our domestic uses. But this is a subject on which I am a very bad judge.

J. W. C.

The little controversy between Sir Walter Scott and Mr. Croker caused no interruption to their friendship, although it was represented by Miss Martineau, and repeated blindly by others upon her authority, that they had a deadly quarrel, brought about, of course, by the violence and injustice of Mr. Croker, and healed only by the magnanimity of Scott. There could not be a greater tissue of misrepresentations. The following correspondence explains all that needs explanation on the subject. A portion of one of the letters —with a few variations in the text—was published in Lockhart's 'Life of Scott,' but it is necessary here to show the true state of Scott's feelings, and a letter of 1827 is added for the same reason :—

Sir Walter Scott to Mr. Croker. Extract.

March 19th, 1826.

My dear Croker,

I received your very kind letter with the feelings it was calculated to excite, those of great affection mixed with pain, which, indeed, I had already felt and anticipated before taking the step which I knew you must all feel as unkind, coming from one who had been honoured with so much personal regard. I need not, I am sure, say that nothing but an honest desire of serving this country by speaking *out* what is generally felt here, especially among Lord Melville's warmest and oldest friends might have some chance, howsoever slight. Depend upon it, that if a succession of violent and experimental changes are made from session to session, with bills to amend bills when no want of legislation had been at all felt by the country, Scotland will, within ten or twenty years, perhaps much sooner, read a more fearful commentary on poor Malachi's epistles than any statesman residing out of the country and strange to the habits and feelings which are entertained here can possibly anticipate. My head may be low—I hope it will—before the time comes. But Scotland, completely liberalized, as she is in a fair way of being, will be the most dangerous neighbour to England that she has been since 1639. There is yet time to make a stand, for there is yet a great deal of good and genuine feeling left in the country. But if you *unscotch* us you will find us damned mischievous Englishmen. The restless and yet laborious and constantly watchful character of the people, their desire for speculation in politics or any thing else, only restrained by some proud feelings about their own country, now become antiquated and which late measures will tend much to destroy, will make them, under a wrong direction, the most formidable revolutionists who ever took the field of innovation.

With respect to your own share in the controversy, it promised me so great an honour, that I laboured under a strong temptation to throw my hat into the ring, tie my colours to the ropes, cry, "Hollo there, Saint Andrew for Scotland," and try what a good cause would do for a bad, at least an inferior, combatant. But then I must have brought forward my facts, and as these would have compromised friends individually concerned, I felt myself obliged, with regret for forfeiting some honour, rather to abstain from the contest. Besides, my dear Croker, I must say that there are many and too direct personal allusions to myself, not to authorize and even demand some retaliation *dans le même genre*, and however good-humouredly men begin this sort of "sharp encounter of their wits," their temper gets the better of them at last. When I was a cudgel player, a sport at which I was once an ugly customer, we used to bar rapping over the knuckles, because it always ended in breaking heads; the matter may be remedied by baskets in a set-to with oak saplings, but I know no such defence in the rapier and poniard game of wit. So I thought it best not to endanger the loss of an old friend for a bad jest, and sit quietly down with your odd hits, and the discredit which it gives me here for not repaying them or trying to do so. I can assure you, Malachi's spirit has been thought meanly of for his silence, and this ought to be evidence in my favour that my temper at least is unconcerned in this unhappy.dispute.

Yours affectionately,

WALTER SCOTT.

March 26th, 1826.

MY DEAR CROKER,

I have your kind letter, and can assure you that when putting a more personal interpretation on some passages of your letter than I ought to have done, I did not consider them offensive, and if I had replied under the impression I had adopted, I would have taken particular care not to have executed the *moderamen inculpatæ tutelæ*. But it is much better not, and so *transeat cum cæteris erroribus*.

I enclose a letter for your funny namesake and kinsman,* whose work entertains me very much.

Believe me always,

Yours affectionately,

WALTER SCOTT.

April 25th, 1827.

MY DEAR CROKER,

As I trouble you with a packet for Lockhart, I cannot but add my sincere gratulation upon your keeping a good house over your head in this stormy weather which has bared so many biggings. The numerous rumours which reach me in this quarter are so varying that had I time, I believe I would come to London merely to see how the cat jumped. And I am as well where I am, since the present disputes seem to have divided most of my personal friends. The disposition seems as if some Yankee general had given the command, *Split and Squander.* My own feeling is much that of an old Scotch Judge called Lord Elchies, who when he heard a case keenly debated, and foreseeing it was to give him some trouble

---

* [T. Crofton Croker, who had just published the first volume of his ' Fairy Legends and Traditions of the South of Ireland.']

in deciding it, used to exclaim to the lawyers on each side most piteously, " Oh, Sirs, gar them gree—gar them gree— canna ye for God's sake gar them gree ? "   But his Lordship's good wishes were usually as useless as mine would be on the present occasion,   Well ! God's above all, and so concludes a letter which need never have [been written ?]   I send the Portefeuille de Buonaparte which you wished to ha**v**e ; but to my thinking there ought to be two parts, and there may be one lost at binding, I suppose.   As the volume contains some tracts which are now not of every day occurrence I will thank you to preserve it, as it would break a pretty large set of things of the kind, but if the Portefeuille be of interest to you, do not hesitate to break the binding and return the others.

Always, my dear Sir,

Yours truly obliged,

WALTER SCOTT.

P.S.—You are aware that Mr. Canning has forfeited all pretensions to the character of a statesman by the manner in which he has behaved to Lockhart.   For Dean Swift, you [are] aware, says that if a true statesman is led by circumstances to suspect an individual of something of which he is innocent, no species of explanation should remove his dislike, because that would be to acknowledge the possibility of a failure in judgment.   It is a sad thing for a premier to commit such a blunder in the outset of his career, and I am afraid it will be a poor counterpoise that I recognise in the frankness, candour, and nobleness of his proceeding the man of high honour that my regard so long thought him.

Confidence was gradually restored to the markets, but the country remained in an agitated condition.   There was great distress among the poor, and already a loud and general outcry had arisen against the corn laws.   Lord King anticipated Mr. Cobden by declaring that these laws were maintained exclusively in the landed interest, and were the " most gigantic job in the whole history of misrule."   In May, a measure was passed permitting the importation of 500,000 quarters of foreign corn, without any limitation as to price.

This, however, did not suffice to allay popular discontent. " The political sky looks very cloudy," wrote Mr. Croker to Lord Hertford, in October. " The three C's—Corn, Currency, and Catholics—will perplex, if not dissolve, the Government. If the Catholic question has a majority next session, I do not think the Cabinet will stick together. The Chancellor [Eldon] and Peel will go, and Westmoreland and Liverpool must follow, and all will be at sea."

But there was still another great question which required public consideration, and it was brought forward once more by Canning in a celebrated speech. The Spanish aggressions and intrigues of France had always been regarded by Canning with impatience, but the public mind was filled with apathy, and Canning knew that nothing could be done until this was shaken off. Hence he made speeches from time to time with the design of getting a strong force of popular opinion to support him in the course he desired to take, and each one of these speeches undoubtedly produced a great effect. French influence had been highly prejudicial to English interests in Portugal ; and when the intelligence was received that troops which had been organised in Spain were marching upon Portugal, it was generally perceived that the long-expected crisis had come. The Portuguese government formally requested assistance from England, to enable it to repel invasion from Spain ; and Canning announced on the 12th of December, that the request had been granted, and that British troops were actually on their way to Portugal. " We go," he said, " to plant the standard of England on the well-known heights of Lisbon. Where that standard is planted, foreign dominion shall not come." It is to these circumstances that the next letter relates.

Mr. Croker to Lord Hertford.

December 13th, 1826.

MY DEAR LORD HERTFORD,

I am sorry that I cannot be with you till *Sunday* at dinner.
As the troops for Portugal are all to be sent by this Department, I have my hands full of work and shall have till the
end of the week.

Canning made a brilliant and warlike speech last night,
but he was outdone in his warlike flourishes by Baring, and
above all Brougham, who made a most tedious repetition of
what Canning had said so much better.

I do *not* expect *war*. *De deux choses l'une—either* Spain
will submit, or Portugal will have exhibited a unanimous
desire for the absolute Don Miguel.

Despatches arrived last night, while we were in the House,
which lead me to adopt the latter supposition. The *Constitutional* Chambers are, it seems, not unanimous in approbation
of the *Constitution* under which they exist. If this be the
case, and if, as we have heard, the people are averse to it, I
contemplate the possibility of all being settled before our
troops can get out, and then we shall be in rather a puzzling
position. We shall know in a day or two how the royal
army feels: there are strong apprehensions about it; if it
fails, *adieu paniers, vendanges sont faites.*

Yours ever,

J. W. C.

It is only necessary to add in this place that the despatch
of troops at once answered the purpose which was intended.
The Spaniards were quickly driven out of Portugal, Ferdinand
recognised the Portuguese Government, and France ceased to
instigate Spain to a policy of aggression. The British force,
however, was not withdrawn until 1828.

The other letters of this year are of a more miscellaneous
character, and sufficiently explain themselves.

Mr. Croker to Mr. Henry Goulburn.

August 30th, 1826.

Since I wrote to you of the Duke of York's very alarming state* he has made a turn, and continued for a week or ten days mending in a very unexpected way; but I fear that the amendment is but temporary and fallacious, for although his appetite, his spirits, and his strength are *all* improved, the disease does not decrease, and when I saw him the day he came to town, he said: " I am *generally* better, but you see my body is more swollen than it was." He knows his situation, and looks at it like a hero. I doubt whether *he* has any hope, but he maintains a decent cheerfulness, and a very unaffected composure. I have reason to hope that his mind has been employed in serious and, I trust, satisfactory contemplations, but there is no outward show of any alarm ; the aide-de-camp at Brighton did not know what was the matter with him ; the public has not as yet any notion of his danger, and as little of what his disease is. The sad truth will come upon them by surprise, for though they know that there is something wrong, they have no *distinct* apprehension about him.

Yours, my dear Goulburn, most affectionately,

J. W. C.

Mr. Croker to the Right Hon. F. Robinson.

November 1st, 1826.

When we were heart-broken by a calamity similar to yours,† our first relief was by escaping from the scenes which reminded us of our lost happiness. If yours and poor Lady Sarah's feelings be the same, Mrs. Croker's apartments at *Kensington*, or mine at the *Admiralty*, are ready to receive you without the *slightest* inconvenience to us. You need not write—no answer will be a negative ; and if you accept, send your people to say which house you will have, and to make your arrangements—both houses are completely furnished.

* [He died on the 5th January, 1827.]
† [Referring, of course, to the loss of a son.]

You will judge how sincerely Mrs. Croker and I sympathise with you and Lady Sarah; your affliction revives all our own.

Yours affectionately,

J. W. C.

Mr. Croker to a young Naval Officer.   *Extract.*

November 13th, 1826.

Now, my dear Follett, attend to my advice. Do not gallop through my letter and throw it aside, but read it *over and over again*, and recollect that I am your best friend, and resolve to repay all I have done for you by strict attention to what I write, and go over each particular item of my advice until you have executed those which are temporary, or *fixed in your mind* those which are of more general application.

1st.—Your conduct on board the *Cyrene* † will, I hope, be *modest*, and you will take care not to hurt the feelings of the officers whom you leave behind by any assumption of your new rank. Captain Campbell (as the *Cyrene* will probably be detached from the Admiral) will, I have no doubt, facilitate, as far as his duty will allow, your joining the Admiral or the *Fly*. Make him my compliments, and thank him for the kind mention he has made of you to General Campbell.

2nd.—When you join the *Fly* your conduct must be still more cautious, and, if possible, more modest. You are very young, very fortunate; you will come over the head of senior officers, who cannot be expected to receive you with as much good humour as if you had been their senior. I know the custom of the Naval Service reconciles these ways of getting over one another's heads; they, probably, were made over the heads of their own seniors; but nevertheless such an advancement must always give a certain degree of pain to those who suffer in the individual instance; and good taste, good manners, and good sense require you to do all you can to soften the mortification which those officers must feel. Be, therefore, very kind and civil to them—not cringing, nor

---

* [Lieutenant Follett Pennell, who was promoted to the rank of Commander in 1826.]

† [The ship which Captain Pennell was about to leave; the *Fly* was the vessel to which he was appointed.]

giving up your station or authority, or seeming to feel that you were not worthy of your rank, but as one who, having had good fortune, treats others as he would wish to be treated had the superior good luck been theirs.

Your first lieutenant is an old officer for the first of a sloop. You will, of course, pay him all the deference which his length of service entitles him to; to respect others in their several ranks and stations is the surest mode of being respected in your own.

3rd.—Alter as little as possible the routine which Captain Wetherell had adopted. Make no sudden changes—confirm, in the first instance, all his orders. Desire that everything may go on as in his time; if, in practice, you find that alterations be necessary, introduce them slowly, by silent degrees, and as occasion may occur.

4th.—At the Admiralty we consider that much punishment is a proof that the captain does not understand the true discipline of the service. You will succeed to the command of a well-disciplined and orderly ship; you must endeavour to keep her so; an increase of punishment will convince us that you do not know how to manage a ship's company. Moderation towards your men, good humour with your officers, and *a command over yourself*, are the three essentials towards your being a respectable officer.

Let me repeat to you that *economy*—that is the *living within one's income, whatever it may be*—is the foundation of all true respectability; and I shall not think well of you if you have not saved at the end of two years two or three hundred pounds. Captains on other stations contrive to live, and some even to *save*, out of their pay; you may surely do so when your pay is double.

As to *writing*, I beg of you to take pains with your *hand*, and learn to write like a gentleman. Nothing gives a more unfavourable impression than an ill-written, ill-spelled, ill-folded, ill-sealed letter.

Mr. Croker to a Consul Suspected of Jobbery.

December 18th, 1826.

I have already had to complain of your indiscretion, but I can hardly suppose you mad enough to meddle in such an affair as this; I only warn you that I shall go to the Foreign

Office immediately on my return to town, and if I find *there,* any traces of your recommending one of your relations to be Vice Consul at Morlaix, I shall submit to Mr. Canning the expediency of immediately appointing another consul.

I shall personally regret the ruin of you and your family which I am aware will follow this step; but I will do my public duty; and as I placed you in your present office for public benefit, so I shall take care to have you *removed the moment* I learn that you are meddling with private jobs.

I am, yours,

J. W. C.

Anecdotes and Conversations from Mr. Croker's Note Books.

October 24th, 1825.

Moore in his lately published 'Life of Sheridan' has recorded the laborious care with which he prepared his *bons-mots.* Madame de Staël condescended to do the same. The first time I ever saw her was at dinner at Lord Liverpool's at Coombe Wood. Sir James Mackintosh was to have been her guide, and they lost their way, and went to Addiscombe and some other places by mistake, and when they got at last to Coombe Wood they were again bewildered, and obliged to get out and walk in the dark, and through the mire up the road through the wood. They arrived consequently two hours too late and strange draggled figures, she exclaiming by way of apology, " Coombe par ci, Coombe par là; nous avons été par tous les Coombes de l'Angleterre." During dinner she talked incessantly but admirably, but several of her apparently spontaneous *mots* were borrowed or prepared. For instance, speaking of the relative states of England and the Continent at that period, the high notion we had formed of the danger to the world from Buonaparte's despotism, and the high opinion the Continent had formed of the riches, strength, and spirit of England; she insisted that these opinions were both just, and added with an elegant *élan,* " Les étrangers sont la postérité contemporaine." This striking expression I have since found in the journal of Camille Desmoulins.

The conversation turned on the Court of Berlin, and Lord Liverpool asked if M. de Ségur, then ambassador there, was related to the old family of Ségur, of whom his lordship mentioned one whom he had known. She answered laughingly that they were related "du côté des syllabes," meaning that they were *not related*, though their *names* were the same. Lord Liverpool did not see what she meant, and repeated his inquiry in the form of asking whether they were of the same family. She replied with great readiness, " Milord, ils sont du même alphabet." Nothing could appear more extemporaneous than this double jest, yet it must have been prepared, for every one now knows that the M. Ségur of Berlin was one of the old Ségurs, and he was in fact the very man that Lord Liverpool was inquiring about. Madame de Staël had the phrase, *cut and dry*, as the expression is, ready to be used on any of the occasions, then very frequent, when strangers inquired if such or such of Buonaparte's chamberlains or diplomatists were of the old stock whose names they bore ; and the phrase of " du même alphabet " I have since seen somewhere in print.

She was ugly, and not of an intellectual ugliness. Her features were coarse, and the ordinary expression rather vulgar, she had an ugly mouth, and one or two irregularly prominent teeth, which perhaps gave her countenance an habitual gaiety. Her eye was full, dark, and expressive ; and when she declaimed, which was almost whenever she spoke, she looked eloquent, and one forgot that she was plain. On the whole, she was singularly unfeminine, and if in conversation one forgot she was ugly, one forgot also that she was a woman.

Some one was laughing one day at the titles of the Haytian Empire, the Count de Lemonade and the Duke de Marmalade. " This would come," said Madame de Staël, " with a bad grace from us French, who see nothing ridiculous in the titles of the Marquis de *Bouillé* and the Duke de *Bouillon*. Nor ought the English to be very facetious on that point, who see nothing absurd in Lord *Boyle* and Mrs. *Fry*."

October 26th.

General Becker was an Alsatian, and, I know not why, in the confidence of Fouché, who at the second abdication placed him as superintendent of Buonaparte's movements, and I have no doubt that the General had orders to get Buonaparte out of France *bon gré mal gré*. I visited Paris between the Battle of Waterloo and the embarkation of Buonaparte, and was at one or two meetings with Lord

Castlereagh, the Duke of Wellington, Fouché, Talleyrand, and M. de Jaucourt, Minister of Marine, when we discussed the best method of laying hold of Buonaparte. I took the liberty to advise an order to our Admiral to advance suddenly under the white flag, and in concert with the King's officers to seize the ex-Emperor. I calculated that it would take *ten minutes* before the authorities could be induced to fire on the white flag, and in that time our sailors and marines would be in possession of the town. This was finally agreed to, and a letter to Sir C. Hotham, who commanded our squadron, was prepared to that effect, with this remarkable notification that it was very desirable to take Buonaparte alive, and with as little violence or even inconvenience to him personally as possible, *but that he was to be taken;* and that the life of any British sailor was as dear to the King of England as that of Buonaparte. This was the way I stated it at the meeting, and it was in substance implied in the despatch, but not so crudely, but we were anxious to frighten Fouché, whom we suspected still of some intrigue with Buonaparte, and we thought it likely that he would apprise him of our violent resolutions—or something to this effect. This despatch was entrusted, as well as the corresponding powers on the part of France to Captain de Rigny. There seems every reason to suppose that Fouché, by the telegraph or some other means, communicated to Buonaparte these determined measures, for he immediately after these resolutions were taken, but before the arrival of De Rigny, suddenly changed all his plans, and gave himself up to Sir C. Hotham.

General Becker returned to Paris as soon as he had gotten rid of his perilous charge, and the day he arrived I met him at dinner at M. de Jaucourt's. He, it seems, had had little previous knowledge of Buonaparte, and was certainly not much impressed with reverence or even with ordinary respect for his character or conduct. The vulgar familiarity of his manners was still known only to a narrow circle, and Becker was greatly surprised, and not much flattered, to find his imperial prisoner pinching his ears as they walked in the grounds of Malmaison. He found him, he told us, very unlike what he had expected, a great gourmand, very anxious about his dinner; lazy, apathetic, and sensual. Whether it was really the General's opinion, or whether he thought it a safe prophecy to make I cannot tell, but he more than once told us that the ex-Emperor was apoplectic, decidedly apo-

plectic, and that on the journey he more than once thought
he would have died of an apoplectic stroke. I could not help
whispering to Madame de Jaucourt that I suspected the
General had had "l'apoplexie dans sa poche," and I was afterwards assured that Fouché's orders were that Buonaparte
should be got rid of, *coûte que coûte.* The General, I think,
told us that he had pistols in his pockets the whole time.

The day Becker arrived there was a great review of the
Austrian Cavalry. I asked him whether he had come to town
in time to see it, and what he thought of the Austrian
Cuirassiers. " Ils sont," said he, " les plus beaux *autocrates*
de l'Europe."

A crowd of people came in the evening to hear the news—
amongst others, La Place, the savant. He was so civil as
to recognise me as a *colleague*, because I was an F.R.S. God
knows how he knew that; we got into conversation; his was
certainly not brilliant, nor was there, I ought to add, any
opportunity for brilliancy, but a little trait of character
escaped him. We talked of the King's administration before
the *Cent Jours.* He did not approve of the tone which had
been adopted and still less of the measures, but there was one
thing which was so gross a blunder and folly that it exceeded
all the rest, and was indeed the chief cause of the return of
Buonaparte. I pricked up the ears of curiosity at this exor-
dium, and felt no small interest to hear what this portentous
blunder had been. It was that instead of making Buonaparte's senators all *hereditary peers*, some of them had the
peerage for the same term they had their senatorship only,
viz., *for life.* M. le Comte de la Place was only a *peer for life.*
The King, however, soon adopted this new system, and made
all the peers hereditary, and never did a more unwise thing.
La Place, for instance, is as fit to be a peer of France as he is
to be drum-major of a regiment of the line. He was, however, a respectable man, and the thing was tolerable in his
personal case, but it is different when his sons and all the La
Places to the end of the chapter must be the colleagues, not
of F.R.S.'s like me, but of the Noailles, Montmorencies,
and Birons. A peerage without either gold or blood!

Sudbourne, September, 1826.

The Duke of Glo'ster is a great asker of questions. He
asked the Duke of Grafton who, though sixty-six, does not

look above fifty, "how old he was," before a large company
in a country house. The Duke of Grafton did not like the
inquiry, but answered. Some time after the Dukes met again,
and the Duke of Glo'ster repeated this question, to which the
Duke of Grafton dryly replied, "Sir, I am exactly three weeks
two days older than when your Royal Highness last asked
me that disagreeable question."

May 6th, 1826.

The Duke of York, Duke of Wellington, Lord Huntly, and
some others dined with me at the Admiralty.

Some discussion arose as to the value of cuirasses; whether
the confidence they gave to the individual soldier counter-
balanced their weight and other obvious disadvantages. The
Duke of Wellington thought it might in single men or in
small bodies, but in great masses the confidence and spirit of
the men arose from other considerations. On the whole he
did not like the cuirass. Some one asked whether the French
Cuirassiers had *not come up very well at Waterloo?* "Yes,"
he said, "and *they went down very well too.*" He then went
on to tell us of a regiment of Cuirassiers that had charged up
the great high-road at Quatre Bras, and had turned into a
farmyard or inclosure which had no exit on the other side.
The Duke was not aware of *this*, else he could have taken
them all; they immediately came out again, but on their
retreat along the same road, the British, who were in line
along the cross-road, and "particularly your regiment" (the
92nd), said the Duke, turning to Lord Huntly, "gave them
a couple of volleys which brought them all to the ground, and
there those that were not killed were so encumbered by their
cuirasses and jackboots that they could not get up, but lay
sprawling and kicking like so many *turned* turtles."

Sudbourne, December, 1826.

Every one knows the story of a gentleman's asking Lord
North who "that frightful woman was?" and his lordship's
answering, that is my wife. The other, to repair his blunder,
said I did not mean *her*, but that monster next to her. "Oh,"
said Lord North, "that monster is my daughter." With this
story Frederick Robinson, in his usual absent enthusiastic
way, was one day entertaining a lady whom he sat next to
at dinner, and lo! the lady was Lady Charlotte Lindsay—the
monster in question.

When Huskisson was attached to Lord Stafford's embassy in 1792,* he and Mr. Fergusson (tried afterwards with Lord Thanet), since a barrister at Calcutta, and now M.P., used to dine at Beauvilliers's, where there was a smart young waiter, whom, however, these two Englishmen used to *row* exceedingly. At last Beauvilliers told them one day that they had driven the *pauvre garçon au désespoir*, and he had gone and enlisted. It was a lucky persecution for him. The young waiter made rapid advances in his new profession—he was Joachim Murat, King of Naples. This Huskisson told us.

Mr. Fergusson after the Maidstone affair,† was to have gone with Lord Lauderdale to India, and at last, though Lauderdale did not go, Fergusson did. He has made more money than it was thought was ever before made at the bar. For the last years he was Attorney-General to the Company, and this business with his private practice produced *one year* 25,000*l.* He has brought home, they say, near half a million. He went the other day into the House of Lords, and the Lord Chancellor, who was Attorney-General in the Maidstone trials, good humouredly recognised him, and congratulated him on this good fortune.

Sudbourne.

In the Peninsular War, infantry officers not allowed forage, used to buy forage for their mules and horses. They could always buy forage from our cavalry, and even from the stables of the staff; but the German Legion never could be tempted to part with their forage, every man made common cause with his horse, and nothing could induce the honest Germans to defraud their fourfooted colleagues of their due provision. Comparisons are odious !

Count Staremberg, when he was in England, used to play at the Union. His English was not quite so good as his luck.

---

* [Mr. Huskisson was Private Secretary to the British Ambassador in Paris, Lord Gower.]

† [The Earl of Thanet, a Whig nobleman, and Mr. Cutlar Fergusson, were tried before Lord Kenyon, in 1799, for a riot in attempting to facilitate the escape of Arthur O'Connor before his trial at Maidstone. They were found guilty and condemned to a year's imprisonment, and a fine of £1000 in Lord Thanet's case, and £100 in Mr. Fergusson's. The prosecution was conducted by Sir John Scott (afterwards Lord Eldon), Attorney-General, the defence by Mr. Erskine.]

Playing one night at *trente et un*, the late Lord Barrymore was at the table, and not much delighted with the success of the Count. His Excellency was not very nice in his person, and it was ludicrous to hear him proclaim the state of his hand by saying, "I am *dirty !* I am *dirty !* " At last, when he had achieved the best possible hand, he was so elate, that he almost embraced Barrymore, exclaiming, "I am dirty, I am *dirty-one*, I am *dirty-one*." Barrymore, who lost by the Count's success, and had no liking for the nasty embrace, said, "Damn it, sir, so you are ; but that's no reason why *I* should be *dirty too*."

Conversations with the Duke of Wellington.—Mr. Croker's Notes.

I shall here set down what I remember of a visit to Sudbourne,* as nearly as I can in his own words, from the notes that I made every evening.—J. W. C.

The Duke offered an Estate in France.

I will tell you an odd story of the old King (Louis XVIII.). One day, after the restoration, when I waited on him at the Tuileries, he paid me some compliments on my share in the events which brought it about, and he took the ribbon of the St. Esprit off his own body and put it on me. I, of course, expressed my thanks, but I said that before I could venture to accept or wear this mark of his royal favour, I must have the consent of my own sovereign ; and added that I should write that evening, and had little doubt that the Prince Regent would signify his approbation. Shortly after I returned home, the Duke of Richelieu, then Prime Minister, followed me, and after alluding to the affair of the St. Esprit, said that as I was going to write about that, the King wished me to take the same opportunity of writing about another matter upon which he supposed I should also require my sovereign's consent ; this was, His Majesty's intention to present me with a more solid and lasting mark of his gratitude, in an *estate in France*. Grosbois was the place intended, and the

* [The seat, it will be remembered, of the Marquis of Hertford, with whom the Duke of Wellington and Sir Robert Peel were on terms of quite as close an intimacy as Mr. Croker.]

Duke stated some of the *agrémens* which that seat particularly possessed, and some circumstances which made the King think it a proper reward for my services to France. This took me quite by surprise, and was for the moment rather embarrassing, for I could not decently refuse point blank from Louis XVIII. what I had accepted from King Ferdinand; but a little consideration sufficed to convince all parties that the cases were essentially different, and above all, in the spirit and temper of the two nations and the circumstances of the two cases. In Spain I had been the victorious general of their own armies. In France, my merit with the King was that I had beaten their army. It would have been impossible to have made a falser step, and so there was an end of Grosbois; when I look back at this offer I am still more surprised than I was at first, that it should have been thought of.

The Grandees of Spain.

I am a Grandee of Spain! They have the privilege of being covered in the King's presence. Formerly there was but one class; there now are three, which differ from each other by some such forms as these—all referring, as you will see, to the covering. The first class enter the royal presence already covered; the second, I think, enter uncovered, but cover unbidden, after they have advanced a few steps; the third do not cover till the King desires them; but when covered, I believe, all are equal, though not all hereditary. It is strange for a grandee of Spain not to know all these distinctions quite accurately, but I was some years a grandee without knowing even so much. When Ferdinand returned to Madrid, he, on one occasion, showed himself to the people from the balcony of the palace; his suite, and amongst the rest myself, stood in the room behind; the people, I believe, called for me, and the King desired me to come forward, which I did, bareheaded, of course. The King immediately said to me, be covered, and of course I should have immediately done so anywhere else, but in the face of all his people I could not at once bring myself to do it; but the people about us hastened to remind me that I was a grandee of the first class, and that I ought not to have been uncovered.

My grandeeship, title, and estate, were given me by the Cortes, but the King confirmed them in the most liberal way.

At his first court on his return, when the grandees—some newly created, others having succeeded during the usurpation— were to be solemnly admitted to the royal presence, we all assembled in an ante-room ; when the door of the presence-chamber was opened they allowed me, in consideration, I suppose, of my military situation, to go in first ; and the Duke of Alajen, as Captain of the Guards, next ; after which they all rushed in *pêle-mêle* in a riotous confusion, and in the scuffle San Carlos, who was one of the juniors in date of grandeeship, turned up one of the foremost ; some one endeavoured to moderate the tumult, and begged them to place themselves in order, but they cried out that "*there was no order there,* they were all equal." This confusion is a part of the dignity, for they do not even recognise the original date of a grandeeship even in the highest class, which is hereditary.

Ferdinand is by no means the idiot he is represented. He is a good natured man, not deficient in sense. It is his political position, and the state of the Spanish Government and people themselves, which are to blame for what those intelligent gentlemen, the correspondents of the English news-papers, all lay to the account of the poor King.

Talleyrand.

It may seem odd to confess, but I never could discover on what grounds Talleyrand's great reputation as a *Minister* was built. I never found him a man of business, nor, I must say, able in affairs. When things were returning, after the anarchy, to a more settled state, the Directory were glad to get any one of the old school who had any reputation to give a kind of respectability to their Administration. Buonaparte did the same. To have been a member of the Constituent Assembly, and to have outlived the Revolution, was itself a merit in those days. The Revolution was a kind of tontine and Talleyrand, Fouché, and half-a-dozen others, accumulated all its advantages on their own heads by mere benefit of survivorship.

It is easy enough to be a successful Minister for Foreign Affairs to a government which has military possession of Europe. As to his ministry under Buonaparte, it was almost a sinecure ; the *chef de l'état major* was the real Minister of Foreign Affairs, and what he did not do, Buonaparte did himself, and Talleyrand often received applause and censure for things that he never saw nor heard of till they were brought to him for signature. Witness, amongst many other instances which I could give you, that paper which I gave Lord Whitworth, and which he gave to Peel, in which Buonaparte does not trust Talleyrand literally to *walk alone*, but prescribes how far he shall follow Lord Whitworth, and when he shall turn on his heel.

When Talleyrand was discussing with Louis XVIII. the question whether the Deputies should not have an official salary, the King wished that the honour should be its reward, and that the functions should be *gratuites*. "*Gratuites !*" said Talleyrand, "mais ce serait *trop cher.*"

But what amazes one most in him is the boldness of his duplicity. Would you believe it, that at Erfurth, where Buonaparte met the Emperor of Russia, to persuade him to join in overwhelming Austria, Talleyrand, the Minister for Foreign Affairs, who, all day long, laboured under Buonaparte's vigilant eye to carry this object, used to visit Alexander secretly at night, and furnish him with every argument, reason, or pretence which he could discover or invent against Buonaparte's plan.

This Talleyrand himself told me, but, I should not have believed it from him alone, but the Emperor confirmed it to me, and I had it also from the Princess of Tour and Taxis, at whose house these conclaves took place. When a foreign woman once gets a taste for these kinds of intrigues she never gives it up. This good princess, having played a part in the congress at Erfurth, has contrived also to have a share in all the other congresses.

The Battle of Vittoria.

During the movements that preceded the battle of Vittoria, we had heard of the armistice * in Germany. All my staff

* [The armistice was signed at Plesswig the 4th June, 1813—to last to the 20th July; it was afterwards extended to the 10th August. The battle of Vittoria was fought the 21st June. On the 28th June took place the interview between Buonaparte and Metternich at Dresden, which produced the continuation of the armistice. Buonaparte received the intelligence on the 30th June. Bubna, then with Buonaparte, heard it a few days after, and it caused the resolution to denounce the armistice on the appointed day.—J. W. C.]

were against my crossing the Ebro [*]; they represented that we had done enough, that we ought not to risk the army and what we had obtained, and that this armistice would enable Buonaparte to reinforce his army in Spain, and we therefore should look to a defensive system. I thought differently. I knew that an armistice could not affect in the way of reinforcement so distant an army as that of Spain. I thought that if I could not *hustle* them out of Spain before they were reinforced, I should not be able to hold any position in Spain when they should be, and above all, I calculated on the effect that a victory might have on the armistice itself. So I crossed the Ebro and fought the battle of Vittoria. The event showed I was right in my military expectations, and I found afterwards that I was equally right in my political speculations. The victory excited a great sensation in Germany, and particularly at the head-quarters of the allies. Metternich told me that Stadion [†] (I think) woke him in the middle of the night with his tumultuous joy at the news, " Le roi Joseph est —— en Espagne " was one of the softest terms used, and their transports subsided into a determination to denounce the armistice, and to pursue the war till Napoleon himself should be ——.

I hastened my movements at Vittoria because I knew that a reinforcement of 20,000 men was advancing under Clausel, while I had only 6000 coming up under Packenham. Their outposts met, but Clausel did not dare attack him, and I had made arrangements for falling on Clausel with my whole force; and I should probably have overtaken and defeated him and his army, but that, in spite of my positive orders that there should be no wandering, a certain officer of dragoons chose to be taken prisoner while he was at dinner in a country house, and Clausel became thus aware of my movements, and hurried away so fast and in such a direction that I did not choose to follow him. On what slight accidents events turn.

---

[*] [See a repetition of this incident, 17th January, 1837. On *this* occasion, he said, " All my staff, including the two next in command." The two next in command were Graham and Hill, but I think he mentioned Murray on this occasion; my note does not give any name.—J. W. C.]

[†] [He also said something of Hardenberg, but I did not exactly collect what—perhaps that Stadion first called up Hardenberg, and that both called up the rest. On another occasion he repeated the story without any mention of Hardenberg.—J. W. C.]

The Duke's Generals.

I look on Lord Beresford as the best officer we have for the command of an army. To command a division and to command an army are as different as chalk and cheese—they require quite different qualities, though the greater will, of course, include the less. Sir George Murray is a very able man, an admirable Quartermaster-General; but he is not *au fait* of the actual handling of troops—the mechanical process of bringing them into play. He is clever enough to have felt this himself, and had a mind to leave the staff to practise this branch of tactics in the management of a division; but it is necessary to begin still lower. One must understand the mechanism and power of the individual soldier; then that of a company, a battalion, or brigade, and so on, before one can venture to group divisions and move an army. I believe I owe most of my success to the attention I always paid to the inferior part of tactics as a regimental officer.* There were few men in the army who knew these details better than I did; it is the foundation of all military knowledge. When you are sure that you know the power of your tools and the way to handle them, you are able to give your mind altogether to the greater considerations which the presence of the enemy forces upon you.

* [He told me, on an earlier occasion, that within a few days after joining his first regiment (I think he said the 73rd) as an ensign, he had one of the privates weighed in his clothes only, and then with all his arms, accoutrements, and kit in full marching-order, with the view of comparing as well as he could the power of the man with the duty expected from him. I said that this was a most extraordinary thought to have occurred to so young a man. He said, " Why, I was not so young as not to know that since I had undertaken a profession I had better try to understand it." When I repeated this to Colonel Shawe, a great friend of both him and Lord Wellesley, he told me that in the Duke's early residence in India, and before he was in command, his critical study of his profession afforded a marked contrast to the general habits of that time and country. Shawe also added another early anecdote. The Duke inherits his father's musical taste, and used to play very well, and rather too much, on the violin. Some circumstances occurred which made him reflect that this was not a soldierly accomplishment, and took up too much of his time and thoughts; and he burned his fiddles, and never played again. About the same time he gave up the habit of card playing.—J. W. C.]

The Archduke Charles.

[He quoted the Archduke Charles's book, and I asked whether the Archduke was really a great officer ?]

A great officer ? why, he knows more about it than all of us put together.

Croker. What, than Buonaparte, Moreau, or yourself ?

Aye ! than Buonaparte or any of us. We are none of us worthy to fasten the latchets of his shoes, if I am to judge from his book and his plans of campaign. But his mind or his health has, they tell me, a very peculiar defect. He is admirable for five or six hours, and whatever can be done in that time will be done perfectly ; but after that he falls into a kind of epileptic stupor, does not know what he is about, has no opinion of his own, and does whatever the man at his elbow tells him.

Buonaparte as a General.

If I am to believe Ségur's and, indeed all the other accounts of the Russian campaign, Buonaparte committed the most egregious faults of generalship and conduct. Time was everything, and I can show on paper, out of his own reports and returns, that he *lost* seven weeks in point of time in the advance to Moscow. He made also a false movement in changing his line upon Minsk, which had, *inter alia*, the disadvantage of bringing him nearer to the South Russian army, when he might have attained his object in another way [which the Duke explained, but which I cannot pretend to follow], without these disadvantages. He lost a good deal also by what looks like indolence ; he was often absent when he ought and might have been present, for instance, at Valontina, I think it was, when he heard the firing, and sent orders and might have come up ; if he had, he would have put an end to a dispute between his generals, and probably have had a decided success. His personal proceedings previous to and during the battle of Borodino are inexplicable. Some of his apologists attribute it to sudden illness, but that does not account for the details, unless the illness could be supposed so serious as to derange his understanding. His conduct in all these cases is not easily accounted for. I believe he was in more awe of his marshals than was generally supposed—

he acted as if he was not sure of their obedience; for instance, he would order one of them to take another under his command, but he never ventured to tell the other to obey him (of course the two fellows got into a quarrel directly); or was he afraid that any of them, if too successful, might eclipse him? But there were none of them that I know anything about, except Massena, who had any pretensions to a comparison with him.

Buonaparte's mind was, in its details, low and ungentlemanlike. I suppose the narrowness of his early prospects and habits stuck to him; what *we* understand by *gentlemanlike* feelings he knew nothing at all about; I'll give you a curious instance.

I have a beautiful little watch, made by Breguet, at Paris, with a map of Spain most admirably enamelled on the case. Sir Edward Paget bought it at Paris, and gave it to me. What do you think the history of this watch was—at least the history that Breguet told Paget, and Paget me? Buonaparte had ordered it as a present to his brother, the King of Spain, but when he heard of the battle of Vittoria—he was then at Dresden in the midst of all the preparations and negotiations of the armistice, and one would think sufficiently busy with other matters,—when he heard of the battle of Vittoria, I say, he remembered the watch he had ordered for one whom he saw would never be King of Spain, and with whom he was angry for the loss of the battle, and he wrote from Dresden to countermand the watch, and if it should be ready, to forbid its being sent. The best apology one can make for this strange littleness is, that he was offended with Joseph; but even in that case, a *gentleman* would not have taken the moment when the poor devil had lost his *châteaux en Espagne*, to take away his watch also.

All those codicils to his will in which he bequeathed millions to the right and left, and amongst others left a legacy to the fellow who was accused of attempting to assassinate me, is another proof of littleness of mind; the property he really had he had already made his disposition of. For the payment of all those other high-sounding legacies, there was not the shadow of a fund. He might as well have drawn bills for ten millions on that pump at Aldgate. [We had on our way driven past it.] While he was writing all these magnificent donations, he knew that they were all in the air, all a falsehood. For my part, I can see no magnanimity in a lie; and I confess that I think one who could play such tricks but a shabby fellow.

Jonathan Wild the Great.

I never was a believer in him, and I always thought that in the long-run we should overturn him. He never seemed himself at his ease, and even in the boldest things he did there was always a mixture of apprehension and meanness. I used to call him *Jonathan Wild the Great,* and at each new *coup* he made I used to cry out "Well done Jonathan," to the great scandal of some of my hearers. But, the truth was, he had no more care about what was right or wrong, just, or unjust, honourable or dishonourable, than *Jonathan,* though his great abilities, and the great stakes he played for, threw the knavery into the shade.

Buonaparte's System of Secrecy.

I am not sure that the greatest pleasure I ever felt in my military life was not the evening of the day we crossed the *Nivelle.* We took a kind of redoubt, in which was a French battalion and its lieutenant-colonel. I had a mind to be civil to him, and asked him to dinner. He came, but was very sulky. My staff were pressing him with questions, to which he gave no answers, or very dry ones. I, however, interfered quietly, and whispered to them to let him alone, and that after a good dinner and a few glasses of Madeira, our friend would mend. So in the course of the evening I saw he was in better humour, and then I apologised for the fare I was obliged to give him, and still more for the apartment in which it was served—it was a wretched kind of barn; "But you," I said, "who have served all over the world, have probably been used to such things, and indeed your Emperor himself must of late had some hard nights' lodging himself; and, by the way," I added, "where was his *quartier général,* when you last heard of him?" "Monseigneur" said our man, with a tragic grimace, "*Il n'y a plus de quartier général.*" He alluded to the rout of Leipsic, and I then saw my way clearly to Bordeaux and to Paris; for besides what the officer could tell, I calculated that the disaster must have been very great to have reached him at all: for it is truly astonishing in what a degree of ignorance as to all that was passing he

[Buonaparte] contrived to keep all France. We found people who had never heard of the battle of Trafalgar; and the south of France could hardly believe their eyes when they saw us come down the Pyrenees! but he kept the rest of the world in the same ignorance of what was going on in France. I confess the first light I ever received on that subject was from Faber's book,* which was reviewed in the *Quarterly Review,* and which I think you [Croker] sent me. It was a most able, and, at the time, valuable work. It has been doubted whether there was such a *person* as Faber, though nobody doubted the truth of the facts; but there certainly was such a person as Faber himself. He was a German or Alsacian, who had got to St. Petersburg. I think I have heard from some one that they knew him there. The book was of considerable use to me when I entered France, and, as far as I had an opportunity of putting it to the test, I found it true.

Posterity will hardly believe the success and extent of that system of darkness which Buonaparte spread over France, but it was so complete that even I, who had been for so many years in contact with his armies, and was now, for months, on his frontier, was glad to glean from any precarious and humble sources some knowledge of the real state of the interior.

The Priest of St. Pé.

There is a little village called St. Pé, where I was stopped a day or two by very bad weather; I was lodged at the Curé's, a good old man, from whose conversation about the state of France I received lights which had important results. He was very clever and well informed, and took not only *right*, but *large* views of things; he confirmed all I had read in Faber, and gave me such valuable intelligence as to the state and spirit of the whole south of France, that I repeated it in a dispatch to Government at home, and I read the dispatch to the Duke de Guiche, then an officer in our army, whom I purposely sent home with it, and whom I authorized to tell the contents to Monsieur (Charles X.). I concluded by suggesting the appearance of one of the princes with my army. This dispatch, all founded on my conversa-

---

[* 'Notices sur l'Intérieur de la France, écrites en 1806, par M. Faber,' St. Petersburg, 1807. Reviewed by Mr. Croker in the *Quarterly*, August, 1811, vol. vi. p. 235.]

tions with this old priest, appeared so satisfactory and convincing that the Duke of Angoulême, now Dauphin, came out immediately. When the business was done, I did not forget the old priest. He would not quit his little parish, but the King did something for him which made him happy. He did not, however, live long to enjoy it. He was a man of superior talents and sagacity ; he had in his early life lived in good society. I think he had even been about Versailles, and my meeting him in that remote and muddy village, and spending two rainy days with him, had perhaps some influence on the destinies of the House of Bourbon.

The Duke and the Horse Guards.

I can't say that I owe my successes to any favour or confidence from the Horse Guards ; they never showed me any, from the first day I had a command to this hour. In the first place, they thought very little of any one who had served in India. An Indian victory was not only no ground of confidence, but it was actually a cause of suspicion. Then because I was in Parliament, and connected with people in office, I was a politician, and a politician never can be a soldier. Moreover they looked upon me with a kind of jealousy, because I was a lord's son, " *a sprig of nobility*," who came into the army more for ornament than use. [N.B. — He more than once in the course of conversation with me mentioned this reproach of his having been " *a sprig of nobility*." I have no doubt that the phrase had been applied to him at some early part of his career by some one, from whom it had made an impression, but unluckily I omitted to ask him about it.] They could not believe that I was a tolerable regimental officer. I have proof that they thought I could not be trusted alone with a division, and I suspect they have still their doubts whether I know anything about the command of an army, for I dare say you will be surprised to hear that in all the changes made since the war in the regulations of the army, I have never been in the most trifling or distant degree consulted on any point. As to the dress, I say nothing ; though that is a matter on which one who had dressed so large an army for so long might have some experience, and an opinion as to what would wear best, and be most convenient and healthy. But upon any change in the arms and accoutring, on the establishing cuirassiers or

lancers, and on things of this sort, you would have thought
that I had had a good deal of practical knowledge, having had,
as you know, something to do with lancers in Spain and
cuirassiers at Waterloo.   Well, I never knew that the Blues
or any other regiment were to have cuirasses till they were
actually in them.   Then there was published a new book of
manœuvres and movements ; as it had been my luck to
move and manœuvre a greater portion of the British army
than any officer in the service, and in the field too, you would
hardly credit, what I nevertheless assure you is the fact, that
I never heard any more about it than you did.

The " Dry Nurses " of the Horse Guards.

When the Horse Guards are obliged to employ one of those
fellows like me in whom they have no confidence, they give
him what is called a *second in command*—one in whom they
have confidence—a kind of *dry nurse*.   When I went to
Zealand they gave me General Stewart as second in command,
that is, in reality intended for *first in command*, though I was
the first in name.   Well, during the embarkation, the voyage
out, and the disembarkation, General Stewart did everything.
I saw no kind of objection to anything he suggested, and all
went *à merveille*.   At last, however, we came up to the
enemy.   Stewart, as usual, was beginning his suggestions
and arrangements, but I stopped him short with " Come,
come, 'tis my turn now."   I immediately made my own
dispositions, assigned him the command of one of the wings,
gave him his orders, attacked the enemy, and beat them.
Stewart, like a man of sense, saw in a moment that I understood my business, and subsided with (as far as I saw) good
humour into his proper place.   But this did not cure the
Horse Guards ; when I went to Portugal they gave me Sir
Brent Spencer as *second in command*, but I came to an immediate explanation with him ; I told him I did not know
what the words " *Second in command* " meant, any more than
third, fourth, or fifth in command ; that I alone commanded
the army, that the other general officers commanded their
divisions ; that if anything happened to me, the senior survivor
would take the command ; that in contemplation of such a
possibility I would treat them, but him in particular, as next
in succession, with the most entire confidence, and would leave
none of my views or intentions unexplained ; but that I would

have no *second in command* in the sense of his having anything like a joint command or superintending control; and
that, finally and above all, I would not only take but insist
upon the whole and undivided responsibility of all that
should happen while the army was under my command.

The Convention of Cintra.

After the Convention of Cintra, there was a pretty general
desire in England that a general should be shot, after the
manner of Byng, and as I was a politician, I was, of course,
the person to be shot, which would have been rather hard, as
I was the winner of the two battles which had raised the
public hopes so high, and had nothing to do with the subsequent proceedings but as a subordinate negotiator under
orders of my superior officers. Even the Government were
inclined to give me up. When I came back, the old King was
to have one of his weekly levées ; I asked Lord Castlereagh
to carry me " as I must present myself on my return from
abroad " and happened to have no carriage in town. Castlereagh hemmed and hawed, and said that there was so much
ill-humour in the public mind that it might produce inconvenience, and, in short, he advised me not to go to the levée.
I said, " When I first mentioned it, I only thought it a matter
of respect and duty to the King ; I now look upon it as a
matter of self-respect and duty to my own character, and
I therefore insist on knowing whether this advice proceeds in
any degree from His Majesty, and I wish you distinctly to
understand that I will go to the levée to-morrow, or I never
will go to a levée in my life." Castlereagh immediately
withdrew all opposition. I went, and was exceedingly well
received by His Majesty.

I had several fellows in the army who misbehaved. One
in particular, a Captain ——— ;* he was ordered for the
storming party at St. Sebastian [I am not quite sure whether
the Duke said St. Sebastian or Badajos]. Though it was
very dark, we perceived that one of the parties was not
moving on, and was suffering accordingly from the enemy's
fire. There was a cry amongst the men in front for the
captain ; there was no captain to be found, he had run away ;
at last, the lieutenant, who was at the tail of the party, heard

---

* [The Editor has struck out the name.]

that the captain was not to be found, and he ran to the front and led the company forward. Next morning, of course, I gave him the command of it. That captain is now in London, and he complains that he is an injured man, and wants to be restored; he is a protégé of Dick Martin's, but if such a fellow were to be forced back into the army I would leave it myself. Yet I know that I am abused for what his friends call my hard-heartedness to this poor fellow.

After this excursion, I met the Duke of Wellington at Teddesley, Beaudesert, Mansfield, and Strathfieldsaye, but I only noted a little of his conversation at Beaudesert.—

Lord Hopetoun.

The late Lord Hopetoun was too rash—over brave—so much so as to be hardly trustworthy. He was always at the outpost, and whenever there was firing he was sure to be in it. Accordingly he was always wounded, and his capture was really a disgraceful affair, and all from too much bravery. On one occasion on which he was wounded and defeated, I came up and rallied the men, and I then was obliged to tell him plainly that such boyish impetuosity *would not do.* He was a fine fellow, and as amiable as he was brave.

Mr. Gleig and the ' Subaltern.'

' The Subaltern ' [Mr. Gleig's book, which I had brought with me and lent the Duke, who had not before seen it] is all true enough. Two points which fell under my own personal view are quite so. I mean the scene in which he describes my meeting his regiment, and my rallying the army after Sir John Hope was wounded. But the Subaltern talks too much of his own personal comforts, and too little of his men; if you believe him implicitly, you would imagine that he thought of nothing but his own dinner; but this is the usual fault of journalizers, who are naturally struck by what immediately concerns one's self; and in fact, a subaltern in an army can in general have little else to tell. I hope, and indeed know, that the regimental officers were in general much more attentive to the comforts of their men than the Subaltern tells us; but he is a clever, observing man, and I shall inquire about him.

Bringing an Adjutant-General to reason.

Charles Stewart (third Marquis of Londonderry) was a sad *brouillon* and mischief-maker. I was obliged to get rid of him. He used to harass the cavalry to death by constant patrols and reconnaissances. This I was obliged to forbid, but he did not obey me; but this was not the real cause of my rupture with him. It was produced by a foolish pretension he set up as Adjutant-General of the army, that the examination of prisoners belonged exclusively to him. It happened one day that some prisoners were taken, and my aide-de-camp, happening to be on the spot, examined them immediately, and, to save time, brought me the result. But in consequence of this, Stewart refused to execute the rest of his duty as to these prisoners, and declined to take any charge or care of them whatsoever; and he left them to escape or to starve as far as his department was concerned. This was too much; so I sent for him into my room. We had a long wrangle, for I like to convince people rather than stand on mere authority; but I found him full of the pretensions of this department of his, although he and it and all of them were under my orders and at my disposal. It was in vain that I showed him that an accidental interference under emergent circumstances with what was ordinarily his duty could not be considered as any affront to him. At last I was obliged to say that, if he did not at once confess his error, and promise to obey my orders frankly and cordially, I would dismiss him instanter, and send him to England in arrest. After a great deal of persuasion, he burst out crying, and begged my pardon, and hoped I would excuse his intemperance.

Intrigues against the Duke.

After this he intrigued in the army against me, and with the assistance of Robert Crawfurd, had turned every one of the general officers against me, except Lord Beresford, who, like a good soldier and honest fellow as he is, discountenanced all these petty intrigues. You will be surprised to hear that all this was grounded on a project of poor Castlereagh's going into decided opposition. His ground was to be the impossibility of doing anything in Spain, and the expediency of withdrawing the army, and this doctrine Charles Stewart preached, it seems, amongst the officers. It was therefore impossible to keep him in the army, and when he was going to England he imparted to me this notable scheme of opposition, in which his brother was about to embark. I told him that I had no right to advise him or his brother, but that, as I had a regard for both, and particularly for Castlereagh, I charged him to tell him that I looked on any such project of opposition as alike unworthy in its object and unfounded in fact, and that, like all pretences—for it was only a pretence—it would recoil on those who adopted it. However, Castlereagh soon after joined Mr. Perceval, and the threatened opposition was no more heard of. I cannot believe that this was the project of Castlereagh's own mind. I suspected always that it was suggested, or perhaps only *attributed* to him, by Charles. It is wonderful what influence he had over him, and not only influence, for that might be produced by brotherly love, but Castlereagh had a real respect for Charles's understanding, and a high opinion of his good sense and discretion. This seems incomprehensible to us, who know the two men, but the fact was so.

Poor Crawfurd was a dissatisfied, troublesome man, who fell quite naturally into this sort of intrigue, and I believe he pushed it to a very blameable extent, for when he was mortally wounded he sent for me, and there, in the way one has read of in romances, he solemnly asked my forgiveness for injuries of that kind which he had done or endeavoured to do me.

I believe there was a good deal of this sort of spirit at one time, before I had laid hold of the public opinion, both in the army and the country, but I kept never-minding it, quite sure that all would come right in good season. You have expressed this in your poem about me in better language, but however expressed, the fact was that I paid so little attention to this small malice, that there was, I have no doubt, much that I never knew, and almost all I ever did hear, I have forgotten.

One evening at Beaudesert, when we were talking of Quatre Bras, some matters of fact were mentioned upon which, to my surprise, I found that the Duke and Lord Anglesey entirely differed. Such differences invalidate all history. Their two aides-de-camp, Lord March and Fitzroy Somerset, who were playing billiards in the next room, were called in and appealed to ; they also differed, but each, I think, was against his own general. In the course of this discussion Lord March stated that three colours were taken at Quatre Bras. The Duke had never heard of it. Lord March saw them, and had them, but could not tell what became of them. A French officer of cavalry had *lost his head* (not his *caput*, but his capacity), and had rode through our line, and was galloping wildly about in our rear. Our soldiers began to fire at him. Fitzroy Somerset tried to ride up to him and to save him, but he could not catch him. Lord March and Curzon made a similar attempt, but before they could reach him he was shot. They, however, caught the horse. Curzon, who was on foot, jumped up on him, but in a few minutes was himself killed. March then succeeded to the fatal horse, but no more mischief happened ; he rode him to Paris, and there sold him for forty-five dollars.

Duke.—The best of all the publications [about Buonaparte] is that of Baron Fain. All the dictations to Montholon, Gourgaud and Las Casas are of little real authority. They are what Buonaparte on after consideration thought it expedient to represent things to have been, and not what they were. Any accurate reader will find them to be what *made-up* stories always must be, full of contradictions, but we who know the affairs of our time know that they are full of false-hoods; but Fain's book, if not absolutely true, is at least sincere ; that is, Fain may be mistaken in some facts, but he is generally correct, and bating a little natural leaning to Buonaparte, very fair. That is the *real book*, the rest are all fabricated apologies.

Sir Sidney Smith.

Of all the men whom I ever knew who have any reputa-tion, the man who least deserves it is Sir Sidney Smith. During my embassy at Paris (where he was living to avoid his creditors in England) I saw a good deal of him, and had eternal projects from him as long as I would listen to them. At first, out of deference to his name and general reputation, I attended to him, but I soon found he was a mere vaporizer. I cannot believe that a man so silly in all other affairs can be a good naval officer.

While our expedition against Algiers, under Lord Exmouth, was going forward, Sir Sidney asked an audience of the old King, Louis XVIII., and after some delay obtained it. His business was to acquaint the King that the expedition must fail; that the force was insufficient, and bad of its kind; but that, above all, the commander was ill-selected; that he knew Lord Exmouth well, having served with him, and that whatever qualities he might have as a mere sailor, he was the most unfit man in all other respects to command such an enterprise; that he himself was, from a variety of considerations, the only person who ought to have been selected; and, finally, by this omission an affair so vitally important to the civilised world must, to an absolute and demonstrative certainty, fail. The old King was sly, and had a quiet kind of humour; he listened to Smith without interruption; and when he had concluded a very long speech, he told Sir Sidney that he was very much obliged to him, for the information that he was so good as to give him, that he quite appreciated his *lumières* and his motives, but, he added, I am sure it will give you additional pleasure, as it has done to me since I have heard your opinion, to learn that we have this morning heard, through Marseilles, that what you fear is impracticable has been accomplished with the most complete success!

C.—But has not Sir Sidney the merit of enthusiasm—a main ingredient towards making a great man?

Duke.—No, not even enthusiasm; but a degree of egotism and vanity that looks like enthusiasm; but he has no enthusiasm in the world except for what relates to Sir Sidney Smith.

[N.B.—I myself knew Sir Sidney Smith, and though I thought him, as most people did, a little crazy—perhaps with vanity—I, though with some difficulty, prevailed with Lord Melville to employ him as second in the Mediterranean Fleet, which was, I thought, due to his former distinguished services, and the noise he had made in the world, and I thought that, having been so long unemployed, he had a peculiar claim to be brought forward at that time. The seamen at the Board were rather averse; for certainly he was not what is called a sailor. I must add that the Duke only knew him at Paris, when his eccentricity, or levity, or vanity, or whatever it may be called, had grown so remarkable that I am not surprised at the unfavourable impression he made on the Duke. When I first went to the Admiralty, Sir Roger Curtis, then .commander-in-chief at Portsmouth, who had previously been an acquaintance of mine, through the Howes and Lady Sligo, and was so kind as to favour me with his advice, said to me, "My dear friend, beware of *Heroes*—the more you come to know them, the less you will think of them;" and certainly he was right as far as my experience went with many who set up for *heroes.* The grand exception was the *real hero*—the Duke—who in mind and manners was the same, exactly the same, when I first knew him in 1806, as he is now, and rose in my admiration every hour that I saw him—always simple and always great.—C.]

Louis the Eighteenth.

I said that Louis XVIII. understood English, but I did not think that he spoke it readily—at least, not very willingly. I had had the management of the embarkation at Dover on his first restoration, and though he had numberless occasions to speak to the English, he never did so in English, and I remember that having said something to one of the people of the yacht, who did not understand him, I was obliged to repeat it in English.

Duke.—That only proves that he did not like speaking English; but I assure you he has often spoken it to me, and very well too. He was clever, and well informed, and a *diseur de mots.*

I said that on that occasion at Dover one of the *girouettes,* who came over to salute the King, was the Duke de Liancourt, but the King would not receive him. M. de Liancourt applied to me for a passage back. I did not know that the King had refused to see him, but as I knew something of the Duke's career, I was not sure whether the King would wish for his company on this occasion. So I went to the King, and asked him what he wished. The King answered, sharply, "You may put him where you will, Mr. Croker, except in the same ship with me." This was in the cabin of the yacht, at the door of which the Duc de Duras was exercising his old office of *Premier Gentilhomme de la Chambre,* and as I was going out he told me that the King had declined to see M. de Liancourt. M. de Duras's own appearance there in that office was sufficiently singular. He had held it before the Revolution, and was in attendance on Louis XVI. when the mob prevented his going to St. Cloud. He had emigrated, and had been appointed to the same office by Louis XVIII., but he returned to France, and lived in retirement till this great change of circumstances called him to resume his duty at the King's door at Grillon's Hotel, and here again in the yacht, which he seemed to fall into as naturally as if there had been no interruption since the 18th April, 1791.

Duke.—I remember M. de Liancourt's haste to kiss the King's hand was much ridiculed, and, I think, caricatured. It was a strange escapade for him, for the King and he had an old grudge. I fancy he had always been eccentric and over busy.

The Duke in Spain and Portugal.

Strathfieldsaye, October 20th, 1825.

The Duke.—Batalha, like Battle Abbey, was founded by King John I. of Portugal to commemorate his great victory over the King of Spain. He, like our Conqueror, was illegitimate, but the founder of the reigning family. My army encamped there on the very anniversary of the battle [14th August, 1385].* There was also some nominal similarity in the circumstances, for there was then an alliance between the Portuguese and English against the French and Spaniards. The monks were not as cordial as I expected. He then mentioned some remonstrances and opposition on their parts which I omitted to note.

He told us the history of the blowing up of Almeida and Brenier's † escape. It was a great disgrace. Col. Bevan ‡ too late, Col. Douglas too soon, § General Campbell's ‖ regiment of

---

* [His army encamped there the night between the 13th and 14th August. I think he said that himself and staff lodged within the abbey. His dispatch of the 14th August is dated Alcobaça, and says the army had arrived there that morning. A later dispatch states that he marched from Leyrias to Calvarie on the 13th, and on the 14th to Alcobaça; Calvarie, I suppose, was adjacent to the abbey, probably the *Calvary.*—J. W. C.]

† [Brenier had been made prisoner at Vimiera; I think the Duke added that he was a very impudent fellow, and on his capture asked the Duke to lend him 500*l.*—C.]

‡ [Colonel of the 4th Regiment.—C.]

§ [Lieut.-Colonel Douglas, of the 8th Portuguese.—C.]

‖ [They called him "*Jingly Pat*," or some such name; I forget why, unless it was from a trick he had of *whistling*, which he would do interjectionally in the midst of serious matters. I had more than once business to do with him, and there was always an accompaniment of whistling. The Duke was not satisfied with him about Almeida.—C.]

dragoons taken, freed by an infantry picket. Albuera—
Blake's vanity, arrogance, and insufficiency. He claimed the
post of honour and lost it. "Not write history because truth
cannot be told?" So I said to Jomini, and so I wrote to
you when I told you that a battle was like a ball—that one
remembered one's own partner, but knew very little what
other couples might be about; nor, if one did, might it be
quite decorous to tell all he saw. So that, besides almost
inevitable inaccuracy, there was the risk—indeed, the certainty—that you could not tell the whole truth without
offence to some, and perhaps satisfying nobody.

He repeated the arguments in favour of the Convention of
Cintra in the great and urgent advantage of getting the
French out of Portugal *at once*, which by battles and sieges
might not have been accomplished in a whole campaign; and
all direct and forward movements in favour of Spain would
have been paralysed.

The First Portuguese Campaign.

General Foy's history of the Peninsular War, which just
includes the first of the Duke's Portuguese campaigns, was
mentioned—[here unluckily my note was interrupted, which
is much to be regretted, for I recollect that his exposure of
Foy's presumption in matters of opinion, and of his gross
misstatements of matters of fact was very complete, though
very good humoured and candid as to Foy's talents]. He
concluded :—

But after all, though I admit neither his conclusions nor his
statements of facts, he was a very distinguished officer. He
was only a colonel at Vimiera, though he had seen a great
deal of service. I fancy his politics kept him back. He was
made a general, I think, immediately after. His wife was a
handsome woman, keeping a salon and *faisant les délices à
Lisbon*. She can have nothing to do with the book, though
her name is on the title-page.

The Guards and " White's Window."

The Duke often expressed a high opinion of what we call
the *gentlemanly* spirit. After some pleasantries on Cooke, and
dandyism, and so forth, to which Cooke replied with great
readiness and good humour; he said the Guards (meaning
the officers) were the most troublesome people in the army

when there was nothing to be done, and he had constant
occasions to be vexed with them when in quarters and in the
intervals of active operations, but when these recommenced,
the Guards were the best soldiers in the army. None of
them, he said, ever misbehaved when there was any duty to
be done. *White's window would not permit it.* [N. B. *White's
window* was at this time the fashionable tribunal of the
dandies.]

National Characteristics.

The national character of the three kingdoms was strongly
marked in my army. I found the English regiments always
in the best humour when we were well supplied with beef;
the Irish when we were in the wine countries, and the Scotch
when the dollars for pay came up. This looks like an epigram,
but I assure you it was a fact, and quite perceptible ; but we
managed to reconcile all their tempers, and I will venture
to say that in our later campaigns, and especially when
we crossed the Pyrenees, there never was an army in the
world in better spirits, better order, or better discipline. We
had mended in discipline every campaign, until at last
(smiling) I hope we were pretty near perfect.

The Ford at Assaye.

It was on this occasion that he gave me an instance of the
importance of a very ordinary degree of thoughtful common
sense. He described his very critical position on the march
before the battle of Assaye, when his small force was
threatened by an overwhelming deluge of native cavalry, and
his only chance, not of victory only, but of safety, was his
getting to the other bank of the river (Kistna), which was
a few miles on his right. He had some of the best native
guides that could be had, and he made every possible effort to
ascertain whether the river was anywhere passable, and all his
informants assured him that it was not. He himself could
not see the river, and the enemy's cavalry was in such force
that he could not send out to reconnoitre. At last, in extreme
anxiety, he resolved to see the river himself, and accordingly,
with his most intelligent guides, and an escort of, I think he
said, all his cavalry, he pushed forward in sight of the river
in the neighbourhood of Assaye, which stood on the bank of

another stream that ran nearly parallel to that which he wished to cross. When they came there, he again questioned his guides about a passage, which' they still asserted not to exist; but he saw through his glass, for the enemy's cavalry were so strong that he could not venture to get closer, one village on the right, or near bank of the river, and another village exactly opposite on the other bank, and " I immediately said to myself that men could not have built two villages so close to one another on opposite sides of a stream without some habitual means of communication, either by boats or a ford—most probably by the latter. On that conjecture, or rather reasoning, in defiance of all my guides and informants, I took the desperate resolution, as it seemed, of marching for the river, and I was right. I found a passage, crossed my army over, had no more to fear from the enemy's cloud of cavalry, and my army, small as it was, was just enough to fill the space between the two streams, so that both my flanks were secure, and there I fought and won the battle of Assaye, the bloodiest, for the numbers, that I ever saw; and this was all from my having the common sense to guess that men did not build villages on opposite sides of a stream without some means of communication between them. If I had not taken that sudden resolution, we were, I assure you, in a most dangerous predicament."

An Enigma in Buonaparte's Career.

There was something in Buonaparte's hasty return out of Spain [in December and January, 1808–9] that I have never understood. When Moore retreated, he followed him closely as far as Benevento and Astorga. He had a greatly superior force, two to one he gave out; and I should have thought, as he was afterwards so anxious *de se frotter* against *me*, he would at that time have been still more anxious to have personally performed his threat of driving the leopards into the sea; but he stopped, all of a sudden, committed the command of the armies to Soult, who pushed Moore as hard as he could, while Buonaparte returned to Valladolid, where he remained a week or ten days, doing nothing that we know of while Soult was following Moore; and I think it was about the very day that the battle of Corunna was fought that Buonaparte set out from Valladolid for France, riding post through Spain, and making a wonderfully rapid journey to Paris.

The reason given for all this was that he had received news of the bad disposition of Austria, which rendered his presence in Paris very urgent; but that does not explain his quitting his army at Astorga, at the moment that it had come in contact with Moore, and it was clear they must soon fight a regular battle; and his returning to waste, as far as I can see, ten days or a fortnight before he set out for Paris. Was he disinclined *de se frotter* against Moore? Did he wish that Soult should try what stuff our people were made of before he risked his own great reputation against us? or did he despair of driving us out of Corunna? and was the bad news from Vienna (he generally kept bad news a profound secret) now invented or promulgated to excuse his evident reluctance to follow us up? I cannot account for his not having subtracted from the three weeks he spent in Spain after his return from Astorga, and the three months that, I think, he spent at Paris, half-a-dozen days for so great an object as a victory over the English won by himself in person. My own notion is that he was not sure of the victory. He was certainly at that time greatly displeased with Talleyrand, and made him a *scène* on his arrival in Paris; and it is possible, and even probable, that the extreme haste of his return may have had some political cause, foreign or internal; but even this does not explain my difficulty of why he did not in person attack Moore, or, at all events, why he was not rather with the army the ten days that he lingered at Valladolid.

CHAPTER XII.

1827.

THE year 1827 marked at once the culminating point and
the close of Canning's career. Scarcely had he realized the
most ambitious of his dreams when death summoned him
to relinquish the power which he had attained, by means
that his warmest admirers were not always prepared to
defend. For years previously, he had looked forward with
confidence to filling the office of Prime Minister of England,
and when Lord Liverpool was seized with the illness from
which he never recovered, Canning saw that his opportunity had come. The Eldon section of the Tory party,
with Peel and Wellington, were opposed to his plans, but
with equal art and determination, he swept aside every
impediment in his path to success. The narrative of the
political events of that time has often been written, though
never perhaps with all the clearness and fulness that could

be desired. Mr. Croker's letters contain much that will be of value to the historian who may hereafter undertake the task. He was consulted on almost all sides at every stage of the negotiations, and he could see, from his peculiarly advantageous point of view, a good deal that was hidden from the persons more directly and more nearly concerned in the moves that were being made. He was, it will be observed, very anxious that Canning should bring himself to act cordially with Wellington and Peel, but this was impracticable for many reasons, the chief of which was that Canning was resolved to be in the foremost place, while neither Wellington nor Peel was willing to see him there. Canning's superior generalship carried the day—thanks, partially, to the influence he had already acquired over the King.

The Conyngham family were, on their side, rendered friendly to Canning by the appointment which he secured for Lord Conyngham of the Chamberlainship, and for Lady Conyngham's son of an Under-Secretaryship in the Foreign Office. He had also shown a most friendly disposition towards Mr. C. R. Sumner, the tutor of Lady Conyngham's son, who was afterwards made Bishop of Winchester. At the same time, he was careful to gain the good will of Madame de Lieven and Sir William Knighton. With these powerful forces in his favour, unpopularity at Court was no longer an element which it was requisite for him to take into account.

The question of Catholic Emancipation was embarrassing, but it seems to have occurred to Canning that this also might be disposed of without difficulty. For his own part, he was prepared to undertake not to bring the subject forward during the lifetime of the King, but he began by advising the King to form an Administration based upon his own views, of

opposition to the Catholics, believing, as a critic who is
usually allowed to be impartial* has said, "such a Government to be impossible, and also convinced that if possible it
would be ruinous to the State." Few of Canning's avowed
assailants have pronounced upon him a harsher sentence than
this. The result of the carefully considered series of steps
was that Canning became First Lord of the Treasury, and
Wellington and Peel, acting with the anti-Catholic party
generally, resigned their offices. Special efforts were made
by Mr. Croker to persuade Peel to remain with Canning, and
Peel was at one time disposed to take that course; but, as
Mr. Disraeli remarked,† "between Mr. Canning and Mr.
Peel there existed an antipathy: they disliked each other;
Mr. Canning was jealous of Mr. Peel, and Mr. Peel was a
little envious of Mr. Canning." Thus repulsed by his old
political associates, Canning sought support from the Whigs
and found them ready enough to join him, with the important exception of Lord Grey, who remained hostile, and discharged barbed arrows at the new Prime Minister, every one
of which rankled deeply in the wound. The Tories attacked
him severely, and the reproaches which he had to endure for
treachery towards his former friends undoubtedly affected
him deeply, and increased the ill-health from which he had long
been suffering. "He could not possibly disguise from himself," remarked an acute political observer of the time,‡ "the
humiliating truth that he had formed a coalition with that
party and those persons against whom he had been sincerely
and victoriously engaged during his whole political life upon

---

* Sir George Cornewall Lewis; the 'Administrations of Great Britain,'
p. 443.

† 'Life of Lord George Bentinck' (1852), p. 286.

‡ In the *Quarterly Review*, vol. xliv. 1831, p. 282. This article, it
may be as well to state, was not written by Mr. Croker.

every question of importance, the single one excepted, upon which neither he nor they deemed it prudent to try their strength against the known opinions of the King, and the undoubted feeling of the country."

In four short months, the rule of Canning was ended by death, and for a little more than five months, his successor, Lord Goderich passed a harassed life, amid perpetual brawls and disagreements; dissatisfied with his colleagues, his colleagues dissatisfied with him ; a perpetual cloud of resignations in the air, and a battle incessantly raging over personal " claims " which the Premier was too weak a man either to quell or to reconcile. There is scarcely a more pitiable figure to be seen in the whole of political history. When, at last, fairly badgered out of office, Lord Goderich went to take leave of the King, it was said that he burst out crying, and that the King offered him his pocket handkerchief*—an incident which brought this ludicrous *entr'acte* to an appropriate termination.

Mr. Croker's diary and letters explain in detail much that has hitherto been in doubt, or has been known only in a general form. His record of the year begins with the death of the Duke of York, who was attacked with gout and dropsy in December, 1826. The King went to see his brother twice, and was much affected.

Mr. Croker to Lord Hertford.

January 4th, 1827.

He sent to-day for Taylor† and Stephenson, who had not seen him for some days, and said, "I feel I am dying and have sent for you to bid you good bye." He then appeared

---

* 'Colchester Correspondence,' iii. 540.

† [Sir Herbert Taylor, who had been the Duke of York's military secretary, and had also acted as amanuensis for George III. when blindness first overtook him.]

to move his lips as if in prayer, and then made a motion with his head as if to bow them away; so, at least, his servant interpreted the gesture, and they retired.   He did not take their hands.

Princess Sophia is, they say, confined at home by illness. Ill she may be, poor thing, but I believe she stays away because it is painful, and useless, and injurious to both that she should see her brother.   She saw him yesterday, and he held her hand half an hour without speaking.

The Dukes of Clarence and Sussex are constantly in the house, but have not seen him these two or three days.

To Lord Hertford.

January 6th, 1827.

The scene is closed, and the most kind and best natured of Princes is no more.   I need not tell you any particulars—the papers are full of them.

He was fully sensible to noon at least, as at that hour he insisted that his legs should be dressed, and expressed some impatience at the delay which, he saw, was intentional.

The Dukes of Clarence and Sussex were in the ante-room, and both showed very much of good feeling.   Taylor went off to the King with the melancholy tidings, and is not yet come back, so that we are in doubt what his Majesty will do about the mourning.

A few weeks after the Duke's death, his guns and pistols were sold at Christie's.   Mr. Croker estimated that they had cost about 4000*l.*, for there were " four-score fowling-pieces and as many cases of pistols."   What they brought in the auction room he does not state.   The Duke of Wellington succeeded the King's brother as Commander-in-Chief, but the King himself desired to fill that position, and was only deterred from his purpose by the unusually vigorous remonstrances of Lord Liverpool.   George IV. was far from being in vigorous health, and there seeemed a probability that the Duke of Clarence, his brother, would soon be called upon to succeed him.   " He had" wrote Mr. Croker to a friend, " some affection in his legs, and the itching is so troublesome that he cannot help scratching himself to pieces. His legs, from his ankles to his knees, are sore (not *broken*) from the operation of his own nails."

The Corn Laws were again brought before the House by Canning, who proposed to adopt a sliding scale, the duty on corn being increased or diminished as the price fell or rose. Huskisson had suggested the device, and before Lord Liverpool's illness he had fully approved of it. But it was not thought advisable to allow Huskisson to bring in the Bill, in consequence of the opposition he had aroused among the country party. In writing to Peel, Mr. Croker speaks of "your" resolutions, but in reality Peel opposed them. His anticipation with regard to the opposition the Bill would have to meet with was, of course, fully borne out by subsequent events.

Mr. Croker to Mr. Peel.

March 1st, 1827.

DEAR PEEL,

I should have seen you had I not been confined ever since Sunday, but my cold is better, and I shall go to the House to-morrow, or to-night if wanted.

I hear from the people who have called upon me that the opposition to your Corn Resolutions (*if they are to make any sensible alteration*) will be very great, particularly in the Upper House, where anything under 70s. will be, they say, rejected; *this* may be an exaggeration, but, depend upon it, there is a spirit of opposition gathering in the Lords which will be formidable.

I dare say that your Resolutions are reasonable, but you will find your noble auditors *un*reasonable.

I think it right that you should know this; although I do not think that it can have any effect on your measures, it may have on your speeches.

Yours affectionately,

J. W. C.

Lord Liverpool was first incapacitated by an attack of
paralysis and apoplexy on the 17th of February, and for
several weeks the Government remained with only a nominal
head.

From Mr. Croker's Diary.

Saturday, Feb. 17th, 1827.—Lord Liverpool was this morning struck with an apoplectic or paralytic attack at Fife
House. He had received his post letters at the usual hour,
and had opened them with his two private secretaries—
a few which he wished to consider he took away with him
into the room where he generally breakfasted. This was a
little after ten. The servant who took in breakfast observed
that he was sitting in rather an unusual way, and had not
spoken to him, but did not suspect that anything was amiss,
and he left the breakfast, but a considerable time having
elapsed, the servant went in again, and found him extended
on the floor without sense or (apparently) life. It happened
that his physician, Dr. Driver, was in the House at the time.
He was immediately called in and bled him. Sir Henry
Halford was also sent for. Dubious whether the disease was
of a fatal character or a mere temporary attack, those about
Lord Liverpool resolved to keep the matter secret as long as
they could, and succeeded wonderfully, for it was not known
even to the Ministers till between one or two.

Sir William Knighton has been some days seriously ill in
Hanover Square, and the Duke of Wellington and Arbuthnot
went to him to consult as to the mode of communicating this
melancholy event to the King. Sir W., and indeed every one
else, was very anxious that the Duke should go, but he positively refused. He said it was not his business, and that on
no occasion did he wish to do what was not his business, but
particularly he would not so in a case like this. He proposed,
and it was settled by such of the Ministers as were at hand,
that Peel, as Secretary of State for the Home Department, was
the fittest person to go down. A messenger was despatched
to Brighton about half-past two to break the matter to the
King, and Peel followed about five.

I dined at the Speaker's second official dinner, where there
was not only no grief, but not even a decent pensiveness. In
short, no one seemed to think or care about poor Lord Liverpool. I sat next Wilmot Horton. He seemed to think that

Canning's health, habits, and taste would all render it impossible for him to be First Lord of the Treasury and Chancellor of the Exchequer. For my own part, I cannot see how he can be anything else, or how anybody else can be placed in these offices as things are now circumstanced. Two months ago, before the Duke of Wellington had accepted the command of the army, he might have been made First Lord of the Treasury, but I look upon it as now quite out of the question. Some weeks ago, when some one, I forget who, was expressing how much the Duke's appointment (to the Horse Guards) had increased his weight and diminished that of Canning, I said, what I am now confirmed in thinking, that it was quite the reverse, as it removed Canning's only rival for the situation of Prime Minister to a place which was so appropriate to him, that he could not leave it even to be First Minister.

Lord Liverpool had spoken the night before in the House of Lords, and was not so clear as usual. Lady Isabella Blachford, who called to pay Mrs. Croker a morning visit at Kensington *before the thing was known*, said that Lord Liverpool had made a strange speech the night before about the Duchess of Clarence, and had called her "a worthy and deserving object." I daresay that he was already a little confused, yet next morning, half an hour before he fell, his secretaries did not see any difference in his mind or manner.

Sunday, Feb. 18th, 1827.—As I came into town from Kensington, I called on the Duke of Wellington, whom I found at breakfast. After a few words about some other business, we began to talk of the state of affairs. He was quite open and confidential, and his views were, what they always are, clear, moderate, and generous. He said that all he wanted was to keep the Government together, not merely for their own sakes, but for that of the country, for that "after them *comes chaos*." I said that a few weeks ago that would have been comparatively easy, as all pretensions might have been persuaded to give way to him, and all parties in the Cabinet might without dishonour have united under him, but that I could not but feel that his late appointment seemed to render any arrangement of that kind impossible.

He said at once, and in his frankest manner, "Yes, yes, I am in my proper place, in the place to which I was destined by my trade. I am a soldier, and am in my place at the head of the army, as the Chancellor, who is a lawyer, is in his place on the woolsack. We have each of us a trade, and are in our proper position when we are exercising it." This encouraged me to say that I thought the way—the best way—I feared the only way—of keeping us together was to make Canning Minister, and to give Robinson the Foreign Office, with, if they wanted assistance in the Lords, a peerage. This, I said, would make the least change, and would, I thought, answer all expectations, provided Mr. Canning should engage to take the Government on the same terms and in the same spirit in which Lord Liverpool had held it.

The Duke seemed to assent to what I said about Mr. Canning, but to doubt about Robinson; and he asked, generally and without making any distinction as to the points of my proposition, whether I thought Peel would assent to that arrangement? I said I did not know, but that I thought *he ought*; that I was sure it was the course which would ensure his becoming Minister in due time. The Duke spoke handsomely of Canning in all their personal intercourse, and seems inclined if possible to go on with him, but I see that he doubts Canning's prudence, and fears the restlessness of his disposition.

I said that I agreed with him that the Foreign Office would be a severe trial, and perhaps too high a step for Robinson, and that I threw it out only because it would make the least displacement, as he and Canning would only have to change sides of Downing Street. Palmerston, I thought, would be a better Secretary of State, but he had not yet been in the Cabinet; Robinson, after being Chancellor of the Exchequer, could not be well postponed to Palmerston, and as he, Palmerston, had made no difficulty about Robinson's present position, I thought it likely that he would make none as to my proposed arrangement, which would be the nearest possible approach to the *status quo*. If once we began a general move, I agreed with him that chaos was not far off.

Some time after this, while matters were still in suspense, Peel called on me at the Admiralty (as he often did) to ask me to take a walk. I had told him all along of what I had said to the Duke of Wellington on the above occasion, and some other accidental meetings, and though he never made any direct declaration, I had no reason to doubt that he would acquiesce, if the Duke did, in Canning's promotion. This was strongly confirmed during this walk. Huskisson, who was Canning's *alter ego*, had been ill and confined to his house,

and Peel proposed that we should begin by paying him a
visit at Somerset House, which we did, and nothing could be
more cordial ; and to those who know Peel's *very peculiar
manners*, this volunteered visit and cordiality at that moment
will be conclusive that he had then no idea of separating himself from Canning.   After we had paid a long and cheerful
visit to Huskisson, we pursued our walk over Waterloo and
Westminster Bridges, and through the parks, talking of
various matters, and now and then of the crisis in which we
were.   Just as we got two-thirds of the way up Constitution
Hill, our talk about the latter had grown more explicit, and
we were discussing in a light problematical way the course
that different members of the Cabinet might take if Canning
was placed at the head.   I mentioned Lord Westmoreland as
likely to resist.   Peel pooh-poohed that difficulty.   We were
just then opposite to Lord Eldon's, and pointing to his house,
I said, " Would *he* stay," upon which Peel squeezed my arm
tightly under his, and said, "*he will if I do.*"   I had, and
could have, no longer any doubt that Peel had no disinclination to such an arrangement—the squeeze of the arm seemed
to say, " I have settled all that."   I never heard, and Canning
told me that he never knew, what had changed Peel's disposition
—for a change he, like me, thought it was.   Peel never again
spoke to me on the subject, and I was as ignorant of and as much
surprised at his resignation, indeed more so than the public,
and up to that time I had taken no part in the affair, and I
don't think I had even seen Canning in private.   I never
mentioned the subject to the Duke because I did not think he
had treated me with confidence in not telling me his change
of opinion ; but his kindness to me continued not only un-
altered, but I might say was increased, and I really believe
that he did not wish that I should resign, which if he had
mixed me up in the matter I probably must have done, though
certainly not for Peel's reasons, as *I* could not object to
Canning's former inclination to Catholic emancipation, as I
was in the same category.   So was Lord Melville ; and why
he went I never could guess—I suspect that there must have
been some old grudge between him and Canning.

March 16*th.*—Dined with Mr. and Mrs. Peel.   I fear that
he is quite indisposed to serving under, not Canning he says,
but a *Catholic* Premier.   He would like the Duke or Lord
Bathurst, or even Lord Melville.   I observed to him that
Lord Melville was a *Catholic.*

Mr. Croker to Lord Hertford.

March 27th, 1827.

On Friday evening Lord Liverpool showed the first symptoms of political recollection, and again on Saturday evening. He asked after the result of the Catholic Question, and then added in a faint voice, "who succeeds?" Lady Liverpool told him of the King's forbearance, and expressed her own hope that he would be soon able to do business. He said, "No, no, not I—too weak—too weak."* After this he relapsed into unconsciousness. This, however, relieves Ministers from the silence to which delicacy to Lord L. had imposed upon them, and I have no doubt that the King will be spoken to in a day or two. Canning and Lord and Lady Granville and the Lievens go to Windsor to-day.

Mr. Huskisson to Mr. Croker.

Somerset Place, April 12th, 1827.
11 P.M.

My dear Croker,

I was at your door about half an hour ago, but found no admission. I therefore conclude that you are gone to Kensington, and your servants to bed.

Canning has so many engagements to-morrow (besides the probability of having to wait upon the King) that he cannot name any time; but he desired me to say that, if you will call in Downing Street, taking your chance, he will be very glad to see you.

He does not ask to see Lord Hertford (though it would afford him great pleasure to have an opportunity) for two reasons: 1st. He is under so much uncertainty as to the disposal of his time; and 2nd. He does not wish to do anything which might be misconstrued into an attempt to canvas in support of the King's right to name the individual who is to be at the head of the Administration. It is against this right that the present effort is directed. The King, you may rely upon it, feels *this*, and not the Catholic Question, to be the only question at issue in the present struggle; and *they* will find themselves much mistaken who expect to overcome that

* ["He had been exceedingly harassed for the whole of the last two years by the intrigues then carrying on."—*Colchester Diary*, iii. p. 477.]

impression, or to dictate to the feelings by which it has been so strongly excited. When C. left the King this evening, H.M. was apprized of the full extent of the difficulties thrown in his way. This knowledge has only confirmed the King's determination not to yield to them; and I think you will agree with me that with the King resolved to be firm, Mr. C. is not likely to desert the duty which H.M. has imposed upon him.

Every truly yours,
W. HUSKISSON.

Mr. Canning's efforts to create a Ministry were impeded by many circumstances, and Mr. Croker was apparently desirous that he should not increase his difficulties by disregarding the influence of the great territorial lords, who exercised so great a sway in the House of Commons, and consequently over the Government, before the Reform Bill of 1832. It was with a view of reminding him of this power, which necessarily had to be reckoned with, that the next letter was written. The allusion in the latter part of Canning's letter was probably aimed at the Duke of Wellington, but it has always been understood that " insult," if there were any, was offered by Canning to Wellington.

Mr. Croker to Mr. Canning.

April 3rd, 1827.

DEAR MR. CANNING,

Some gentlemen and particularly our friend Sir George, talk so slightingly of *Blue-ribbands* that I think it right to send you a memorandum which will show you, in one view, how impossible it is to do anything satisfactory towards a Government in this country without the help of the aristo-cracy. I know that you must be well aware of this, yet the following summary may not be useless to you, though I know that it is imperfect.

Yours, dear Canning,
Most truly,
J. W. C.

Number of members returned to the House of Commons by the influence of some of the Peers :—

Tories—Lord Lonsdale 9, Lord Hertford 8, Duke of Rutland 6, Duke of Newcastle 5, Lord Yarbro' (for W. Holmes) 5, Lord Powis 4, Lord Falmouth 4, Lord Anglesey 4, Lord Aylesbury 4, Lord Radnor 3, Duke of Northumberland 4, Duke of Buccleuch 4, Marquis of Stafford 3, Duke of Bucks (2) 3, Lord Mount-Edgcumbe 4—70 ; besides at least twelve or fourteen who have each two seats, say 26—96.

Whigs—Lord Fitzwilliam 8, Lord Darlington 7, Duke of Devon 7, Duke of Norfolk 6, Lord Grosvenor 6, Duke of Bedford 4, Lord Carrington 4—42 ; with about half a dozen who have each a couple of seats, 12—54.

Mr. Canning to Mr. Croker.

April 3rd, 1827.

Am I to understand, then, that you consider the King as completely in the hands of the Tory aristocracy as his father, or rather as George II. was in the hands of the Whigs ? If so, George III. reigned, and Mr. Pitt (both father and son) administered the Government in vain.

I have a better opinion of the real vigour of the Crown when it chooses to put forth its own strength, and I am not without some reliance on the body of the people.

And whether in or out of office (an alternative infinitely more indifferent to me than you perhaps imagine, and with the inclination of my choice, if anything to the latter) I will not act (as I never have acted) as the tool of any confederacy, however powerful; nor will I submit to insult (without resenting it according to the best of my poor ability) from any member of such confederacy, be he who he may.

There are my opinions. They are purely *defensive* ones, but there are limits beyond which defence cannot be purely passive.

Yours,

C.

Mr. Croker to Mr. Canning.

[Same date.]

I really did not mean to attach any importance to the list of the aristocratical members, nor do I surmise that they have,

at this moment, any peculiar influence with the King, for I
positively know nothing of any of the opinions except what I
hear in the streets, into which I seldom go, and excepting also
those of one person whom I mentioned to you.   All I meant
to do was to show, in one view, how powerful the aristocracy
is, and how necessary it is to have a fair proportion on the
side of a Government.   You will observe that I included the
Whigs as well as the Tories, and I reckon Lord Seaford's and
Lord Wharncliffe's interests, as well as those of the older
peers, and I arrive at this conclusion, and a very important
one it is, that the *old Tory* and the *steady Whig* aristocracies
have at least 150 members in the House of Commons, not by
influence or connection, but by direct nomination, and that
no Government which did not divide them could stand for
any length of time.   I think the peers, &c., who are not
either old Tories or old Whigs may have about a dozen
members.

I assure you, on my honour, that I never heard anything
like *insult* or even *disrespect* towards you, but I really know
little of what folks are saying or doing; for except the one
person I have already alluded to, I have not had a conversation, much less any *confidential* communications as to the line
of politics that any one was likely to adopt; my regard and
gratitude to the Duke of Wellington, who first brought me
forward in public life—my private love for Peel—and my
respect and admiration for you, made and make me most
anxious that you should all hold together.   Neither political
gratitude nor private friendship blind me to the fact that in
such a union your present and relative station entitles you to
expect the lead, and that such an arrangement would afford
the best chance of keeping the Government together.   At
least, so I think; and these have been long my opinions;
but I feel that it is almost presumptuous in *me* to have *opinions*
on such subjects.   I have no political weight, either personal
or official; and although I am most anxious to see my friends
kept together, and would do anything within my humble
means to effect so desirable an object, I have not the vanity
to suppose that I can conduce to it, otherwise than by saying
as I always have done, that in my private intercourse with
each, I had never seen any thing but good-will and generous
sentiments towards the other two.

I have been betrayed into this rather *rigmarolish* note by
an expression in your note which seemed to imply that I knew

or apprehended some hitch in the progress of the arrangement which I most wish to see—and I hope you will forgive my tediousness.

Yours, dear Mr. Canning,

Most truly,

J. W. C.

Mr. Canning to Mr. Croker.

April 4th, 1827.

Your list is good for nothing without commentary. Add therefore, if you can, to these names the *price* that Government pays for their support, in Army, Navy, Church, and Law, Excise and Customs, &c.

And then calculate what number of unconnected votes the same price distributed amongst others would buy in the market if the Crown were free ?

[*Enclosed in the foregoing letter.*]

Lord Lonsdale 9, Duke of Rutland 6, Duke of Newcastle 5, Lord Powis 4, Lord Falmouth 4, Lord Anglesey 4, Lord Aylesbury 4, Duke of Northumberland 4, Duke of Buccleuch 4, Lord Mount-Edgcumbe 4—48.

Mr. Croker to Mr. Canning.

April 6th, 1827.

I send you a memorandum which, I think, will surprise you. The aristocracy, powerful as it is, does not enjoy any great share of political *office* in the House of Commons. So that, in fact, a Government has less to give to them, or take from them, than at first thoughts one would have supposed. Depend upon it, the aristocracy is the *unum necessarium*, or, at least, an *indispensable* ingredient, and that in order to conciliate and manage *it*, the union of the Duke, Peel, and yourself is absolutely necessary.

I know very well that many of these grandees are very unreasonable, and I believe there has been too much indiscreet and even offensive talk (though I have not myself heard any), but indiscretions and offences are, I suppose, inseparable from the excitement which a state of things like the present naturally produces. If you, Peel, and the Duke are once agreed, all the rest will soon subside into their accustomed channels, and flow along without even a murmur, which God grant.

Yours most sincerely,

J. W. C.

PATRONS.	Number of Members.	Number of *such* Members holding Political Office.
Lord Lonsdale	9	2 (Becket).
Lord Hertford	8	2 (Croker).
Duke of Rutland	6	0
Duke of Bucks	6	1
Holmes's Trustees	5	2 (Canning, Phillimore).
Duke of Newcastle	5	0
Duke of Beaufort	3	1
Duke of Northumberland	4	0
Lord Powis	4	1 (Holmes).
Lord Aylesbury	4	1 (Nichol).
Lord Falmouth	3	0
Lord Anglesey	4	1
Lord Shaftesbury	3	0
Lord Bath	3	1 (Cockburn).
Lord St. Germains	4	1 (Arbuthnot).
Lord Somers	3	0
Lord Mount-Edgcumbe	3	0
The Bullers	4	0
Lord Strafford	3 (24)	0
Lord Sandwich	3	1 (Calvert).
Johnston Trustees	3	1 (Wallace).
Lord Huntingtower	3	0
Lord Beverley	2	1
Dorset Trustees	2	1 (Strathaven).
Lord Pembroke	2	0
Lord Westmoreland	2	0
Lord Exeter	2	0
Lord Radnor	3	0
Duke of Leeds	2	0
Lord Londonderry	2	1 (Harding).
Lord Harrowby	2	0
Lord Donegal	2	0
Bridgewater Trustees	2	0
	116	18

So that of 116 members, returned by the Tory aristocracy, only 18 hold political office, and of those 18 no less than 12

2 B 2

are persons on whom the patrons confer that favour at the request of the Government.

There are about 30 Tory Peers, who have each one seat. Two Tory Commoners have each 4. Sixteen Tory Commoners have each two seats, and about seventeen Tory Commoners who have one seat each. Total, 203; in the hands of what may be called the Tory aristocracy. The Whig seats are about 73.

Mr. Canning to Mr. Croker.

Foreign Office, April 18th, 1827.

1. I have written to North * to offer him a seat, without contest or expense. What can I say more?

2. It is a little too much to leave us aground; and then to make our *not calling for other help* the condition of coming back to us.

I will however suspend everything till to-morrow.

Ever yours,

G. C.

Mr. Croker to Lord Lowther.†

April 14th, 1827.

DEAR LOWTHER,

I hasten to tell you that Mr. Canning has received a proof of his Majesty's determination to support him, which will lead to most important results. The Duke of Clarence is declared Lord High-Admiral, and the whole of the late Board, Protestants and all, remain with his Royal Highness as his Council.

No true Tory will like to commit himself in opposition for two generations, and I hope and trust that most of them will consent to go on in the King's service. I am anxious that you should know this important event as soon as possible, as I cannot doubt that such a mark of the King's personal feel-

* [Mr. North had been a candidate for Dublin University against Mr. Croker, dividing the Conservative vote.]

† [Lord Lowther appears frequently at a later date in this correspondence as the Earl of Lonsdale. He resigned his office in 1827, declining to serve under Mr. Canning.]

ings will have some effect on you. It grieves me to think
that in addition to so many other afflicting disunions I should
have any—even *political* differences with you—*personal* I
hope there never will be

Yours affectionately,

J. W. C.

Mr. Croker to Lord Lowther.

April 16th, 1827.

DEAR LOWTHER,

Your letter is a most sensible and able one, and states the
case with great fairness.* I will only make one observation,
that dreading as you do Whig-men and ultra-Liberal measures,
you ought not (in strict argument) to contribute to force Mr.
Canning to such men and such measures. Mr. Canning is
making, they say, every effort to obtain Tories and Protestants
to join his Administration. If so, what can Tories and Protestants want more ? and if they will not help to assert their
own principles, who is to blame but themselves ? I am a
Tory as sincere, though not so important, as you are ; and if I
were as important, I should think I best served my principles
by asserting them in council, and maintaining them in practice.

My only hope now is that Mr. Canning may be able to
form such a Government, and be able to pursue such measures,
as may obtain your approbation.

Your friend Copley is Lord Chancellor ; Lord Anglesey, they
say, Master-General ; Tindal, Attorney-General. I have not
heard that Beckett or Granville Somerset have resigned—nor
Macnaghten, nor Herries, nor Holmes ; so that there is a
sprinkling of Protestants.

I have not heard of any Opposition man being applied to,
although it is evident that if none of the Tories can be prevailed upon to come, recourse must be had to some of the
moderate Whigs.   Public opinion has pronounced most loudly
for Mr. Canning.   You know how I despise popularity, and I
set no store upon so fugacious and hollow a support, but it
will in this instance probably last long enough to enable
Mr. Canning to form a Government strong enough to forfeit
it with impunity.

For myself, I have no motive or object, but a desire to

---

* [This letter is not to be found.]

keep my public friends together, and to keep my private friends still indulgent to me.

I lament that I am not now addressing the First Commissioner of Woods and Forests,* but I do not the less love you because you do not take the same view of that subject that I do.

Yours affectionately,

J. W. C.

Mr. Croker to Mr. James Daly, M.P.

April 17th, 1827.

My dear Daly,

The turn things have taken is indeed extraordinary, and to me, in respect of Peel and the Duke, most afflicting; but I suppose it could not be helped. His Royal Highness the Duke having offered me his confidence, I have consented to remain not merely out of respect to him and out of duty to the office, but, I will add, out of regard to the new Government itself, which I think has been a little hardly dealt with by having such a burst of resignations showered on it at once.

My chief consolation is that no one raises even a whisper of reproach against Peel, whose conduct has been, *consensu omnium*, most admirable.

Yours most sincerely,

J. W. C.

During the progress of these negotiations, it happened that Peel became distrustful of Mr. Croker, without the slightest cause, as he subsequently discovered. It is evident from the foregoing letters that Mr. Croker acted with entire loyalty towards his friend, but Peel's suspicions were aroused, and for some few months there was a coldness on his part toward Mr. Croker. " Peel will not believe," wrote the latter, "that all my communications with Canning were not directed against his interests." Before the close of the year, however, this misunderstanding was cleared away, although Peel's letter of

---

* [Lord Lowther was again appointed to this office in 1828.]

reconciliation scarcely made amends for the unnecessary suspicions which he had entertained.

Mr. Peel to Mr. Croker.

Drayton Manor, October 3rd, 1827.

MY DEAR CROKER,

The suspension of my intercourse with you was caused by the part which I had reason to believe you were taking in those arrangements which were connected with the dissolution of the late Government. In consequence of unreserved communications with you, you were in possession of my opinions and fixed intentions in certain contingencies, and I certainly think that under all the circumstances I might have expected from you at least a total abstinence from any interference, direct or indirect, in what was passing at the time of which I speak.

Mr. Canning declared to more than one person that there was no one to whom he was so much indebted for suggestions as to the course which he should pursue as he was to you.

Such an avowal by him, or indeed the fact of your being in confidential communication with him at the period in question, was a sufficient reason for my declining to hold any intercourse with you on matters of a public nature.

I am perfectly ready to bury in complete oblivion the causes of misunderstanding and alienation, and it is clear that nothing can more contribute to this—particularly considering the relations in which we respectively stand to the present Government—than a total oblivion when we meet, of politics also.

Believe me, my dear Croker,

Ever very faithfully yours,

ROBERT PEEL.

It is quite certain that throughout this period Mr. Croker neither sought nor desired to gain any advantage for himself. The foregoing letters prove how thoroughly disinterested he was, and what was the real nature of his advice. He had in every way sought to bring Peel into prominence rather than to keep him down. Had he desired promotion to higher office, he could easily have secured it. "I was so satisfied," he wrote in after years, "with my post at the Admiralty that I twice refused Privy Councillor's office. Mr. Canning offered me any that I should choose, but I peremptorily declined. I preferred remaining at the Admiralty, where I was master of my business, and not unacceptable to the public. I thought it my duty to remain with and support Mr. Canning on public grounds." On public questions his views had undergone no change. He was engaged in a contest for the representation of Dublin University—an honour which he had much coveted for years past, and which he soon had the satisfaction of obtaining. He took occasion once more to declare his views concerning Catholic Emancipation, and avowed that they were the same as they had ever been. On the Corn Law Bill he was less in sympathy with the views of Canning than with those of Wellington. In the Upper House, the Opposition was very strong, and the Ministry was not greatly strengthened by the elevation of Mr. Robinson to the Peerage under the title of Viscount Goderich. The "sliding-scale" scheme was twice defeated in the Lords, to the great vexation of Canning. The following letters touch upon this subject, and upon certain topics of social interest, such as the account of the two fêtes which enlivened the summer of 1827.

Mr. Croker to Lord Hertford.

June 26th, 1827.

The messenger is still embargoed, and I shall therefore despatch two packets more: one to St. Petersburg,* containing only a note and a newspaper; the other to wait at Berlin with any addition Ward may have to make. Our House is

* [Lord Hertford was at this time Ambassador at St. Petersburg.]

adjourned, and we are to be prorogued on Saturday or Monday.

You will be sorry at all the bother about the Duke of W.'s amendment to the Corn Bill.

The King, they say, comes to town on Friday or Saturday to settle the Speech ; but he will not go in person, though he is quite equal to do so in point of health.

The Speaker has had a fall from his horse—his face much bruised and disfigured. He was hardly able to speak on Saturday, but he would get into the Chair for ten minutes to forward the business; he is better, but will look for a fortnight to come as if he had been a performer at Moulsey Hurst.*

J. W. C.

It will be observed that in the next letter there is the first allusion to Canning's rapidly failing health.

Mr. Croker to Lord Hertford.

The great " Carousal " of the year has been the fête at Boyle Farm † on Saturday last. It would fill three letters to give you any account of this entertainment, and of all the impertinences which preceded and accompanied it. It was *exclusive* to the last degree ; the founders of the feast, Alvanley, Chesterfield, Castlereagh, H. de Ros, and Robert Grosvenor ballotted, it is said, for every name proposed for invitation. The wags say that Lord and Lady Grosvenor had four black balls ; on which Robert Grosvenor said that really he could not be of it if he were not to ask papa and mamma. Upon this he was allowed to invite them, but on an *engagement* that they should not come. People who were shabby enough to ask for invitations were well served in the answers they usually got ; the men were rejected because they were old or vulgar, and the ladies because they were ugly. It was really amusing to hear at the Opera the reasons which the excluded ladies gave for being seen at so unfashionable a

* [Where the prize-fights were usually held.]

† [Boyle Farm was the residence of Lord Henry Fitzgerald, and afterwards of Lord St. Leonards. The fête here referred to was celebrated in verse by Thomas Moore and by Lord Francis Egerton.]

place as the Opera was that night. I will not make you stare with all the fables which are reported; roads watered with Eau de Cologne—500 pair of white satin shoes from Paris to counteract the damp of the green turf. More gallons of Roman punch than Meux's great brewing vats would hold. Fireworks ordered on this scale—the Vauxhall man was asked what was the *greatest* expense he *could* go to, and then ordered to double it; and so I need hardly add that I was not invited; but it really, and without exaggeration, was a most splendid fête. Alex. Baring calculated the expense at 15,000*l.*; but no one else that I have heard carries it higher than 3000*l.* or 3500*l.*

Canning looks tired, but his intimates say that he is *only* tired; the Opposition say that he is really ill. The Duke of Devonshire has lent him Chiswick, as his father did to Mr. Fox. I hope it may not be ominous.

People are staying longer in town than usual, I think, and are therefore prolonging what they call the pleasures of the season; breakfasts and water parties which, (on account, I presume, of the chief motives of such gatherings,) find so little countenance from the heavens above, that every day that has been fixed for one of these things, down goes the mercury, and down comes the rain. The Speaker made us laugh by a practical illustration of these (really) " contretemps." While he was dressing, the other morning, in a bright sunshine and perfect white-trousers-weather, he heard a noise of music on the river, and on inquiry from his servant found that the Corporation were going on the water for a day's pleasuring. "Are they so?" said the Speaker, "then give me a pair of cloth pantaloons," and, to be sure, the day changed to as dirty a one, as the sailors call it, as ever drenched silk or blew away feathers.

To-day has been tolerably fine, although there is a pic-nic breakfast at Putney—a real pic-nic. They have hired or borrowed a lawn for the occasion, and each person brings a dish and a bottle. The Duchess of Leinster is the founder of the feast—'tis a mighty economical mode of entertaining the town. Her Grace needs only bring a cheese-cake and a bottle of soda-water—that fulfils the requisites; and then one might hope that her Grace of St. Albans would bring a round of beef and a bottle of brandy. This *fête champêtre* was held, or I should say more truly, is now holding, at a villa at Putney called the Cedars, from some large trees which you may remember; but those who either would not go, or were not asked, are called the *seceders*, so that it looks like a party thing. They say that Lady Glengall has persuaded Leach to attempt a kind of Vauxhall party in the Rolls garden—a place about ten feet square at the back of Fleet Street. It will be more fruitful of jokes than of anything else: they talk already of light let into Chancery—smelling of the oil—that the garden is really the *court*—and "hot rolls in the month of July." I spare you many more. Mrs. Fox was saying the other day at dinner that the Master of the Rolls had given a dinner-party to Lady Glengall, Mrs. Fox herself, and half a dozen other women. "And really," said Lord Dudley, "were there no *men* but the Master of the Rolls and Lady Glengall?"

I forget whether the ladies had burst out into flower before you went; they now wear bouquets like our grandmothers, and not merely in their bosoms, but they carry them about in their hands as large as brooms, and when they sit down to dinner they stick their nosegays into the water glasses and the table looks like a bed of flowers. Some one was saying that young Lady Londonderry has relays of them, and that when she dines out a page follows her with a fresh bouquet. They talk of reviving the fountains in which our grandmothers used to carry their flowers about their persons. If they succeed, we may repeat Horace Walpole's jest and say, "What a number of sore throats there will be from the over-setting of the fountains." But all this fashion will be gone before you return; at least, it is to be hoped so. This fountain-spilling would be dreadfully inconvenient.

In the month of August, as a passage in the above letter states, Canning went to the Duke of Devonshire's villa at Chiswick only to die—in the same room, as is well known, where Fox breathed his last. It was "a small low chamber, once a kind of nursery, dark, and opening into a wing of the building, which gives it the appearance of looking into a courtyard." The circumstances are fully described in the subjoined letters:—

Mr. Croker to the Duke of Clarence.   *Extract.*

August 6th, 1827.

I must not conceal from your R.H. that I hear from private information that there are no hopes whatsoever of Mr. Canning's outliving the day. It is said that mortification has advanced—that he is, and has been, for some hours insensible—that his breathing is difficult, and that, in short, there are all the symptoms of approaching dissolution.

Mr. Croker to Lord Hertford.

August 7th, 1827.

Mr. Canning is still alive, but that is all. I saw Sir W. Knighton to-day, who says that he looks on recovery as next to, if not impossible, and has of course no hope.

Mr. Canning has not been well ever since the Duke of York's funeral. He there caught cold, and was teased, as you know, for some months with rheumatism and lumbago ; this lumbago has some peculiar symptoms, being accompanied by obstructions arising from intestinal inflammations and his mode of life (for he ate and drank too heartily), which kept these bad symptoms alive. He also changed his doctor, and got one Mr. ——, who has now a great vogue ; this —— was all his life a naval surgeon, and as the majority of his cases in that practice had required mercury, he has got accustomed to that remedy, and he gave Mr. C. so much that he actually salivated him: this, it is thought, added to the disorder and indisposition, and dining about ten days ago at the Chancellor's at Wimbledon, he sat in a draught and caught cold again, and about this time I saw him, and he said, with a strong expression of melancholy, that he had not been well or had one day's health since the beginning of the year.

Sunday, the 29th, Warrender spent with him. He thought him weak, languid, and out of sorts, but nothing serious. On Monday he went to Windsor. On Tuesday he came to town and did business. He was looking very ill, but still nothing very serious appeared. Sir William Knighton saw him that day, and told him that he looked ill, but Mr. Canning answer-

* [Whom Canning had made Lord High Admiral, to please the King.]

.ing that he had seen Maton that morning, Sir William supposed that all that was necessary would be done, and interfered no further.

On Thursday Sir William Knighton called at Chiswick, and observed Mr. Canning so much altered for the worse that he insisted on his calling in some additional advice, and he himself good-naturedly drove to town and brought back Sir Matthew Tierney, and either Holland or Farre, I know not which. They found positive inflammation so far advanced and the patient so reduced by four months' alternate quacking and indulgence, that he was unable to undergo the sudden reduction which they thought necessary. It seems as if the real seat of the original disease was not well ascertained, but it now had spread to the lungs, and by noon on Friday his life was evidently in danger; that night the danger became imminent, but the medical measures had had some effect, and he was *better* on Saturday morning; perhaps I should say *easier*, for *better* I doubt that he was, as ulceration of the lungs was proceeding rapidly.

Mr. Canning was not sensible for the last eighteen hours, and for some days had been a little wandering at times. I told you that he had finished a long paper on Portugal on Thursday. On Friday, in an interval of quiet, he called to Stapleton* and desired him to send the paper (it *had* been sent the day before) to *Goderich* and *Robinson*, and to desire them to cut it up and not to spare it—and he desired Stapleton to write this down that he might make no mistake. Stapleton saw that this was a wandering of his mind, and pretended to write, and Canning desired to have what he had written read to him; upon which Stapleton began, "Send that paper to Goderich and Robinson," upon which Canning said "*Goderich* and *Dudley*. Now you see how necessary it was to make you write it down, you would else have thought that I was talking nonsense."

On Saturday he walked across his room, and when the doctors offered to help him into bed, he said, " No, no, not so bad yet; I think I can do that without help; and when he got into bed he said rather gaily, " Well, I feel that if I can get through to-day I shall do." But later on that day he said to Sir Matthew Tierney that he had

* [Canning's private secretary, and afterwards the historian of the official part of his life.]

struggled with the disease for a long while, but that he now felt that it had quite mastered him.

To Lord Hertford.

August 8th.

I sent you a long letter yesterday to tell you of Mr. Canning's increased illness, and a short one this morning to acquaint you with his death; but as the Austrian courier does not go till this evening, I shall add a few lines which he will deliver if he should chance to come upon you *chemin faisant*.

Mr. Canning is no more *—and that is all I can tell you; though the event must have consequences that will be felt all through England, and all through Europe, no one is as yet composed enough to contemplate the probable results.   For my own part, I do not doubt that the King will eventually give his chief confidence to the Duke of W., and then, whether he will himself take the first post, or give it to Peel's younger hands, or agree on a *fagot*, under whom all may serve without renouncing individual pretensions, no one I think can foresee.   I think the first course the most probable and the most easy.   Some people think that Dudley, Sturges, and the Duke of Portland, who only stayed in to oblige Mr. Canning, will be glad to be released, and that their vacancies, with Bexley's, would leave room enough for the Tories; but will the Tories act with Lansdowne and Carlisle, or they with the Tories?   But all these are speculations quite *en l'air*; for my own part, I expect a complete Tory Government, with which I wish Lord Carlisle could act, nay I should not be sorry for Lord Lansdowne; but I do not think they can well coalesce with the Duke and Peel—it will then come to the old Administration, *minus* Mr. Canning—but query whether *minus* Mr. Canning's *friends—that* will depend mainly on the Catholic Question.   An exclusive Protestant Government cannot, I am satisfied, stand; there would be an Opposition of 250, which would stop all public business.   If Lord Liverpool's Government can be patched up, with the Catholic Question open, the Administration may go on.   Why should I tease you with these *ifs*, which you, in Poland, are just as capable of suggesting as I in Whitehall.

I suppose the King will, out of respect to his present

* [Mr. Canning died on Wednesday morning, the 8th of August.]

Ministers, send for some of them before he takes any other step. The Chancellor seems to be the natural person to send to, but I have just heard that Goderich has gone down to Windsor—that may perhaps be as an ambassador from the Cabinet.

Everybody happens to be in town except Lord Melville and, I believe, Lord Bathurst, and we shall have all the intricacies of April to unravel again.

Yours ever,

J. W. C.

Mr. Croker to Lord Lowther.

August 16th, 1827

Dear Lowther,

I am just returned from following Mr. Canning to his grave. Nothing could be more solemn or affecting—the people in the street behaved with great decency, though there was nothing like a general wearing of black ; but the crowd was respectful in its demeanour. The Dukes of Clarence and Sussex attended—the latter voluntarily, the former (but this is a great *secret*), on a suggestion that he ought. Lord Conyngham and Knighton also attended. The Duke of Devonshire was remarked as being particularly affected.

Some surprise and dissatisfaction is expressed that Peel, at least, did not attend the funeral yesterday. I own that I wish he had, even though he, of the late Ministers, had been alone.

On the death of Mr. Canning, Mr. Croker hoped to see the Duke of Wellington form a Ministry, with Peel leader of the House of Commons. But the King sent for Lord Goderich, and Mr. Herries was eventually appointed Chancellor of the Exchequer, "with the consent of Lord Lansdowne and his friends," as Mr. Croker wrote to the Duke of Clarence ; but this appears to have been a mistake, for Lord Lansdowne at first resigned, and the Whigs were evidently offended at Mr. Herries' appointment. On the 11th of August, Lord Goderich consulted Mr. Croker as to the formation of his Ministry, and the latter once more urged the adoption of the plan to which he had so pertinaciously adhered—the introduction of Wellington and Peel into the Government, and the coalition of the Tories with the moderate Whigs. To effect this arrangement, he offered, as it will be seen, to resign his own office—worth " 3200*l.* per annum, with one of the best houses in London." His fidelity to Peel, and to his political opinions, needs no greater proof than his willingness to make this sacrifice. It will be remembered, however, that Lord Goderich chose to pursue a different course, and his Government was doomed almost from its birth.

Mr. Croker's Memorandum of a conversation with Lord Goderich.

Admiralty, August 11th, 1827.

I began by saying that the King's having sent for him to be his adviser in the formation of a new Cabinet, had imposed upon him a most difficult and complicated task, and that every information which he received, though perhaps not available, or of much importance at the moment, might in the course of events be turned to some account. I said that I understood, and could not help saying, regretted that considerable difficulties existed in the way of a reunion of the late Ministers with a portion of Mr. Canning's Cabinet ; that it was thought (I did not inquire how truly) that the King felt some degree of displeasure against them—for *that* of course I could have no remedy, but that we had abundant examples that royal displeasure was not inexorable, and that I was sure that due explanations and proper representations of the advantage to his Majesty's quiet, of a strong government would overcome all difficulties of that nature.

But it might also be surmised that Lord Lansdowne and his friends might be unwilling to see the return of the Duke of Wellington and Mr. Peel ; to this I should say that, even if it came to that, there ought to be no difficulty in making a choice between the two sets of men ; but it occurred to me that there was a point on which the wishes of Lord Lansdowne and the Duke might unite, and which might contribute to an approximation between them—I meant the accession of Lord Grey to office. Lord Lansdowne, whatever he might privately feel about Lord Grey, was so far connected with him in public opinion that a junction with him would be, in the eyes of the public, a sufficient price for his uniting with the Duke and Mr. Peel; while, on the other hand, I could not but believe that in the late short campaign there had been enough of co-operation between the Duke and Lord Grey to make the Duke not only willing but desirous to introduce Lord Grey into any Cabinet of which he should form a part.

Lord Goderich here said that he had no reason to suppose this; that no doubt Lord Lansdowne and his friends could of course not object, and would even be pleased at the accession of Lord Grey, which would appear to give additional strength to their party; that Lord Grey himself professed not to be in opposition, nor to have any connection whatsoever with the Outs, and that he (Lord Goderich) knew that the Duke of Wellington disclaimed, with warmth, any kind of connection with Lord Grey.

I replied that he might be better informed, but that I could not help thinking that if ever he came into details of this nature with the Duke of Wellington, he would find Lord Grey not disagreeable to the Duke, which I conceived rather fortunate, because Lord Grey was, no doubt, a very able man, and the chief objection that could be made to his coming into office would be obviated by the concurrence of the Duke in that measure. I added that if the Duke, Peel, and Lord Grey could be introduced into the present Cabinet it would make one of the most powerful and, as far as I could foresee, the most popular Governments that could be formed. Lord Goderich said that he had no communication whatever with Mr. Peel, but he doubted whether it was possible that he could come in after having stated that his sole reason for not serving under Mr. Canning was, not any personal objection, but because he could not act under any person voting for the Catholics; and indeed in the discussion which Lord Goderich himself had with Mr. Peel previous to his resignation, he understood from Peel himself, he thought in distinct terms, that Peel would have objected to serve under him (Goderich), or any other person professing the same Catholic principles. I said that we were not yet arrived at the consideration of who should be under or over, and that as to the rest, of course I was not in Mr. Peel's confidence, and still less could I contradict Lord Goderich's impression of what had passed between them;

but I had formed in my own mind a different opinion. I believed that if it had been brought to that point, Mr. Peel would not have gone out on the mere question that the head of the Government should be a Protestant. He would, I had no doubt, have taken into consideration the personal qualities and character of the individual proposed, and the degree of security which that personal character might give for his impartiality with respect to the Catholic question. Lord Goderich said that he had understood that Peel's declaration in the House of Commons had been explicit on that subject in the sense in which Lord Goderich had himself understood him. I said that passages in his speech had certainly that aspect, but that there was one remarkable part which I observed particularly (though I had not heard it much noticed since), which appeared to me to afford the true key of Peel's present position. He had stated that " there was a general objection to having any but a Protestant at the head of the Government; but,"he added, " that that objection was peculiarly strong in his individual position, for that the Secretary of State for the Home Department not only had the responsibility of all Irish affairs, but he was, from official forms, the instrument by which all the patronage of the first Minister was exercised." He went on to say that "it might be objected to this motive for his resignation that he might have got rid of the difficulty by changing his office, but," he said, " the public were so ready to suspect the reasons which persons might have for adhering to office that he feared such a change would seem to be a mere trick or evasion, the imputation of which would be derogatory to the character of fairness and sincerity which he felt he deserved."

I showed Lord Goderich that it flowed as a corollary from this passage, that Mr. Peel felt and admitted that any other than the Home Office would have been less inconsistent with his feelings on this point; and that if he were placed in such an office without anything that could raise an imputation of trick or evasion, he would not have felt any insurmountable difficulty in having a moderate Catholic head to the Government; and that I had even heard that there had been some overture made in April for placing Lord Melville there. I begged of Lord Goderich to recollect that, however smooth his course would be in the House of Lords as to the distribution of business, that in the House of Commons he would have great difficulty in finding a leader—that at last he

would find himself driven to the alternative of Peel or
Brougham ; and that if he now so played his cards as to be
forced to take the latter, every thing like a Tory, even down
to so insignificant a person as myself, would immediately
quit the Government, and the great majority of the House
would, I thought, mutiny.

Lord Goderich admitted that Brougham would never do.

I then went on to say that Huskisson's health, I thought,
as well as his disposition and habits would prevent his
accepting—certainly his executing satisfactorily—so laborious
a task.   Tierney also had not health, nor, I think, any desire
to become so prominent.   Palmerston was better, but I
doubted whether he would or could undertake it ; and, in
short, I came back to what I said that he would find at last
that he was in a dilemma between Peel and Brougham.

Lord Goderich dropped some expressions as if his Whig
colleagues would not consent to admit Peel, and he said that
honour and gratitude and good faith required that he should
maintain the principles and persons of Mr. Canning's Government.   I replied that I could not presume to say to what his
honour pledged him, but on the other hand, I must plainly tell
him that without a junction with the Duke and Mr. Peel he
would never make a King's Speech ; and as there were vacancies
which must be filled up, I saw no inconsistency or impropriety
in filling up from those with whom Mr. Canning and himself
had so long acted, and whom Mr. Canning had so strenuously
endeavoured to keep in his Cabinet.   I repeated that he
would soon discover that it was utterly impossible that he
and his Whig colleagues could go on as they were—that he
and they ought to be delighted if any arrangement could be
made under which the Duke and Mr. Peel might be induced
to return to office—that I saw that his own position might be
a difficulty with them, but that, considering that they had
offered to arrange with Mr. Canning on the footing of a kind
of elected head to the Government, I thought that his own
conciliating disposition, and the important fact of his being
already in the King's confidence, might probably get over that
difficulty.   On the whole, I ventured, as an old and disinterested friend, to press upon him the expediency—the
necessity—of endeavouring to induce the King to send for
the Duke of Wellington to offer him the army, to request of
him to undertake the trouble of the Ordnance and the Cabinet,
and if he listened to the proposition of continuing Lord

Goderich at the head, to promise him in the Cabinet all that deference which his rank, his talents, and his experience entitled him to. He should also, simultaneously, write to Peel to acquaint him of the proposition to the Duke, and to offer him the Chancellor of the Exchequer, or anything else which he might prefer, and which could be offered to him; and to both I advised him to say that Lord Melville might come to the Colonies, and that on all minor arrangements, he would be glad to discuss what they might have to propose with a cordial desire of doing whatever was possible to reunite the various subordinate claims.

Lord Goderich here rather interrupted me by saying that there were no minor arrangements to make—that there were no vacancies. To which I replied that that was not quite the case, that when I recommended Sir Edward Owen as Surveyor-General of the Ordnance, I did so because, in addition to his fitness for the office, he had the advantage of being removable with very little difficulty, as a professional command would always be an honourable retreat for him; that Clerk would probably follow Lord Melville as Under-Secretary to the Colonies. Thus there would be room for Hardinge and another of the Duke's friends.

"But what," asked Goderich, "would you do with Horton? Besides, only two Under-Secretaries can be in Parliament." I replied that if the great points of a union with the Duke and Peel could be arranged, all the rest was trash and lumber which might be easily disposed of—that the only things which, in the first instance, pressed were the Ordnance Board, and room in the Treasury for Peel's personal friends; that if we were to descend to the consideration of minor points, I could myself help the arrangement, for which purpose I, without any reserve or affectation, begged to place *my office* at his disposal; that I did not want to retire, but that I had been at the Admiralty a long while, and should under any circumstances have easily consoled myself if I were to be put out; but for so great an object, and one which I had so much at heart as the bringing back the Duke and Peel, who could not come with honour if they did not replace in office some of the friends who had resigned with them, I should resign with more real pleasure than I felt even when I came in. I begged him not to think that I spoke lightly or loosely, that I spoke advisedly, and that my office was high both in emolument and confidence, and one which might, I thought, be likely enough to become useful in helping to satisfy some of the pretensions which he might have to deal with.

He answered me with personal kindness on this point, but seemed to me not to contemplate the possibility of his making any arrangement which would require such a sacrifice on my part.

I then reverted to Peel, and said that there was one point on which he would feel so strongly, both publicly and privately, that I thought it would induce him to sacrifice a great deal to bring it about—that was the appointment of Mr. Saurin to the Irish Seals. Lord Goderich stopped me at once; he said that his colleagues would never listen to that— that indeed they could not without dishonour; that after what had passed with regard to Lord Plunkett, it was quite impossible. I said I was sorry to find him so fixed, that I admitted there was much in what he said, but I did not think the difficulty insuperable; that some move might be made amongst the Irish Chief Judges which would make room for Saurin, and that, at all events, I thought, that any arrangement for Saurin (who was really deserving attention on his own account) would be a great step towards an accommodation with Peel.

But he said, "We have nothing to offer Peel but the Chancellor of the Exchequer, which I suppose he would not take."

I replied that I could not tell, but that Mr. Peel was a reasonable man, and that I thought he would be—or, at least, ought to be—contented to take that if there were nothing else arrangeable; that moreover that office, with the lead of the House of Commons, was a very prominent station—one in which we recollected how Mr. Perceval had distinguished himself; and, finally, that at all events the offer to Mr. Peel would satisfy the Tories and me in particular (if amongst such great interests I could venture to name myself), but I did so, not only on account of the familiarity of our old friendship, but because I knew that many persons connected with the Government thought as I did on the subject, and that without such an arrangement, the Ministry could not meet Parliament, and that I myself individually felt that my own position would become untenable. Remember, I added, these my last warning words—without the accession of the Duke and Peel, you *will never make the King's Speech.*

Here we ended. I, all through, endeavoured to prevent Lord Goderich making me any confidence—I only asked him to listen to my suggestions, and not to answer them.

I laughed a little at such a perplexity falling on *him* of all men, and he in return heartily wished that I was in his place, and was lamenting his difficulties very pathetically, when I said, laughingly, that "If I had the misfortune he wished me of being in his difficulties, I knew one or other of two ways out of them—the first, a junction with the Duke and Peel ; and, if that failed, my own resignation."

Mr. Croker to Lord Goderich.

My dear Goderich,

I think it right to repeat to you, in this more *formal* way, what I told you in the course of our conversation this morning, that so convinced am I of the importance to the interests of the country and to the King's own quiet and satisfaction, of having the Duke of Wellington and Mr. Peel in the Government, that if my office can be in any way disposed of to facilitate that object, it is *most freely and frankly* at your service. If my personal fondness for office were stronger than it is, I should feel it due to such *vital* national objects to sacrifice my private feelings, but I assure you these private feelings are not so strong as to make the sacrifice so great as it would have been some years ago ; and I promise you that I shall, out of office, give you as zealous and, I feel, a much more *useful* support than I could do in my present position.

As my office is 3200*l.* per annum, with one of the best houses in London, it might satisfy tolerably high claims ; and although I cannot well spare so great a loss of income, I shall not think it any hardship to be obliged to practise a little economy when I see, on the other hand, so important and, in my opinion, so essential a public benefit as the re-union of the Tory party and its junction with the moderate Whigs under the auspices of one whom I have loved so long and sincerely.

Yours ever,

J. W. C.

Mr. Croker to Lord Hertford.

September 3rd, 1827.

At first Goderich's Government seemed to go on swimmingly. The Duke of Wellington accepted the army, Huskisson was to lead the House of Commons. No more Whigs were to be admitted, and all was quite prosperous, when a little black speck arose on the horizon, which soon swelled into a thunder cloud that threatened for the last fortnight the whole with destruction.

Robinson as First Minister, as well as the head of the immediate department, had fixed on Herries to be his Chancellor of the Exchequer. He had, however, neglected to obtain the consent of his colleagues to this step, and on the day, and at the hour, when Herries was waiting in the anteroom to come in and receive the seals, Lansdowne and Tierney objected, and said that they would resign if such an insult were put upon them. This quite bewildered poor Robinson, who is as firm as a bulrush, and he was obliged to desire Herries to refuse what he had just settled that the King should offer him. Herries, greatly vexed and perplexed, went in to the King, and resisted manfully the King's pressing offer of the seals, which were lying on the table, and which H.M. over and over endeavoured to put into Herries's hand. The King then sent for Goderich, who mumbled some excuses, but said that the Government would be dissolved if Herries were appointed, so the King had no resource but to submit to *a delay*, for he pledged himself that he would not ultimately give up the point, and of *his own accord* ordered Herries to be sworn of the Privy Council.

The *mezzo-termine* agreed upon was to suspend the arrangement till Huskisson should arrive, and that then the seals of the Exchequer should be offered to him. I ought to tell you that Herries very modestly declined the place when Goderich first offered it. He said he was too young in political life, that it would be too great a jump for him, &c., and he rather pressed to be Vice-President of the Board of Trade under Charles Grant, and Goderich had actually offered the Exchequer to Palmerston, who had accepted it; but after all he veered round again, got the King to write with his own hand to insist on Herries taking the office, and took down

Herries in his carriage to Windsor to kiss hands, when the extraordinary scene I have just described took place.

Upon all this, the *Morning Chronicle* published an article grounding the opposition of the Whigs on Herries's connection with Rothschild. This made matters irreconcilable. Herries now said that though he had not wished for the office, and had rather have had a humbler one, his honour was now attacked, and though ready to have no office at all, he would accept no other office but that of Chancellor of the Exchequer. The Whigs—that is Tierney and his immediate friends—talked equally big, and up to this morning the public, who saw the King pledged on one side and the Whigs on the other, were of opinion that the Government must necessarily fall to pieces. However, after a world of shifts and discussions, Huskisson and Sturges Bourne having both declined positively to be Chancellor of the Exchequer, it was settled that there was no other person who could be, but Herries; and the King undertook to see Lord Lansdowne yesterday, and talk him over, which he did, and the Whigs remain in, with, however, it must be admitted, no great accession of *character*. There are a thousand details, all more extraordinary than could have been believed, of the vacillation and wavering of Goderich, and of the firmness of the King; but the substance is as I have told you.*

To Lord Hertford.

December 31st, 1827.

Goderich, I hear, still continues in the fool's paradise of fancying that he is Minister. "On the contrary quite the reverse," as he himself says. Neither Whigs nor Tories will go on with him, and he will find himself like the *bat* in the fable, he will not be admitted either as a beast or a bird. They talk to-day that the Whigs are obtaining an ascendency at Windsor, that Lord Holland is to come in, that Brougham is to be Attorney-General, and Scarlett Chancellor. Palmerston and Charles Grant are to *profess* to be Whigs, and, what I more regret, Huskisson!

* [The negotiations which ended in the appointment of Mr. Herries as Chancellor of the Exchequer, are fully narrated in the 'Memoir of the Public Life of John C. Herries,' by his son, Edward Herries.]

It does seem strange, but I assure you that this report meets some degree of credit amongst the best informed. It seems certain that the King is exceedingly vexed at the *outgoers*, and will not take them but on compulsion.

My own private opinion is that the King will not try a *pure* Whig until he shall have failed to make a *mixture*, and I think the first shop he will go to for his mixture will be Lord Wellesley.

What fools, fools, fools, our Tory friends have been!

Yours affectionately,
J. W. C.

The end of Lord Goderich's experiment was clearly foreseen by others besides Mr. Croker, but the Ministry lingered on till the first days of the following year, when the Prime Minister fulfilled the prediction contained in the following letter :—

Lord Lowther to Mr. Croker.

August 14th, 1827.

My dear Croker,

I cannot write all I feel or think upon the late events, but from your letter I conclude the present Cabinet will hobble on upon crutches till the meeting of Parliament, when Lord Goderich will be frightened and bolt. Some of the Cabinet, like old Tierney, will stick to the last, as they have little chance of again gaining six months' salary or patronage.

In my humble judgment Lord Goderich has not talent, nerve, or audacity to conduct or regulate so large a machine. Tierney or Huskisson have not health for every night's work; a long night debate has afflicted both with illness the last three or four years, and I think Huskisson will not like a visit to Liverpool. I agree with you, and I understand Brougham has announced it on the circuit, that either himself or Peel must have the Commons. The King has vowed Brougham shall never kiss his hand, but he is very forgiving. The Tories would really muster against Brougham. Brougham's vanity, I suppose, would induce him to give up his profession for a seat in the Cabinet, but

Pollock has beat him two to one in the number of briefs on the circuit.

The King seems to be taking his revenge upon his late refractory Tories. It must mortify them to be overlooked, and yet, at the same time, it does not appear the King feels very keenly on the Catholic question.

I wish the world to go on. I thought once I should like office, but I doubt whether my digestive powers are sufficiently active to combine business with the feasting consequent upon an official station, and I begin to like being my own master as well as I did at twenty-one.

I have been at Carlisle with the exception of a few hours ever since I left London, and as the weavers seem inclined to create riot and confusion, it is not improbable that I shall be detained here ten days longer.

Truly yours,

L.

CHAPTER XIII.

1828.

Fall of Lord Goderich—Administration of the Duke of Wellington—The " Great Rock " of the Catholic Question—The Prospects of the Whigs —Anecdote of Lady Holland—Ministerial Difficulties—The Duke of Wellington and Peel—Crockford's " Fairy Palace "—Mr. Herries and the List of the New Ministry—Burke's Dagger Scene—Mr. Croker's Proposals for Gradual Reform—The Vaults of St. Martin's Church— Dinners with Sir Walter Scott, Lord Lyndhurst, and Charles Grant— The Royal Academy Dinner of 1828 — Debates on the Catholic Question—The Duke of Wellington and Mr. Huskisson—Madame de Lieven—Mr. Croker appointed Privy Councillor—The Duke of Clarence at the Admiralty—Anecdotes of the Duke of Wellington and Talley-rand.

WHEN the tottering Administration of Lord Goderich fell to pieces, it was generally believed that the Duke of Wellington was the only man likely to succeed in forming a Government containing any element of stability. It was a responsibility which, as the world has been told on his own authority, he did not covet. He " detested politics," and, as he wrote to the Prince of Orange, the duties which he was asked to undertake were " very disagreeable to him." But the King desired him to place himself at the head of an Administration, and he felt bound to make the attempt. His first step was to entreat the " co-operation " of Peel in " this interesting commission." " I have declined," he wrote, " to make myself the head of the Government unless upon discussion with my

friends it should appear desirable." *   Peel states that he
obeyed this summons, "though not without great reluctance,"
for he foresaw great difficulties in connection with the state
of Ireland and the Catholic question.   The King stipulated
that no attempt should be made to construct a Cabinet with
especial view to the Catholic question.   In the end, Peel
accepted office as Home Secretary, Mr. Goulburn being made
Chancellor of the Exchequer, while Mr. Herries accepted the
office of Master of the Mint.   Mr. Huskisson acted as
Colonial Secretary for a few months, and then resigned with
the other " Canningites "—including Lord Palmerston—under
circumstances which are described in the various papers
contained in this chapter.   Mr. Croker's own opinions were
expressed in a short form in an article which he wrote for the
Quarterly Review in 1831.†   "At first sight no Ministry
could look stronger ; the confidence in the Duke was universal and unbounded ; and he was seconded by men who
stood deservedly high in public opinion for integrity, sound
principles, Parliamentary talents, and official habits.   But
the seeds of disunion existed, and sooner or later must have
grown to disastrous fruit. . . . There was the great rock of
the Catholic question, upon which it was easily foreseen that
the Ministry must eventually be driven and wrecked."   The
defeat of Mr. Vesey Fitzgerald at Clare by O'Connell was the
decisive stroke which convinced the Ministry that the question which had so long stood in the way must at last be
frankly dealt with.   But decisive measures were necessarily
postponed till the following year.

　　Mr. Croker's letters were supplemented in 1828 by a
journal, which he begins with this note : " I have always
regretted the not having kept a regular diary, though I have

---

* 'Memoirs by Sir Robert Peel,' vol. i. p. 12.
† Vol. xlv. p. 523.

often attempted to do so. I have, however, not been able to persevere. I hope I may be able to succeed a little better in this fresh attempt." The diary was kept in a fairly methodical way till towards the end of the year, when it became intermittent. The entries were evidently hurriedly written, in a small and scratchy handwriting, often closely "crossed;" and they are exceedingly hard to decipher. A selection will here be made from the most interesting passages.

From the Diary.

January 1st.—I called on Herries, and had a long confidential talk with him on the embarrassing situation of the Government. We have been in a good deal of confidence since he, as well as I, consented to stay with Mr. Canning, and having both been originally attached to Mr. Perceval, we have an additional bond of intercourse. He thinks the Whig party in the Cabinet, instigated and guided by Brougham, will attempt (and perhaps for a time succeed) to make a Whig Administration. He thinks that Huskisson has been looking to be himself Premier, and has for this object chimed in with the Whigs, and that the Chancellor, Bexley, Ch. Grant, and he must go out. Goderich perplexed between them, but more perplexed by Lord Holland and Brougham.

January 2nd.—Saw Herries again. We talked about a paragraph in the *Standard* newspaper of about ten days ago, which proclaimed that the Tories could not come in without stipulating for the dismissal of the Lord Steward [Lord Conyngham]. We agreed as to the mischievous effect of that paragraph, as it was known that the Duke of Wellington and Peel countenanced that paper, and he told me that a certain person took care that it should go down express to Windsor the very night it was published. I had seen the paragraph at Sudbourne, and had shown it both to Lord Hertford and the Duke of Wellington. The former agreed with me that it looked like a manifesto of the party, and one which would defeat all their hopes. The latter said: "What can we do with these sort of fellows?" (meaning the newspaper editors). "We have no power over them, and, for my part, I will have no communication with any of them." Yet his grace had desired Lord Hertford to take in that very paper, which Hertford did reluctantly.

In the evening with Nony at an assembly given by the Duchess of Clarence to Dom Miguel, who seems a civil, modest, and unaffected young man, short and slight in figure, not unlike Lord Marcus Hill. All the people in town at this assembly. I whispered the Duke of Wellington that the paragraph had, as I feared it would, gone to Windsor.

January 3rd.—Planta [Mr. W. Planta, Secretary of the Treasury] called on me. Agrees that Goderich cannot stand. His vacillation has lost him both sides, and there would be an absolute majority against him in the Lords. Planta hopes that Goderich's eyes are at last opened to this, and that he will take some early step to get out of so false a position. Planta had endeavoured to dissuade him from revoking his former resignation. The Chancellor and Anglesey are going down to Windsor to state to the King the perilous circumstances in which the Administration is placed. The difference between Huskisson and Herries has acquired such solidity that it will force one or other out.

In the evening with Nony to Princess Esterhazy's ball for Dom Miguel. He had dined with his own ambassador, Palmella, and came about eleven. The ball began with a waltz. Prince Esterhazy and the Duchess of Clarence, Dom Miguel and Princess Esterhazy. I came away very soon. Prince and Princess Lieven not there. Duke of Clarence says they were not invited, but Lieven himself told me that he had a previous engagement to Claremont, and that Prince Leopold could or would not put off his party. Rothschild introduced to the Duke of Clarence, and asked him whether there would be a war. "Upon my word, Mr. Rothschild," answered the Duke, "I must give to you the same answer Lord North did to such an inquiry. Not having had time to read the newspapers to-day, I cannot tell you."

Mr. Croker to Lord Hertford.

January 1st, 1828.

The prospect of a pure Whig Administration (if anything Whig can be called pure) becomes more distinct. I do not profess to understand how it is to be brought about, but some of the best informed and the most interested think that it is the most probable result of the present crisis. The King is so displeased with Peel, and so indignant at that paragraph in the *Standard* which I pointed out to you, that he is, they say, resolved to try the Whigs, that is, resolved to continue what he calls a mixed Government, but from which *all* Tories will secede. We hear no more of Lord Wellesley. The King is for him, the Lady *contra*. Lord Mountcharles is a decided Tory, and will resign if another Whig comes into power. In the meanwhile Brougham boils the pot and keeps stirring up the ingredients, and is, in fact, at the bottom of all the intrigues. Huskisson I do not understand. He has declared that he will not serve under Wellesley, but, I learn, is quite disposed to go on with the Whigs, though the Chancellor and Herries should go out—in short, that he looks to be first himself. I cannot believe all this, but I tell you what I hear.

Yours ever,

J. W. C.

January 2nd.

The rumours of a change more favourable to the Whigs continue, and I know that the Tories in the Cabinet believe that they are entitled to some credit; but upon what can they be founded? The Whigs are certainly not stronger (not, I believe, so strong) either in Lords or Commons than they have been for some years. The country is at least as hostile as ever—on what, then, can they ground their hopes? I can see nothing but the supposed personal favour of the Crown, but it is only a fortnight since Lord Goderich was forced to resign because His Majesty would not listen to his proposition of even a single Whig. His Majesty, I fear, is very angry with all the seceders, and specially with Peel and the Duke of Wellington. He is also, I know, a good deal affected at that unlucky paragraph in the *Standard* and the Lady (either by that paragraph or some other concurrent cause) is indisposed to the ex-Tories; but it seems to me quite incredible that even these motives should overcome the King's resolution against Lord Holland, and his personal antipathy to Brougham. Yet such is the complexion of the day's news. Perhaps His Majesty hopes that by the accession of Lord Wellesley he may without danger be in a condition to assent to the admission of Lord Holland, but that would be very shortsighted, because Lord Holland will not now come alone.   Be assured he will have Brougham at his tail.

January 3rd.

I am enabled to tell you to-day something that I think may be depended upon, and something also that, though not absolutely to be depended upon, may be possible enough. I think I know that Goderich has opened his eyes to his situation, and has nearly made up his mind to resign. He is gone with his wife to Blackheath, but returns to-morrow, and I hope and believe that he will to-morrow tell the King that he cannot go on.   It is surmised that to save his honour he may take advantage of a new incident which has just occurred, and which worse confounds the confusion.

Old Tierney, under the authority of Goderich and Huskisson, undertook to negotiate with Lord Althorp and the Spencer family that Althorp should be Chairman of the Finance Committee.   There was a good deal of delay and discussion about this arrangement, and at last Althorp consented, and it was after this that the matter came accidentally to the knowledge of the Chancellor of the Exchequer (Herries), who remonstrated with Goderich on the slight put upon him as the Finance Minister.   Goderich threw it all on Huskisson. Huskisson disclaimed all intention of slight to Herries, but insisted that he, as leader of the House of Commons, was solely responsible for the nomination of the Committee. Herries replied that at least he should be previously consulted as to a Committee which so nearly touched his own office as the Committee of Finance.   Huskisson adheres to his nomination, and Herries adheres to his opposition, and one or other will, it is said, resign.   If Huskisson were to go, the Government is broken up at once.   If Herries goes, Bexley will follow, and perhaps the Chancellor, and certainly Tindal, and then Brougham comes in, and then out go all the rest of the Tories, and there will remain a Whig Administration.

Lady Holland was saying yesterday to her assembled coterie, " Why should not Lord Holland be Secretary for Foreign Affairs—why not as well as Lord Lansdowne for the Home Department ?"   Little Lord John Russell is said to have replied, in his quiet way, " Why, they say, Ma'am, that you open all Lord Holland's letters, and the Foreign Ministers might not like *that !*"

From the Diary.

January 6th.—The Duke of Clarence tells me that Huskisson is actually out, and that Lord Wellesley has understood from the King that he is to be the head of his Government. There cannot be at this moment the least ground for either of these reports. Huskisson and Herries are no doubt at variance, and I am sorry for it, and probably one or other will retire, but matters are not yet advanced to this point. As to the latter statement, I never can believe it. Goderich must go, and the Duke of Wellington must either be, or designate who shall be the Ministers.

His Royal Highness talked to me of his own political feelings, and particularly on the Catholic question. He says that it is not ripe for full concession—that *he* would be ready to grant all even now, but that public opinion is not so far advanced—that what he would do therefore at present would be, 1st, to place the English Catholics on the same footing with the Irish ; 2nd, to introduce a bill to legalise intercourse with the Court of Rome, with a view to negotiation. His Royal Highness said that as long as the Duke of York lived he had, out of respect for his judgment as well as for that of the King, refrained from voting on that question ; but he was always, as he still is, satisfied that the concession must and ought to be made. His Royal Highness is for a Government founded on a union of parties. He says the names Whigs and Tories meant something a hundred years ago, but are mere nonsense nowadays. I agreed with His Royal Highness that Whigs in power soon assimilated themselves to Tories, and that Tories in opposition would soon become Whigs, but that I still thought that there were two marked and distinct parties in the country, which might for brevity be fairly called Whig and Tory.

January 8th.—The Duke of Clarence's news of yesterday was, as I expected, quite unfounded. Goderich is gone down to Windsor to resign, and he will find the King, if not unprepared, at least unprovided.

The King, as soon as he had seen Goderich, sent off an express for the Chancellor, who went immediately to Windsor. Goderich's resignation is therefore at last *fait* and *parfait.* His real friends never wished him in the situation of First Minister. We shall now have all the uncertainties and anxieties of last April over again, but there is but one *exit,* viz., the Duke of Wellington and Peel; but the Duke will be reluctant to leave the army, and Peel alone will not be able to re-unite the Tories; and I therefore expect that it will be rather accession on their parts than an entire new frame of Government.

January 9th.—The Chancellor returned from Windsor in the night, and went back at nine this morning, in company with the Duke of Wellington.

The Duke of Wellington came back about six o'clock, and immediately sent an express for Peel, who was at the Wilderness these last two or three days, but is by this time, I suppose, gone back to Maresfield. It seems incredible, but is quite true, as I hear, that the Duke and Peel have been so ill-informed of what has been going on as to be taken quite by surprise.

Mr. Croker to Lord Hertford.

January 10th, 1828.

The Duke, who went down with the Chancellor yesterday morning, returned from Windsor last night, and immediately sent an express for Peel, who came to town this morning, and at ten had an interview with the Duke. What passed can be as yet, of course, known only to the initiated, of whom I am not one; but that Peel was disposed to enter into the negotiation may be inferred from the fact of his having consented to see the Chancellor, after his interview with the Duke; and this fact came to my knowledge by a very ludicrous adventure, which, as an episode in these dry political discussions, may amuse you. An acquaintance of Peel's and mine was invited to be at Maresfield to-day—a man (whom you do not know) of no politics or party, but rather a droll fellow. He went on this visit in his gig, and slept last night at Godstone, halfway to Maresfield, intending to drive on this morning. At breakfast, however, the landlord of the inn told him that Mr. Peel had passed up to town very early in the morning. Upon this intelligence my man thought it most prudent to put about ship and return to town also; but on his return, about noon, he thought it right to call at Peel's house to inquire whether he had done right, or whether he was expected to go back to Maresfield. On knocking at Peel's door, it was opened by a servant, who, it seems, did not know our friend's person. (I suppose all the

old servants are in the country.) To the inquiry of whether
Mr. Peel was at home, the man replied that he was out of
town. "Oh no," said the visitor, "I know he came to town
this morning." This altered the porter's note, who immediately, in a most respectful whisper, asked, "Sir, are you
the Lord Chancellor?" Our waggish friend (meaning no
mischief) answered, "Why—no—not yet—but I hope to be
so soon." "Oh, sir, in that case, my master has desired that
you should be admitted." And admitted he was, to the
great astonishment of the politician, and the great amusement of the friend, who lost no time in calling over here to
tell us of the state secret into which he had so unwittingly
fallen.*

But glad as I am on every account that the Duke of
Wellington and the Chancellor are called upon to advise the
King, I cannot but foresee great difficulty in making a satisfactory arrangement. Who are to be the orators in the
Lords or in the Commons? Peel in the latter, helped by
Herries and Goulburn (supposing even Herries to stay), will
hardly be a match for the vehemence of an exasperated
Opposition in which it is thought that Mr. Canning's own
party will enrol itself; but in the Lords what is to be done
if, as I understand, Lords Grey and Lauderdale are (as
a basis) to be excluded? Who is to stand up in that House
against those Lords and Lansdowne, Holland, &c.?

January 21st, 1828.

The Duke and Peel satisfy all *my* private and public
feelings, but if we lamented that Mr. Canning was driven to
coalesce with Lord Lansdowne, what shall we say of the
introduction of Lord Ellenborough?

Herries *is* at the Mint—reluctant and feeling, I believe,
that he is degraded, but with no alternative between that
and standing quite and utterly alone.

I am afraid that the Duke means to keep the army with
the Treasury. That will not do!

I met Peel and Goulburn yesterday, *mighty cordial.* I have
heard the appointment of Goulburn to an office, for which he
is thought incapable, extolled as a masterstroke of policy in
Huskisson. I cannot suspect Huskisson of such an inten-

---

* [The hero of this incident was Alexander Cockburn.]

tion, but I mention the fact to show you what people think of Goulburn's appointment.

Westmoreland and Eldon have been put into the dirty clothes basket with Wynn and Bexley, and *thrown overboard* —thrown overboard for Lord Ellenborough.

January 24th, 1828.

I have seen the Duke, and this is what passed : a friendly greeting, and then he wished to see me to express his hope that the arrangement he had formed was such as to conciliate my confidence and support. I replied that I had never ceased to wish that his Grace were in the Cabinet, and that knowing, as I did, his opinions on the subject, I presumed that the force of circumstances alone obliged him to be at the head of it * * * He stated how he was beset and plagued with importunities and remonstrances, and compared himself to a dog with a canister tied to his tail. "There," he said, pointing to a formidable heap of green bags and red boxes, "there is the business of the country, which I have not time to look at—all my time being employed in assuaging what gentlemen call their *feelings*. In short, the folly and un-reasonableness of people are inconceivable." He then let out the true secret of his arrangements by saying that—"What Peel said is perfectly true—those who are for forming an exclusive Ministry, expect that I am to go into the House of Commons with *half a party*, to fight *a party and a half.*"

Lord Yarmouth is in town—just come. I saw him yester-day evening with John King when I went into Crockford's to look at his fairy palace, which certainly beats the drop-scene of a pantomime. The lamp in the staircase cost £1200, and so in proportion. The whole house is as splendid as marble, scagliola, gilding, and glasses can make it. I cannot think that it has cost less than £50,000. Who's to pay ?

From the Diary.

January 11*th.*—They have a report that it is intended to place Lord Melville nominally at the head. This would appear to me quite monstrous if I did not recollect my conversation with Peel last year, in which he said he would serve under Melville. The necessity of getting over Hus-kisson, and the difficulties he makes, may have suggested

this mezzotermine, as he has always kept up a friendly intercourse with Melville; but what is to become of Peel's
speeches and pledges about the head of the Government
being Protestant? Besides, the country will not bear a man
of straw; and Melville himself, though not bright, has too
much good sense to undertake it. The difficulties are very
great, but this expedient will not solve them.

One day this last week, talking with the Duke of Clarence
about Mr. Burke's manifesto against the Queen after the
Regency—(the whole history of which the King himself
had told me)—His Royal Highness said that so much
violence was a little inconsistent with Mr. Burke's conduct
in a particular that regarded himself (Duke of Clarence)
about the same time. His Royal Highness was advised to
apply for an increased allowance, and Mr. Burke was selected
to pen the demand. While he was writing the letter in the
Duke's presence, he stopped, and, looking up at His Royal
Highness, said, in his Irish accent and quick manner, " I vow
to God, sir, I wish that instead of writing letters of this kind,
you would go every morning and breakfast with your father
and mother. It is not decent for any family, but above all
the Royal family, to be at variance, as you all unhappily are."

January 20th.—It is reported that the list circulated on
Friday evening, and which was in the *Morning Chronicle*
of Saturday, was communicated by Herries to Maberley.
The new Cabinet is in a fury, and the Duke of Wellington
has required an explanation from Herries. There is some
ground for this complaint. Herries's confidential clerk, it
seems, saw the list, and did communicate it. This is very
unlucky for Herries, as it seems to accredit complaints of the
same kind which some of his late colleagues made against
him. I can say that though I have had a great deal of
confidential conversation with him, he never in the slightest
way gave me any information of a Cabinet nature.

I called on him about this, and to tell him that we had
had the list as early as four on Friday, which was two hours
before Maberley saw his clerk; but I since learn that the
list we saw came also from the said clerk (Shearman).
I regret all this.

I scolded him also for taking the Mint, and told him that
in quitting his finance he had surrendered his Martello-tower.
He agreed in all I said, but he showed me that he must be
what he was or nothing; that he alone could not set up

a Tory Opposition, and that he could not join the Whigs.
All true enough.

I met Peel and Goulburn accidentally at Hyde Park
Corner—the first meeting with Peel on friendly terms since
April—very cordial.

January 28*th.*—Dined with Peel, to hear the Speech.
Thirty-two at dinner in his gallery, which looked very handsome, and thus accomplished one of the purposes for which
I designed it originally. I sat next to Hardinge, and had
a great deal of confidential chat with him. Fitzgerald and
Wilmot, who sat opposite, were very pleasant. Talking of
the *Times* newspaper, and the paragraphs supposed to have
been furnished to it by the late Ministers, and which had
done them so much harm in public opinion, Wilmot, in his
candour, said that he really believed that it was none of
their doing. "At all events," replied Fitzgerald, "it has been
their undoing." I was the only person present in George III.
Windsor uniform, which I always wear on these occasions
—the only occasions on which one could nowadays wear the
fashion of the last reign.

January 29*th.*—Cecil Jenkinson moved the address very
badly. Robert Grant seconded it very well; but nothing
remarkable. Brougham diffuse and weak, but, when compared with those about him, he is a giant. Calcraft said
a few words in his ordinary neutral style; and I could see
that Normanby, Dr. Lushington, and Brougham interchanged
sneers at what he said. He is, as he has so long been, only
waiting an opportunity to leave the Opposition side of the
House. The House was full; all except the rows behind the
Treasury Bench. It is evident that the minds of Members
are not made up, and that a strong floating squadron could be
easily erected, and, indeed, perhaps will not be easily prevented.

February 10*th.*—A curious anecdote, which explains several
particulars in the conduct and feelings of the Hanover family
since their accession. Princess Augusta said lately to a
private friend: "I was ashamed to hear myself called
Princess Augusta, and never could persuade myself that
I was so, as long as any of the Stuart family were alive; but
after the death of Cardinal York, I felt myself to be really
Princess Augusta." Yet, after all, the Modena family has as
good a title to the throne of England as the Stuarts had, and
Princess Augusta's title is no better now than it was while
the Cardinal was alive; indeed, it is rather worse, for the

Modena title is antecedent to James II.'s abdication, and, if they were Protestants, would be consistent with all that was done at the Revolution.

February 22*nd.*—Examined for near three hours before the Finance Committee. Baring and Stanley showed intelligence and good sense. Parnell is a pedant, thinking of nothing but political economics, and of them very confusedly. Hume and Maberley are two blockheads. The latter asked me if the entry books and records of the office could not be copied by a *machine* to save clerks! And all his other questions were of the same force.

Dined with Lord Hertford with Duke of Wellington, Count and Countess Ludolf, Mr. and Mrs. Arbuthnot, Lord and Lady Londonderry, Mr.,* Mrs., and Miss Mitchell, Mrs. George Fox, Lords Lauderdale, Chesterfield, and Shaftesbury, Col. Armstrong, Sir H. Coote, Sirs George Warrender, J. Shelley, and J. Beresford. Vesey Fitzgerald was kept in the House of Commons in attendance on the army estimates. I sat next to Lord Londonderry, and we talked of his forthcoming work on the Peninsular War up to 1813.

February 23*rd.*—The town has it that in consequence of observations made in the House of Commons as to his intrigues (of which Herries is supposed to be the instrument) to effect the dissolution of the late Administration, Sir Wm. Knighton has suddenly gone abroad. He certainly is gone. But he went before these explanations, and he has for the last few years made several similar excursions, all of which (except one when he went to the poor late Mountcharles) were enveloped in mystery. His last and the present journey have been, by those who think they know best, attributed to the state of the Duke of Cumberland's health. But the town chooses to fancy that it is the result of Tom Duncombe's having denounced him in the House of Commons. He was gone before.

February 29*th.*—Renewed debate on Brougham's motion relative to the state of the law. Solicitor-General made a clear but feeble answer, disproving thoroughly, but with little effect, some of Brougham's cardinal cases. Scarlett, jealous that Brougham should run away with all the honour of these amendments, which have been in discussion in West-

---

* [A well-known Russian merchant of the day, living in Charles Street, Berkeley Square. He was famous for going nowhere without his sister.]

minster Hall these some years, sneered at the length and
infinite extent of Brougham's speech. It seems that Lord
Tenterden has had two bills ready drawn for remedying some
of the grievances complained of by Brougham. This the
Solicitor rather *let out* than *stated triumphantly*, as he should
have done. Brougham, as appeared by his grimaces and
gesticulations, was furious with Scarlett; but the latter left
the House, rather shabbily, I think, before Brougham replied,
and Brougham had time to cool. Had he spoken at once,
there would have been hot work.

March 2nd.—The King is obliged to be carried to and from
his carriage; and instead of the open railed gate to the
Garden of St. James's, through which His Majesty has driven
of late years from the Park, they have in the last two days
substituted a close gate to prevent the people's seeing the
operation of moving His Majesty in and out of his carriage.

Vyvyan, who is one of His Majesty's equerries, tells me
that he thinks that this will be his last visit to London. A
bill is to be brought in to enable him to hold a council for
the Recorder's Report out of Middlesex. This may be necessary in compliance with established practice, but in principle
I believe the King's consent to execution is only necessary
when the King happens to be present. The old proverb says,
"the King's face gives grace;" and I believe that when His
Majesty is at Windsor, criminals in London may be executed
without his consent, and in Windsor *not*.

March 4th.—The King came to town at ten o'clock last
night—well, except the weakness in his knees and ankles.

Sir Thomas Thompson, Treasurer of Greenwich Hospital,
died yesterday. He commanded the *Leander* in the battle of
the Nile, but was taken on his way home with the dispatches,.
after an action in which he was so badly wounded in the leg
that he had a pension for the injury. At the battle of Copenhagen this same leg (which gave him a deal of trouble and
pain) was carried clean off, to his great happiness, and he had
another pension for the loss of the leg. He was Comptroller
of the Navy when I came into office. He was a good-natured,
single-hearted fellow, and by no means a bad Comptroller.

Dined at Warrender's with Lord Chancellor and Lady
Lyndhurst, Sir S. and Lady Sheppard, Lords Chandos, Lauderdale, and Dudley, Mr. William Adam, Quintin Dick, William
Courtney, and old Jekyll. The latter was very agreeable,.
and he and Lauderdale gave us many anecdotes of Fox, Burke,.

Hare, and above all Fitzpatrick. Lord Lauderdale told us
he was in Parliament in 1780, before I was born, so that he
must be at least sixty-nine. Jekyll described Burke's conduct
the night of the dagger scene. He had since his quarrel with
Sheridan sat in the place on the floor below the gangway on
the left side, where old Bankes has sat of late years. Jekyll,
coming a little late, saw a place vacant next Burke, and took
it. When Fox spoke, Jekyll cheered violently. Burke told
him that he was nervous, and begged him not to cheer so
loud, as it agitated him. He had bundles of paper, and the
dagger wrapped up in paper beside him, and apologised to
Jekyll for the inconvenience they caused him. When he
threw down the dagger the House laughed, and some asked
where the fork was. It quite failed. Jekyll, of course,
thought so, but Lord Sidmouth told me the contrary. I said
that I had heard from some one, but could not recollect
whom, but it was one who knew Fox, Burke, Sheridan, and
Fitzpatrick intimately, that he thought Fitzpatrick the *first*
of all of them. Jekyll replied : " Well, and I should say so
too, but his delivery in the House of Commons was so
inefficient that he never made any figure there."

March 6th.—Went from the House of Commons to dine
impromptu with Holmes. We were, besides Lady Stronge and
Miss Tew, Colonel Cuffe, Capt. à'Court, Mr. Harrison of
Liverpool, a young officer of the name of Browne, and
Holmes's brother. As we were going to dinner through
Cockspur Street, Holmes caught a pickpocket with his hand
in his pocket. The poor devil had no shirt, and was so
humble and penitent that he let him off. He was a mild-
looking young man, in squalid misery.

March 14th.—House of Commons. Peel and I went up to
dine at Kerr's, but were interrupted by a call for a division
on Penryn Disfranchisement Bill, on which Peel ran down to
speak. He had had a meeting in the morning at the Home
Office of Palmerston, Huskisson, Goulburn, Herries, Fr. Lewis,
Fitzgerald, Planta, Dawson, Wm. Peel, and myself, to consider
how to deal with these bills, and he proposed (as I had
suggested to him by letter in the morning) to postpone
a decision on Penryn Bill till we knew whether we should
have also to dispose of the franchise of Retford, and if we had
both, to satisfy the agricultural and manufacturing classes by
giving two members to the hundred, and two members to one
of the great towns.

Mr. Croker to Mr. Peel.

March 14th, 1828.

Dear Peel,

There is a great feeling *for* and *against* Retford, and there *will* be about Penryn. The High Tories will be exceedingly reluctant to transfer the franchise of the former to any other place; on the other hand, there will be a considerable feeling against throwing the borough into the hands of two or three great landowners. I have always been (as an anti-reformer) inclined to give the representations which might fall in by disfranchisement, to the great towns having populations of 100,000, and I should, individually, be glad to see both Retford and Penryn transferred to Birmingham and Manchester; but I fear that would be thought too *reforming*, though *I* am sure that, in fact, it would tend to stave off reform. If, as they tell me, a case can be made for the hundred in which Retford is situated (from the riches and population of the district, and there being only eight members for the whole county, and no contiguous borough)—if, I say, a case can be made for Retford, why not try a compromise, and give Retford to the hundred, and Penryn to one of the great towns? I know something also may be said for Penryn hundred, as it includes the considerable unrepresented town of Falmouth; but as Cornwall has forty-two members and Notts but eight, and as Falmouth and Penryn are surrounded with boroughs, there does seem to be some difference in the cases; and I therefore think the proposition I have made worth consideration, even on a mere view of the two cases.

But it seems to me to have other and less obvious advantages. If the hundred system is to be maintained in *both* cases, we shall have a great and, I think, not unfounded outcry. The crowd in and out of the House will exclaim that the popular side has no longer any hope of gradual reform, and will renew the cry for radical reform with the more effect; and those who look deeper will say that in order to evade a proper reform, you are in truth making a real innovation on the Constitution, which had apportioned the representation between town and county—between freemen and burgesses on one hand, and freeholders on the other; and you are now, when the manifest evil is that great town population is inadequately represented, about to transfer four members from town election to county or freehold election; on the other hand, if both boroughs be transferred to great towns, the Tories in general will be dissatisfied, and Parliament will be, I think, *concluded* in all future cases by precedent. Having luckily now two boroughs to dispose of, you may, if not satisfy, at least conciliate both parties, and, which is still more important, you will keep open the future power of Parliament to adopt one or the other course on a view of the individual circumstances of each respective case.

It does not seem to me of any great importance, but I may as well mention that Manchester did once send members to Parliament.

Yours ever,

J. W. CROKER.

From the Diary.

March 16*th.*—Lord Hertford left town this morning to spend a few days at Brighton. I called on Sir Thomas Lawrence to look at his picture of the Duke of Clarence, and the others he is finishing for the exhibition.

I also called on Mr. Briggs about the picture he is painting for the Institution, of the King visiting the fleet after the 1st June.

I also called on Mr. Wood, a young painter whom Sir T. Lawrence has recommended to me, to make some copies I wanted. I find he has taken to portraits, and paints them miserably.

I ended my tour of painters by a visit to Mr. Shee, where I saw an old picture of Chief Baron Lord Yelverton—I think the best I ever saw of Mr. Shee's. It is left on his hands.

Dined at Lord Camden's with Lords Sidmouth, Colchester, Elliot, and Brecknock, Sir Geo. Cockburn, Sir Edward Owen, Sir Rowland Hill, Sir H. Hardinge, Sir Ed. Knatchbull, Sir George Clerk, Mr. Duncombe of Yorkshire, and Mr. Barrow. A very good dinner—like the house, a little old-fashioned, but of a stately old fashion.

March 17*th.*—I attended the funeral of my old friend Mr. Bicknell. I observe that there are three degrees of mourning on these occasions—cloaks, with crape hat-bands ; crape scarves and hat-bands ; and *silk* scarves and hat-bands. His remains were neither buried nor interred, but deposited in the vaults of St. Martin's. The coffins are placed in irregular piles on the floor of the vaults, five or six over each other. The greater part of the service was read in the Church (as it was at Kensington the other day), after which we descended into the vault. When the minister came to "dust to dust," one of the undertaker's men stepped up on the lower coffin of the pile, to enable him to throw a handful of dust on poor Bicknell's. This looked very irreverent, and the sight of these piles of mouldering coffins excited most disagreeable ideas. Some of them were falling to pieces, and I almost dreaded to see them burst open and lay bare the awful secrets of our dissolution.

March 18th.—Dispatches by express from Portugal. Dom Miguel is about to make himself absolute King. The Constitutionalists and the English are in danger, as they think, and Sir Fred. Lamb, the ambassador, has stopped the final return of our ships and troops. I saw the Duke of Wellington upon this subject. Prince Lieven was with him when I went in. When Lieven was gone he told me that the Greek and Turkish questions were in a sad mess. Russia persists in her design, and the Duke does not see his way out of it. He laid the blame on the treaty of London. I could not help hinting at the Protocol. As to Portugal, he disapproved of Lamb stopping the troops, and he wishes we were out of that scrape too.

In the House of Commons Peel has given up the Test and Corporation Acts for a declaration, which means nothing, and which will never be taken by any one. This is another step to Catholic Emancipation. The Duke of Clarence asked me about the Duke of Wellington's opinion on the Catholic question. I said that I supposed, and indeed believed, his Grace was convinced that something must be done. His Royal Highness said that he *knew* that the Duke was making inquiries on the subject from some of the Foreign Ministers, and His Royal Highness further observed on the inconsistency of the King's refusing in Ireland what he granted in Hanover. I said the cases were not quite the same. The King held Hanover by hereditary right, but England only by the Protestant Settlement.

The Duke of Clarence frequently harps upon a notion that Prussia is to take the first opportunity of seizing Hanover, and he does not seem so much adverse to it as might be supposed. He has never liked Hanover, perhaps because his education was exclusively English, but I think that I see the jealousy of the sons of his two brothers of

Cumberland and Cambridge, who are the heirs presumptive of Hanover. He, like Macbeth, repines at the barren sceptre to which no son of his is to succeed.

March 19th.—We have been in a bustle all day with the Greek and Portuguese questions. *The King,* that is Huskisson, has directed that Codrington shall receive orders direct from the Secretary of State. There are many precedents, even as late as the last Copenhagen expedition; and if it had been done in July last, no one could have objected, but doing it now does look like disapprobation of the conduct of the Lord High Admiral, and he so feels it. Orders are gone that the army should evacuate Lisbon; but a line-of-battle ship, a couple of frigates, and the Marines to garrison Fort St. Julien, remain a little longer. Two or three sloops go to Oporto. I was to-day *ten* hours at my desk without intermission, except to see people on the business I was engaged in.

March 21st.—Saw Peel about the dispute between our and the French fishermen at Jersey, and besought him not to allow this *pimple* to be scratched into a *sore.* Talked of East Retford. He complained that the Tories and country gentlemen cared about nothing but the Corn question; that they complained if Ministers yielded, complained more if Ministers were in a minority, but would not take the trouble of attending to put them into a majority. He showed me a fine picture of a lion devouring a wild boar, which he has lately got from Spain. It is very good of its kind, but I don't like the kind.

March 23rd.—Had a long conversation with Herries about the Greenwich pensions. He wishes me to state to the Finance Committee what I have stated to him.

Dined at the Lord Chancellor and Lady Lyndhurst's with Lord and Lady Morley, Mr. and Mrs. Sidney, Lord Dudley, Sir F. Burdett, Mr. Luttrell, Jekyll, R. Ward, Wrangham, Wm. Russell, and the Knight of Kerry. A very agreeable day. Talked of the arts and the stage, but of course no politics. From the heat of the room, which is a small one, with only light from the ceiling, Rob Ward was obliged to retire before the ladies; but after a walk round Hanover Square he came back again; but when we got up to go to the ladies, Mr. Wm. Russell fainted twice. The first time he fell and cut his head; when he fainted again, I held him. I afterwards took him to his doctor's, and afterwards home to

Lincoln's Inn, in my carriage. I was unwilling to let him go alone, as I was afraid that he might have fainted a third time.

March 26th.—Cecil Jenkinson gives me a melancholy account of both Lord and Lady Liverpool. He is rather worse than better, less intelligible, and more irritable. He is sensible, and his great annoyance is the not being able to make himself understood. He has had of late a kind of monthly relapse, in one of which he will probably go off. Lady Liverpool has, from her anxiety and attendance, been dangerously ill.

March 29th.—Mrs. Croker and Nony left Kensington for Windsor at half-past twelve to-day, in our carriage. I followed them at three, in one of Hutton's coaches, and I arrived about an hour after them; and at a quarter-past six we put up at the Castle Inn, which is worse than ever. They went by Datchett; I came by Englefield Green. Before I left town I attended a meeting of the subscribers to Mr. Canning's monument. About fifty met. Agreed to the two statues—one colossal in bronze, one in marble for the Abbey. Stapleton was ready to show fight for Chantrey. Several persons, and particularly Lord Harrowby and Spring Rice, begged me to use my influence with Chantrey to make him take the marble statue. I will try.

March 30th.—We attended divine service at St. George's Chapel at eleven. Any well-dressed persons obtain seats in the stalls. I suppose they all pay something. I gave the sexton half-a-crown. Servants and inferior persons seemed to sit in the lower seats and benches on the floor, without any special leave. More of the service chanted than is usual in cathedrals. Most of the prayers and the Nicene Creed. It was all very well done, but very long—about two and a half hours. Dr. Clarke and Mr. Proby the canons present. The latter preached tolerably—a sermon appropriate to the season.

We afterwards called on Mr. Wyattville, and walked over the new works of the Castle with him. They are in many respects handsome, and not inconvenient, but the repairs, &c., have already cost £500,000, and I confess I do not see more than I should have thought one-fifth of the sum might have produced. It is true that all the external work has been done so exactly in the old style, and with stone and mortar so stained to assimilate, that there is no great show of new work. After all, the rooms are by no means what they ought to be; they are very handsome, and even noble, but they are neither in number and size what might have been produced for much less expense. They are, moreover (except the corridor and dining-room), in the style of Louis XIV., which does not accord with the general character of Windsor. The King's stairs too rich and massive for its size. The dimensions are almost mean, and the labour of workmanship extravagant. Mr. Wyattville told me that it would cost £700,000 more. He has committed some gross faults, such as machicolations over inclined bases and over inferior buildings, and the sameness and meanness of the masonry has a bad effect on so large a front.

March 31*st.*—Grant opened the Corn resolutions in the Commons in a very apologetical speech, in which his principal object was to justify his resolutions by a supposition that Mr. Canning, if he had lived, would have consented to such a modification, and he concluded with a studied panegyric and tribute to his memory, which was not well taken by the ultra-Tories, though cheered by the rest of the House. The country gentlemen seem but half pleased, although they have got the good price of 64*s.*, which they proposed last year, and were beaten.

April 12*th.*—Nony and I dined with Mr. and Mrs. Lockhart in Sussex Place, to meet Walter Scott. We had besides Miss Scott and Lady Davy, Mr. Henry Ellis and Mr. Charles Scott. In the evening some ladies came whom we did not know. After dinner one of the pipers of the 72nd Regiment (which is to embark on Monday for the Cape), who had been Sir Walter's piper, came to take leave of him—a fine fellow (of the name of Bruce), in full uniform, who played his pipes walking up and down the room. They are sad discordant things, and I believe every one, even the Scotch themselves, was glad when he had done.

April 21*st.*—Dined with us at Kensington, Sir Walter Scott and Mr. Lockhart, the Knight of Kerry, Sir H. Hardinge, Mr. Hook, Mr. Locker, Mr. Chantrey. A very agreeable day. Hardinge told us the circumstances of Sir J. Moore's wound and death. He was speaking to him when he was shot. Moore's countenance assumed a great severity, and it was evident he made a great effort over himself to avoid showing the anguish he felt. He also told us of the Duke of Wellington's visit to Blucher's army just at the beginning of the battle of Fleurus,* and the Duke's foreseeing, from the errors of the Prussian disposition, that they were sure to be beaten. The day month on which his [Hardinge's] arm was amputated in a wood in Flanders he was sleeping in Marie Louise's state bed at St. Cloud. Blucher had selected and insisted on his using this apartment.

Sir Walter said he hoped never to hear a friend of his tell a ghost story, as the only two persons on whom he could rely, and who had told him such stories, had put an end to themselves. One was Lord Londonderry, and his story was that of the " radiant boy."

April 23rd.—The King's drawing-room. Mrs. Peel was to have presented Nony, but she is ill, and Lady Anne Beckett presented her. The King recognised her, and spoke affectionately to her, and told me as I passed by afterwards that he had had a great curiosity to see his " little friend" after so long an interval.

The Duke of Cumberland was there, and his son Prince George. This little pickle is about nine, and was dressed in the uniform of the 10th Hussars. He looks intelligent, and they tell me is so. He was surprised into screams of laughter at the Judges' wigs, nothing like what he had ever before seen. He has a slight cast in his eye, and has a strong resemblance to his grandfather the late King. He is what every one would call a fine boy.

A great crowd at the Drawing Room, and the absence of hoops brings the ladies into such close contact that some of them quarrelled, and were near pulling one another's feathers.

Dined at Charles Grant's with the House of Lords. There were Lords Cassilis, Wicklow, Grantham, Sydney, Goderich, Farnborough, Malmesbury, Stanhope, Clare, and Falmouth. The only Commoners were the host, Vesey Fitzgerald, Robt. Clive, and I.

Fitzgerald told us that when one of Plunkett's friends was lamenting how little he had got, Burke said : " Come, come ; he has not had all he deserved, but he has done *pretty well for a failure.*"

April 27th.—Dined with me at the Admiralty, the Duke of Wellington, Lord Aberdeen, Lord Dudley, Lord Lowther, Huskisson, Wilmot-Horton, Vesey Fitzgerald, Sir George Warrender, Jekyll, Walter Scott, and Holmes. Scott was not

* [Better known as the Battle of Ligny.]

in force, but the Duke was, and very frank and amusing. He said all troops ran away—*that* he never minded; all he cared about was whether they would come back again, and he added that he always had a succession of lines for the purpose of rallying fugitives.

April 30*th.*—Dined at Lord Hertford's with Lord and Lady Salisbury, Lord and Lady Tankerville, Sir J. and Lady Anne Beckett, Mr. and Mrs. Agar Ellis, Mr. and Mrs. Parnther,* and Countess St. Antonio, Lords Clare and Glengall, Sir G. Warrender, Messrs. Rogers and Luttrell, Poodle Byng, and Col. Walpole. Went in the evening to Warrender's, to a concert. The great curiosity of the day is Mademoiselle Sontag. How she got famed for *beauty* I cannot guess. She is short, stumpy, with a very common set of features, and a rather vulgar expression. The face is, like most others, a little better when she smiles; but Clanwilliam must have been already mad before he could fall in love with this face or figure.

May 2*nd.*—Test and Corporation Repeal Bill passed, our House agreeing to the Lords' amendments. I said a few words against the Bill, as likely inconveniently to affect the members of the Church of England.†

May 3*rd.*—Dined with the Royal Academy. Sat between

* [Then of Grafton Street.' The Parnthers were great friends of the Duke of Wellington.]

† [Mr. Croker said he regretted that the Bill was not returned to them in the same state in which it was sent up to the Lords. He did not think that those who made the present alterations saw the results to which they were likely to lead. He felt confident that the consequence of them would be to render an annual Act of Indemnity still necessary, though the great object proposed by the measure was to get rid of that necessity. It would have been better if this declaration had been allowed to be taken at the same time and in the same places as the other oaths and declarations required from persons admitted to office. Six months were allowed by this Bill, whereas the other oaths, connected with the holding of office, were to be taken within three months. Why might not the declaration be made in His Majesty's Courts of Exchequer or Common Pleas? When the measure came into operation he had no doubt it would be found impossible to stand by the provisions of it, and that Indemnity Acts would be still necessary. So much confusion would arise from the present provisions of the Act that no declaration at all would be taken, and an Act of Indemnity would be the very first measure it would be necessary to propose next session.]

Mr. Rogers and Sir A. Hume on one side, and Lords Farn-borough and Cawdor on the other. Opposite were Herries, Walter Scott, Davies Gilbert, and the Speaker. We had a good deal of talk and laugh in our circle. Lawrence made a speech in praise of Turner and Danby. He and Scott made a neat short speech on the toast of the latter's health. Prince Leopold spoke, or rather croaked, out some broken English, the chief point of which was that in a hundred years the English school of to-day would rival the Dutch School of a hundred years ago. Aberdeen, honestly enough, mentioned nothing but Lawrence's own works as worthy of notice. It is a very poor Exhibition. After the dinner was on the table, we waited a good half hour for the Dukes of Clarence and Sussex, who did not come, and never intended to come.

May 4th.—The Duke of Clarence treated me with his usual dish of Catholic question politics. His chief subject of anxiety now is about Sir J. Newport's notice of a motion for repealing the Acts forbidding intercourse with the See of Rome. I got tired to death of his confidences and questions. I wish I could get back to distance and mere civility.

May 6th.—Dined at Lord Hertford's with the Duke of Cumberland, Prince and Princess Esterhazy, Dowager Lady Salisbury, Lord and Lady Lonsdale, Lady A. Beckett, the Duke of Wellington, Lord Beresford, Lord Eldon, Baron Bulow, Sir H. Cooke, M. de Neumann, and Capt. and Mrs. George Seymour. The Duke of Cumberland was very gracious and tiresome, and kept us sitting till eleven o'clock, so that the *operatists* (of whom he was one) got there very late. Esterhazy told, and Neumann confirmed, an account of the Prince's (Esterhazy's) having magnetised by the mere motion of his hands a German lady, who immediately fell asleep, and did not wake for twenty-four hours, and was only recovered by slow degrees and medical means from this nervous stupor. It happened at a villa the Esterhazys had near town.

May 9th.—Catholic question—adjourned debate. Young Villiers Stuart was fluent, and showed some talent. Brownlow had a few brilliant and many absurd passages, and occa-sionally talked almost insanely. Mackintosh was long and laborious, and puzzled himself and tired us with references to papers. Peel made a good argument on the treaty of Limerick, but really one might as well, at this time of day talk of Noah's flood as of the treaty of Limerick. Lord William Paget said a few words to explain his conversion, which were very well conceived, and delivered with modesty and taste. Lamb made a short and fine burst for conciliation and harmony; after which the House would hear no more, and Lord Sandon moved an adjournment, on which every one got up and walked away.

Saturday 10*th.*—Dined with the Drapers' Company in their fine hall. The building I should guess to be of the days of Anne or George I. The ceiling and other ornaments of the hall are, I think, by Sir W. Chambers, or out of his school. They do not assort very well with the original design of the room. The ceiling, the twelve signs, and then a kind of architectural circumflex, including under each of the four seasons its three proper signs. A very good dinner, and very tolerably served, except that the tin covers marked with the name of the adjoining tavern were not equal to the rest. Dreadful tedious toasts and speeches ensued, even down to me, and the poor University of Dublin was hooked in to afford an excuse for the latter.

May 15*th.*—Our melancholy anniversary. I stayed at home. Mrs. Croker paid her sad visit to Wimbledon.

The King had a childs' ball, to which Nony, *having been presented as out*, was not asked—nor, indeed, if she had been, could we have gone this day.

May 16*th.*—Navy Estimates. A long and tiresome Committee squabble. The Finance Committee attacked by Calcraft and Knight of Kerry, but more damaged by themselves. We see now the folly, as we before saw the cowardice, of putting Hume and Maberley on this Committee. They are more troublesome than ever, because being placed on the Committee has redeemed their characters, and increased their information. I whispered this to Peel, whose act it was, and he was very little pleased with the remark. "Il n'y a que la vérité qui blesse." But it is the turn of his mind to endeavour to get over adversaries by concession. He always gives more importance, and weight even, to a public enemy than to his own supporters.

May 18*th.*—Dined with us Mrs. T. Chaplin, Capt. and Mrs. Fleetwood Pellew, Col. Shawe, Sir Thomas Hardy, Mr. Hook, Col. Ellison, Mr. Lambert of Galway. A very agreeable dinner. Both Mrs. Chaplin and Mrs. Pellew are gay and clever in conversation. Col. Ellison has great good sense, a very good tone, and a neat expression. Hook is always excellent, and though he did not shine *peculiarly* this evening, we had a very pleasant day, except that we discussed Nash and his architectural monstrosities a little too much.

May 19*th.*—The rest of the Navy Estimates voted with little trouble. I went home, expecting nothing important on the East Retford bill, on which I was resolved not to vote, altogether disapproving of it. But in a division on it, Huskisson and Palmerston (Charles Grant absent) divided with the Opposition against Peel and the rest of the Government. This created a great sensation. In the debate Peel, they tell me, had the worst of it, from young Stanley particularly; and he certainly was inconsistent in some degree, but Huskisson ought to have avoided an open abandonment of the leader.

May 20*th.*—Huskisson has sent in his resignation. This is known only to a most select few, but the general state of the case is notorious enough, and creates great sensation. I know the Duke took his letter to the King in order to have His Majesty's authority to end the negotiation as he might think best, before he entered into it. This His Majesty granted. Palmerston did not send in his resignation, but he is in the same boat. They both came late into the House, and it was reported that they had both been dismissed, but nothing has been settled. I hope and believe that matters will be arranged, for there really are excuses both for Peel and Huskisson.

May 27*th.*—Wrote to the Duke of Wellington. Had a great deal of conversation with Hardinge. He had seen the Duke, and told him that he understood from me that I was willing to make way for Wilmot-Horton, if that would facilitate his arrangements, as Wilmot cannot, they say, vacate. He added that he had mentioned that he (Hardinge) thought that I would accept Ireland, and that he thought me very fit for it. I said I ratified both his suggestions. We had a great deal of very confidential conversation on all men and all places. I think less favourably of the Duke's position than he appears to do. I told Hardinge the motives that now would induce me to accept the Secretaryship in Ireland, which I would not formerly have done.

Lord Hertford advised me to ask the Duke for Ireland, but I would rather not move.

May 28*th.*—I wrote to Hardinge that, as we heard that

Dudley, Grant, and F. Leveson were gone, I thought the political weather looked very bad; but on that very account, I was the more ready, if the Duke of Wellington wished it, to go on with his Grace for better or worse. The Duke was my first, and is my natural, if not only, *political* connection; and as Lord Hertford will adhere to the Duke, this will place all my public and private feelings in unison. But I have repeated, what I said before, that I would not change my office. I regret Huskisson's resignation. I think he was somewhat hardly dealt with; and even if I wished for a change of office (which I do not), I should be sorry to obtain it in consequence of his removal.

May 29th.—Left town for Ireland in the coach called the Wonder. We left the turnpike at Islington at six precisely, and, breakfasting at Market Street, and dining at Birmingham, reached Shrewsbury at twenty minutes past eleven. Slept at the Lyon Inn.

June 1st, Dublin.—Attended service and received the holy sacrament in the College. The anthem from Handel's 'Messiah.' I did not like it. A sermon from Dr. Singer on the Trinity. I did not much like it either. He said the mystery of the Trinity, like many operations of nature, was inexplicable, though in a *different degree.* Is not this a bull?

Drove to the Phœnix Park to call on the Lord Lieutenant. He was not returned from Church, so I went on and saw Gregory, and told him my London news, viz. that Wilmot and Calcraft have declined office, that F. Lewis * and Francis Leveson had resigned, and that Courtenay and Twiss had been brought forward. Gregory was delighted to have escaped Lewis as Secretary here.

Lord Anglesey was very glad to see me, and entered into the whole of the political game with me. He had on his table open a letter he had just received from the Duke of Wellington, with copies of the correspondence. He read me the Duke's letter, which said little more than that he sent them for his Lordship's *private* information, and that he did not expect in return any observations on them. Lord Anglesey had not read the correspondence, but he was quite aware of their contents, and he thought that there had been too much haste on both sides. He told me that Huskisson, Lamb, Sir Geo. Murray, and the Duke had all written to him, and then he went fully and most confidentially into

* [Rt. Hon. T. Frankland Lewis, Vice-President of the Board of Trade, father of Sir G. C. Lewis.]

all the circumstances of his own position and views, and he read me copies of his letters to the Duke, to Lamb, and to Lord Holland, in which latter he seems to put the highest confidence—so high, indeed, as to leave him the arbiter of whether he is to stay in office or not. The sum of his various statements is this, that he is happy here, and not only well with both parties, but in their confidence; that the Catholics had agreed, out of deference to him, to moderate the Associationists, and to stop the simultaneous meetings; and on the other side Sir H. Lees had given up, from the same motive, his Orange meetings in the North.

June 4th.—They say there are no nightingales in Ireland, but a bird with a note very like a nightingale (I suppose a thrush) woke me at half-past one in the morning, and sang till daybreak. No nightingale could have been more untimely. Mr. Fitzpatrick came down to Howth with me, where we breakfasted with Sir Harcourt and Lady Lees. I started on board the *Harlequin*, Capt. Davies, at half-past eight, and landed at Holyhead in six hours and six minutes. The wind and tide were favourable, but the water was not smooth, and the vessel rolled a good deal. I dined with Capt. Davies, and left Holyhead about twelve o'clock. I had waited there to get back my Monday's letters, which had gone to Dublin by the morning's mail, and which now came back to me by the afternoon mail, which arrived by half-past ten. Travelled in the mail coach.

June 7th.—As I was coming out of Huskisson's, I met a messenger from the Duke of Wellington desiring to see me. I went across, and met Lord Beresford in the anteroom, who says that he thinks Dom Miguel will be beaten in Portugal. When I went in to the Duke he told me that Lord Anglesey had written to him to the same effect as his note to me, occasioned by the rumours which had reached Dublin of my appointment. His Grace said civil things of me, but added that he was afraid my appointment would not do. He was proceeding to give me reasons, but I stopped him, saying that his opinion was enough, and that I was satisfied he was right; but then I said I must ask him as a private friend, if he would allow me to call him so, and a man of honour, whether he thought I could remain at the Admiralty. He looked startled. He said that he looked on the Admiralty to be, after Ireland, the most important place out of the Cabinet, much superior to the Privy Councillor's office, which had little or no official duties. He added that

the income also was so much better. I agreed also to that,
and said that I was aware of, and concurred in, all he said, but
that public opinion must be the guide, as it was the best
reward of public men, and that Privy Councillor's office being
considered the post of honour, I could not, with a due regard
to my honour, acquiesce in my official inferiors and juniors
being thus put over my head, without affording me the
option ; that I knew that by any change I must lose income
and official importance, and would certainly have a reluctance
about any change, but that I would lose both rather than lose
character, if I submitted to the slight of not having been
even thought about. We talked it over long without arriving
at any conclusion, except that he begged of me not to resign
hastily, and to wait at all events a few days.

The Duke entered fully into Huskisson's affair. He said
that he had no doubt that he meant seriously to resign, until
Dudley's visit next day induced him to wish to recall it : that
he had been goaded by Planta and others, as he went home
the night of the division, and had made what he considered
a complete resignation. The Duke was quite ready to permit
him to withdraw the letter, but would not invite him to
remain. " In short, I told Dudley and Palmerston that I had
no objection, nay, I wished, that they and Huskisson could
get out of the scrape, but that I begged on my own part to
decline taking a *roll in the mud* with them. This was not
a very elegant expression, but it was a sincere one."

The Duke of Clarence is again, or rather still, confident
that there is to be a war. He told me to-day that Mme. de
Lieven had said to the King the other day : " Sire, vous voulez
la guerre ; eh bien, vous aurez votre contentement." I do
not believe it, but it is certain that she said a much more
offensive thing to the Duke of Cumberland the other day.
She was talking with His Royal Highness of our domestic
politics, and of the Catholic question, and supposing that
there should be a majority in the House of Commons against
the Ministers ; and replied the Duke, " Nous les renverrons."
" Eh puis ? " said Madame de Lieven, " si la majorité vous
soit encore contraire." " Nous les renverrons encore." " Eh
puis ? " asked the lady, in her gentle, respectful way. " Nous
les renverrons encore !" " Eh puis ? " " Nous les renverrons
encore !" " Eh puis ? " This went on till the Duke saw the
absurdity of his position, and stopped, after uttering his last
" Nous les renverrons encore," with a certain tone of com-

mand; on which Madame Lieven, sinking her voice to the lowest possible tone of gentleness and humility, whispered, as a finale, "Eh puis—l'Hanovre!!!" She, I hear, endeavoured to give this *mot* all possible misinterpretations; but it is too clear and clever to be misunderstood, and I suppose it has given rise to the report that the Lievens are about to be recalled.

June 9th.—They say that Madame de Lieven did really say something to the King about the change of his Ministry, and that His Majesty answered her that if his ambassador at St. Petersburg should presume to criticise the conduct of the Emperor in the interior affairs of his empire, His Majesty would instantly recall him.

Peel tells me that the Duke of Wellington has seen the Duke of Clarence, who makes no kind of difficulty about my being sworn of the Privy Council, and the Duke of Wellington went to St. James's to propose it and the other arrangements to the King, and that there should be a Council on Monday.

June 15.—Received a letter from the Duke of Wellington explaining his reasons for not having offered me other office, but proposing that I should be of the Privy Council.

June 16.—Kissed His Majesty's hand, and then shook hands with each Privy Councillor at the table.

June 17th.—The Duke of Clarence's answer to mine, very civil and congratulatory, reached me by post, and was the first letter I received by my new title.

Courtenay made a miserable figure in the House of Commons on General Gascoigne's motion about the decrease of seamen and shipping. He said that his mind, as well as Mr. Fitzgerald's, was on that great subject a "sheet of blank paper." He meant to say *unprejudiced,* but folks laughed at an expression which was in the injurious sense fully borne out by his speech.

Mr. Croker to Mr. Doyle, Dublin.

June 16th, 1828.

My dear Doyle,

You will be pleased to hear that I have been this morning sworn of the Privy Council. This mark of his Majesty's favour and of the confidence of his Government has been given to me rather than remove me to one of the usual Privy Councillor's offices, all of which are in *income* and official *importance* inferior to that which I hold, and which now, by this additional rank, is all that I could possibly desire. I should feel real gratification if my dear father had lived to see me in a situation which he would have considered so exalted; but alas! the circle of those who are personally interested in me is sadly narrowed. It is some satisfaction, however, to me that you, the oldest and one of the dearest of the friends of my father and myself, still survive to enjoy whatever gratification this increase of honour can give us.

Believe me to be, my dear old friend, with great sincerity, most affectionately yours,

J. W. C.

From the Diary.

June 24th.—I went with Mrs. Croker and Nony to look at a cottage and farm at West Molesey which Mr. Jesse recommends me to take—a pretty place, but much neglected and dilapidated. He thinks I can have the cottage and fifteen acres of land for £50 or £60 a year. If so, I think we shall take it, though it is rather farther than I should have wished, viz., fifteen miles.

June 25th.—Dined at Lord Farnborough's with Sir Geo. Cockburn, P. Courtenay, S. Perceval, Sir Robt. Inglis, Sir W. Gordon, Col. Trench, Col. Wood, Mr. Twiss, Mr. Robt. Ward. Dull enough. Perceval and Ward * were preaching craniology, and Ward gave instances of Deville's guessing from his *bumps* details of his character without knowing who he was, so absurd as that he was *religious* but *not* a Methodist. These nice moral distinctions are, I think, quite beyond the powers of expression by bumps. Perceval, who is an enthusiast, took my head in hand, and found that I was a lover of ghost stories—the only stories, if I know myself, which I do *not* care about!

June 27th.—We had a long and useless debate about East Retford. As the bill cannot by possibility pass this year, I do not see why we need have fought the postponement as we did. All the reason I could gather from the Cabinet

---

* [Plumer Ward, as before explained—author of 'Tremaine,' and other works.]

Ministers was that they did so for the sake of impression—but impression may be good or bad. I regret the whole thing.

The accounts from Ireland that O'Connell means to stand for Clare make a great sensation.

The Duke of Clarence, in allusion to an unreasonable request made to him by Lord Wellesley, told me a story which I had not heard before, of old Provost Hutchinson. When Lord Townshend was Lord Lieutenant of Ireland, he one hot day asked for a cool tankard, and when he had drank, and the cup was placed on a side table, the aide-de-camp in waiting came in to announce that the Provost was in the anteroom, and requested an audience. "Ah," said Lord Townshend, "he is coming to ask something which I dare say I can't give him, so take away the tankard, for if he can get nothing else, he will ask for *that*, which I could not decently refuse." This is almost as good as the Isle of Man for a cabbage garden.

June 28th.—We hear a curious story, almost like a scene in a novel. Lady Londonderry gives a fancy ball on the most extravagant scale, both of design and expense, on Monday; but they are so distressed, notwithstanding the union of their immense fortunes, that their horses and carriages were taken in execution *yesterday*, and it is thought that executions are actually in the house, and that the splendid gala of Monday will be held under the special (but modestly concealed) patronage of the Sheriff's officers. This surprises me. I thought Londonderry was very rich. He has nominally £60,000 a year; but as he is strictly tied up, it is possible that having spent, as they say, £200,000 on Wynyard, and £100,000 on the house in town, besides several other follies, he may be in want of ready money, but hardly, I should have thought, to such an extremity as is reported.

July 1st.—I hear that Lady Londonderry's fête last night was splendid, but dull. The first *coup d'œil* was very gay, and as long as it looked like a pageant it was well enough. When, however, the Leicesters and the Burleighs began to move about, the velvets and embroidery made but poor amends for the want of ease and vivacity. We heard of a lady of quality who asked to be allowed, as one of the characters of Queen Elizabeth's Court, to appear as Lady (Rachel) Russell.

July 9th.—Fitzgerald writes to me that the Sheriff has made a special return, viz., that O'Connell had most votes, but that he had declared himself to be a Roman Catholic.

July 11th.—The Duke of Wellington sent for me to read me a letter to the King * which he had drafted, and on the facts of which he wished my opinion. He talked of Irish affairs, and said that though of a sanguine temper, and not used to despair, he confessed that he was at last puzzled what to do or what to think. He lays great stress on the power of the Roman Catholic clergy, and says it is the same everywhere—in France, in Spain, in Portugal. The case of O'Connell is, he says, the least part of his difficulty. It is bad enough, but the state of things which it proves is the real anxiety.

The Duke sent to me again in the evening to read me the final letter to the King, in which he had made use of the suggestions and facts I had furnished him with. It is wonderful with what facility and accuracy he scanned all those facts, and with what clearness and force he embodied them in his letter.

July 12th.—The Duke of Wellington sent for Cockburn † and me, to read to him his Grace's letter to the King of yesterday, and to both of us the King's answer. The King answered *on the moment,* quite agreeing with the Duke of Wellington, and saying that an extinguisher must immediately be put on the Duke of Clarence's attempts at rendering himself independent of all authority.‡ He read to us also a draft of his letter to the Duke of Clarence on the subject in which I ventured to suggest that he should be a little more explicit on His Royal Highness's assumption of a military command. I had hardly got back when Peel sent to beg to see me. It was on O'Connell's case. He seems not to see his way, and is unwilling to commit the House with

* [This letter is printed in the 'Wellington Despatches,' New Series, vol. iv. p. 514.]

† [Admiral Sir G. Cockburn, Lord of the Admiralty.]

‡ [Mr. Croker had strongly resented the undue interference of the Duke of Clarence in his department. "I have heard my father say," writes one of Mr. Croker's relations, "that the Duke of Wellington came out to Kensington Palace at this time, and that he and Mr. Croker walked up and down the broad walk for a couple of hours in earnest conversation, when it was decided that the Duke of Wellington or the Duke of Clarence must resign." Mr. Croker's conduct all through this affair suffices to prove that he was no time-serving politician.]

O'Connell, and on the whole would wish to postpone the question to next Session. I said that if the law officers were clear as to the state of the law, I thought that the *return*, by stating O'Connell to have declared himself a Roman Catholic, obliged the House of Commons to vindicate the law ; that I thought a *timid* or temporising course would create great dissatisfaction and future difficulty ; and that his own personal character would suffer by it ; and that I did not see what was to be got by postponement, as the case would be just as embarrassing at the opening of the next Session as at the close of this. While we were but entering on the subject, the Duke of Wellington sent for both of us. It was to read to me the alteration which, in consequence of my suggestion, he had made in his letter to His Royal Highness, which perfectly agreed with what I had said. There were present at this conversation Lord Bathurst, Peel, and Goulburn.

July 13th.—I called on Peel by appointment at ten, and we resumed our conversation on O'Connell's case. We were each of the same opinion as yesterday, but both agreed that Fitzgerald's report and opinion as to the state of feeling in Ireland would have great effect in swaying our judgment on the question. Peel seemed to me to wince at my expression of a *timid* and temporising policy, which I could not help repeating to him.

July 23rd.—Dined at Sir H. Hardinge's, where, besides Lady Emily, we had Lords Brecknock, Lowther, and Downe, Sirs H. Taylor, Robt. Farquhar, Messrs. Calcraft, Planta, Holmes, Col. Cradock. Talking of beautiful women, I told the anecdote that I had separately asked the King and Sir Thomas Lawrence, who they thought the most beautiful woman they had ever seen, and before I gave their answer I asked the present company to guess whom they had named. Sir Herbert Taylor and Holmes both agreed in saying Lady Charlotte Campbell ; and it was Lady Charlotte that both His Majesty and Sir Thomas had selected. I have never met any one, except the Duke of York, who had known her in their youth, who did not represent her as the most beautiful creature they had ever seen.

July 24th.—Dispatched orders to the senior officers in the Tagus and Douro to return five days after the receipt of my letter with all the ships to England. This gives me great pleasure. I think the whole of our policy as to Portugal has been wrong for ourselves, wrong for the Portuguese, and wrong with reference to the laws of nations.

Mr. Croker to the Duke of Wellington.

August 14th, 1828.

MY DEAR DUKE,

The Duke of Clarence came to the Council to-day, and did the usual business; after that was over, he made us a speech, under the influence of a good deal of ill-suppressed agitation, stating that he had resigned; and only carried on the business till another arrangement could be made. He said that he looked upon himself as a military officer—that if he were a civil officer like a First Lord of the Admiralty, he would have many observations to make on the cause of his resignation, but that, in his military character, he could only say that he had resigned and would give no reason for it.

This speech was very confused, and we did not, and do not, very well see what H.R.H. meant by his civil and military distinction. I believe his idea was *to assert his right to hoist the military flag,* and so maintain his point; and at the same time to hint that his silence as to the cause of his retirement was the consequence of his military obedience to the King.

H.R.H. spoke with an eager look and an impassioned voice, and it was doubtful whether anger or a feeling of regret was prominent in his mind.

He afterwards sent for me into his room, and there said, he wished to say to my face what he had often said behind my back, that he was unexceptionably pleased with my conduct, &c., &c. He mixed his praise of me with violent complaints against *others,* and pointed clearly at Sir George Cockburn, and when I was about to express my regret at what had happened, and particularly at the view he thus stated himself to have of the causes of it, he interrupted me (though not at all uncivilly) and put an end to our interview.

He subsequently came into the Board Room and did business as if nothing had happened. At his first appearance he treated Sir G. Cockburn with marked displeasure, but at the second interview he was more civil, and charged him with some communications to the different departments.

Believe me to be, my dear Duke,

Most faithfully yours,

J. W. C.

From the Diary.

August 25th.—Dined with me at Kensington Mr. and Mrs. Lockhart, Mr. Strode, Sir A. Grant, Mr. Horace Twiss, Mr. Hook, Mr. Wilkie—an agreeable day. Hook was talking of his bribing postilions to go a great pace; Sir A. Grant said, "But, Mr. Hook, don't the ghosts of murdered horses come to disturb your slumbers?" "You mean *nightmares*, I suppose," rejoined Hook.

August 26th.—The Duke of Clarence came to town, and did business with remarkable good humour and affability to everybody, which seems to me to portend some new attempt on his part to find a salvo for staying in office.

The Chancellor sent to me for Prince George's portrait as L.H.A., in order to compare it with the D. of C.'s; this also looks like what I have hinted at above.

September 1st.—Got up early, and met Lowther at Lord Hertford's to shoot in the Regent's Park. He killed two hares and a pheasant, shooting very ill. I killed four hares, shooting very little better. We saw, I suppose, thirty hares and a good many pheasants, and but one partridge—a stray red one, I believe, from Lord Hertford's.

September 17th.—I called on the Duke of W. to settle about his visit to Sudbourne, which we fixed for the 12th October. His Grace promised to write to Sir F. Wilson to get the King's signature to the warrant and bill for the new patents. H.M. is not well, and at all times has a great aversion to arguing. The Duke told us that when His Majesty went to Hanover, the Regency signed upwards of 10,000 papers, and that the King has not signed an army commission since. I know he signs all our papers and commissions very regularly. The Duke talked to me of the necessity of appointing an officer to affix some kind of signet which should be equivalent to, and supersede the royal signature. I said this was the origin of the Privy Seal, and that that officer might be entrusted with this duty. "Oh, Lord, no," said the D. "The King would not admit Lord Ellenbro' or Lord Westmoreland into his presence freely enough for that—it must be some one of those familiarly about him who should be sworn never to affix the signet but in His Majesty's presence, and by his special and instant command. This seems as if he had Lord Westmoreland in his mind for Privy Seal. His

Grace appointed to call on me at five o'clock, to walk up to Hyde Park Corner to look at the alterations of his house. We walked up the park, and as we went talked of the King and of his wonderful knowledge of character and his art of guessing what any one is about to say to him. The Duke told me that when he went with the Chancellor on the 9th of January to the King to accept the Government, His Majesty was in bed, and when they first went in was groaning and appeared very miserable and unhappy, but as the conversation went on he grew better, sat up in the bed, and began to tell all his communications with his late Ministers, mimicking them all to the life, and exhibiting such a drama, so lively, so exact, and so amusing, that the D. never saw anything like it.—Goderich, Lansdowne, and, above all, Anglesey, whom he positively made himself look like. I myself had seen many similar exhibitions, and though I have seen better mimics than the King as to the mere voice and manner, I never saw any who exhibited the niceties of character with so much discrimination. As a mere imitator the King has some superiors, but I have never seen his equal for a combination of personal imitation, with the power of exhibiting the mental character.

September 18*th*.—Mr. Hook and I took boat at Whitehall at three o'clock and went a tour into the City. We visited St. Paul's, and were shocked at the abundance and ill-taste of the modern monuments there. Johnson and Howard, both by Bacon, and the figure of Lord Rodney, by Flaxman, as I think, are the only tolerable ones; the rest are in various degrees contemptible. We then went to Christ's Hospital, and saw the fine new hall that they are just finishing there; thence to the Charterhouse, where they seem to be rebuilding almshouses; thence to St. John's Gate and Clerkenwell Green, and back by the Post Office, which is a most unsightly structure in my judgment, and the two side porticoes, or colonnades, are mere excrescences, which were much better away. We dined at Dolly's on beefsteak and toasted cheese, and in order not to derogate from the primitive simplicity of the place, drank port. After dinner we walked home over Blackfriars and Westminster Bridges, and went into the Coburg Theatre for an hour, where we saw a vulgar but in some parts droll piece, called 'Wives by Advertisements.' The house was crowded in a most extraordinary degree, and there were, I think, twice as many women as men, and the piece created a curiosity and an enthusiasm in the audience very unlike England. The audience seemed exclusively tradespeople of various degrees.

September 21*st.*—Left town at half-past seven in the blue coach for Woodbridge, where I arrived at quarter-past four, and at a quarter before six arrived at Sudbourne.

Lord Hertford is better in general health and spirits, but cannot even attempt to walk. Raikes was amusing us after dinner with some stories of the laxity of the world in pecuniary matters, and mentioned particularly one gentleman to whom a creditor (after in vain appealing to his honour and generosity for the repayment of a debt which partook of the nature of a debt of honour), indiscreetly wrote at last that he would put it into the hands of an attorney to recover. The gentleman took advantage of this, and immediately wrote back to say that, as a debt of honour, this sum had stood high on his list for early payment, but that as the creditor had chosen to make it a matter of business, he had struck it out of the post of honour, and placed it at the bottom of the list to await the fate of all the other affairs of business. This story, which was well told, excited a good deal of merriment; and when that had subsided a little, John King exclaimed, "Yes! and I'll tell you who the party was—you yourself, Tom Raikes!" I never saw a surprise in a farce make more effect. We hardly knew how to look, and not at all what to say. Raikes stammered and hesitated, and seemed to doubt whether he ought not to take it seriously; but King stuck to his point manfully, and added that the other party was Crockford, the blackleg, and we were all glad to drown the altercation in bursts of laughter, which, indeed, we could no longer have suppressed.

October 5*th.*—It was about this time that by a letter from Broadstairs I authorized Mr. Jesse to conclude for a lease of the cottage at Molesey which we had been to see in June, and which I at first called Rose Lodge, as I could not find that it had hitherto had any distinctive name, but I since find that it was commonly called Molesey Grove. Lord Hotham's father, when Col. Hotham, resided in this cottage, and Lord H. was born here. I wonder how, in the state it then was, any gentleman's family, however small, could have been stowed away in it, as there are but two best bedrooms, and they are small. I intend to add three bedrooms.

October 11*th.*—Called on the Duke of Wellington; he

comes to-morrow to Sudbourne. We had a long and confidential talk on public affairs. He is very much perplexed what to do about Ireland. He speaks to me unreservedly and with the most entire confidence on all points.

The Duke is in excellent spirits, and very entertaining. He told us to-day that having once expressed to *Isquierdo* his wonder at the enormous number of *charlatans* that there were in the world, Isquierdo quietly said, "I beg your pardon; I do not think there are *enough—in proportion to the number of dupes.*"

Oct. 17*th*—The Duke began to talk of incidents in the Peninsular War. . . .

The French and English armies, as they became better acquainted by frequent contact, grew to be very civil to each other, particularly after we had passed the Pyrenees, and the advance posts and picquets were on the most friendly terms. There was a small public-house beyond the Adour, where the English used to cross over and sup with the French officers; and in the line before Bayonne, a French officer came out one day to our advance posts, and, saluting the officer, inquired whether one of our parties had not possessed themselves of three muskets and three sets of accoutrements of a French party. Inquiry was made, and the arms, &c., were found. It appeared that the English soldiers had given the French some dollars to buy them some bottles of brandy, but, not trusting entirely to the honour of the enemy, had insisted on keeping three muskets, &c., as a pledge that the brandy should be forthcoming. The dollars were returned, and the Frenchmen got their accoutrements again.

The advance posts always gave notice to each other when they were in danger. On one occasion, when the French army was advancing suddenly and in force, the French posts suddenly cried out to ours, "Courez vite, courez vite, on va vous attaquer."

"I always encouraged this; the killing a poor fellow of a vidette or carrying off a post could not influence the battle, and I always when I was going to attack sent to tell them to get out of the way.

"Lambert once carried off a post, but he had given them warning that they had come too far, and that if they did not go he should be obliged to carry them off; they did not take the hint, and he next day did as he had threatened, and the French said it was all fair.

"When Gozau came to me before Toulouse from Soult, I said I was glad to see him, for that I was just going to attack him again, and that I felt the arrangements would come on his part with a bad grace if it was to be made after the attack had actually commenced. 'Oh, yes,' said Gozau, 'I knew that you were going to attack us, for I saw that you were bringing up 'la ligne, la sixième' [and a couple of other divisions, whose numbers I forget]. In short," said the Duke, "he knew as well as I did the corps that were coming on."

December 6th.—To town. Went with Cockburn and Lowther to Guildhall to meet the New London Bridge Committee on the subject of the approaches—a very difficult one. I suggested carrying on the level of the arch over Thames Street as far as Fish Street Hill and Miles Lane, and having also arches at those streets. This seemed to meet most people's ideas, and Mr. Rennie, who immediately approved of it, was ordered to make plans and estimates accordingly.

I showed them that even if the shape of the ground did not suggest this mode of crossing Thames Street, it was *on principle* better that two such immense thoroughfares should not meet on the level.

December 26th.—The publication of a letter from the D. of W. to Dr. Curtis on the Catholic question makes a good deal of sensation, though it really says little, and absolutely nothing which the Duke has not said in Parliament, viz., that he *wishes* something could be done, but sees no prospect of it. And if there be any chance, it would be to leave the question to rest awhile, so that party animosities might have time to subside, and arrangements could be considered. But on the whole this letter is favourable to the Catholic claims, because it admits the *principle*, and the difficulties alluded to are of a temporary nature.

END OF THE FIRST VOLUME.

LONDON : PRINTED BY WILLIAM CLOWES AND SONS, LIMITED, STAMFORD STREET
AND CHARING CROSS.